The Blood Waltz

By Rob Kenyon

Dedication

To my paternal Grandmother, Mrs Margaret Kenyon (Nee Bruen) who taught me how to read and used to buy me comics as a child fuelling my imagination, thank you.

Margaret Kenyon 1926 – 2013

Acknowledgements

Thank you to my lovely wife, Nicola, who has been my rock and given me the encouragement to carry on with this novel, it has taken 6 years from start to finish and it has been hard to keep plugging away with it but now it's done. Thank you to my parents and all my family and friends whom I didn't tell about this novel but I'm sure will all go out and buy it.

Prologue

A British Soldier slowly waves a metal detector over the dusty ground whilst walking forward hesitantly with his body profile casting a long shadow across the barren ground, he is 5ft 11", slim build, mousy brown hair with a short blonde wispy beard and his face is weathered a lot more than it should be for someone of 22 years of age. The wrinkles on his sunburnt face along with the stresses and strains of war make him look in his early 30's.

Following him cautiously are 11 other soldiers, each of them dressed for cold weather which looks rather strange due to the sun beaming down on them, scorching their skin giving them a reddish coloured tinge to their complexion, this is Winter in Afghanistan.

Each of the troops carry an L85A2 rifle and scour the area in different directions. Some of the older soldiers still don't trust the L85A2 or SA80 as it's also known despite the modifications made to the rifle over the years, it had gained a bad reputation during the late 1980's and early 90's and was colloquially nicknamed 'The Politician' as it hardly worked and you couldn't fire it, but most of the soldiers in the troop hadn't been in the army long and they had a much deserved faith in the rifle as it had proved itself in the theatre of war over the last 10 years.

The soldiers walk slowly beneath the clear blue sky in a fallow field each following the same path as the soldier who is leading them harnessing the metal detector.

Towards the Northern edge of the field, around 100 metres away are trees and foliage with various sized dwellings, presumably a very small village but as the troops look over to it they fail to see any civilians and from previous experiences this has proved to be a warning for an impending ambush from the Taliban with the civilians fleeing whichever area they're in upon the Taliban entering.

'Fucking gobshites' cursed Jay in his broad Liverpool accent 'they know something's wrong, that's why they've all fucked off'

Jay looks back to the soldiers walking behind him searching for someone's facial expression to acknowledge his opinion, then he looks back over to the small village.

'We're here...fighting for their country...and they've all fucked off' said Jay as he spits on the floor

Walking slightly behind is another soldier who looks a few years older and a rank higher than Jay. This is Karl Sampson, a 31 year old Lance Corporal and section 2nd in command from Leeds who joined the Royal Engineers 14 years previously, around a time in the UK when there was high unemployment especially for the generation just leaving school, Karl had embarked on an apprenticeship in joinery but the company he worked for went bust one year into his apprenticeship and without a company to work for and pay for him to go the technical college he was thrown off the course, Karl worked in numerous dead end jobs such as packing sandwiches into the triangular containers, putting chocolate bars into groups of four ready to be packed and other mundane tasks until his application to join the Army had gone through.

He had reached the rank of Corporal three years previous but had been bumped back down to Private after an altercation in a bar in Ayia Napa with a Royal Marine after things got heated after Karl had beat the Marine at the punch ball machine gaining a higher score on numerous occasions and making fun of the defeated Marine, fists were thrown and Karl was arrested by the Military Police.

'Shut up Jay' said Karl nonchalantly

'It's bullshit though, we…' said Jay

'Hey' interrupted Karl with venom 'shut the fuck up'

Further down the line is Corporal Bradley Clyde, a 6ft 3" well-built and tough looking soldier, Jay looks back at Clyde and then straight back to the floor, Clyde is an intimidating presence among the troops due to his well-deserved rise through the ranks over the years serving in Northern Ireland, Kosovo, Iraq and Afghanistan. Many of the troops in his command where still learning the alphabet whilst Clyde was a fresh-faced teen patrolling the mean streets of Belfast during the Troubles in the mid 1990's.

Corporal Bradley Clyde hails from a small mining village called Haydock in St Helens in the County of Lancashire, Clyde is in his early 30's and had joined the Royal Engineers at the same time as Karl and over the years had become extremely close friends due to them coming from a similar background where both of their Fathers had been put out of work when the coal mines closed in the early 90's, they both came from working class backgrounds as most regular soldiers did but they both played and loved Rugby League, with Karl being a fan of Castleford and Clyde supporting Wigan.

Clyde was a little older than Karl but had joined the Army under similar circumstances in the mid 90's, Clyde had hoped to follow his Father at the local coal mine but since they had closed down a year before he left school there wasn't many manual jobs going spare, he could never see himself working in an office as it just wasn't manly enough so his Father had pushed him in the direction of the Army as a way to learn a trade and see a bit of the world as his Father had served in the Army during the late seventies.

Clyde was from a tough background and was the eldest of four brothers with each brother being well known in the village as being tall, tough, athletic and a good rugby player with a mischievous side. He was a good soldier and maybe ready to press on and take the plunge and join the SAS but he wasn't that way inclined, he enjoyed the soldiering and was getting enough of that being in the Royal Engineers and also learning a trade ready to go back to civilian street after he'd done his 22 years' service with a nice lump sum and a decent pension to fall back on, with that being said he enjoyed his time in the Army and had no immediate desire to leave.

'Fuck it' mumbled Jay under his breath as he turned away from Clyde, just one look from Clyde was enough to see Jay succumb to his authority.

Clyde aims his rifle looking toward the foliage through the rifle scope and looks to have spotted something, he scans the bushes but can't spot anything other than the leaves moving in what little wind there is, dismissing the movement he lowers his rifle then proceeds to follow the other troops.

'Smithy, get onto 2nd platoon, we'll be back in half an hour approaching from the East' said Clyde

'Yes Corporal' said Smithy obediently

Smithy can be heard speaking to the other platoon over the radio, Clyde's platoon and the one at the FOB (forward observation base) share the job of patrolling the area in which they are in with today being Clyde's platoons turn to take on those duties.

Clyde turns around and looks behind to the direction in which they had just walked from and looks through the scope on his rifle, he then lowers his rifle and turns around walking just behind Smithy. The other soldiers in the platoon walk slowly whilst scanning their hostile surroundings.

Karl stops and pulls out two cigarettes and starts to walk backwards in front of Clyde as he puts both cigarettes into his own mouth and lights them, then puts the lighter back in his pocket and inserts one of the cigarettes into Clyde's mouth, Karl turns around and smokes his cigarette as he walks in front.

'Nice one' said Clyde

An explosion is heard further up the line and dust fills the air making it impossible to see anything, the sound of rifle fire cracking in the distance accompanies the sound of cries of agony further up the line from the unfortunate casualty. Clyde and Karl both dive to the floor along with the other troops.

'Contact, contact' shouts Clyde as the cigarette falls from his mouth

The sound of rifle fire in the distance alerts Clyde to the location of where it is coming from, many of the soldiers pass the message back that Richards is the casualty.

'Contact right, contact right' shouts Clyde

The soldiers are all lay on the ground facing towards the tree line where they believe they are being attacked from.

'Open fire' shouts Clyde

The soldier's fire intermittently towards the tree line as the dust settles gradually around them. The cries of agony can be heard still further up the line along with other voices shouting and as gun fire cracks overhead Clyde looks to where the explosion happened and spots Jay tending to the casualty.

'Jay' shouts Clyde 'who is it?'

Jay is lay down next to Richards helping the medic tend to his wounds looks back over his shoulder to Clyde.

'It's Richards' said Jay

Clyde raises his head slightly trying to locate Smithy, Smithy is firing his rifle towards the distant treeline with half an eye on Clyde as he knows he will ask him to get medical help for Richards by means of a helicopter casualty evacuation or CASEVAQ as it is abbreviated to in the military.

'Smithy, Smithy, get a CASEVAQ ASAP' said Clyde

'Yes Corporal' said Smithy

Clyde slowly crawls up to the start of the patrol where Richards is lay on the floor with his leg missing and is bleeding profusely, he is slipping in and out of consciousness as the blood congeals in the dusty soil like a dark red porridge. Another soldier, Crosby, is dressing the wound and another, Leach, is writing on Richards head with black marker to indicate to whoever takes on the medical duties after he has that he has administered morphine to the casualty.

'Come on Richards mate' said Crosby as he wraps the tourniquet around the end of the bloody stump just below Richards knee.

Richards's looks shocked as he is lay on the floor with blood mixing with the dust congealing at the base of his leg stump, Clyde looks back to find Karl then looks to his right and around 30 metres away there is a small compound around the size of half a football pitch with mud walls and small dwellings inside, from previous experience they make good places to take cover whether in a fire fight or as a patrol base, the key thing is making sure that the enemy has not booby trapped it as a way of pushing the patrol into it, Clyde is experienced enough to know that the compound needs to be checked if they are to use it as cover.

'Karl, get everyone into that compound, you and Jay get inside and secure it first' barked Clyde

'Yes Corp' shouts Karl

Further down the line Karl is passed the metal detector, he stands up then scans the ground quickly towards the compound as Jay follows, Karl approaches the compound entrance and turns around to the rest of the soldiers who are lay on the ground firing in the direction of the tree line in the distance.

'Squad, when I say so, take cover inside the compound' shouts Karl

Karl reaches the compound entrance and whilst he is scanning the floor and walls to the door way Jay is aiming his rifle over Karl searching for any Taliban inside.

After a quick scan of the area with the metal detector and after Jay has rushed about inside to make sure the compound is empty Karl rushes back to the compound entrance and crouches whilst aiming his rifle towards the enemy.

'Squad, on me' said Karl

The rest of the squad stand up and rush towards the compound as Karl, Jay and Clyde provide covering fire towards the tree line.

Sporadic rifle fire is still coming towards them as they are taking cover lay on the floor, bits of dirt fly up into the air as the bullets hit the ground close to the makeshift medical team.

'Fuck' reeled Leach 'that was close'

Crosby looks to Clyde.

'Let's get him inside' said Crosby

Clyde looks towards the compound entrance.

'Karl!' shouts Clyde

'Yes Corp?' replied Karl as he cautiously leans around the entrance to the compound.

'30 seconds rapid fire' shouts Clyde

'Yes Corp' said Karl

Karl turns way from the entrance and Clyde fires sporadically towards the tree line.

Inside the compound Karl kneels up and looks above the compound wall, by now the rest of the squad are lined up against the compound wall firing sporadically towards the buildings and trees in the distance, Karl turns to the soldiers.

'30 seconds rapid fire' shouts Karl slowly and precisely making sure everyone can hear him clearly

The sound of gun fire intensifies as the soldiers provide rapid fire for covering support whilst outside Clyde lowers his rifle and looks to Crosby.

'Ready?' said Clyde

'On 3' said Crosby as he looks to Clyde '1, 2, 3'

Crosby and Leach pick Richards up as Clyde quickly aims his rifle towards the tree line and fires a volley of shots as he stands up and slowly jogs behind carrying the injured soldier's rifle over his shoulder.

'Come on, get him inside' encourages Clyde

Crosby and Leach carry Richards holding one of his arms over their shoulders and hold a leg each just under Richards' thighs, they walk as fast as they can over the route made safe by Karl earlier on. Slightly behind is Clyde who continues to stop, turn and fire a volley of shots towards the distant tree line.

Crosby and Leach carry Richards inside the compound entrance and lay him on the floor a few metres away from the entrance, Karl rushes over and crouches next to the casualty and notices that he doesn't look good, he'd lost a lot of blood and the colour has drained from Richards' face. From previous experience of these injuries Karl knows it's touch and go depending on how quick they can get the CASEVAQ there and get a few pints of blood back into his system.

'Come on Richards mate' said Karl

Richards gives an unconvincing smile, Karl looks at Clyde and raises his eyebrows unconvinced Richards will live much longer, Clyde looks around to the soldiers and spots Smithy with the antenna on his rucksack and he is using the radio, he struggles to hear over the noise of the rifle fire beside him.

'Where's this fucking CASEVAQ Smithy?' shouts Clyde

Smithy is mid conversation on the radio and is nodding his head, Smithy looks to Clyde.

'Twenty minutes Corporal' said Smithy whilst being muffled by the sound of gunfire nearby from the other soldiers.

'Fuck me' shouts Clyde who is clearly disappointed as he shakes his head and looks around the compound then back to Smithy, time is precious in these situations and 20 minutes seems too long.

'Can you get us some air support?' said Clyde

'Yes Corporal' said Smithy 'I'll see what I can do'

Smithy struggles to communicate over the radio due to the noise in the background and wanders about in the compound trying to find an area in which he can hear clearly.

Clyde looks at the soldiers firing over the wall then moves quickly over to them whilst ducking to Jay who is carrying a Javelin missile launcher and taps him heavily on the shoulder, Jay stops firing and looks back.

'Jay, get that Javelin set up on the roof of that building' said Clyde who then pats Jay on the back twice.

Jay puts his rifle sling over his shoulder whilst Clyde unpacks the Javelin from his back. Clyde looks over the compound wall towards the treeline and village in the distance.

'Have we got a positive ID on their position?' said Clyde

A rocket hits the compound wall filling the area with dust, the gun fire from the soldiers dies down due to the shock of the blast.

'Fuck me' shouts Karl in his thick Yorkshire accent as the dust covers him making him cough

The soldier's each stand up gingerly from the blast and begin to fire back at the enemy, luckily nobody was hurt due to the compound wall shielding the blast.

'Baxter?' called Clyde who looks around for Connor Baxter who is carrying the heavy machine gun

'Yes Corporal' said Baxter in his Scottish accent

'Get your fucking arse up onto that roof and lay down some fire' said Clyde

'Yes Corporal' said Baxter who laboriously lifts the machine gun from resting on the wall so he can carry it

'Take Leach and Jay with you and get a PID on their position' said Clyde.

Baxter trudges past Clyde and up the stairs whilst carrying his heavy gimpy (General Purpose Machine Gun) with Leach and Jay just behind him. Clyde walks over to Smithy and crouches beside him.

'What's happening Smithy?' said Clyde

'CASEVAC 15 minutes, still waiting on the air support' said Smithy

Clyde takes a deep breath and purses his lips, looks away and then back to Smithy as he had higher expectations for the call out time for air support.

The sound of gun fire in the background is suddenly intensified as the sound of Baxter's machine gun starts to fire subduing the counter fire from the enemy, Clyde runs over to the building where Baxter, Jay and Leach are and calls up to them.

'Have you got a PID on their positon?' said Clyde

Jay leans down and gestures to Clyde but struggles to have himself heard due to Baxter firing his machine gun.

'To the right, to the right, next to that fucking big building' shouts Jay

Clyde looks around to see a soldier firing his rifle and has a mortar tube on his backpack.

'Jimmy' calls Clyde

Jimmy keeps firing towards to tree line oblivious of being called by Clyde.

'Jimmy!' shouts Clyde a bit louder so he can be heard and walks towards him and smacks Jimmy on the shoulder, Jimmy looks around and back to Clyde who is pointing towards the enemy location.

'Get some mortars fired onto that fucking building' said Clyde as he points to the distance

'Which one Corp?' said Jimmy

'The one to the right of the big building' said Clyde

The sound of gun fire fills the air with cracks and zips, a small explosion goes off in the distance, a voice can be heard on a radio not too far away and the voice is calling out numbers for the grid reference, Karl shuffles over to Clyde.

'So we wait here, ride it out until the air strike?' said Karl

Clyde nods at Karl.

'Corporal' said Smithy

Clyde acknowledges Smith by lifting his head and eyebrows slightly.

'It's a no for now on the air strike, they're providing air support for the Irish Guards in Nad-e Ali, ETA 1 hour' said Smithy

One hour? Fucking hell. What are we going to do?

As Clyde contemplates the time the air strike will take a small explosion goes off just outside the compound presumably from an RPG (rocket propelled grenade) due to the size of the explosion.

Jesus, they've got fucking rockets. Where the fuck is that Javelin?

Clyde turns and looks up at Jay.

'Jay, get that fucking Javelin fired' said Clyde

Jay leans over the building slightly and looks at Clyde.

'Yes Corporal' said Jay

Mortars. Where are our mortars? We need mortar fire.

Clyde looks towards the compound wall and then back five metres to see Jimmy setting up the mortar tube with another soldier.

'Jimmy. Ready when you are' said Clyde

'I'm ready now Corporal' said Jimmy

The cracks and the zips from the rifle fire is now accompanied by a short thud followed by an explosion in the distance as Jimmy fires mortars at the enemy position. Leach and Jay are setting up the Javelin on the roof of the compound whilst Baxter provides covering fire with aggressive bursts from his machine gun. Up on the roof Jay is sitting down cross legged and lifting the Javelin onto his shoulder.

'Let me fire it' said Leach

'Piss off, it's my turn' snapped Jay sullenly

Jay sits cross legged on top of the building and props the Javelin tighter onto his shoulder and towards his head as he brings it closer so he can see through the sight to aim it towards the enemy.

'I've been carrying the heavy bastard all day' said Jay

Clyde and Karl look back up to see the Javelin teetering slightly over the edge of the building.

On top of the building Jay is aiming the it towards the enemy position in the distance, then a plume of smoke comes from behind the Javelin and the rocket fires out making a loud whoosh as it flies, it takes seconds to reach the building before it explodes and reduces the building to smoke and rubble, the soldiers all cheer.

'Fucking have some of that' shouts Jay

The gun fire quietens down to the odd crackle from inside the compound.

'Cease fire, cease fire' shouts Karl

The odd round is fired by one of the soldiers next to the compound wall, another soldier gives him a nudge to alert him to the cease fire order.

'Cease fucking fire' shouts Karl

Clyde looks up to the roof of the building and notices Baxter continuing to fire sporadically towards the treeline, Clyde and Karl look at each other and Clyde nods in the direction of the back of the building.

Karl and Clyde run around to the back of the building and climb the stairs that lead onto the roof and shuffle along the floor towards Jay, Leach and Baxter. Jay notices Clyde and nudges Baxter who then stops firing then looks to Jay and then back to Clyde and Karl.

'What's the verdict then chaps?' said Clyde

'We nailed them boss' said Jay who seems pleased as punch

'Is there any movement around the treeline?' said Clyde as he looks through the scope of his rifle towards the smouldering rubble in the distance

'No, I've not seen anything' said Baxter who squints as he looks towards the distance over the top of his machine gun sights

Jay looks through his scope towards the tree line, Clyde does also and the building which has just been destroyed, Clyde lowers his rifle and looks to Leach.

'Did you see anything Leach?' said Clyde

'I saw movement in the treeline' said Leach 'they can't be civvies or they'd have already got the…'

'…got the fuck out of there yes, I know' said Clyde

Got to be fucking Taliban, fucking sneaky twats.

Clyde aims his rifle towards the treeline and looks through the scope, Karl also does the same but neither of the men spot any movement.

'No. Nothing' said Karl

'Me neither' said Clyde 'keep your eyes peeled for any shifty looking fuckers'

Clyde and Karl lower their rifles, Clyde notices Crosby tending to Richards just below so he leans slightly over the edge and looks over.

'Crosby. How's Richards?' said Clyde

Crosby looks backwards and around unable to pinpoint where the voice came from, then eventually looks up to Clyde on the roof.

'I've stopped the bleeding, he's still with us' said Crosby who hands and uniform was now saturated in blood

The compound falls silent as that bit of information sinks in with the rest of the squad and the faint sound of a chinook can be heard in the distance. Clyde and the other soldiers look to the direction of the chinook, Clyde then looks towards the back of the compound where there is an area in which the chinook can land, this is the L.Z. (Landing Zone), he then leans back over the side of the building to find Smithy.

'Smithy, get them to land behind us, we'll mark it with purple smoke' said Clyde

Smithy starts to relay the message over the radio and then looks up to Clyde and sticks his thumb up to him.

'Five minutes to landing Corporal' said Smithy

Clyde looks towards the chinook and then to the other soldiers on the roof.

'Right. Leach and Jay get Richards and bring him to the L.Z, Baxter stay here, me and Karl will secure the area' said Clyde

Jay, Leach, Clyde and Karl shuffle over the building's roof then stand up and run down the stairs.

Jay and Leach run over to Richards whilst Karl and Clyde run to the rear of the building aiming their rifles as they walk to make sure there aren't any Taliban hiding in wait for them making sure they can fire a quick burst of shots before they dive for cover.

Karl scans the floor with his metal detector making sure there aren't any more IEDs hidden in the ground as it would be catastrophic if the chinook landed on one plus it would be a massive trophy kill for the Taliban.

As Karl continues to scan the ground with the metal detector Clyde rustles through his webbing pouch and pulls out a smoke grenade, he pulls the pin then throws it into the middle of the field, the smoke bomb starts to bellow out purple smoke, Karl picks up a bleep from the metal detector as he hovers it over a section of the field which would be used as the L.Z.

'Whoa, hang on a minute' said Karl as he drops to his knees and pulls out his knife and starts to prod the ground.

Shit, I shouldn't have thrown the fucking smoke grenade yet, shit.

Karl prods the ground and pulls out a rusty flattened coke can from just below the soils surface, he picks it up, smiles and turns to look at Clyde as he holds it out in front of him.

'Thank fuck for that' said Clyde who was unimpressed, he was glad it wasn't an IED as that would have held up the CASEVAQ.

Karl stands and starts again scanning the area and after a couple of minutes has secured the immediate area to be used as the L.Z.

Clyde looks up and starts walking backwards to see if he can see the chinook over the nearby trees. The sound of the chinook gets louder as it comes into clear sight overhead and the purple smoke starts to swirl due to the down draught from the chinook. Clyde and Karl kneel on the floor whilst guarding their eyes against the swirling dust and grass.

Jay and Leach approach Clyde and Karl carrying the stretcher with Richards lay on it who is now unconscious, Crosby is running alongside the casualty holding his rifle and a drip which is connected to Richards.

The chinook slowly gets lower until it lands in the field with a bump, as it lands Clyde and Karl stand up and slowly approach the chinook whilst crouching, Crosby, Leach and Jay follow with Richards. Dust, purple smoke and dried grass dance around in the down draught and make it hard to see as they approach the rear of the chinook, the Weapons Systems Operator (WSOP) on the chinook briskly walks down the rear ramp to usher the soldiers onto the helicopter and inside is medical equipment and a host of doctors and surgeons gowned up and waiting to provide emergency medical care. Jay and Leach lay Richards onto the floor inside the chinook as Crosby looks to the surgeons but struggles to have his voice heard over the sound of the chinook.

'He stood on an IED (Improvised Explosive Device) approximately 30 minutes ago, he's lost a lot of blood but I've stopped the bleeding, he's had morphine and keeps slipping in and out of consciousness. His blood type is O' said Crosby

The medic on the Chinook nods at Crosby then ushers him off the helicopter as the other medical staff rush to work on Richards.

The soldiers quickly exit the chinook and aim their rifles covering the surrounding alien landscape as the chinook takes off. The dust, purple smoke and down draught get more intense as it hovers above them then moves off slowly into the distance.

The dust settles slightly and the sound of the chinook eases up, Clyde stands up as do the other soldiers.

'Right, let's get back to the compound and wait for this airstrike' said Clyde

As Clyde and the other soldiers approach the compound to where the rest of the troops are Smithy gives the thumbs up to Clyde.

'Not long Corporal, air support is on its way' said Smithy

'Good stuff, we may not need it though. Has there been any movement?' said Clyde

'Fiji said he saw movement in the tree line a few minutes ago' said Smith

'Is that right Fiji?' said Clyde

'Yes Corporal' said Fiji

For obvious reasons, he is nicknamed Fiji due to that being his place of birth and is the typical Fijian, around 6ft tall, 100kgs and a decent Rugby Union player.

'Right, let's check it out' said Clyde

The sound of the chinook fades and a whistle sound grows louder very quickly and there is an explosion inside the compound close to Clyde.

Chapter 1 - Discovery
Present Day – German Countryside

A worried farmer knocks on the window of Clyde's car.

'Are you ok in there?' asks the farmer

Clyde quickly turns to the farmer.

'Are you ok?' asks the Farmer

Clyde stares at the concerned farmer whilst coming back into reality from his day dream, Clyde looks around and then back to the farmer who looks worried about the state of his mental health but also a bit scared in case he himself is harmed.

'Erm, yes, yes thank you' said Clyde who seemed embarrassed

Fucking hell, I must have zoned out again.

'Ok' said the Farmer who cautiously steps back from the vehicle

The farmer takes a further step back as Clyde opens to the door of his car and Spike jumps over his lap and out through the open door, Clyde follows.

'You see I didn't want to startle you if you were having a nap, it's just…you were awake but staring into space' said the Farmer 'Are you sure you're ok?'

Just fuck off out of my face.

Clyde nods as he closes the door of his car and locks it.

'Yes, honestly I'm fine' said Clyde.

Clyde starts to walk away from the Farmer into the fields, the worried farmer still stares at Clyde.

'Ok then, well…you enjoy your walk then' said the Farmer

Knob head.

'Will do' said Clyde as he smiles at the Farmer

Clyde walks through the countryside, there are many woodland areas around but Clyde sticks to walking in the field as Spike runs around the area stopping every so often to look towards his master to make sure he is still there, Spike is a typical Springer Spaniel and wants to run around furiously investigating every area in which they walk.

The grass is dewy as it's early in the day and the underside of Spike is wet due to running in the longer grass next to the woods. Clyde spots a rabbit at the edge of the woods further up ahead, Spike turns to look at Clyde and then looks to the rabbit. Spike sees the rabbit and slowly trots towards it with hunched shoulders and head low.

'Spike, no' said Clyde

The rabbit spots Spike and turns quickly and runs back into the woods, Spike immediately sprints towards the fleeing rabbit.

'Spike, Spike………bollocks' said Clyde

Clyde starts to run after Spike and runs into the woods knocking back low hanging branches in the pursuit, as soon as he gets a few metres into the woods he loses sight of Spike as his eyes adjust to the difference in the light as it's much darker in the woods.

'Spike, Spike, where are you boy?' calls Clyde

Clyde searches the woods as his eyes adjust and he can see a white shape move in the distance, it's Spike who's further ahead still chasing the rabbit.

'Spike!' calls Clyde as he jogs towards his preoccupied dog 'fuck'

After a few minutes of jogging up a hill inside the woods Clyde stands at the top of it and looks down to see Spike barking outside a hole in the ground at the bottom of the hill, Spike is trying to get his head inside the hole and starts to dig away at the outside foliage in front of the hole.

Don't you fucking dare go in there.

'Spike' shouts Clyde

As Clyde runs down the hill very fast due to the decline he approaches Spike who then wriggles himself inside and down into the hole.

'Fucking hell' said Clyde as he runs up to the hole and crouches to the floor and reaches into the hole to try to grab Spikes hind leg if he can but he is out of reach, Clyde pulls his arm out of the hole reaches into his pocket and pulls out a torch, he then shines his torch into the hole and looks inside but can't see his dog in the earthy darkness.

'Spike. Come on boy' calls Clyde hopingly

Clyde looks behind him to get his bearings but is deep into the woods, there isn't much light due to the heavy foliage, despite it being early in the day the torch helps him see. He kneels down in front of the hole and starts to pull away at the foliage around the hole and it opens up slightly then holds his torch in his right arm and pushes his way into the hole with his right arm in front of him and his left arm behind so he can squeeze through.

As he gets his shoulders inside and shuffles along he notices the hole is large enough to kneel up inside so proceeds to do so until it gets large enough to stoop inside and finally large enough to fully stand up.

'Spike' shouts Clyde

The dull sound of Clyde calling out stops dead inside the dark hole, he shines his torch around carefully and realises he is in something a lot larger than a rabbit hole, maybe it is a cave, he rubs his foot on the floor and shines his torch

14

down at the floor and sees that it's made of concrete, he looks up and around shining his torch around the area as his eyes adjust to the dimly lit room.

'Spike' calls Clyde

Clyde shines his torch up to the ceiling and he notices it has a concrete ceiling with light fittings and steel conduit on the ceiling.

Lights? Steel conduit? What is this place?

Clyde starts to walk with more confidence in the hole as he shines his torch in front of him and notices tables, chairs, filing cabinets and so on scattered around the room in a disorganised manner.

'Jesus' said Clyde as he looks closely at what's on the desks and notices the ash trays and stationary all have swastikas emblazoned on them.

'No fucking way' said Clyde

He can't believe it, he has found an intact German bunker from the Second World War, 99% must have been found and destroyed since the end of the war and because he's only 20 miles from the nearest built up area he wonders how this wasn't found.

Still, with Swastikas being banned in Germany there is a black market for this type of memorabilia so maybe he can make some money out of the find. Some of the squaddies at his base would buy them for sure, maybe he could get in touch with some German collector who may offer a tidy sum for the items. He could retire early if there's enough memorabilia to sell or buy a house, he could buy a business for when he leaves the army.

This stuff could be worth a fortune. I'm going to be rich.

Suddenly, Clyde hears something move nearby and then brush against his leg, he shines his torch down quickly as he has been startled.

'Spike' said Clyde gleefully as Spike sits in front on him and barks.

Clyde reaches into his pocket and pulls out the dog lead.

'Come on boy, let's put your lead on' said Clyde as he bends down and attaches the lead back onto Spikes collar and then shines his torch further back into the bunker.

He spots some dusty rifles propped in a rack against the wall, the rifles look a bust rusty but still once cleaned he could make some money on the black market, he'd have to be careful selling the equipment especially weapons as it could see him discharged from the Army and he would be waving goodbye to his pension which he had worked so hard for but still, Clyde thought, there's money to be made here.

'We need the lights on, don't we buddy?' said Clyde as he shines his torch towards the ceiling and traces the steel conduit from the light fittings back to a light switch on the wall, he then walks slowly over to the light switch with Spike following cautiously behind.

'Come on boy, get a move on' said Clyde as he jolts the lead towards himself, then walks over to the light switch and flicks it on and waits for a moment, he knows these types of lights take a while to warm up but the filament lights up slightly so you know it is working but not fully warmed up, this doesn't happen so after a couple of seconds staring at the lights to see any sort of encouraging light he is met with pure darkness, surely a fuse may have blown he thought.

He traces the steel conduit from the light switch and traces this back through another room which looks like it was a canteen for the bunker and through the kitchen area into what looks like a plant room, there is a large oil-fired boiler, compressors, diesel powered backup generators and water tanks in the room so it must have been the plant room for the bunker.

He shines his torch around the room and can faintly see a coal fired boiler in the corner and a large supply of coal which has been interweaved with cob webs and just to the right of that Clyde spots the main electrical fuse board.

'Jackpot' said Clyde

He walks over to the fuse board and tries to open the door to it, the door is around 3ft x 3ft and the battleship grey paint finish has turned to a deep brown rust over the years, he grabs the walnut handle and tries to twist it, the handle doesn't move despite the effort he puts into turning it.

'Come on you fucker' snarls a frustrated Clyde

The handle isn't moving any time soon so Clyde puts the torch into his mouth and aims the torch at the handle with his mouth and uses both hands to try to open the fuse board door, under the strain of Clyde's strength the handle snaps off cutting his right hand and causes him to drop the torch from his mouth.

'Argh you fucking twat' curses Clyde as he holds his right hand where he has just injured, Spike barks, Clyde turns to look at his dog and then bends down to pick up his torch then uses it to see how much damage has been done to his hand.

'Bastard' said Clyde bluntly

The large red graze on his right hand in between his thumb and his fingers isn't bleeding but it looks painful, he licks his wound then aims his torch back at the fuse board, Spike barks.

'Hey!' said Clyde

Spike barks again and looks guilty for doing so.

'Hey!' snaps Clyde as he points his finger at Spike 'stop it'

Clyde shines the torch towards Spike and it casts its light onto an axe next to the coal pile, the axe is sticking out from a chopping block used for chopping wood when starting the fire for the boiler, he notices this and walks up to it grabbing the handle and stepping onto the chopping block simultaneously pulling the axe out.

He then looks around the boiler and spots a large metal tool box which is open with a lump hammer, wrenches, ring spanners, crow bar which are all visible from where he is, he walks up to the tool box and throws the axe onto the floor disregarding it leaving it beside the tool box as he hopes there may be something better to use to gain access to the fuse board, he shines his torch over the tools.

That crowbar will be better.

Clyde tries to close the tool box but it had rusted solid, he picks up the open tool box and carries it over to the fuse board dropping it to the floor creating a large jangle from the metal tools banging around inside, Spike barks.

'Hey!' said Clyde

Clyde bends down and pulls out the crow bar and lump hammer, he puts the torch into his mouth and slides the crow bar into the fuse board door then starts to hit it with the lump hammer so that the crow bar just slides inside, Clyde drops the lump hammer onto the floor then starts to pull on the crow bar and with a loud snap the fuse board door opens, Clyde drops the crow bar onto the floor creating another jangle then he takes the torch from his mouth, Spike barks.

'Spike!' said Clyde who was growing tired of his dog barking every couple of seconds

Clyde points the torch into the fuse board and notices all of the fuses have blown, he then looks into the toolbox and spots a wooden handled screwdriver and picks it up. He holds the screwdriver by the handle with his finger and thumb horizontally so that the metal of the screwdriver bridges the gap where the fuse had blown, a blue spark flashes from the screwdriver but the room doesn't light, he continues to the next and the same thing happens but this time the pumps from the hot water tanks start buzzing which breaks the eerie silence, Spike barks.

'Spike' shouts Clyde

Spike is inconsolable as he barks in the direct of the moaning and gurgling pumps attempting to pump the rusty sludge that now fills the pipework, Clyde pulls the screwdriver away.

'It's ok boy, it's ok' said Clyde

Clyde bends down to console Spike.

'It's ok' said Clyde

Clyde then gives Spike one last rustle of his fur then aims his torch back into the fuse board, Clyde now bridges the gap on the fuses on the fourth one and with the blue spark the lights in the plant room switch on as do the lights in the kitchen and canteen.

'Yes' calls Clyde triumphantly

Spike starts to wag his tail and trots closer to Clyde rubbing his head against his leg.

Although the rooms are lit over half of the light bulbs don't work but there is enough light to see the whole area, Clyde struggles to see properly though as his eyes adjust to the light and looks around the plant room and back to the fuse board to see what he needs to do to permanently leave the lights on.

Inside the fuse board are coils of fused cable left there just in case one day they did blow and need replacing and after 30 minutes he manages to wire the fuses in then switches on the lighting for the structure.

He then walks back the way he came in and through the kitchen noticing the old ovens and grills but doesn't stay too long and moves into the canteen, he has no intention of investigating the mess area as he spotted the rifles and Nazi memorabilia in the main bunker so heads to that direction, after all, there may be something worth selling on the black market in the main room rather than 60-year-old stainless steel cutlery.

As he walks into the main room he notices the rotten corpses which are now skeletons wearing white jackets with swastikas on their lapels, there are also skeletons of SS officers and regular soldiers lay around the room and some with missing limbs, maybe due to an explosion in the bunker he thought.

Fucking hell, this is unreal.

Spike is kept close to Clyde as they walk slowly through the room up to some large oak doors which are closed, Clyde tries to open the doors but they are jammed shut due to the pressure being put onto the sunken lintel above the door.

'Shit' said Clyde

Clyde holds the handle and hits the door with his shoulder, the door moves slightly, he does this again and the door moves a little bit more and loosens some dust which falls onto his head and shoulders, he spits out the dust which went into his mouth and steps back and starts to kick the door and it gives him a little more room allowing him to squeeze through into the next room, Spike walks up to the gap in the doors and peers his head through, on the other side Clyde turns to Spike and encourages him to join him.

'Come on lad' said Clyde

Spike squeezes through the gap into the other room they both walk inside carefully around a much larger room, this new room has a lot more space inside and has a red light on top of a room made out of steel, the prominence of the red light attracts Clyde to it more than the promise of other hidden treasures as a piece of technology or engineering may fetch more than uniforms or trinkets.

He walks slowly towards the room with the red light on top not taking any notice of anything else in the room and as he approaches he notices a large door which is ajar to the metal room and shines his torch inside to where there are numerous rabbits huddling in the corner trying to protect themselves from the intruder, Spike barks and attempts to run into the room only to be held back by Clyde sticking his leg in the way to prevent him from going after the rabbits.

'Spike, sshh' said Clyde

Inside the steel room is a large switch on the wall, Clyde has a look outside of the room and there is another large switch on the outside wall and is an exact replica of the one inside. Thinking that this is the light switch for inside the steel room Clyde approaches the switch outside and puts his hand on it and pulls it down, the room fills up with red light and a loud noise that sounds similar to a large jet engine fills the air, the sound gets louder and the light gets brighter so much so that Spike barks profusely and Clyde covers his ears and closes his eyes. The noise gets louder until there is a bright red flash and the light and noise disappear.

'Whoa' said a shocked Clyde who can only hear the remains of the noise ringing in his ears and he struggles to see as his eyes adjust to the darkness once again, he shines his torch inside the room to look at the rabbits and they seem to have disappeared, he then strains his eyes as they adjust to the now dim light and the rabbits have disappeared.

Where the hell have they gone?

Chapter 2 - Flashback

Now Clyde can see a lot better he opens the door fully to get inside to investigate thoroughly to see what had happened and the rabbits had gone.

'Jesus' said Clyde

He closes the door to the metal room and looks around outside the room to see if the rabbits had run out through a gap, then the room is filled again with a red flash but this time there is no sound and the light is only a red flash, Spike barks and Clyde holds his hand up towards the light as to protect his eyes. The light dies down and Clyde slowly walks up to the steel room and opens the door and shines his torch inside to find the rabbits have returned, albeit one maybe two were missing from the initial group but he couldn't be certain as he never counted them at the start.

'What the fuck?' said Clyde

He slowly walks inside the room as the rabbit's huddle closer together in the far corner, Spike bows his head as if he is about to enter the room and stops to look up at Clyde awaiting his master's permission.

'Come on boy' said Clyde as he walks towards the rabbits whilst Spike is sniffing profusely at the rabbits huddling together in the corner, Clyde bends down and manages to pick one up as the other scurry out of the room with Spike attempting to go after them as he turns and his claws scrape and slip on the polished metal floor.

'Spike, stay' calls Clyde with assertion

Spike stops and cowers looking up to Clyde who holds a rabbit and strokes it.

'Calm down, I'm not going to hurt you, let's just see if this works' said Clyde

Clyde bends down unclips Spikes collar, Spike barks at the rabbit which Clyde is holding.

'Spike, calm down' said Clyde

Spike looks a little coy and walks backwards slowly then sits down and starts to sniff the air in the direction of the rabbit, Clyde puts the dog collar around the rabbit's waist and tightens it so it can't slip off.

'Spike. Out' instructs Clyde

Spike trots out of the room stopping and looking back not wanting to miss out on anything, Clyde follows and then places the rabbit onto the floor inside the metal room and closes the door, he pulls the switch and turns away from the room and the same happens again, the room is filled with a loud noise and a bright red flash.

Once the flash and noise had finished Clyde turns around, opens the door and the rabbit had again disappeared.

'No fucking way' said Clyde

Clyde exits the room and closes the door and waits outside, a minute later there is another red flash and he opens the door to see the rabbit inside wearing Spikes collar.

I don't believe it, it's not possible.

He walks over to the rabbit with Spike quickly behind him and picks up the rabbit and removes the collar, he turns to his dog.

'Sit' said Clyde

Spike again sits down and sniffs in the direction of the rabbit, Clyde puts the rabbit on the floor of the room to which the rabbit takes the opportunity to run to the corner of the room, Clyde grabs hold of Spike around the neck and puts his collar and lead back on. Spike tries to sniff the rabbit cowering in the corner of the room and attempts to walk towards it.

'Spike' said Clyde

Spike stops and looks up at Clyde then begins the sniff the floor, Clyde gives a gentle tug of the lead.

'Come on boy' said Clyde as he exits the room and closes the door keeping the rabbit inside, he then exits the main room and enters the first room they entered and looks towards the direction of the hole in which they initially crawled through as the light from outside shines through slightly and walks towards it.

Walking towards the exit Clyde looks at the rifle rack with a fully stocked rack of bolt action rifles propped up in there, he grabs one of the rifles and holds it up to his eye as he aims towards the exit, then he tries to load the rifle but the action on the rifle has ceased, Clyde puts the rifle back into the rack then heads towards the exit. Spike walks on in front through the hole and Clyde follows on behind crawling on all fours holding the torch and dog lead with his right arm held in front of him.

Spike is first out of the hole and Clyde squeezes himself out of the hole and back into the woods, they walk out of the woods and back onto the field, Clyde gets out his mobile phone, he looks at his phone which has no signal so he continues to walk towards where he parked his car.

After a few minutes Clyde has signal on his phone, he picks out Karl's number from his phone and calls him.

Karl is in the gymnasium on the Army base completing his own made up circuit of thirty press ups, thirty sit ups, thirty burpees then thirty star jumps followed by thirty punches of whatever comes natural on the heavy punch bag, naturally he trains hard as he is a soldier and he completes the circuit from thirty and drops down in fives until complete, Karl is on his last five star jumps and notices his phone ringing lay at the side on the floor, with Karl being strict with his training regime he increases the pace and hits the heavy bag five times in lightning speed before rushing over to his phone before Clyde gets impatient, Karl is out of breath when he answers.

Clyde waits for Karl to answer the phone he looks back to see were the hole was but looks a little confused.

'Hi mate. What are you up to?' said Clyde excitedly

'Nothing, just finishing in the gym, why?' said Karl

Karl notices Clyde seems a little excited by the tone of his voice.

'Listen, if you're not doing anything get down here now' said Clyde

'Why? What's up?' said Karl

'Listen, just bring a torch with you and make your way to where I park when I walk Spike in the Countryside. Do you know where I mean?' said Clyde

Karl thinks to himself, he's sure he remembers where it was but the Countryside all looks the same to him, he could maybe wing it or at least make his way somewhere near and then phone Clyde.

'I think so' said Karl unconvincingly

Clyde doesn't want to spend the next hour or two trying to direct Karl to where he is, the suspense is getting higher the longer he keeps the bunker secret, he's desperate to show Karl.

'Head South East towards Seesen then turn onto the K65 towards Gittelde. Do you remember?' said Clyde

'Yes, a few miles past the dairy farm? On the same road near to the National Park?' said Karl

'Yes, I'll meet you near my car. Hurry up' said Clyde

'Will do, keep your hair on' said Karl

Clyde puts his mobile phone in his pocket and starts to walk towards his car with Spike trotting beside him, he can't wait to show Karl the bunker as he had thought earlier on they could make a lot of money selling the memorabilia and as both Clyde and Karl are popular members at their base in Hameln they have their fingers in quite a few pies and are in to gambling, drinking and selling things that have 'fallen of the back of lorries' so to speak.

An hour later Clyde is sat at the front of his car resting on the bonnet and Spike is inside the car sat on the passenger seat, Karl approaches in his own car and gives the thumbs up then parks behind. Karl gets out of his car and walks over to Clyde who is walking to meet him.

'So, what is it then, what's the big fuss?' said Karl as he locks his car

Clyde smiles then starts to walk towards the woods as if he's trying to put on a show and keep his best friend in suspense, Karl doesn't seem keen to play along with this masquerade.

'You'll see in a bit' said Clyde

Karl stands still not willing to carry on with the silly game Clyde seems to be playing.

'Come on. What is it?' said Karl

Clyde turns to look back at Karl.

'Follow me and you'll find out' said Clyde

Karl shakes his head then begrudgingly follows Clyde.

'It better be worth it; I was just about to go to the pub' said Karl

Clyde turns and nods his head.

'Don't worry, you'll like it, I promise' said Clyde

'It better not be anything weird' said Karl half-jokingly

Clyde shakes his head, smiles and continues to walk towards the forest with Karl quickly catching up.

After half an hour, they both come to a standstill in the woods unable to locate the bunker, Clyde is searching in the woods looking in vain to see the rabbit hole, Karl watches on and looks disinterested.

Karl thinks to himself '*what the hell have I come all this way for? I've wasted a couple of hours on this, what the hell is Clyde up to and why won't he tell me what the surprise is?*

In the meantime, Clyde thinks to himself '*where the bloody hell is it? I bet I look like a liar in front of Karl and he will take the piss out of me for this wild goose chase'*.

'It was around here somewhere' said Clyde

'I bet it was, is this some sort of joke? Is this a way of getting me out of the house so you and the lads can do a practical joke on me?' said Karl

Clyde laughs and thinks maybe that would be a good idea but one for the future.

'Honestly mate, when you see it you will be amazed' said Clyde

Karl rolls his eyes clearly fed up.

'Well you'd better find it quickly or I'm going back, it's nearly beer time' said Karl

Karl looks back to the direction they came and really wants to call it a day and go back to the barracks, meanwhile Clyde keeps looking around and seems to have spotted something.

'Hang on a minute, it's over here, I remember now this is where I walked into the woods chasing Spike, follow me' said Clyde

Clyde starts to run away and further into the woods, Karl follows apprehensively, he wants to go back but he didn't pay much attention to whereabouts in the woods he was, he needed Clyde to guide him back to his car once they were finished.

'Wait up will you?' said Karl

Karl chases after Clyde, as Karl brushes past some low hanging branches he spots Clyde in the distance crouching in front of a small hole, Karl jogs up and crouches beside him.

'This is it Karl, this is what I was telling you about' said Clyde as the beaming smile covered his face

Karl stands up, takes a step back and looks at Clyde.

'You've got to be having a laugh?' said Karl disappointedly 'all this way for a bloody rabbit hole?'

Karl pulls out a cigarette and lights it and takes a step further back and sits down on a fallen tree.

'A bloody rabbit hole?' said Karl

Expecting a different reaction Clyde wants to tempt Karl inside as he knows his reaction will change once he sees inside the bunker.

'It's not just any old hole, wait until you see what's inside' said Clyde

Karl shakes his head, he had just had a shower after the gym and changed into the clothes he was going to go to the pub in after the jaunt in the woods with Clyde.

'We won't fit through, plus I'm going out in a bit I'll get my clothes full of shit' said Karl

Clyde looks back at Karl shakes his head then looks towards the hole.

'Your clothes look shit anyway mate, I wouldn't worry about getting dirty' said Clyde

'Knob head' said Karl as he laughs as he knows Clyde sense of humour.

'Anyway, of course we'll fit, I've been down it myself' said Clyde

Clyde is now lay on the floor in front of the hole holding his torch in front of him, he turns around and looks at Karl.

'Well come on then, follow me' said Clyde

Clyde squeezes through the hole and into the bunker, Karl throws his cigarette onto the floor, gets on all fours then follows Clyde down into the hole. As they get further inside Clyde stands up and shines his torch back at Karl and helps him stand up.

'What is it then, a cave?' said Karl

'Not just a cave, it's a bunker' said Clyde

Karl pulls his torch from his pocket, turns it on and shines it around the bunker, Karl is still stooped but once he shines his torch around he gains the confidence to stand up straight.

'So, is this going to be where you bring all your ugly girlfriends then? So us lot can't take the piss?' said Karl as he laughs.

'Fuck off, have a closer look' said Clyde

Karl shines his torch around and has a closer look inside and spots the Nazi memorabilia and walks over to it and picks a letter opener up and turns to Clyde.

'Jesus, we could make a few quid from all this you know' said Karl

'I know; come into the next room I want to show you a little something' said Clyde

Karl puts the letter opener into his pocket.

'I don't want to see your dick mate' said Karl

'Bullshit you don't, anyway, now's not the time for silly games. What's in this next room is amazing, you wouldn't believe something like it could exist' said Clyde

Clyde leads the way over to the large wooden doors, Karl shines his torch around and spots the corpses of the dead Nazis.

'There's bloody dead Nazis in here' said a shaken Karl

'I know, just keep walking' said Clyde

'There's rifles as well' said Karl

'I know' said Clyde dismissively 'We'll look at them later'

As they reach the wooden doors Clyde and Karl squeeze through the large oak doors and into the larger room and straight away Karl notices the red light.

'What's that red light for?' said Karl

Clyde turns to look at Karl and smiles.

'That's what I'm talking about' said Clyde

Clyde and Karl walk through the dimly lit room over to the metal room, Clyde opens the door and ushers Karl to look inside.

'Here, have a look inside' said Clyde

Karl peers around the doorway and looks inside the room and spots the rabbit.

'A rabbit?' said Karl who raised his eyebrows not knowing what the deal was with the rabbit, he was expecting something else, maybe Nazi gold bullion, stolen art or something along those lines

'Yes, but watch this' said Clyde

Clyde nudges Karl back and closes the door then pulls the switch down. The loud noise fills the room as does the red light and as it gets louder and brighter Karl and Clyde cover their ears and close their eyes.

'Fucking hell' shouts Karl

There is a bright red flash and then the room returns to normal, clearly Karl is impressed.

'Fucking hell, what was that?' said Karl

'Open that door and tell me if the rabbit is still in there' said Clyde

Karl looks Clyde up and down not knowing whether it is some kind of trick, he then slowly opens the door and steps inside and starts to look around but can't see the rabbit, it looks to either disappeared or simply run off due to the noise and light.

'How did it get out? Is there a hole in the wall?' asked Karl naively as he looks around the room for a hole or something that the rabbit could have escaped through.

'No I've looked, there's nothing' said Clyde

'So how did it disappear then?' said Karl

Clyde steps inside the room.

'I pulled the switch like that one outside, there was a loud noise and a red flash and then it disappeared, then it came back a few minutes later' said Clyde

Karl looks confused and shakes his head and looks to the switch on the wall inside the room.

'I'm not having that, surely there's a hole it escapes through because it's scared of the light and noise' said Karl

Clyde walks to the other side of the room and searches the walls and corners trying to prove there are no flaws in the fabric of the room and there are no tricks or secret passages for the rabbit to escape.

'Look, there's no holes' said Clyde

Clyde looks up to see Karl grinning as if he knows something Clyde doesn't and he's holding the switch.

'You pulled this and it disappeared?' said Karl

Clyde holds his hands up and is scared that Karl will pull the switch as it would be something he would do, he would do it to try and call Clyde's bluff.

It was Karl's rebellious nature that meant he always had to do what he was strictly told not to do, for instance, if someone told him not to get the hottest curry or drink the most potent alcoholic drink as a bit of friendly advice he would take it as a personal challenge, which sometimes backfired on him as some of the lads in the platoon used to wind him up this way and get him doing all kinds of stupid and painful things.

'Don't fucking touch it' said Clyde

'Nothing will happen' said Karl as he grinned

'Don't be fucking stupid' barked Clyde as he starts to walk towards Karl to prevent him pulling the switch.

'Bollocks, you're full of shit' said Karl as he laughed

Karl pulls the switch.

'You fucking…argh' shouts Clyde

The room fills with a bright red light, Karl and Clyde start to levitate and they hold their hands over their ears and close their eyes and scream in pain as their body temperatures rise and it feels as though there are millions of needles sticking in and out of them all over their bodies, then there is a bright red flash and Karl and Clyde disappear.

Chapter 3 – Into the Unknown

Clyde and Karl are lay on the grass unconscious in the middle of a field next to a forest, both show no signs of injury.

There are birds singing in the trees and the sky is clear with the odd white cloud and its quiet, apart from the sounds of nature and after a few minutes the faint hum of diesel engines in the background is enough to bring Clyde around. He opens his eyes whilst still lay on the floor and looks up to the sky and struggles to see anything other than shadows.

A diesel engine seems to be moving closer and there are German voices shouting in the same direction of the engine. Clyde leans up and as his vision is getting better he has a look around and spots Karl on the floor next to him, he hits Karl's leg with the back of his hand in order to wake him up.

'Karl, get up' said Clyde still angry about Karl pulling the switch, although it seems they are both ok, things could have been worse.

Clyde then aggressively pushes Karl and he then wakes up slowly, Clyde's vision is getting better and can make out the forest behind them and spots a figure in the distance in the direction of where the diesel engine seems to be coming from. He stands up uneasily and struggles for a moment to keep his balance and Karl leans upright but is still sat on the floor.

'What happened?' said Karl groggily as he squints trying to find Clyde

'I don't know but we're outside in the fields now' said Clyde

Karl rubs his eyes as Clyde looks around and blinks a lot to make his vision better, Clyde can hear the diesel engine and a German shouting but can't make out what they are saying.

'I can't see a fucking thing' said Karl

'Me neither' said Clyde

Karl looks to the distance and squints even though he can't see anything he can hear the diesel engine.

'Ssshh. What's that noise?' said Karl

Clyde stands dead still and attempts to listen and look into the distance.

'I can't see anything, it sounds like a tractor' said Clyde as he tries his best to listen 'hang on, it sounds like it's a German shouting something'

'Probably the farmer pissed off because we're on his land' said Karl

Karl is still sat on the floor; he struggles to stand up without the help of Clyde to pull him to his feet.

'Just tell him to…' said Karl

'Hang on a minute' interrupts Clyde 'it sounds like they're telling us to get down or they will shoot us'

'What? Fuck off, let's get out of here' said Karl nonchalantly

Karl turns and starts to walk away towards the forest then stops and turns to Clyde. Clyde can see a lot clearer now and looks to where the diesel engine is coming from.

'Which way is it to the cars?' said Karl

Clyde ignores Karl and continues to look towards where the engine noise is coming from and holds his hand up to Karl as if to tell him to be quiet.

'Hang on a minute. It looks like a German half-track from the 2nd World War' said Clyde

Karl tries to look towards the direction of the half-track.

'It's probably war re-enactors. Just tell them to fuck off, we've probably stumbled into their pathetic games' said Karl who was lighting a cigarette

A shot is fired hitting the ground next to Clyde.

'Jesus' said Karl who takes his first drag and blows out the smoke

'Hey. What are you playing at?' shouts Clyde

Clyde's vision gets back to normal and he can make out the German halftrack which has left a convoy a mile in the distance. The convoy consists of around 20 half-tracks each full of troops with a few tanks and auxiliary vehicles in tow, Clyde thinks this can't be war re-enactors, not on this scale anyway, sure if it were a few overweight middle-aged men running around then it could be, but the size of the convoy and the fact they had been shot at makes Clyde think that these guys could be real. Or could be some paramilitary organisation like the Red Army Faction or some other far right terrorist group on exercise.

'Fuck' said Clyde

Karl looks at Clyde in anticipation of what he has just spotted seeing as he at present has the better eyesight and vision.

'What's up?' said Karl

Clyde looks shocked, he looks back to Karl then back to the half-track.

'I don't know what's going on but I don't think they're play fighting, there's a massive convoy about a mile away' said Clyde

'Who the fuck are they?' asked Karl

'Fuck knows' said Clyde with a hint of worry in his tone 'it might be a German paramilitary group or something'

Another shot hits the ground next to Clyde as the halftrack can de distinctly seen and heard.

'Get your hands up!' calls a German Soldier on top of the half track

Karl cannot speak German whereas Clyde can fluently.

'What's he saying?' said Karl who was growing angrier by the minute, it was his nature to hit first and ask questions later but he couldn't understand what was said and he couldn't see properly

'He said get our hands up' said Clyde

Clyde takes the soldiers seriously but because Karl cannot see them or the convoy and neither can he understand them he doesn't want to stick around.

'Sod that. Come on let's get back to the car' said Karl

A shot is fired again hitting the floor next to Clyde.

'Shit' said Clyde

'Get onto the floor' said the German Soldier

'Hey Karl. We better do what they say, they're not messing around' said Clyde

Clyde raises his hands then places them onto his head and starts to kneel onto the floor, Karl notices as his eyesight is getting better and can make out the half-track approaching them.

'Fucking hell mate, what's going on?' said Karl

Karl also kneels to the floor raising his hands then places them on top of his head.

'I don't know but they're firing live rounds. Let's play along with them and if it gets a bit silly we'll beat them up and get the hell out of here' said Clyde

'Sounds like a plan to me' said Karl

A 2nd World War German half-track is now 20 metres away, the German soldier manning the machine gun on top is competing with the sound of the half-tracks diesel engine to be heard. Clyde's vision is now completely back to normal and Karl's isn't far behind either.

'Hands behind your heads' said the soldier

'What did he say?' said Karl

'Just put your hands behind your head, they've got weapons and there's a few of them' said Clyde

Karl's vision has returned to normal now.

'I know' said Karl 'my visions back to normal'

Clyde and Karl are kneeling up with their hands behind their heads and are awaiting the approaching altercation.

Two soldiers jump from the back of the half-track armed with bolt action rifles and walk towards Clyde and Karl whilst aiming their rifles at them. A third soldier jumps from the back of the half-track, it's a German officer who looks quite young, maybe a little wet behind the ears Clyde thinks. The young officer walks slowly and slightly aloof over and stops in front of them whilst the two soldiers walk slowly behind them.

'What are you playing at?' said Karl

A German soldier behind Karl hits him in the temple with his rifle knocking him to the floor unconscious.

'Englander?' said the Officer who smiles smugly

Clyde moves to take his hands from his head to open his arms out and attempts to speak to the officer in German.

'Listen, we've…'

Clyde is hit also in the temple with the soldier's rifle knocking him unconscious to the floor next to Karl.

Clyde opens his eyes as he is being dragged along the dewy grass by his feet by the two soldiers and his hands have been tied behind him with rope as have Karl's, they lift him up onto the half-track and as Clyde looks around he spots Karl sat in the half-track fully awake with a bleeding nose, Karl looks disgusted mainly due to the fact that if they attempted to fight back at this stage it would prove pointless and they have to grin and bear it.

The door on the back of the half-track is slammed shut by the last soldier to board the vehicle, then the soldier walks around to the front of the vehicle and climbs into the driver's seat. The driver then proceeds put the vehicle into gear and slowly drives away, Clyde looks back to see whereabouts they are to see if he can see their cars in the distance but he can't, he doesn't recognise his new surroundings and that worries him as the forest in which lies behind them as they drive away is only small, maybe one acre so it can't possibly be the national park in which they had entered where the bunker is.

In the distance Clyde can see the end of the convoy driving off into the distance and notices the half-track in which they are being held captive is driving into a different direction. The half-track drives over a small ditch shaking all aboard the vehicle and with Clyde and Karl's hands being bound they struggle to stay seated upright with Clyde falling forwards from his seat into one of the soldiers, the soldier shoves Clyde back aggressively into Karl.

'Get off me you prick' shouts Clyde bitterly

The soldier stands up and attempts to strike Clyde with his rifle stock but the half-track again drives over a small ditch which causes the soldier to fall into another soldier who is seated. The seated soldier pushes the fallen soldier away and he struggles to keep upright and drops his rifle, Clyde and Karl smirk as the soldier struggles to get to his feet.

'What the fuck are you two laughing at?' said the soldier who then punches Clyde and then punches Karl in the face which angers both men, Clyde now with bulging eyes, gritted teeth and a slightly red cheek leans towards the soldier who hit him.

'Take these ropes off so we can sort it out like men' said Clyde

The soldier smirks then loads his rifle and aims at Clyde, the officer notices and leans back to hold his arm over the soldier's rifle pushing it down.

'Baum' said the officer softly in the same manner as a Grandmother might chastise a toddler

'Sir' said Baum

'Behave yourself' said the officer

Baum begrudgingly lowers his rifle and keeps his eyes locked to Clyde's.

'Yes Sir' said Baum

Baum then sits down and stares at Clyde, Clyde winks back knowing he isn't afraid to fight anyone as he'd had a tough upbringing and was known to be quite a good fighter and knows he could beat him in a fight.

'Schwuchtel' said Baum under his breath as he looks away and to the direction of where the vehicle is heading

The half-track is now jostling over an uneven farm track. Karl still looks disgusted and is staring at Baum, Clyde looks at Karl who looks back at him and nods towards Baum as if to gesture that it was him who gave him the burst nose.

The officer is sat close to the front of the half-track and is smoking a cigarette, he looks through his binoculars to the sky as the faint hum of a group of Messerschmitt's fly overhead, he then turns around to look at Clyde.

'I can safely say it's all over' said the Officer

Clyde looks at Karl and then back to the Officer in bewilderment.

'I don't know what you're talking about' said Clyde

The Officer smiles, then glances up to the Messerschmitt's then back to Clyde.

'You know exactly what I'm talking about' said the Officer

Clyde glances up at the Messerschmitt's flying overhead then back to the Officer and slowly shakes his head.

Are they Messerschmitt's? What the fuck is going on? Where are we?

'No, I really don't' said Clyde

The Officer raises a smug grin as he looks at Clyde with distain.

'You don't have any identification, you're clearly English *and* of a fighting age' said the Officer as he takes a drag on his cigarette and blows out the smoke in an effeminate manner 'that to me either says spy or deserter'

Clyde leans forward towards the Officer as if to clarify what had just been said, Baum notices and drops his cigarette which he had recently lit and clutches his rifle tighter ready to hit him with the stock of the rifle again.

'Whoa, hang on a minute…' said Clyde

Clyde attempts to stand up and is kicked in the ribs by Baum who is still seated. Karl attempts to stand up to help Clyde but is kicked with a sweeping kick by the other soldier taking his legs from underneath him resulting in Karl falling awkwardly to the thick steel floor.

'You fucking bastard' said Karl

The other soldier loads his rifle and aims it at Karl whose face then turns from anger to shock, the Officer again turns around.

'Not yet Gunter' said the Officer who holds his slim line cigarette holder between two fingers and blows out smoke 'we need them for interrogation'

Karl, Clyde, Baum and Gunter exchange poisonous looks at each other as all four men really want to have their shackles unleased both physically and metaphorically and fight their opposite number.

I'll fucking kill him thinks Clyde as he stares at Baum like a tiger ready to pounce.

The minor fracas is interrupted when the half-track approaches an old man who wasn't far off being aged 90 who is walking with his back towards the half-track, the old man is walking in the middle of the dirt road dodging the puddles and the driver of the half-track is beeping the horn to make the old man move out of the way but the old man doesn't seem to take any notice, he's either ignoring the half-track or is hard of hearing.

The young Officer has a point to prove in front of his troops and doesn't want to be upstaged by a belligerent old man, the officer who is in no mood for messing about as he has two British spies and is keen to get back to base to let his superiors know of his findings in the hope that good fortune will come his way as a result of it.

'Hey, move out of the way' shouts the Officer

The old man continues to walk in the road slowing the half-track down to a slow pace just a few metres behind him with the driver beeping the horn profusely to alert or scare the old man into moving.

'Get out of the way, you old fool' shouts the Officer

The old man glances over his shoulder then moves out of the way but stands in a puddle of water soaking his foot. The old man isn't happy that the village he has lived in all of his life has now been taken over by an invading army and is personally being bullied out of the road by an obnoxious foreign Officer that is still wet behind the ears.

'Thank you' shouts the Officer

The old man stands reluctantly at the side of the road and glances at his soaked shoe, the puddle was deep enough for the water in it to spill over the top and enter into his shoe soaking his foot, this old man wasn't happy as he himself had fought in the Franco-Prussian war 69 years ago when he was 18 years old and the French were defeated, this bore a deep grudge in the old man against the Germans but the young officer wouldn't know this and didn't show any respect towards the old man so as the halftrack approaches him the young officer stares at him.

'Stupid old fool' said the officer

The old man smiles at the officer and as the halftrack drives past, the old man spits at the officer hitting him in the face with a large amount of dark green warm phlegm.

The Officer is shocked, he wipes the sticky gunge from his face and smears it along his eye lid as he clears it from his eye and cheek then turns and looks at the soldiers in the back of the truck, then looks at the driver not knowing what to do next, he didn't expect this.

'Stop the truck' shouts the panicking officer

The halftrack stops forthwith and the old man looks sheepish as he realises he may have done something stupid that may result in harm to him but nevertheless he stands and stares at the officer defiantly.

The officer stands up inside the half-track and looks at Baum and Gunter as if to gauge their reaction, he then turns to face the old man whilst pulling out his pistol and shoots the old man in the chest. The old man drops to the floor and his lifeless body pours blood out of his chest into the newly trodden tracks in the dirt road. Clyde and Karl look at each other worryingly as the Officer sits back down in his seat emotionless.

'Drive on' said the Officer coldly

The Officer pulls out a handkerchief from his pocket and wipes his face, then turns to Clyde who by now along with Karl aren't the antagonists they were just five minutes earlier, after what had just happened it was safe to say they would behave themselves for the time being.

'Let that be a lesson to you both' said the officer calmly

Clyde and Karl look to the floor, the officer turns away and Baum starts to smile, Clyde looks up and notices Baum smiling.

'Not so cocky now are you?' said Baum as he grinned with his fat red cheeks bulging

Clyde looks down at the floor as does Karl, Baum leans in to Clyde.

'I'm going to chop you both up and feed you to the pigs when we're finished with you' whispers Baum callously then starts laughing, Gunter notices and smiles at Clyde and pats the knife on his webbing.

Clyde is distracted by the sound in the distance of a squadron of Messerschmitt's flying overhead then looks back around to where they are driving towards and spots a building fifty metres away, the building looks to be a farm but this one has a large radio mast outside. Clyde looks to Karl then nods in the direction of the farm, Karl looks towards it.

As they get closer, the farmhouse which has been turned into a communications post for the German Army stands dominantly in the countryside with a hastily engineered watch tower overbearing them as they slowly drive through the entrance into the courtyard of the farm and come to an abrupt halt, the farm house is riddled with bullet holes and the windows are smashed, the sound of a diesel generator can be heard which is connected to the radio mast and a thick black armoured cable runs into the house through a small window.

The driver exits the vehicle and walks to the back of the half-track opening the doors, Baum and Gunter stand up and look to Clyde and Karl who are looking up at their captors sheepishly.

'Get up' instructed Baum bluntly

Clyde slowly stands up as does Karl and as quickly as they both stand up they're pushed from the back of the half-track and fall to the floor due to having their hands bound, Baum and Gunter climb down behind them.

'Up, up, up' shouts Baum quickly and aggressively

Baum kicks Karl hard in the arse, he then does the same to Clyde.

'Come on' shouts Baum

'Let's go' said Gunter

Clyde and Karl are pulled to their feet by the driver and are led into the house by Baum and Gunter. The driver of the half-track and the officer walk in through the door in front of Clyde, Karl and the two soldiers.

'Lock them in the bathroom, I'll call it through to Captain Jaeger' said the officer

The officer and the driver walk away into another room in the house and the two soldiers push Clyde and Karl up the stairs, onto the landing and then throw them into the bathroom and lock the door.

Inside the bathroom, Clyde and Karl stand up and look out of the small window and into the distance where the Messerschmitt's are dive bombing a position which is followed by an explosion and a cloud of black smoke as if a tank or a truck had been hit with one of its bombs.

'Fuck. This can't be right' said Karl

'I know. I don't know what the fucks going on' said Clyde

Both men must be thinking the same, they must have travelled back in time to the 1940s but how? It surely isn't possible, it would be a stupid idea to suggest but the reality struck home when the old man was shot as both men had seen men shot so knew it when they saw it and the old man was shot and killed for real, these soldiers who had taken them captive were no war re-enactors. The question about travelling back in time needed to be asked no matter how silly it sounded.

'We can't have… can we?' said Karl

'We must have; we must be back in 1940' said Clyde

'We can't be, surely' said Karl

'How do you explain it then?' said Clyde

'Fuck knows' said Karl as he shakes his head in disbelief 'I'm not stopping here though'

Clyde turns his back to Karl and holds out his bound hands behind his back.

'Here, cut me out of these' said Clyde

'What with?' said Karl as he looks at the ropes confused

'Have you still got the letter opener?' said Clyde

'Hang on' said Karl as he starts to check his pockets 'No, they must have searched me'

'We've got to get out of here now, we're going to have to kill them all' said Clyde

'What are we going to do?' said Karl

'I'll smash this ceramic basin, pick up a piece and cut me loose' said Clyde

Clyde kicks a ceramic basin in the bathroom knocking it off the wall smashing it in half on the floor, Karl walks up and crouches picking up a small piece of the ceramic basin, Karl stands up and they stand back to back whilst he cuts Clyde's ropes, outside the bathroom Baum notices the commotion going on inside and pulls out his keys from his pocket ready to go into the room to quell the commotion from the prisoners.

'Hey, what are you doing?' shouts Baum outside the bathroom

Keys can be heard rattling outside the door as Baum attempts the select the right key for the door. Clyde is cut free and Karl starts to cut his own ropes, Clyde starts to pull back and forth on a lead water pipe that supplied the basin and pulls back and forth on the pipe to snap a piece off.

'Karl, you stand over there, I'll stand to the side of the door and when he walks in I'll smash him in the face' said Clyde

Clyde pulls the lead pipe and breaks off a piece of pipe which is two feet long which results in water spraying out from the broken pipe towards the door,

Clyde quickly runs to the side of the door as it starts to open. Baum walks into the room and aims his rifle at Karl and looks at the water spraying out.

'Hey, hands up' shouts Baum as he loads his rifle

Clyde swings the lead pipe with maximum force hitting Baum in the throat. Baum drops his rifle and grabs his throat as he drops to his knees, Clyde picks up the rifle and both Karl and Clyde pause for a moment to look at the soldier who is struggling to breathe, they both lean over the body of the dying soldier.

'Who's the big man now?' said Karl

Baum looks to be choking due to his crushed windpipe and his face is turning blue.

'We're going to feed *you* to the fucking pigs' said Clyde

Clyde holds Baum's rifle and aims it towards the doorway, Karl spits at Baum.

'Hey, what's going on?' calls Gunter's voice further down the hall

'Karl, I'll get this one and the officer, you get the other one' whispers Clyde

Clyde aims the rifle down the hall as Karl steps over Baum who is bleeding heavily from his mouth and is getting sprayed with water from the broken pipe. Clyde walks slowly down the hall with Karl directly behind and as he approaches the stairs Gunter pops his head up from the stairs and fires his rifle towards the prisoners, they both duck and Clyde returns fire with a single shot which drops Gunter to the floor with a thud, Clyde and Karl scurry over to Gunter's body, Clyde picks up his rifle and passes it to Karl.

'You go and get the other one, I'll get the officer' said Clyde

Karl rushes off in a separate direction as Clyde walks briskly down the stairs and into the hall and kicks a door open, inside is the young officer who is using the radio.

'Yes, there's been a disturbance…' said the panicking officer desperately trying to get the point across that they were struggling at the outpost with the prisoners

The officer turns to look at Clyde and attempts to grab his pistol from his holster but is struggling to due to him using the radio with the other hand, Clyde aims the rifle at the officer and pulls the trigger, nothing happens as Clyde had forgot to reload the rifle as he is not used to bolt action rifles, the officer stops using the radio and attempts to release his pistol from its holster so Clyde throws the rifle at the officer knocking his concentration and runs at the officer who has now stood up.

Clyde rugby tackles the officer who by now has released his pistol and they wrestle on the floor, the officer struggles to aim the pistol whilst Clyde has him in a choke hold whilst also holding the officers hand with the pistol in and points it away from them both.

The Officers' legs are kicking out and both men are struggling mid fight, then a gunshot is heard elsewhere in the house and there is a voice on the radio reporting back.

'Please continue with the last message over, you said you had a disturbance at the outpost?' said the voice on the radio

The officer screams out for help but Clyde pulls him tighter in the choke hold, the officer manages to fire a few rounds at the ceiling whilst Clyde is squeezing his neck and then stops struggling after one last tight squeeze followed by a crack and then his body goes limp.

Footsteps can be heard running to the communications room where Clyde is, Clyde picks up the pistol and shuffles along the floor backwards hiding in the corner of the room and aims the pistol towards the doorway expecting to have to kill whoever walks into the room next.

A rifle slowly moves around the door frame aiming it around the room, Clyde holds the pistol tighter as he aims it at the doorway ready to fire at whoever walks through the door.

'Clyde?' said Karl cautiously

Clyde breathes a sigh of relief and lowers his pistol.

'Fucking hell mate, you scared the life out of me' said Clyde as he stands up and Karl lowers his rifle and walks into the room.

'I've killed the driver' said Karl excitedly

'I've done three of them so that must be it then' said Clyde

'Please repeat last message, you wish to report a disturbance, over' said the voice on the radio

Karl and Clyde look at each other, Clyde stands up quickly and picks up the chair which had been knocked over in the fight and sits down in front of the radio and puts on the headset and glances back to Karl with worry hoping his rusty German accent will do the trick in reassuring the person on the radio that everything is fine at the outpost.

'Yes, there's been a disturbance' said Clyde

Clyde looks around to Karl and then raises his hands whilst shrugging his shoulders then turns back to the radio, Clyde stares at the radio trying to think of a good excuse and cover story.

'Yes, one of the guards has gone berserk and shot another one of the soldiers' said Clyde

Clyde looks at Karl and shrugs his shoulders, Karl raises his eyebrows as if to agree with Clyde's makeshift tale.

'Received, has the disturbance been quelled?' said the voice on the radio

Clyde leans further towards the mouthpiece on the radio.

'Yes, he's dead. I shot him' said Clyde brazenly

Clyde leans back in the chair and folds his arms awaiting the response.

'Do you require medical support?' asked the voice on the radio

Clyde leans towards the mouthpiece slowly.

'No, no, they're both dead. Myself and the Private are fine' said Clyde

Clyde turns and nods at Karl then leans back in the chair and folds his arms.

'Who am I talking to please? Name and rank' said a new voice on the radio

Clyde looks at Karl then looks to the body of the dead Officer, Clyde quickly searches the body and pulls out a wallet, and Clyde opens the wallet.

'Lieutenant Lukas Wolf' said Clyde

Clyde looks at Karl.

'Very well Lieutenant Wolf, Captain Jaeger will be attending your position in the next few hours to investigate' said the voice on the radio

Clyde allows the last message to sink in then realises he had heard the Officer mention 'Captain Jaeger' earlier on and Clyde's wants more information and thinks that if he is posing as an Officer maybe he can pull rank on the radio operator and scuttle the plan for 'Captain Jaeger' to drop in on them allowing them time to escape.

'Sorry, who am I speaking to?' said Clyde as he waits patiently expecting the voice on the other end to be a Sergeant at best.

'This is Brigadier Freidrich' replied the voice on the radio

Clyde leans forwards quickly.

'Apologies Brigadier, I shall meet with Captain Jaeger shortly' said Clyde

'Very well. Over and out' said Freidrich

Clyde rubs his hand through his hair and lets out a deep breath then takes off the headset and turns to look at Karl who is now pacing the room.

'We've got to get out of here' said Karl

'We don't even know where we are' said Clyde

Karl stares at Clyde and then looks at a map of Northern France on the wall.

'We must be in Northern France' said Karl

The thought that not only were they in a different country but they are more than likely in another time, Clyde allows that thought to sink in for a moment then looks at Karl.

'We don't even know what year we're in' said Clyde

Karl takes that information in and struggles to accept it as even if they had ended up in Northern France whatever the year they had to get out of the farmhouse as they'd just killed four men between them, either way they had to move out of the area and quickly.

'Does it matter, either way we're in the shit as we've just killed four men' said Karl

Clyde rocks back on his chair and thinks what if they are in present day, they have just killed four men, it could be classed as self-defence but how can they be in present day? They're in France and had seen the old man shot dead, they saw the Messerschmitt's and the convoy, they must be in 1940 around the time of Dunkirk.

'We must be in 1940' said Clyde

Karl appears to say something but then hesitates and shakes his head.

'I…I don't care where or when we are. We need to get the hell out of here, and fast' said Karl

'I really do think we may have somehow…' said Clyde

Karl looks at Clyde awaiting his next words, Clyde is apprehensive about saying the next words as he knows Karl will brush it off or laugh at him for suggesting it.

'…time travelled' said Clyde

Clyde's expectation of Karl's reaction is wrong; Karl shakes his head quickly.

'I agree; I think we have. I also think we need to get the fuck out of here now' said Karl

Clyde always fantasised about time travel and thought it would be a great way to make money, become powerful and make the world a better place, albeit in his own eyes. He had always dreamed of travelling through time but on his terms and being prepared not thrust into the deep end. Clyde had always thought time travel to be impossible, for the people who did invent it may prevent others including him from travelling from dimension to dimension wreaking havoc and changing the future.

Or he wondered whether he had received a head injury or died in the bunker and all this is made up but it couldn't be, he'd felt the pain when punched and also this was more real than any dream he'd ever had, it couldn't be a dream, he thinks that maybe he had died and this is some sort of dream he's having as his brain operates until it fails and all over in a millisecond in real time.

Whatever had happened there was a very good chance that both Clyde and Karl were in Northern France in May 1940 and were under threat.

'Fuck it, let's get in the half-track and make our way to Spain' said Karl

Clyde stands up and lights a cigarette for Karl and one for himself, he passes one to Karl.

'If we take off now, they'll realise something's wrong and they'll search for us, and if we're not captured by the Germans either the French or the RAF will take us out' said Clyde

Karl shakes his head whilst still pacing the room, he takes a look through the window then looks at a large map on the wall and runs his finger to their location.

'We're here, it's about 700 miles to Spain, if we set off now in the half-track, get as far as we can then make up the rest of the distance by foot during the night we'll be alright' said Karl

Clyde steps closer to the map to get a better look at it.

'I agree, but this *Captain Jaeger,* I'm guessing from the Gestapo, is on his way. He's only one man so let's kill him then we'll escape' said Clyde

Karl shakes his head and steps back whilst holding his hands up in disagreement with Clyde.

'What if he isn't alone' said Karl

'If anyone else turns up we'll kill them too. If we wait for Jaeger, then we'll maybe have better transport to get us to Spain. He may be driving a car, that's a little bit more inconspicuous than a big bloody half-track trundling down the road waking everybody up. This Jaeger may be driving a squad car so we could get to Spain a lot quicker' said Clyde

Karl looks to the floor in deep thought then looks back at Clyde.

'That's true, driving a car would be better' said Karl

Clyde stares at Karl now knowing that's he's convinced him to stay put and not act to rash in escaping unprepared and with the Gestapo on their way to investigate.

'Right, let's dump their bodies then get changed into their clothes ready for Jaeger, we'll wear their uniforms and lure him into the house then kill him' said Clyde

Karl looks at the map then back to Clyde and nods.

'Come on then' said Karl

Clyde and Karl each undress the dead Officer and leave his body wearing only his underwear and socks.

'You ready?' said Clyde

Karl nods at Clyde.

'Let's move him then' said Clyde

Clyde and Karl cumbersomely pick up the officer's body and struggle slightly due to the dead weight of the body.

'Bloody hell he's heavy' said Karl

'Tell me about it' said Clyde

Clyde has the top half and Karl has the legs of the Officer, they slowly carry the body out of the room.

'Where we going to dump it?' said Karl

'Let's just drop him outside for a minute and then have a look around' said Clyde

Clyde and Karl carry the body outside into the courtyard and drop the body onto the floor, the lifeless body thuds as it lands on the ground and the officer's body is lay in what would be an uncomfortable position if it was a living person. Karl leans back whilst stretching his back by thrusting his pelvis forwards sharply.

'Bloody hell, I've nearly put my back out' said Karl

Clyde looks over to a barn and Karl notices and looks in that direction too.

'We'll stick him in there' said Clyde

Karl nods and bends down to pick up the dead officer's legs.

'Righto' said Karl

Clyde bends down and picks up the dead Officers body holding the body under the arm pits, they slowly but steadily carry the body over into the barn and then drop the body at the entrance.

'Jesus, he's bloody heavy' said Karl

'Don't be so soft' said Clyde

Clyde looks around in the barn and notices a wooden fence further down the barn so starts to walk over to it, as he gets closer he hears the sound of pigs grunting and turns to Karl.

'This must be where the pigs are' said Clyde

Karl starts to walk over and Clyde walks further up and can now see four pigs in a pen.

'Yes. Definitely pigs said Clyde

Karl walks up alongside Clyde and stands next to him looking at the pigs.

'Didn't that bastard Baum threaten to feed us to the pigs?' said Karl

Clyde nods.

'Aye, he did' said Clyde

Karl continues to look at the pigs then looks to Clyde and as he does so he passes Clyde a cigarette and puts another in his own mouth and lights it.

'Are you thinking what I'm thinking?' said Karl

Karl holds his lighter out in front of Clyde and lights his cigarette, Clyde takes a drag and exhales.

'Let's do it' said Clyde

Clyde and Karl walk over to the officer's body and each grab one leg and pull the officers body along the floor to the gate of the pig pen, by now the pigs are crowded around the entrance to the pig pen grunting and oinking at them both. Clyde throws his cigarette onto the floor and stubs it out with his foot.

'Let's pick him up and throw him over' said Karl

'Bollocks to that he's too heavy' said Clyde

Karl remembering Clyde had teased him earlier for commenting on the weight of the body responds in typical witty fashion.

'Oooh don't be so soft' said Karl

Clyde looks at Karl and shakes his head as he grins as Karl has broken the tension at last.

'You distract them around the other side and I'll drag him in' said Clyde

'Ok' said Karl

Karl stubs his cigarette onto the floor and walks around the other side of the pen clapping his hands.

'Come on pigs. Come on' said Karl

Some of the pigs notice Karl and trot over to him.

'Come on pigs' said Karl who continues to clap

Karl reaches over into the pen and starts to pat them, Clyde looks around the barn and notices there is a wheel barrow full of turnips a few yards away.

'Karl. There's some turnips over there' said Clyde

Karl looks over to the turnips then back to Clyde.

'Throw me a couple of them, I'll distract them with the turnips' said Karl

Clyde walks over to the wheelbarrow and picks up three turnips then walks over to the body looking at Karl who is unaware Clyde is about to throw a turnip to him and try to catch him off guard.

'Karl. Catch' said Clyde who throws a turnip and Karl catches it, quickly followed by another turnip which he catches then the third which he drops and rolls into the pen. Clyde shakes his head as the pigs push each other out of the way to get at the turnip.

'I've seen better hands on a digital watch' said Clyde

This was Clyde teasing Karl on his ability to catch, more precisely teasing his ball handling ability with both men being Rugby League players before they had joined the army. To have 'a good pair of hands' or 'good hands' meant that you were good at passing and catching and with Karl dropping one this left it wide open for Clyde to pass comment.

'I'm still better than you' said Karl

This was a quip at Clyde as Karl had played for the Army Rugby League team whereas Clyde had only played for the Royal Engineers.

Karl smiles as he looks to Clyde then throws the other two turnips into the pen. All of the pigs in the pen are now pushing each other to eat the turnips, Karl runs around to the entrance and opens the gate, Clyde grabs one of the legs of the dead officer and Karl grabs the other and they pull the officer into the pen. They both drop the legs and exit the pen with Clyde locking the gate as they go.

Clyde looks to the wheelbarrow and back to Karl who is again stretching his back by thrusting his pelvis forwards and sideways sharply.

'When you're finished snake hips, let's use that bloody wheelbarrow for the rest of them' said Clyde

Karl has his hands perched on his hips and is thrusting his pelvis sideways and stops suddenly.

'Well that'd make sense, my backs knackered' said Karl

An hour or so later Clyde and Karl wheel the last dead body into the barn then cumbersomely dump it into the pig pen, by now the pigs have started to eat the officer and had made good progress in doing so which revolted both men and they try hard not to show it.

Karl and Clyde both have rags tied around their faces covering their mouths and noses due to the stench not only of the pigs but of the bodies. Clyde locks the gate for the last time on the pig pen, he pushes the wheelbarrow into the corner so that it skids along the floor unaided crashing into the side of the wooden barn wall.

Clyde and Karl both exit the barn quickly and on reaching the fresh air outside pull their makeshift face masks away and gasp in the clean and fresh air. Both Karl and Clyde bend over and put their hands on their thighs, Karl starts to vomit, Clyde notices and starts laughing.

'You bloody big girl' said Clyde

Karl vomits and looks to Clyde and struggles to speak.

'It… it bloody stinks' said Karl

Clyde continues to laugh and Karl dry wretches then vomits.

'Come on. We had better get used to using the weapons' said Clyde

Clyde and Karl walk over to the half-track and Clyde reaches into the back to pull out two rifles, he passes one to Karl and keeps hold of one for himself, he loads it then looks to the courtyard wall where there is a small sign post attached.

'I bet you can't hit that sign' said Clyde

Karl wipes his mouth and takes a minute to gather himself as he still feels nauseous, Clyde spots a chance to get one over on Karl and tease him once more.

'Are you ok? Do you need a minute to recover?' said Clyde jovially

'Fuck off' said Karl abruptly

Karl shakes his head, spits onto the floor then loads his rifle and aims it at the sign, takes a breath then fires hitting the sign making a loud ping as the bullet hits the metal, Karl looks at Clyde.

'There you go' said Karl cockily 'What do I win?'

Clyde aims his rifle at the sign, takes a breath then fires also with the loud ping of the bullet hitting the metal, he then looks at Karl.

'I'll get you a goldfish the next chance we get' said Clyde

Karl walks to the back of the half-track and climbs up into the back, in the back is an MG34 which is a light machine gun, he picks it up and turns to look at Clyde.

'Look at this' said Karl

Clyde looks up at the MG34.

'It's a beauty' said Clyde

Karl places the MG34 on the edge of the half-track to support its weight whilst he loads the weapon. Karl aims the MG34 towards the sign which both men had previously shot at then looks to Clyde.

'Ready?' said Karl excitedly as he wanted to fire the machine gun

'Go ahead' said Clyde

Karl bends so that he can look down the sights aiming at the sign, he then pulls the trigger letting out a short rasp of fire at the sign hitting it numerous times almost disintegrating the sign. Clyde and Karl both smile.

'Bloody hell. This has got some power' said Karl

Clyde walks over to the half-track and leans over to open a wooden crate and pulls out a German stick grenade, Karl notices and lays the MG34 down to one side and picks up a grenade looking it over struggling to see where the pin is.

'How do you use these grenades?' said Karl

Clyde turns the grenade upside down and starts unscrewing the cap from the bottom.

'You unscrew the cap on the bottom, pull on the cord then throw' said Clyde

Karl nods his head as if he has taken in the information.

'No problem' said Karl

Clyde unscrews the cap, pulls on the cord and throws the grenade towards the sign then hides behind the halftrack peering towards the grenade, Karl ducks and peers out from the top of the half-track. A few seconds later the grenade explodes spewing soil into the air, Karl turns to Clyde and laughs.

'Decent bit of kit this eh?' said Karl

Clyde nods in agreement.

'Top quality' said Clyde

Karl picks up the MG34 and some ammunition and walks to the edge of the half-track, sits on the edge then shuffles off and stands next to Clyde whilst holding the MG34.

'So, what's the plan then?' said Karl

Clyde looks to the fields and then back to the farmhouse and looks at the bathroom window upstairs then back to Karl.

'You cover with the MG34 from the bathroom window. When Jaeger knocks at the door I'll shoot him with the pistol and you take care of his driver or whoever turns up with him. If you need any help I'll grab the rifle and flank them on the left' said Clyde

'Ok' said Karl

'Just be careful if he shows up in a car, we need that to escape' said Clyde

'Obviously' said Karl as he rolls his eyes

'Well I'm just saying' said Clyde

'I won't shoot the getaway car, don't worry' said Karl

Clyde nods whilst Karl grins.

'Once Jaeger or whoever he is turns up with are all dead, we'll throw them to the pigs…'said Clyde

'No, fuck that. Just leave them' interrupted Karl as he doesn't want to stay in the area any longer than they have to.

Clyde thinks about Karl's comment and thinks he has a valid point, they've already waited for Jaeger before they escape, maybe they can just hide the body slightly rather than mess about wheeling however many bodies up to the pigs in the barn.

'Ok, we'll leave them then change back into civilian clothing then get into their vehicle and make our way to Spain' said Clyde

'Aye, ok' said Karl

Clyde looks at his watch then looks around the courtyard to the farmhouse kitchen window.

'Change into German uniform then gather some food, water and get the weapons ready. I'll sort out the route' said Clyde

'Ok, will do' said Karl

Clyde walks back into the house and heads for the communications room whilst Karl grabs some ammunition from the half-track and carries it into the house and lays it on the table in the kitchen, once in the kitchen he changes into one of the dead soldier's uniforms then opens the cupboards in search of food and drink. Karl picks up a backpack which is on the floor and starts to fill the rucksack with tins of food from the cupboards.

Meanwhile, Clyde is in the communications room changing into the Officers uniform and sat looking at a large map of Northern France on the table. Once dressed Clyde draws in red pen the route which he thinks they should take to Spain. Clyde looks at the compass on the table and continues to draw lines and crosses on the map to indicate places to avoid, he is in deep thought as he looks at the map and looks at his watch then writes at certain points of the map as to where to rest on their journey.

Once Clyde has finished, he folds the map up to the size of an A4 sheet then walks into the kitchen to where Karl has prepared two rucksacks with food, water and ammunition for their weapons, Karl looks at Clyde.

'Have you sorted out the route?' said Karl

'Yes. Have you got the supplies?' said Clyde

'Yes. I've also got some valuables from the house which we can barter with' said Karl

Clyde nods and opens the rucksack on the table and looks through the items and pulls out an old watch taken from one of the dead soldiers.

'Good thinking. We'll need to barter with some sailors at San Sebastian to take us to England' said Clyde

'Sshh' said Karl as he notices a noise outside

Karl holds his hand up to silence Clyde, both men hold still for a moment then they look towards the kitchen window. The hum of diesel engines in the distance alerts Karl to rush over to the kitchen window for a better view of what is going on.

'Shit' said Karl

'What's up?' said Clyde

Clyde moves quickly over to the kitchen window and stands beside Karl looking out to see a small convoy of heavy trucks around 500 metres away travelling towards the farm.

'Shit!' said Clyde

'Jesus. It looks like there's a few of them, are they coming here?' said Karl

'I bloody hope not, let's just see if they pass' said Clyde

The small convoy of around five trucks get closer to the farm, by now the sound of diesel engines can be distinctly heard in the farm kitchen.

'There heading this way, let's move now' said Karl as he picks up the rucksack from the table and slings it over his shoulder and moves towards the back door and opens the door slightly.

'Wait' said Clyde

Karl stops and looks back.

'What?' blurted Karl with disgust

'We can't move; they'll spot us' said Clyde

Karl starts to put the rucksack over both of his shoulders and it tapping his hand on the top of the door as he stands half way through the door with one arm on top and one holding the handle on the inside.

'Fuck it, we'll just take the bare minimum and go on foot. Come on!' said Karl impatiently

Clyde turns from Karl and looks out towards the convoy, by now the convoy is 100 metres away, Karl opens the back door fully and is looking towards the nearby woods approximately 100 metres away in the total opposite direction of the convoy, Karl thinks no matter how fast the convoy moves if they run now the farm house will shield their escape.

'Let's move now. We can make it to those trees before they get here and by the time they find out anything has happened here they'll not find us. We'll be long gone' said Karl

Clyde looks towards to convoy which is now 50 metres away and back to Karl.

'It's too late now, you wait here and I'll deal with them. I'll tell them to move on' said Clyde

'Clyde. Come on, let's fucking go!' said Karl impatiently

Chapter 4 - From the Frying Pan into the Fire

The convoy pulls up outside of the courtyard but one truck strays and drives inside the courtyard stopping outside the farm house. Karl and Clyde both look through the window in shock at the surprise convoy.

'Jesus man, we've got to hide' said Karl

Outside in the courtyard a German SS Officer stands up in the truck, this is Lieutenant-Colonel Otto Stechen.

'Go inside and fetch them' ordered Stechen

A soldier jumps off the side of the truck. Clyde turns away from the window inside and turns to look at Karl.

'You're Private Schmitt, I'm Lieutenant Wolf, I'll do the talking' said Clyde

The SS Soldier walks into the kitchen, stops and salutes Clyde who in turn salutes back.

'Sir, Lieutenant-Colonel Stechen orders you to leave your station and accompany us in the convoy' said the SS Soldier

Clyde looks at Karl and then back to the soldier and gets ready to use his authority for the first time.

'I'm under strict order to remain here' said Clyde

The soldier looks back to the truck to Stechen who by now has climbed from the truck and is walking towards the kitchen door, Clyde turns to the SS Soldier.

'Brigadier Freidrich has ordered us to stay and wait for Captain Jaeger of the Gestapo' said Clyde as Stechen walks into the kitchen.

'I'm over ruling those orders. You should have constructed this outpost by now and by the looks of it you have. You need to come with us to assist us should we need any engineers' said Stechen

Clyde and Karl look at each other deflated that they won't get their chance of escape and they can't take on the convoy of troops as there's too many of them, Clyde looks back to Stechen who has started to walk back out of the kitchen.

'But Sir…' said Clyde

'Come on. Chop chop' said the obnoxious Stechen

Stechen turns and walks back out into the courtyard as does the SS soldier and they get back into the truck, Clyde turns to Karl knowing their escape plan is now futile or at least it is for the time being and deep down both men know that they will need to go with the flow for short term survival.

'Listen, we have to go with them, we'll leave at the next opportunity I promise' said Clyde

Karl looks out through the open kitchen door out towards the woodland and then back to Clyde.

'Can we not just throw a few grenades at them and make a run for it?' said Karl

Clyde leans in to Karl, both men are agitated and scared of the prospect of being alongside more German soldiers and their cover being blown for they'd be shot as spies.

'There's too many of them. We must go with them. I promise, the first opportunity we get we'll leave' said Clyde

Karl shakes his head and steps backwards as he's not as keen as Clyde is with teaming up with the SS.

'Fuck this, I'm making a run for it' said Karl

Karl attempts to walk towards the back door, he had always been very impulsive, Clyde grabs his arm and pulls him back.

'Listen' said Clyde sternly 'If they get a whiff of us being English we're fucked'

Karl looks out to the soldiers in the truck.

'We're fucked either way' said Karl aggressively

'Come on!' shouts Stechen

Clyde stoops as to make eye contact with Karl as he is looking towards the floor.

'We've got to go with them. Just keep quiet and do what they say. The first chance we get we'll make a break for it ok?' said Clyde

Karl nods then looks away.

'This isn't right. This just doesn't feel right' said Karl

Karl picks up his MG34 and Clyde picks up a rifle then they walk out into the courtyard holding their weapons and are pulled up into the truck and sit down inside, the truck begins to move away. Stechen turns back to Clyde and smiles then turns looking forwards. Clyde and Karl are sat at the back of the truck next to each other and Karl leans closer to Clyde.

'What about when Jaeger turns up?' said Karl

'What about him?' said Clyde

'What he if finds something in the barn?' said Karl

Clyde pauses and then turns to look at the barn and then back to Karl.

'It's too late to do anything now' said Clyde

Clyde and Karl both look back towards the barn scanning the area just in case they can see anything, it doesn't matter if they do as they were helpless to do anything given the circumstances.

Moments later, the truck joins the convoy of the other trucks at the back of the line and moves off down the dirt track leading back to the main road. The truck jostles over the uneven terrain and joins up with a larger convoy on the main road, the truck is full of SS Soldiers as is every vehicle in the convoy. The crackles in the distance indicate a battle a few miles away and accompanied with the sound of Messerschmitt's dive bombing and strafing locations around the same location this can only mean one thing, this is war.

Stechen finishes speaking over the radio and puts the radio down and turns around to look at Clyde who is sat behind him and reaches out his hand.

'Lieutenant-Colonel Stechen, 3rd SS Division Totenkopf' said Stechen

They shake hands and Stechen strikes Clyde straight away as an impatient and driven Officer. Stechen is short in height, blonde hair and a slim build with a small scar where his eyebrow meets his nose, probably from falling from horse Clyde thinks as with Stechens accent and the way he holds himself Clyde can tell he'd had a privileged upbringing and must have got the scar from doing something fancy rather than fighting.

'Lieutenant Lukas Wolf, 43rd Sturmpionier Battalion and with me is Private Schmitt' said Clyde

Stechen barely looks at Karl but stays nodding and looking at Clyde.

'May I ask where we're going?' asked Clyde inquisitively

Stechen smiles at Clyde and seems to have finished judging him.

'We're supporting the rest of 3rd Division further north, we may need your support as combat engineers' said Stechen

The convoy is travelling at a good speed and is making decent progress, Stechen looks at Karl and then back to Clyde.

'So, what did Brigadier Freidrich say to you?' said Stechen

'He said to wait at the farmhouse Sir' said Clyde confidently in the hope that name dropping Freidrich may prompt Stechen to change his mind and stop the truck and allow both Clyde and Karl to walk back to the farmhouse.

'Any reason for that?' said Stechen

Clyde looks to Karl then back to Stechen.

'Captain Jaeger was going to pay us a visit Sir' said Clyde

Stechen lowers his eyes brows and holds his chin with his finger and thumb looking puzzled then looks at Clyde.

'Ah. So the disturbance must have been at your post?' said Stechen as if to show that he is in the know with everything that goes on

How the fuck does he know?

'Yes Sir' said Clyde as he wonders how the hell he found that information out

'So, what happened?' said Stechen

Clyde looks at Karl and then back to Stechen.

'One of the privates went a bit crazy and shot our Corporal Sir' said Clyde

Stechen stares at Clyde wide eyed as he seems to enjoy the gory details involved in death and knows that if he presses, Clyde will give him all the details.

'Then what happened?' said Stechen

'Then I shot him Sir' said Clyde

Stechen nods his head then turns to the front, Clyde looks at Karl as if to say everything seems to be going well, he then turns back to Stechen who has also turned to face him.

'I like your style Wolff' said Stechen

Stechen nods, he absolutely loves the thought of killing his own troops if they don't obey his orders, in fact he enjoys killing his own belligerent troops more than he enjoys killing the enemy. Though he never actually pulls the trigger, he's too much a coward for that, he usually orders the killings but revels in them nonetheless.

'I'd do the same' said Stechen pompously 'If any man does not fully get behind the war effort he is no good alive'

The radio operator picks up the radio and looks at Stechen.

'Excuse me Sir' said the radio operator

Stechen turns back to face forwards and picks up the radio receiver, Clyde turns to Karl who looks worried, Karl shakes his head at Clyde and leans closer.

'We need to get the fuck out of here' whispers Karl

Clyde looks to the floor then back to Karl who looks intense, he isn't as comfortable as Clyde is as he can't speak the language so doesn't know what is being said and luckily the other soldiers in the back of the truck alongside Karl remain silent throughout the journey.

'We will do mate. Just wait for the right opportunity' whispers Clyde

Clyde looks forward to see that the convoy entering a town which has been decimated by battle, there are buildings that have crumbled into rubble, some are smouldering after being on fire and there are no civilians but there are a few medical units looking after injured soldiers, Karl leans closer to Clyde and speaks in hushed tones.

'Back at the bunker. How long did it take the rabbit to reappear?' said Karl, clearly he had been thinking of a way of getting out of the situation

'A few minutes at the most' said Clyde

'Why the fuck are we still here then?' said Karl

This dawns on Clyde, he hadn't thought about the time it took for the rabbits to reappear back in the room. He along with Karl had been too caught up in it all to think about the possibility of just being transported back to present day.

'I don't know. It must have something to do with our body mass' said Clyde

'We need to get out of here, make an excuse' said Karl

Clyde leans forward to Stechen.

'Excuse me Sir' said Clyde

Stechen turns around to Clyde.

'Yes Wolff?' said Stechen

'Sir, I think it would be a good idea for myself and Schmitt to jump out here and see if there is anything we can do to support in this area' said Clyde

Stechen shakes his head and leans further around to face Clyde.

'Nonsense, you're coming with us. Bethune has been taken, we don't plan on hanging around in this area. We need you further North' said Stechen

Clyde turns to look at Karl and then back to Stechen.

'Sir, there may be booby traps, mines and so on that need clearing, maybe a…' said Clyde

'Ah, ah, ah, ah…let me just stop you there' interrupted Stechen with his usual repugnant manner 'Is there a reason you don't want to go further North?'

Clyde gulps, takes a deep breath and looks around then back to Stechen knowing there's not much he can do in convincing the rude officer that they'd be better of leaving and that he can't rock the boat too much, he needs to keep Stechen on board until they can escape.

'No Sir, I just want to get into the action as soon as I can' said Clyde

'You'll get your chance soon. Just sit down and wait, there's a good boy' said Stechen

Ironically, Clyde wants nothing more than to punch Stechen mainly down to his lack of manners and the way he speaks to people rather than being an SS officer. He knows he will have to swallow his pride and toe the line until he gets his chance to escape.

'Yes Sir' said Clyde

Stechen turns back around and Clyde turns and leans in to Karl.

'He's having none of it, we're stuck with them' said Clyde

Karl seems agitated as he taps his foot on the floor and is looking around the battle ravaged area of Bethune.

'Fuck this, the next chance we get, we need to make a break for it' said Karl

Karl, ever the impulsive one still surprises Clyde despite being in the situation that they find themselves in.

'We need to wait for the right moment' said Clyde

'Fuck the right moment, we need to get out of here, now' insisted Karl as quietly as he could

'Hold on, as soon as we get to where we're going, as soon as it gets dark we'll escape' said Clyde

Karl looks to the side of the road to see three dead British Soldiers and looks at Clyde awaiting a reaction to back up his plan of getting out of the truck as soon as possible with the sight of dead British soldiers pushing Karl over the edge emotionally.

'Listen, you're either coming with me or you're on your own. I'm not staying on this fucking truck' said Karl

'Just a little longer mate…'said Clyde

'Fuck this shit' interrupted Karl

Karl jumps over the side of the truck, the rest of the soldiers in the truck start to shout, Clyde stands up.

'Karl, get back here' said Clyde

Stechen turns to see Karl sprinting away as fast as he could from the convoy, the truck stops.

'Shoot him' called Stechen excitedly as his eyes widened and a smile broke out on his face as he watched on with glee

'No!' said Clyde

Karl is running as fast as he can away from the convoy and is running intermittently in different directions as he suspects he will be shot at and running in this manner is what was taught in the Army to make himself a difficult target to hit, a volley of shots is fired and Karl drops to the floor.

'No!' said Clyde

Clyde attempts to jump from the vehicle and is ready to hop over the side as he holds on to the side and cocks his leg up onto the seat.

'Wolf' shouts Stechen

Clyde turns to Stechen.

'Don't you dare get off this truck, leave him' Stechen said callously

Clyde turns to look at Karl's body in the distance lay motionless with a small pool of blood underneath him gaining in size every second, this is his best friend that has been cut down by the gun fire and Clyde can't believe it, he knew if he tried to do anything he too would be killed along with Karl.

'I know he's one of your men but we won't have deserters' said Stechen

Clyde turns to look at Stechen in disbelief unable to speak as he's still in shock.

'Drive on' calls Stechen

Stechen sits down and the vehicle starts to move away and Clyde looks again to Karl's body lay on the floor then he sits back down.

'That's the only engineer we had… Sir' said Clyde

Stechen continues to look forwards and doesn't turn to face Clyde as that would mean he was having to explain himself to another Officer whom he outranked, he wouldn't allow anyone to second guess him especially in front on his men and had his own way of counteracting challenges to his authority, usually by pulling a few strings with his Uncle Brigadier Freidrich and having the insubordinates sent to the eastern front but he'd took a shine to Clyde, so a sharp tongued put down would be suffice unless Clyde kept up the belligerence.

'We have you don't we?' said Stechen

Stechen turns to look at Clyde knowing he had put him in his place as Officers didn't really get their hands dirty, they just gave orders and Stechen had slapped Clyde down in front of his men in suggesting he take the engineers role, though this wouldn't be a problem to Clyde has he had experience, Clyde nods and looks to the floor.

'All is well then' said Stechen who smiles as though it was friendly banter with Clyde

Clyde clenches his fist and rubs his other hand over his face and lets out a sigh then looks back to see if he can spot Karl but the convoy has now moved way past where the incident happened, Clyde starts to feel hot and his throat gets drier and tighter, he struggles to breathe and is panicking but is trying his hardest not to show it in front of the others. He feels as though as he is being choked by some invisible enemy and loosens his top button on his shirt and slackens it in the hope it will allow him to breathe easier. Thoughts of his best friend Karl lay dead or dying in some far away land with Clyde not being so far away fills him with panic, he still feels hot and is breathing rapidly so pulls out his water bottle and sips from it, he also takes a cigarette out and lights it and randomly stands up in the back of the truck not knowing what to do with himself, Stechen notices.

'Sit down you fool' said Stechen snottily

Clyde doesn't really know what he's doing so gives Stechen an awkward smile and sits down, he feels light headed and thinks about jumping from the truck as Karl did but by now the truck must be two miles away, if he did jump surely he would suffer the same fate. He smokes his cigarette but stumps it out after a couple of drags as he can't smoke it as he has a dry mouth and he is struggling to breathe, he also feels sick. He tries to get over this by sipping the water from his canteen and tries to slow his breathing down before he collapses.

The convoy moves on through the ruins of Bethune the sound of roaring engines and the crackle of gun fire still raging in the distance whilst Clyde battles his demons and struggles with the indecisiveness of staying or going or put simpler, living or dying.

Chapter 5 – Massacre

The convoy of vehicles is moving along a country road approaching a group of farm buildings, experience has taught the driver to be cautious in these scenarios so the convoy slows right down.

In the distance a battle rages on again accompanied with the sound of an aerial battle overhead.

A soldier on Clyde's truck lifts his helmet slightly above his forehead allowing fresh air to blow underneath his helmet onto his perspiring head, the soldier's hair is wet with sweat and as he lowers his helmet he wipes his brow and closes his eyes to momentarily try to appreciate the breeze. Another soldier in the truck wipes the corners of his mouth with his finger and thumb then licks his lips and looks at another soldier's water bottle, the soldier then looks around the trucks floor and then towards the front clearly he'd run out of water and due to the intense mid-day heat he was thirsty.

Clyde looks across the nearby fields and despite the noise from the engines tries to listen to the birds in the nearby hedge rows and wonders whether Karl is dead or maybe still alive, he wonders whether to exit the vehicle now but thinks he'll get shot like Karl did, he still sips his water and struggles to keep calm, on the surface he looks fine but on the inside he is extremely anxious and is recovering from having a panic attack.

Just keep calm…breathe…. everything will be alright, just breathe, nice…and slow.

With thoughts of revenge now on his mind, he must kill Stechen somehow, but at the moment there are too many soldiers to protect him.

You'll get your revenge, just stay calm.

The convoy presses on down the country road when the first vehicle in the convoy explodes and the silhouettes of soldiers on fire in the back scramble out whilst the truck is engulfed with flames, the sound of rifle fire fills the air as soldiers in the second vehicle are caught in the machine gun fire from the ambush and most are killed.

Stechen ducks down in the back of the truck and looks like a rabbit caught in the headlights, he doesn't know what to do and Clyde and the soldiers notice this as they sit in the stationary vehicle.

'Everybody off' shouts Clyde

The truck stops suddenly and Clyde, Stechen and the troops in their truck all exit the vehicle.

'Take cover in the ditch' calls Clyde

The soldiers all gather in the nearby dried out irrigation ditch at the side of the road with each one of them crashing to the ditch with a thud with neither of them returning fire.

Soldiers jump from the rest of the vehicles in the convoy and open fire onto a barn to the right of the convoy where the machine gun and rifle fire is coming from.

Stechen is curled up in a ball flinching with every shot fired, Clyde looks around and the rest of the soldiers are looking to him for leadership and he knows he has to provide it, his natural instincts and training kicks in, he looks further back down the line of troops.

'Mortars' shouts Clyde as he again looks around at the troops to see two soldiers preparing a mortar tube and the base plate whilst another carries a crate of mortars from the back of their truck and lays it on the floor and takes one out ready to drop down the tube once it's set up.

'Get some mortars fired onto their position' calls Clyde intensely

The thud of mortar fire can be heard as the SS troops fire mortars towards the barn exploding and spewing dirt into the air as they land, Clyde turns to four troops next to him.

'You four, give me some covering fire' said Clyde

Clyde looks to Stechen with contempt who now has his hands over his head curled up on the floor then looks to three other troops to his left.

'The rest of you, on three follow me to behind that wall' shouts Clyde

The four troops open fire towards the barn.

'1, 2, 3 go, go, go' calls Clyde as he and the three troops run towards the wall, one of the troops are shot as they scramble out of the ditch, Clyde and the two troops each dive to the floor behind the dry stone wall seeking cover from the rifle fire coming at them from the barn.

'Right. We provide covering fire for the other guys' calls Clyde

Clyde ushers the other troops in the ditch to come out, Stechen notices the rest of his troops are about to make the dash to the wall leaving him behind if he doesn't go with them and he believes in strength in numbers, though a perverse interpretation of that saying, as long as he has troops stood in front of him he stands less of a chance of getting shot is the way he interprets that particular saying.

'Covering fire' calls Clyde

The troops behind the wall open fire towards the barn whilst the four troops run and take cover behind the wall, Stechen also follows but hides from the oncoming machine gun fire behind the four troops, one of them is shot, the troops and Stechen each take cover alongside Clyde.

The sound of cracks, zips and the thud followed by an explosion from the mortar fire in the ditch is accompanied with the sound of cries of agony from the SS troops who were shot in the assault. The wall is hit with rifle fire with bits of the dry-stone wall shooting out bits of dust as the bullets hit it, with every shot hitting the wall Stechen flinches. This is probably the closest Stechen has been to fighting since the phoney war ended just a few weeks before and didn't seem to have adjusted, maybe he had just joined the SS for the glory, he certainly lacked a backbone Clyde thought.

By now troops from the other trucks in the convoy are rushing to hide behind the wall as Clyde seems to be the only officer taking charge in the area, this could be either that he is showing his natural leadership skills honed in battle in Iraq and Afghanistan or could simply be that the other officers in the group have been killed, either way the troops are looking to him for leadership. The strange thing is that at no point during this skirmish does it occur to Clyde that he is fighting for the German SS against the British, his instinct to survive kicks in and he allows it to flow in full force.

A British soldier pops his head around the corner of the barn and fires his rifle, Clyde notices the British helmet and it dawns on him what he is actually doing, he's leading a group of Germans trying to kill British troops.

Shit, what am I doing?

He looks around to see that there are many troops gathered around the wall each taking turns to fire pot shots at the barn and knows he can come up with a plan to quell the fighting to save the British soldiers lives and maybe kill Stechen if he can get him away from his troops for a few minutes.

'Right. I need five volunteers… and you Sir' said Clyde

Stechen is curled up on the floor with his back to the wall with no intention of taking the lead or even taking the risk of firing his pistol towards the enemy in case he gets shot. Stechen is short in stature, small in build and short in courage and this doesn't come as a surprise to the troops who are pinned against the wall, maybe they have witnessed this before.

'Why do you need me?' said Stechen

'Sir. I want you and five troops to flank them on the right, we will provide covering fire, I want to make them think they're surrounded and then smoke them out' said Clyde

Stechen looks around and then back to Clyde, Clyde looks over the wall then ducks, he turns to Stechen who hasn't moved.

'You don't give me orders Lieutenant; you see these pips on my collar' said Stechen acidly

Stechen slumps back further into the wall and Clyde can tell that this guy is shitting his pants.

'Sir, it would be safer for you to flank them than if you stayed here' said Clyde knowing Stechen has the art of self-preservation down to a tee.

Stechen mulls that thought over for a moment, however Clyde thinks if Stechen if flanking the British on the edge Clyde himself may be able to shoot him, after all, he is a very good shot and nobody would know it was him due to the confusion amongst the soldiers caused by the surprise attack, the heat as it is Summer and the disorganisation of the battle.

'Why can't we just wait for the Panzers?' said Stechen nervously

'Sir. We want to capture them, not destroy them' said Clyde

Stechen shakes his head.

'I disagree' said Stechen

Clyde leans closer to Stechen.

'Sir. We don't know how many there are or what ammunition they have, if we surround them they *will* surrender' said Clyde as he tries to convince Stechen

Stechen thinks about surrounding them and maybe that will be a better idea than waiting behind the wall, after all, how long would it be until the British threw grenades or fired mortars at them, if Stechen did lead the team to flank them he'd be slightly further away and safer for sure, it would also give him the chance to really hide but without Clyde there to witness it.

'Ok. I'll go' said Stechen

Stechen nods his head and leans forward slightly so that he can get ready to run to the trees quickly and shuffles to the opposite side of the five troops who will be going with him on the flank getting ready to use them as cover as he did earlier on.

'Ok' said Stechen

Five troops are crouched in front of Clyde.

'Right, we will provide covering fire as you make the dash for the trees' called Clyde over the noise of the battle as the soldiers listened intently 'you six make your way along that ditch and into the woodlands, then spread out and provide rapid fire for 30 seconds'

Clyde and the rest of the troops flinch as an explosion blows a hole in the wall a few metres away, Clyde looks at the hole in the wall and the toppled stones that landed on the soldiers beside the explosion then back to Stechen and the five troops, Stechen crawls along the floor quickly to the ditch and takes cover, he isn't taking any chances so goes before the other troops involved in the flanking manoeuvre.

'Once we have suppressed them with rapid fire their fire will die off for a moment. I will engage the enemy and ask for their surrender' said Clyde

The troops nod in agreement then get set for the dash to the woodlands.

'Rapid fire, 30 seconds' calls Clyde

The troops along the wall provide rapid covering fire as the five troops make a dash through the ditch and towards the woodlands. Stechen makes sure he hides behind the troops as he waits for the five troops to run past him then follows on sheepishly behind.

Clyde pops his head over the wall to look at the barn and then looks over to the convoy where there are mortars being fired from the ditch. The fire from the troops eases as they finish their covering fire and then returns to sporadic firing. Clyde grips his rifle read to aim and looks over to the woodlands in the hope that amongst the rapid fire he can take a shot at Stechen, he can see the five troops but can't see Stechen.

'Where the fuck is he?' whispers Clyde to himself

A shot from the barn hits the wall near to Clyde, this takes his attention away from the flanking troops as he ducks, then looks again in search of Stechen but still no sign of him, he then looks to his troops beside him.

'Rapid fire, 30 seconds' calls Clyde

The troops against the wall and the ones in the woods provide rapid fire upon the barn, one soldier against the wall is shot and falls to the floor. Clyde aims his rifle over to where Stechen should be but he still can't see him, Stechen must be hiding.

Mortars explode all around blowing holes in the roof of the barn and making craters in the ground around it, the sound of gun fire hitting the barn and tearing chucks out of the barn drowns out any other sounds, the fire then dies down as the British soldiers in the barn are suppressed by the vicious barrage of bullets and mortars that have just been fired at them.

'Cease fire, cease fire' calls Clyde

The firing stops apart from the sporadic rifle fire from the barn, Clyde opens a dead soldiers jacket and tears a piece of his white shirt off then ties it around a rifle and then holds it in the air above the wall.

'Hold your fire. Hold your fire' shouts Clyde

Clyde slowly stands up behind the wall, a shot hits the wall in front of him.

'Hold your fire!' shouts Clyde in English at the British troops

Clyde stands behind the wall with a slight hunch anticipating another shot to take him out. The SS soldiers are surprised with what Clyde is doing and watch in anticipation as to what his next move is. Clyde looks over to the five soldiers in the trees and again can't pick out Stechen.

Slippery bastard, where the fuck is he?

'What do you want?' calls an English voice from the barn

Clyde looks towards the barn.

'I want to speak to your commanding officer' said Clyde

Clyde stands behind the wall with his hands in the air but still holding a rifle with the piece of white shirt tied around the end.

'Chance would be a fine thing, he's dead' replied the voice

'Who's in charge then?' said Clyde

'That would be me' replied the voice

Clyde slowly starts to climb over the wall, the other troops are looking at him in shock.

'Hold your fire. I'm just walking slowly towards you' calls Clyde

Clyde slowly walks towards the barn with an arm in the air and the other holding the rifle with the piece of white shirt on.

'I would like to discuss your surrender' said Clyde

'That's not open for discussion' replied the voice quickly

A shot hits the floor in front of Clyde.

'Don't walk any further' came another voice from the barn

Clyde stands still and wonders whether he's placing too much trust in the British soldiers forgetting he's masked as a German Officer and whether the British troops will kill him as a sort of trophy kill. With him being British he wants to make the soldiers surrender before they are blown to pieces by the approaching Panzers.

'You're surrounded. We have a Panzer division on its way shortly and the plan is to blow this barn to pieces if you do not surrender' said Clyde trying his best to convince them to surrender 'I am offering you all a way out of this, so please take it'

Clyde looks back to see a convoy of tanks in the far distance, then turns back towards the barn.

'Well that's awfully kind of you, but we'd prefer to call your bluff' replied the voice

Clyde turns and looks towards the five troops on the flank with Stechen and then is distracted by the faint hum of diesel engines in the distance which can now be heard due to the cease fire, Clyde turns around to look and can see a convoy of Panzers a mile away making its way towards them.

'See for yourself, the Panzers are a mile south' said Clyde

Clyde slowly walks towards the barn but no reply comes from the barn.

'Have you seen the Panzers?' said Clyde

'Yes, we see them' replied the voice

'Please come out with your hands up. You will be captured as prisoners of war but at least you'll be alive' said Clyde

No reply comes from the barn; the Panzers engines grow slightly louder as they head towards the direction of the barn.

'Please, for your own sake, don't be stupid. The Panzers will blow this place to pieces if you don't surrender' said Clyde

Clyde continues to walk slowly towards the barn.

'Stay where you are' replied the voice from the barn

Clyde stops where he is and turns to look at the Panzers, they are now ¾ of a mile away, Clyde realises he is too close for comfort and thinks he should have stayed near to the wall. He doesn't think he's convinced the British soldiers to surrender and if he was in their shoes he'd shoot the officer between the eyes then fight until he couldn't fight anymore then surrender but Clyde had fought in less conventional wars in the present day so that was his way of thinking.

'Should I give the order for the Panzers to fire Sir' shouts a German soldier from behind the wall

Clyde turns to look at the wall, he looks at the Panzers and then back to the barn.

'What do you reckon lads? The panzers are ready to fire. Should I give that order?' said Clyde

The barn door opens slightly.

'Ok…we're coming out. Hold your fire' said the deflated voice inside the barn

Clyde turns to towards the wall and holds his arms in the air.

'Hold your fire, hold your fire, they're coming out' said Clyde

The British soldiers slowly open the barn door and after a short pause one by one they hesitantly walk out.

'Throw your weapons to the floor' said Clyde

The British soldiers each throw their weapons to the floor. Each of the soldiers look tired, hungry, dirty and many have injuries or minor cuts. One by one the soldiers walk out of the barn and Clyde looks around to see Stechen is helping with the gathering of the soldiers, Stechen is lining the British soldiers next to the Barn. Clyde thinks to himself it's very admirable of him to get involved once the threat of being killed has gone.

'Follow the others over to the other barn and line up' said Clyde

The British soldiers each walk out and many of them are smoking and each one of them gives Clyde a dirty look and a few mumble under their breath.

'Jerry bastards' said one soldier under his breath

'Krout' came another

'The Panzers want to know if we need their support' calls a soldier stood behind the wall

Clyde turns to the wall then back to the British soldiers who are now surrounded by the SS troops and are being lined up against the barn by Stechen and his five soldiers.

'Just line up against the barn' said Clyde

Clyde turns and jogs over to the radio operator and as he approaches he leans on the wall looking over to the front of the convoy to where the first burning vehicle is.

'We'll need them to shift the 1st vehicle from the convoy, maybe the second depending on how bad the…' said Clyde

The sound of machine gun fire distracts Clyde from the radio operator and as he turns around two SS troops with MG34 machine guns are firing at the British soldiers lined up against the Barn.

'Cease fire, cease fire' shouts Clyde

The machine gunners can't hear Clyde over the sound of their own machine guns and the cries from the British soldiers, Clyde sprints towards to machine gunners with Stechen standing behind them smiling proudly.

'Cease fire!' shouts Clyde

Clyde runs up next to the machine gunners and prevents them from firing by slapping their hands away from the trigger, all of the British soldiers are lay on the floor, many if not all are dead.

'What are you doing Wolf?' barked Stechen

Stechen stands more rigidly as Clyde has undermined his order to slaughter the British troops, Clyde is clearly disgusted and stands with his eyes bulging as are the veins in his neck.

'What am I doing? What are you doing? Under the Geneva Convention they are prisoners of war… Sir' said Clyde as he remembers the callous nature of the man he is questioning

'Finish them off' said Stechen as he slightly sticks his tongue out as he licks his top lip and walks towards Clyde as the survivors are bayonetted.

Clyde looks at the soldiers bayonetting the survivors with shock and disgust, it was him who convinced the men to surrender and now they're being slaughtered.

Fucking hell, what have I done?

'We haven't the time or resources to keep 90 soldiers' said Stechen bitterly as he walks past Clyde towards to the convoy.

'You've, you've just slaughtered them…Sir' stressed Clyde

Stechen stops and turns back to Clyde.

'Am I detecting misplaced loyalties?' said the wide eyed Stechen still on a high from killing the British soldiers

Clyde looks to the bodies then back to Stechen and gulps as he has seen the ruthlessness of the man, he doesn't want to end up on the pile of bodies himself, he bows his head and looks to the floor.

'No Sir' said Clyde

'Well keep yourself under control' said Stechen

Stechen walks away and the SS troops continue to bayonet any survivors, Clyde watches Stechen walk away and eventually out of sight then walks briskly over to the SS troops bayonetting the British Soldiers.

'Stop that, stop that now, get back to the convoy' said Clyde as he drags the SS troops away from the survivors 'everybody get back to the trucks, on the double'

The SS troops each look at each other then back to Clyde, they had been ordered to bayonet the survivors by Stechen but Clyde is now over ruling those orders.

'Come on, what are you waiting for?' said Clyde to the dawdling SS troops.

The SS troops jog towards the convoy leaving Clyde standing next to the bodies on his own, he makes sure the SS troops are out of view and crouches down and puts his head in his hands, he then vomits a few times until he wretches dry then turns to the soldiers.

'Fucking hell I'm sorry lads, I didn't know that was going to happen' said Clyde

Clyde notices two soldiers towards the back of the group lay under some bodies and they had their eyes open looking at him. Clyde notices and looks around to make sure he's alone and walks over to their location and crouches down.

'I know you're alive. I want to help you' said Clyde

The two soldiers he suspected of being still alive don't move just in case this is a ploy to give themselves away so they stay still and silent. Clyde looks around to make sure he's on his own then looks back to where he suspects there are survivors hidden in the bodies.

'If you make your way twenty miles south there is a farm with a radio mast outside. Inside are supplies, maps, weapons and also a half-track with plenty fuel to get you to Spain' said Clyde

None of the soldiers make Clyde aware that they are still alive.

'If you come across another German soldier on his own on the way named Karl, he is British and may also make his way to the farmhouse and over to Spain, he has been shot so please look after him. Good luck' said Clyde

Clyde then walks away back to the convoy in the hope that the survivors take him at his word and take the offer of escape and more importantly do somehow stumble across Karl and take care of him, by now a Panzer has pushed the 1st truck out of the way and the rest of the SS troops are sat in the trucks, Clyde walks past a truck.

'Wolf!' said Stechen sharply

Clyde looks up to see Stechen leaning out of a truck.

'Get on here' said Stechen

Shit, what does he want? I'll be in the shit for sure now, I may as well kill him there and then if he chirps up. They'll kill me, but fuck it.

Clyde walks to the back of the truck and is pulled into the truck by two SS troops. He moves up to sit behind Stechen.

'No, no. Sit with me' said Stechen who orders him beside him like a dog

Clyde stands up and sits next to Stechen disappointed that he didn't get the chance to kill him, if he had maybe he could have saved the British troops or at least gained vengeance for Karl, however he knew he had to cosy up to conceal himself and in the hope of getting closer to kill him at a later opportunity.

'You did well back there, coaxing out the enemy troops so we could kill them was a grand idea. I'll see that you're rewarded' said Stechen

Clyde looks glum, but there is an element of angst in his eyes along with the feeling of disgust and guilt in his stomach.

Is this guy for real? I can't wait to kill this bastard.

'Sir, Brigadier Freidrich' said the radio operator

Stechen is passed the radio and puts the ear piece on.

'Yes Uncle, I'd like to recommend Lieutenant Wolf for promotion, I think he'd make a great replacement for Captain Hoss' said Stechen

Stechen nods at Clyde who looks back at Stechen with disdain uneasy with the promotion.

'Very well, see you soon' said Stechen

Stechen passes the radio back to the operator and turns to Clyde and reaches out his hand, Clyde looks down at Stechens hand and slowly and limply shakes Stechen's hand.

'Congratulations Captain Wolf' said Stechen

Clyde look towards the barn and then to the distance as he watches the aerial battle rage on in the skies far away wishing he could be far away too, anywhere but there.

An hour or so later the convoy slows down and turns into a farm house courtyard, this is a different farmhouse from the first one where Clyde and Karl had killed the German soldiers.

The first vehicle pulls into the courtyard and then stops, soldiers jump from the vehicle and run towards the backdoor, one soldier kicks open the door and the soldiers file into the farmhouse as they search it to secure it as they plan to use it as a base.

The other four vehicles stop outside the courtyard, moments later a soldier pops his head out of an upstairs window and ushers the rest of the troops to enter the farm house as it has been secured, everybody else gets off the other vehicles and walks into the courtyard, Clyde is walking next to Stechen.

'What's happening Sir?' asked Clyde

'We've been ordered to stay here for the night and await further orders' said Stechen

Stechen walks into the house, Clyde stops and looks around into the distance to the direction of a battle that is in full flow, he cannot see the battle but he can hear it clearly.

I really need to get out of here as soon as I can, but I'm going to kill that bastard before I do. But how do I when there are so many troops here? Fuck it, I'll just do it and take the chance, whatever will be will be.

SS soldiers start to set up tents in the courtyard, some others start to build a fire whilst two soldiers walk back from the other side of the courtyard holding a dead chicken in each hand read to pluck and cook on a spit for their supper. Some soldiers are having their wounds redressed in the courtyard and Clyde looks at a motorcycle inside an open barn as he walks past and the thought of escape springs to his mind once again, maybe he could kill Stechen in his sleep and make his escape on the motorcycle, it would be a lot faster and less obvious than a car, truck or half-track and he could make his way to the original farmhouse and either wait for Karl or try to meet up with the British survivors from the massacre.

'Wolf' calls Stechen as he stands in the doorway of the farmhouse.

Clyde quickly snaps away from his murderous day dreams.

'Yes Sir' replied Clyde as he looks away from the motorcycle towards Stechen.

'Come with me' said Stechen as he snapped his fingers in the air ushering Clyde into the kitchen of the farm house, then they both sit down at the table.

'The British are at Dunkirk fleeing in numbers, I don't think we'll be pushing on' said Stechen

Clyde nods, he now knows he is in Northern France and in 1940, he also knows that after Dunkirk it'll be quiet in the area for a good few years, so maybe Stechen may let him off the hook now so he can go back to the original farmhouse and escape, or so he thought.

'Right, ok, so you won't be needing me here then?' said Clyde

'No, I'll be needing you. You're attached to us now after I promoted you to Captain' said Stechen

Clyde looks out of the window to see a soldier wheeling the motorcycle out of the barn and starts to syphon the fuel out of it into a container and is deflated as another escape plan has gone to rat shit.

'Just relax and enjoy the moment' said Stechen joyously

Clyde looks outside to see the soldier pouring the fuel over some timber that has been stuffed into an old oil drum, the soldier then strikes a match and throws it into the oil drum engulfing the timber with flames sending a cumbersome flume of black smoke into the air.

What am I going to do now?

Chapter 6 – New Beginnings

The morning after, Clyde walks across the courtyard and looks at the nurses walk from the farm house over to the barn where the injured soldiers from the region are being looked after. The farm is now a hive of activity as it's being used as a field hospital for the injured German troops.

Clyde walks through the house into the kitchen which is now a communications room, Stechen is stood next to the radio and smiles at Clyde as if he is a long lost friend.

'Ah, Wolf, I have some news' said Stechen

Clyde strolls over to Stechen and sits down near to him.

'We have both been invited to a presentation ceremony in Lille tomorrow evening' said Stechen

Clyde sits up and takes notice, maybe this could be a means of escape once away from the base, maybe if they go along Clyde can kill Stechen and make a break for Spain.

'How will we get there?' said Clyde

'Don't worry about that I've got it organised' said Stechen patronisingly 'You need to be ready for 3pm'

Again, the cogs in Clyde's mind start turning and he wants to know the intricate details to allow him to plan Stechens assassination and his own escape.

'Who will be accompanying us?' said Clyde

Clyde is now fixated with the plan for the journey to Lille, he knows if he gets the opportunity he *will* kill Stechen and make a break for freedom.

'It's just you and I' said Stechen

Clyde looks to the right and nods, then turns back to Stechen.

'Ok, good. I'm looking forward to it' said Clyde

Clyde walks out of the room and upstairs to his quarters in one of the bedrooms, he sits on the bed and pulls out a small rucksack and puts it onto the bed. He opens the rucksack and pulls out a compass and a map and looks at the map to see where Lille is and measures the distance from Spain, it's approximately 620 miles but he'll have to avoid the German hotspots. If he can make it to the original farmhouse then slip into Vichy France then make his way to San Sebastian, it would be even easier if he had access to a vehicle rather than walking by night over several nights and sleeping during the day until he reaches San Sebastian, if he got the right vehicle he could maybe make his way to Gibraltar which would save the need to bribe one of the sailors at San Sebastian to allow him to hide on one of the ships heading to England.

2:50pm the Next Day

Clyde walks down the stairs holding his rucksack over his shoulder and walks in to the kitchen.

'Are you good to go Wolf?' asks Stechen

'Yes. I'm ready' replies Clyde

Stechen stands up from his chair at the kitchen table and picks up his leather gloves and cap from the table.

'Very well, let's go' said Stechen

Stechen walks outside into the courtyard, it is a bright sunny day with clear skies.

'Fischer' calls Stechen

'Yes Sir' calls a voice beside the truck

'We're ready to go' said Stechen

Clyde looks to the truck where two soldiers are stood at the back and then looks to a squad car, he'd hoped they were going to travel alone or have at the most one chaperone, not three as it would be too risky to kill all of them and escape.

'Sir, I thought it was only you and I going to Lille?' said Clyde

Stechen smiles smugly and raises one eyebrow.

'We're not going to drive ourselves there' said Stechen in his usual snobby manner 'We're officers for God's sake'

Again, Clyde feels as though his plan to kill Stechen has been foiled by the awkwardness of the slippery coward, for some bizarre reason he seems to be so difficult to get alone.

'Sir, I think it would be best to go in the squad car' said Clyde in the hope that perhaps Stechen will prefer the comfort of the squad car rather than have a noisy and laborious ride in the truck.

'No Wolf, the truck will be fine, we can feel the warm breeze as we drive' said Stechen

'I think it would be quicker if we went in the squad car, Sir' replied Clyde

Stechen stops and squares up to Clyde and stands wide eyed but smiles in his usual psychotic way.

'You heard what I said' said Stechen quietly but assertively 'Get in the truck'

Clyde purses his lips and rolls his eyes then clenches his fist and scowls as he walks towards the truck. Clyde looks at Sturm and Muller stood behind the truck, both soldiers look like hardened troops and puts the element of doubt into Clyde's mind at the thought of killing Stechen and escaping.

Fischer walks around to the front of the truck and gets inside and starts the engine as Sturm and Muller each pull Clyde and Stechen up into the back of the truck, another soldier carrying a radio also climbs into the back of the truck. Clyde now knows the escape plan is a no go as there are too many to contest with, maybe when they get to Lille he can make a break for it or maybe by then he will have travelled back to present day, Clyde decides to go with the flow and stay under cover as he desperately wants to kill Stechen for what happened to Karl and the British soldiers.

'Let's go' said Muller to Fischer

The truck starts to move off and Clyde turns to look at the barn where the Red Cross nurses are walking about and the injured soldiers sit resting in the courtyard.

6:30pm Le Grand Hotel - Lille

Clyde walks casually down the stairs and into the foyer, he is wearing a fresh uniform for the event which was provided by the quarter master who had set up stores in the hotel as many officers attending the event had come straight from the field of battle.

As he makes his way down the stairs he can hear a string quartet playing the 'Vienna Blood Waltz' by Johan Strauss J. The grandeur of the hotel and the accompanying music gives Clyde a sudden sense of realisation that he is now on the side of the enemy and now a commissioned officer somehow feels in some ways, a sense of ease, mainly due to his grasp of the German language. He hasn't yet been found out and is anticipating that he won't be there much longer due to either being flashed back to present day or escaping to Spain. Clyde reaches the bottom of the stairs and is guided into the ballroom by a Sergeant acting as an usher for the event.

'This way please Sir' said the Sergeant acting as usher

Clyde is still adjusting to being called Sir and doesn't react initially to the request so he stares at the Sergeant for a moment before realising he's being spoken to.

'Thank you Sergeant' replied Clyde belatedly

Clyde walks into the grand ballroom, the sound of 'Johan Strauss' fills the room, inside are many German officers of all ranks with their wives and mistresses drinking wine and other drinks. There are Sergeants in full dress offering drinks to the new arrivals, Clyde is offered a glass of brandy upon entry.

'Thank you' said Clyde

Clyde takes a sip of his brandy as he scans the room and is tapped on the shoulder, Clyde turns around.

'Come with me' said Stechen

Stechen walks in front as Clyde follows like a lap dog still looking around the room to see the string quartet playing, there are tables set up ready for a banquet. Clyde looks in front to see Stechen stop beside a group of high ranking officers, one of the high-ranking officers turns to look at Stechen and smiles as if he knew him well.

'Uncle, this is Captain Wolf, Captain Wolf this is Brigadier Freidrich' said Stechen

Freidrich looks at Clyde and smiles whilst reaching his hand out, Clyde shakes his hand and now realises that nepotism is the likely reason Stechen had risen through the ranks of the SS without having a backbone.

'Ah Wolf' said Freidrich as he smiles as if he's sharing an in joke with Clyde 'I heard so much about your battle at Le Paradis' again Friedrich smiles and looks to Stechen to gauge his reaction

Clyde shakes Freidrichs hand.

'Yes Sir, what exactly did the Lieutenant Colonel tell you about Le Paradis?' said Clyde

Stechen looks bashful as he turns to Freidrich.

'Otto told me you came under attack from 100 British soldiers, you took command along with Otto and managed to kill them all and with little fuss' said Freidrich proudly as the other high ranking officers listened in

Clyde looks to Stechen as he knows he's told his beloved Uncle a pack of lies and that it was Clyde who had took command whilst his beloved Otto cowered in a ball on the floor and that it was Stechen had slaughtered them all after they'd surrendered.

'I wouldn't say little fuss, we did have difficulties but the full credit for the deaths of the soldiers lies totally with the Lieutenant Colonel, Sir' said Clyde

Freidrich turns to Stechen.

'It was a joint effort; I couldn't have done it without Wolf' said Stechen

'I'll agree with that' said Clyde

'Well Wolf, I'm sure you'll enjoy this evening, we have a special guest in attendance' said Friedrich

Clyde looks around to see if he can see the special guest but as he turns he locks eyes with a beautiful blonde lady, the blonde lady turns away quickly as she'd been staring at him, Clyde continues to look at her, the lady then turns back to look at Clyde and they lock eyes on each other again, the blonde lady smiles at Clyde who then eagerly returns the favour.

'Are you ready to take your seat Wolf' asks Stechen in a politer way than usual seeing as he's surrounded by the high-ranking officers

Clyde looks back to Stechen surprised that he's not being spoken to like a dog.

'Erm, yes Sir' said Clyde

Clyde turns to look back at the blonde lady who has now gone.

'Come with me Wolf' said Stechen

Stechen leads Clyde and Friedrich over to a table, Clyde is distracted searching the room for the blonde lady and as Stechen reaches the table Clyde is still searching the room for her.

'Please Wolf, this is your seat' said Stechen

Clyde sits down and stops looking back and looks forward, the blonde lady is sat across from him at the table and is smiling at Clyde who then smiles back. They both stare and smile at each other with Clyde struggling to speak.

'Captain Wolf?' said a stern masculine voice next to Clyde

Clyde turns to his left to see a Captain from the Gestapo standing from his chair.

'Yes' said Clyde

The Captain reaches his right hand out to Clyde.

'Captain Jaeger. It's nice to meet you' said Captain Jaeger

Clyde stands up to shake hands with Captain Jaeger and knocks a large glass of beer over Captain Jaeger thighs and as the beer lands on Jaegers thighs he stands back quickly making his chair screech across the floor alerting all nearby to the minor fracas.

'I'm sorry Sir' said Clyde

Jaeger picks up a napkin and wipes his thighs, the others who looked at Jaeger all turn around and continue doing what they were doing previously.

'Never mind, accidents happen' said Jaeger

Clyde stands, he picks up a napkin and tries to wipe the beer from Jaegers uniform, Jaeger promptly snatches the napkin from Clyde as he seems embarrassed that another man is trying to wipe him close to his genitals.

'Sorry about that Captain' said Clyde

'Don't worry, I'll go and change my uniform, I won't be long' said Jaeger

Clyde sits down as Jaeger walks away and ushers to the waiter to go with him, the nearby officers get back to what they were doing and Clyde straight ahead to see who is sat on the table and the blonde lady is sat directly across from him, Clyde struggles to hide the surprised and excited look in his face.

'I've never seen you before' said the blonde lady

Clyde is excited that the beautiful woman has spoken to him, he also thinks he stands a chance of getting to know her a lot more intimately as he does have a reputation for doing so in the modern day real world.

'I'm new to these functions, I've just been promoted' said Clyde

The blonde lady twirls her hair as she looks smitten looking at Clyde.

'Hmm, I'm sure your wife will be pleased?' asks the blonde lady

Clyde smiles as he knows she's only asking about his wife so he can tell her he's single, it's the oldest trick in the book.

'I'm not married' said Clyde

The blonde lady raises her eyes brows in faux surprise.

'Oh' said the blond lady in a fake act of surprise 'Your girlfriend maybe?'

Clyde shakes his head.

'No, sorry. I'm free and single' said Clyde

'I'm sure the girls are queueing up?' said the blonde lady

One of the officers on the table turns to look at the blond lady then shakes his head as he disapproves of the flirting that's going on, Clyde notices but doesn't care what the other officer thinks and looks back to the blonde lady and shakes his head.

'Nope' said Clyde

'Aw that's a shame' said the blonde lady

'Don't worry about it' said Clyde

The blonde lady smiles and seems to be thinking something over or building up the courage to ask something.

'Would you like to dance?' asked the blonde lady

Clyde wants to accept but doesn't think he can do the type of ballroom dancing that couples are doing on the dancefloor but he thinks it would get him closer to this fine specimen of a woman and this is the sort of thing people did back in the 1940's.

'Why not' said Clyde

Both Clyde and the woman make their way to the dancefloor, Clyde attempts to hold her around the waist and she adjusts his arms so that they have the correct form then they dance.

'So, are you enjoying it?' said the blonde lady

'Well… I'm not the biggest fan of dancing but…' said Clyde

The blonde lady laughs.

'I mean the event, are you enjoying it?' said the blonde lady as she smiles

Clyde laughs as he realises they were on different wave lengths.

'Yes, it's lovely' said Clyde

They continue to dance with Clyde not doing as bad as he thought, he'd only done this type of dancing at the end of a party and all he thought you had to do was hold your partner lovingly, wobble about a bit and try your best not to stand on their feet.

'You seem a bit nervous' said the blonde lady

'You're the first woman I've seen for a while' said Clyde

The blonde lady smiles.

'Oh really?' said the blonde lady

'Yes' said Clyde

'So, what do you think?' said the blonde lady

'You're a welcome sight, I'll give you that' said Clyde

The blond lady smiles as does Clyde, the blond lady leans forward closer to Clyde so the others dancing nearby can't hear them.

'So where are you based?' asks the blonde lady

Clyde leans forward so that the conversation is private.

'I'm based just outside Lestrem, 43rd assault engineers' said Clyde

'Oh, we have red cross based there' said the blonde lady

'Yes, they've set up a field hospital there' said Clyde

'Hmm, well I might have reason to call in there now' said the blonde lady

'That would be nice, what do you do?' said Clyde

'I'm in charge of the red cross nurses in the region' said the blonde lady

Clyde nods his head preparing himself to ask the next question.

'You're quite welcome to come along anytime you like, I'd welcome you with open arms' said Clyde

'Hmm, I think I'll do that then' said the blonde lady

'Ladies and Gentlemen, please stand' said an Usher

The string quartet cease playing and the others dancing on the dancefloor return to their tables, Clyde and the blonde lady notice and also walk back to their table. Moments later the quartet starts to play the National Anthem of Germany as the other officers hold their arms in the air towards a Nazi flag on the stage, Clyde feels uncomfortable but also follows suit and as the anthem finishes the usher steps forward.

'Ladies and Gentlemen, please be seated' calls the usher

Just as the people in the room sits down, Captain Jaeger briskly walks over to his seat and sits next to Clyde.

'Sorry about that' said Jaeger

'No, it was my fault. I'm sorry' said Clyde

'Never mind, it's ok now. Anyway, it's nice to meet you Wolf, I heard about your struggle at the outpost' said Jaeger

Clyde looks at Jaeger and realises that it was him who was going to be investigating the deaths at the outpost and could blow his cover if he found the bodies in the barn even though the pigs had a good start eating them, Clyde hopes the pigs had a decent appetite and ate every bit of them before Jaeger got there.

'Yes, it was a real mess' said Jaeger

Shit, has he found something? Surely not or I'd have been arrested. But then again, he is sat right next to me...shit thought Clyde

'Yes, it was' said Clyde

'I also heard about your struggle with the British at Le Paradis' said Jaeger

Clyde knows Captain Jaeger is in the Gestapo so it's his job to have his finger on the pulse but he thought he would go under the radar, that's what he wanted, he wanted to stay low, kill Stechen and escape to Spain but at the rate he's going he's making his profile a lot bigger than he'd like it to be.

'Yes, yes, I'm sure Lieutenant Colonel Stechen will tell you all about it' said Clyde as to dismiss any further questions in the hope that Jaeger will either ask Stechen or be too afraid to go sniffing around in his business.

'That too was messy, did any of them survive?' asks Jaeger

Clyde pauses for a moment wondering whether Jaeger is playing games with him and whether he knows full well that there were survivors, maybe he'd picked them up and they'd told Jaeger that an SS Officer had tipped them off about the backpack and the escape plan and Jaeger was at the awards evening just to quiz Clyde and get a feel for him, or maybe it's just Clyde being paranoid.

'No, none' said Clyde

Jaeger smiles pretentiously and nods at Clyde.

'Ok, I'll take your word for it' said Jaeger

Clyde takes a deep breath and turns away from Jaeger and looks over to Stechen who is sat beside a woman and flirting profusely, he hopes to god that Jaeger didn't find the survivors at Le Paradis or the dead soldier's remains in the pig pen.

'I see the Lieutenant Colonel is enjoying his time with General Models daughter' said Jaeger

'It certainly looks that way' said Clyde

Clyde looks to Jaeger and then back to Stechen who is laughing and joking with General Models daughter.

Clyde then looks around the room again to see the high commanders in the German military and thinks that if he could smuggle a bomb into this place, it would set the Germans back months if not years if he could wipe out a few of the high-ranking officers.

Clyde has no access to such explosives yet, but he does back at his base in present day. After Iraq and Afghanistan, he had acquired some plastic explosives among numerous other things such as a claymore, two grenades, a pistol etc and kept them as trophies from his tours, it was a common thing to do in the Army. What he could do would be to bring them back to the 1940's and put them to good use.

'I take it you've met my wife Anna?' said Captain Jaeger

Clyde looks across to Anna who is smiling at Clyde, this is the blonde lady whom Clyde was dancing and flirting with earlier. Again, Clyde thinks he's done everything he could possibly do wrong to make Jaeger suspect something of him and he worries that whether or not Jaeger found anything at the pig pen or Le Paradis he surely must be showing up on Jaegers radar after spilling beer all down his lap at a major function making him look foolish but even more foolish for dancing with his wife. Anna was irresistible but not so much that he'd risk his life for a dance or better if he played his cards right, it simply wasn't worth it.

'Yes, yes we met when you went to get changed earlier on' said Clyde as his cheeks turned slightly red

Jaeger, smiles and nods at Clyde.

'Yes. She is an amazing dance partner eh?' said Jaeger

Inside Clyde was saying 'Fuck, fuck, fuck, fuck, fuck, fuck, fuck, fuck' but on the surface was keeping his composure.

'Yes. Yes, she is' said Clyde as he nervously looked at Jaeger

Again, Clyde listens to his internal voice 'fuck, fuck, fuck, fuck', Jaeger laughs.

'I can't dance due to a gunshot wound in the knee so she has to dance with others you see' said Jaeger

Clyde and Jaeger stare at each other, Jaeger looks to be playing a cruel game with Clyde.

'So don't worry, I'm not the jealous type' said Jaeger

Clyde laughs awkwardly.

'She is accompanying me in the region and is looking after the Red Cross nurses in Northern France' said Jaeger

'Yes, we have a field hospital at Lestrem, there are many nurses who do a great job' said Clyde

'I'm sure they do' said Jaeger

The audience start to applaud, Clyde looks up to see a man walking up to the stage who is short and stout with thick round glasses. Clyde sits forward in his seat whilst clapping looking in disbelief at the man taking the stage as the man is Heinrich Himmler and is stood at the lectern.

'Good evening ladies and Gentlemen, welcome to Le Grand Hotel, Lille' said Himmler

The audience applauds and Clyde looks around to see if there's anyone else of the same notoriety as Himmler in the room.

'Firstly, I want to pass a message on from the Fuhrer' said Himmler as he looked around the room then down to his notes

Clyde stops searching the room to concentrate on Himmler's speech.

'We have driven the British back to their homeland and we have control of France, Holland and Belgium and are making further advances into Poland, Czechoslovakia and the Balkans. The Fuhrer passes on to you his warmest thanks and praise but the effort is not yet over, this is just the beginning' said Himmler

The audience once again breaks into applause, Himmler soaks up the applause and allows the audience to finish.

'After our efforts in the field to take over Western Europe we have had numerous acts of gallantry which enabled this, and that is why we are here tonight' said Himmler

Stechen looks at Clyde with a wry smile, Clyde looks back and sees this and then looks back to Himmler not thinking anything of Stechens facial expression.

'Secondly, I would like to congratulate Captain Lukas Wolf of the 43rd Assault Engineers' said Himmler as Clyde feels his stomach tighten as he is overcome with nerves as the audience again applaud, Himmler allows them to finish.

'Who courageously lead 40 SS troops who were ambushed by 100 British soldiers at Le Paradis, Captain Wolf lead the way to overcome the troops resulting in only 8 deaths and killing the 100 British during a fierce firefight' said Himmler

The people sat at Clyde's table all nod and smile at him, Clyde looks to Stechen who raises his glass to salute him but Clyde takes comfort in staring at the floor and putting his hand on his forehead.

'Ladies and Gentlemen, Captain Lukas Wolf' said Himmler as he searches to room waiting for someone to stand up.

The audience breaks into a rapturous applause and Clyde is still looking at the floor with his hand on his forehead, Captain Jaeger leans into Clyde.

'Wolf, you need to go onto the stage' said Captain Jaeger

Clyde lifts his head to look at the people who are sat at his table, they are all smiling and clapping. Clyde stands up and walks slowly to the stage whilst looking around the room, it seems all eyes in the room are looking at him, and he'd be right as all eyes were looking at him. As he approaches the lectern he looks towards Himmler who is smiling and clapping stood beside him on stage, Himmler salutes Clyde and then pins a badge onto his lapel, Himmler then stands in front of the lectern.

'Captain Lukas Wolf, for your act of gallantry I award you the Iron Cross 2nd Class' said Himmler

The audience carries on applauding Clyde and then all the audience give a standing ovation, Clyde nods shyly then walks briskly back to his seat desperate to avoid the attention thrust upon him.

On his way he is patted on the back by many people and when he approaches his seat Captain Jaeger shakes Clyde's hand, Clyde sits down and Himmler carries on presenting the next award.

'I take it you didn't expect that?' said Jaeger

Clyde turns to Jaeger quickly coming out of deep thought.

'Sorry, I didn't catch that' said Clyde

'I said, I take it you didn't expect to receive the award?' said Jaeger

Clyde shakes his head and looks to the floor then back up to Jaeger.

'No, no I didn't' said Clyde

'You should be happy then' said Jaeger

Jaeger laughs as do the other people on the table, Clyde forces a smile then goes back into deep thought thinking about Karl and whether he is alive or dead, what would have happened if they would have run to the woods when the convoy approached the farm house would they still have made it to Spain and whether the incident at Le Paradis would have still happened.

'Are you ok Lukas?' asked Anna

Clyde looks at Anna and nods.

'Yes, I'm fine' said Clyde

Anna looks at Clyde as if all is not well with him, Clyde again goes into deep thought thinking about Karl and the slaughtered troops.

Later in the evening Clyde, Captain Jaeger and Anna Jaeger are stood near to the bar laughing and joking, most of the people who attended the event have long gone with the ushers and bar staff packing away the chairs and tables in the background, after what had happened over the last few days Clyde took the opportunity to have a good drinking session to help him relax and try to forget about Karl and the troops at Le Paradis.

'It's been a wonderful evening Captain Wolf but we must be off' said Captain Jaeger

'The pleasures all mine' said Clyde as he stares at Anna

Captain Jaeger shakes Clyde's hand, then Clyde kisses Anna Jaeger on the cheek and then the Jaegers walk away, Anna looks back and Clyde winks at her, Anna smiles back.

In the morning, Clyde is stood in the hotel foyer looking up the stairs as Stechen walks down the stairs with a grin on his face. During the night Clyde had thought the best way of killing Stechen would be to cosy up to him, that way he may be able to get some time alone with him then he could kill him then escape, he would have tried to kill him last night but he got into the swing of things and was enjoying having a good drink so had forgot about Stechen unfortunately, this was one of Clyde's faults, once he started drinking he found it hard to stop.

'Good night was it?' said Clyde

'A Gentlemen never kisses and tells' said Stechen

'Ah, so you kissed then?' said Clyde

'We did a bit more than that' said Stechen

Clyde looks around for their driver Fischer whom he had earlier sent on an errand to divert him away so that Clyde and Stechen could travel back to the outpost alone in his newly acquired squad car, that way he could easily kill him and get rid of the body on the long drive back.

'I've acquired us a squad car to travel back to Lestrem, I'll drive' said Clyde

Clyde has visions now of killing Stechen, he has won his trust and maybe they can travel alone back to Lestrem and he can kill him at the side of the road and then make his way to Spain.

'No, it's ok Wolf, I won't be travelling back to Lestrem. After speaking with my Uncle he wants me to oversee the occupation in Paris' said Stechen

Again, Clyde's plan to kill Stechen has been scuppered.

'So you won't be coming back to Lestrem?' said Clyde

'No, my work in the field is done' said Stechen

Clyde looks around and starts to act erratically, he'd missed his opportunity to kill him in the night, he could have smothered him with his pillow in the night but Stechen had sneaked off in the night and Clyde had gotten carried away with the alcohol.

'Why don't we have one last drink in my room before we part' said Clyde trying desperately to convince him 'One for the road you might say'

Maybe Clyde can kill Stechen in his room and then make his escape to Spain, even if he does do a makeshift attempt at it. Just as Clyde finishes speaking Stechen an SS soldier walks up to them, stops and salutes.

'Sir' said Hoffman

'Wolf, this is Hoffman, my bodyguard for the new role in Paris' said Stechen

Clyde looks at Hoffman who is the model of the Aryan race with his imposing 6"3 well-built frame, blonde hair and blue eyes.

'Well Wolf, we shall meet again one day I hope' said Stechen

'Yes, yes. You can sure of that' said Clyde

'Well. Goodbye Wolf' said Stechen

'Yes, goodbye' said Clyde

Stechen walks out of the foyer to outside the Hotel, Clyde puts his hand on his head as he knows he'd missed a golden opportunity to kill Stechen.

Chapter 7 – Sleeping with the Enemy

A few days later, Clyde is stood outside the farm house watching a soldier walk back from the fields with a sack full of carrots, Clyde is drinking water from his canteen and as the water droplet drips down his chin, he quickly screws the top back onto the bottle and wipes his chin. The soldier carrying the sack of carrots see's this and then looks to the floor quickly as Clyde looks at him, he doesn't want to be seen staring at an officer spilling his drink all down his chin.

A rumble of noise can be heard coming into the courtyard as a red cross truck slowly drives in, the big grey truck rumbles slowly past Clyde and a flicker of blonde hair catches his eye.

The truck comes to a halt next to the farm house and the driver jumps from the vehicle, Clyde looks over to see where the blonde hair came from but can't see the passenger, he looks around to the soldiers around him who seemed to not notice the blonde hair, he then looks back over to the truck and then begins to walk over to find out who it was.

As he walks over he sees the blonde woman walk into the barn, Clyde carries on walking over and as he approaches the truck the blonde woman walks out of the barn, this is Anna Jaeger whom he'd met at the awards night in Lille. Clyde spots her but she doesn't see him and attempts to walk past him, Clyde stands in her way.

'It's nice of you to come see me' said Clyde

Clyde has a wry smile on his face and is full of bravado, Anna has a glint in her eye as if she'd planned to visit him.

'Don't flatter yourself' replied Anna with venom 'I was coming here anyway'

'I believe you, thousands wouldn't' said Clyde

Anna rolls her eyes then steps around Clyde and walks to the back of the truck, Clyde smiles then looks over to Anna who by now is stood at the back of the truck struggling to open the back tailgate so he walks over to give her assistance, Anna notices this to tries to open the back of the truck quickly on her own dropping the tailgate down with a loud crash which startles her.

'Take it easy darling' said Clyde

Anna ignores Clyde and reaches forward to grab a box, Clyde also grabs one of the boxes to help her.

'How long do you plan on staying?' said Clyde

Anna turns to look at Clyde who smiles.

'As long as I'm needed' said Anna who then starts to walk away carrying one of the boxes 'I'll be stationed in the area and will be rehoused somewhere nearby'

Clyde lifts the box and starts to walk into the barn alongside Anna. With the flirting going on at the awards night Clyde thinks it would be a good idea to chance his arm and find out where Captain Jaeger is, if he's with her he can ask about him and if he isn't then he could ask Anna out for dinner.

'So where is Captain Jaeger? asked Clyde

Anna looks forward towards the barn and then stops and looks at Clyde and speaks in hushed tones.

'He's been assigned to accompany the Fuhrers entourage while they visit Paris for a few days' said Anna

Clyde smiles.

'Is that so?' said Clyde then he looks around and then leans in to Anna as he prepares to ask a private question 'Well, do you fancy going into Town later?

Clyde leans back and nods as if to coax her into going with him.

'For dinner?' said Clyde

Anna looks around and quickly moves into Clyde.

'That wouldn't be appropriate, I'm a married woman' said Anna

Anna turns to walk away; Clyde quickly blocks her path.

'Come on, live a little' said Clyde

'I can't' replied Anna swiftly

'It's better than army rations' said Clyde

Anna walks around Clyde keen to stay out of his blockade.

'I'll have you back for a decent time, no one needs to know' said Clyde

Anna stops, walks up to Clyde and leans into his ear.

'Ok, only if we're back for a decent time and nobody finds out' said Anna with conviction 'After all, it's only dinner'

Clyde doesn't try to hide the fact that he's happy and it's written all over his face.

'My lips are sealed; I'll meet you back here at 7pm' said Clyde

Later that evening Clyde walks out of the farm house and is dressed smartly, the dark red skies cast a light over the figure of Anna in the distance stood next to the barn. Clyde looks around to see two soldiers walking from the barn towards him, they both salute him, he salutes back and briskly walks over to the barn and approaches Anna who has really made an effort in looking nice, she has on a long tight dress with emphasises her bosom and her hair is long and wavy.

'You look nice' said Clyde

'Thank you' said Anna

'The car is around the other side' said Clyde

Both Clyde and Anna walk around the other side of the barn to where a squad car is, Clyde looks around to see if anyone is watching and then they both get inside, Clyde starts the engine and they drive off.

A waiter walks across a marble floor; the sound of the footsteps is masked by a three-piece band playing easy listening music in the corner. The waiter pours Anna a glass of red wine, Anna is laughing with Clyde and they seem to have been enjoying each other's company over the past few hours and moved from the restaurant and into the now empty bar as the time fast approaches the early hours of the next day.

'Thank you' said Anna

'And one brandy Sir' said the Waiter

'Yes, leave the bottle please' said Clyde

The waiter serves Clyde his drink then picks up three wine bottles and an empty bottle of brandy then walks away, Clyde looks at Anna who starts giggling. Anna leans forward and smiles at him whilst playing with her hair. Clyde looks at Anna and his expression changes to a more serious one, he leans in to Anna and they kiss, Clyde holds Anna's face with both hands as she rubs her hands up the back of his head ruffling his hair as she does.

'Do you want to take this upstairs?' whispers Clyde as he pulls away slightly

Anna stares at Clyde for a moment mulling over whether to go with the flow and end up sleeping with Clyde behind her Husband's back or remain faithful and go home, seeing as though they'd both had quite a lot to drink and Clyde had worked his charm well her thought train was a little skewed.

'Let's go' whispers Anna

The table screeches across the marble floor as Clyde stands and pushes the table away, Anna picks up her drink, Clyde picks up the bottle of brandy and they walk out of the bar with Clyde looking around to make sure there's nobody there to see them, after all, the last thing he needs is Captain Jaeger after him for messing about with his wife.

In the elevator, Clyde grabs Anna by the back of her neck and pulls her forwards towards him and they kiss passionately and whilst he does this he slides his hand inside Anna's dress and feels one of her breasts. Anna continues to kiss Clyde passionately and slowly pulls Clyde's hand out from her dress and pulls away for a second.

'Not here' whispers Anna

Again, they start to kiss passionately again and again Clyde tries to fondle Anna's breasts, Anna slowly slides Clyde hand down to her waist, the elevator stops, a ping sounds out, Clyde slides the doors open and they exit the elevator and he quickly slides them back closed and they rush down the corridor towards Clyde's hotel room and Anna stops.

'Wait, you booked a room in advance?' said Anna

Anna was thinking Clyde had counted his chickens in booking a room in advance thinking that she would be easy to get into bed and Clyde wasn't going to play his hand and go bust, he had a cover story as he had booked the room earlier in the evening when Anna had gone to the toilet but she didn't need to know that, Clyde thought.

'No. I still have the key from the last time I was here' said Clyde

Clyde hoped that Anna accepts the story otherwise he'd be sleeping alone, Clyde opens the hotel room door and Anna looks up and down the corridor to check she isn't being watched and they both enter the room.

As morning breaks, Clyde wakes up in the hotel room with the white sheets tangled around his legs leaving his top half bare, he looks over to the window where the new morning light is pouring into the room and onto the table casting its light over the half full glasses and clothes scattered across the room, he turns to Anna who is still sleeping and still looking as beautiful as she did the night before.

Clyde then gets out of bed naked and walks into the bathroom turning on the shower, he tests the temperature of the water with his hand then steps in. He stands inside letting the water pour across his face trying to refresh himself after the long night of drinking and love making. He leans his head back and opens his mouth to allow the water to pour in. A door slams outside of the bathroom and Clyde spits out the water, opens his eyes and listens.

'Anna?' said Clyde

Clyde listens but there is no answer, he then finishes showering, then steps out of the shower grabbing a crisp white towel from the radiator and ties it around his waist and walks into the hotel room. He looks around the hotel room to see Anna and her belongings have gone, he pauses and smiles in realisation that she'd scarpered whilst he was showering, he then walks over to the window and looks outside to the street below.

Out in the street below Anna quickly walks across the road and is looking at her watch, she gets a set of keys out of her handbag and then gets into the squad car which is parked in front of the hotel, she gets inside and then drives off leaving Clyde no way of getting back, at least they'd not drive back to the farmhouse together as that would really make things look suspicious, Clyde still looks out of the window and smiles to himself.

'Charming' said Clyde

Clyde goes over to the bed and sits on the edge picking up the phone.

'Yes hello, can I order some breakfast please, room 450' said Clyde

Clyde looks around the room to see if Anna had left anything.

'Just for 1 please, no problem, thank you' said Clyde

A few hours later Anna is speaking with a nurse outside the barn stood on the brown crisp leaves which had fallen from nearby trees, the signs of autumn were on their way but summer was still putting up a fight as the sun still shone brightly.

'Yes, I understand, leave it until the end of next month' said Anna

A motorcycle drives slowly up to Anna and the sound of the trotting engine as it drives slowly makes Anna speak a bit louder so that the other nurse could hear her.

'Are you ok with that?' asks Anna

The motorcycle stops behind Anna and revs the engine aggressively with the clutch held in and it startles her, she drops her papers she was carrying and they blow across the yard, Anna and the nurse attempt to pick up the papers as they move about the floor in different directions, Clyde is sitting on the motorcycle behind them both.

'You need a hand?' asks Clyde sarcastically as he grins with delight

Anna is crouched down trying to pick the runaway papers up from the floor, she turns and looks at Clyde with scorn.

'No, I'm quite alright thank you' said Anna

Anna struggles to pick up a piece of paper that blows towards Clyde and she chases after it, the nurse helping Anna is chasing a piece of paper that has blown 20 metres away.

'You sure about that?' said Clyde

'Please, leave it' said Anna

The paper blows away from Anna even further.

'It's making a break for freedom, quick, get it' said Clyde as he laughs

Anna picks the paper up and turns away from Clyde, starts to walk away and can't help but smile but doesn't want him to see.

'So, no goodbye kiss this morning?' said Clyde

Anna turns quickly and walks briskly over to Clyde determined to quell any more talk of the night before.

'I've no idea what you're talking about' said Anna as she prods Clyde in the chest.

'Don't be sorry, you enjoyed it as much as I did' said Clyde

Anna pauses, looks around to see if there is anybody nearby then turns quickly back to Clyde.

'Please, don't say a word about last night, please' begged Anna as she searched the immediate area with her peripheral vision 'Let's keep it between ourselves'

Clyde grabs Anna around the waist and pulls her towards him on the motorcycle, Anna is flustered, she looks around frantically not knowing how to react to Clyde's caveman style grip on her in front of the other nurse, luckily the nurse is still chasing the paper and doesn't witness it.

'So, when are we going out again?' said Clyde

Anna pushes Clyde away, just as she does the sound of a squad car pulling into the courtyard attracts both of their attention, it is Jaeger. Clyde smiles as Anna waves at Jaeger and walks quickly over.

'When the cats away, the mice will play' said Clyde

Anna carries on walking towards Jaeger without acknowledging Clyde.

As Anna approaches the squad car Captain Jaeger steps out of the vehicle and hugs his wife. Clyde nods at Jaeger who nods back whilst Anna hugs him tightly. Clyde puts the motorcycle into gear and moves away slowly to somewhere he can park the bike, Jaeger watches him as he does so with a hint of suspicion in his eyes.

Shortly after the night with Anna, Clyde was posted to the Northern French coast to oversee the construction of sea defences seeing as he is a Captain with an engineering background.

He'd spent the last 11 months on the French coast and his band of forced labour workers from Eastern Europe had made the fastest progress out of all the construction groups as part of the Todt Organisation, he had received numerous visits throughout the year from Fritz Todt, the man in charge of the major civil engineering projects in Germany such as the Autobahn and the Atlantic Wall, to see how the others in the region can learn from Clyde and make the others work just as hard and smart. Due to Clyde's man management skills and modern construction methods had put pay to a few of the other construction officers who were lagging behind, they were reprimanded quite harshly.

With his connections with Brigadier Freidrich through Stechen he is kept in France where all others who upset the apple cart are sent to the Eastern front in preparation to march on Moscow as part of Operation Barbarossa which was due to start in the Summer. Clyde spends most of the year overseeing the construction and writing letters to Stechen to keep up the faux friendship in the hope that he'll drop by, giving Clyde a chance to kill him. He'd made a promise to himself and the memory of Karl and the British soldiers that he wouldn't escape to England or Spain without killing the bastard who committed the atrocity even if it meant sailing close to the wind disguising himself as a German Officer.

Clyde hadn't seen Anna since he scared her with the motorcycle nor had he seen Captain Jaeger though he had heard a lot about his reputation, he hadn't been found out yet with regards to the soldiers back at the original farmhouse in the pig pen or his affair with Anna. He was glad of that as Jaeger had a fearsome reputation as one hell of a bastard who was paranoid by nature and tortured anyone he suspected of being a traitor or informer, so perhaps Clyde's connections had somehow kept him safe for all this time.

He often thought about the possibility of being zapped back to present day, the rabbit was only gone for five minutes at the most and he'd been here months, he asked himself questions all the time 'What happens if I zap back? Will Karl's body zap back too or won't he zap back if he's dead? If he does go back to present day will he attempt to come back to the 1940's to put the record straight with Stechen or will he come back to the exact same time period he did originally and have the chance to escape to Spain with Karl before Stechen or Jaeger gets there?'.

Clyde thought to himself 'only time will tell' and for now only had one thing on his mind, biding his time in order to kill Stechen.

Seagulls fly overhead as the forced labour dig large holes in the sand banks, the labour workers are tired and look to be suffering from malnutrition. The worker's cheek bones are as prominent as the giant bunkers they are constructing on the coast line and their thin arms are as wispy as the vegetation growing in the dunes.

Clyde pulls up next to a tent in his squad car, he gets out of the vehicle holding a ruck sack and starts to walk over to the workers who are digging in the sand. One of the worker's notices Clyde walking over and nudges another worker alongside him nods towards Clyde. A soldier guarding the workers smokes a cigarette whilst loosely holding his rifle slowly turns and spots Clyde who by now is only a few metres away, the soldier drops his cigarette, holds his weapon firmly and salutes Clyde as he approaches.

'Good afternoon' said Clyde as he looks at the cigarette stump still burning on the floor making sure the guard knows he's been rumbled

'Good afternoon Sir' said the guard who was visibly shaken due to him being caught smoking on duty, the guard was new to the area so didn't know how hard Clyde would punish him.

'How are they today?' said Clyde

The guard looks at Clyde and expects him to be angry but he's not that bothered, he knows he has the guard by the balls now and the guard has a lot to do to make things up to Clyde of face the repercussions.

'Sir, we have had 1 more case of Cholera, other than that the work is running on schedule' said the guard

Clyde looks at the workers digging below and notices the two men looking up at him, he then looks back to the guard.

'Good, here's a gift for you' said Clyde as he hands him a carton of 200 cigarettes.

'Thank you, Sir' said the guard as he nervously takes the box from Clyde

The soldier opens the carton and places the packs of cigarettes into his webbing quickly so that nobody catches him doing so. The workers notice Clyde has arrived on site and begin to speak to each other as if to conspire in their native tongue, Clyde notices and walks down the embankment into the pit, the guard notices and his split second first reaction is to warn Clyde about getting close to the workers.

'Sir' said the guard

Clyde turns around to look at the guard.

'Sir…forgive me but, you are aware of the cholera that is going around?' said the guard

Clyde looks to the workers digging in the sand then looks back up the embankment to the guard.

'Yes, I'm quite aware' said Clyde

The guard stops trying to stuff the cigarettes into his webbing and looks puzzled by Clyde's actions.

'Anything else?' said Clyde impetuously

'No Sir' said the guard

'Then turn around and mind your own business then' said Clyde

The workers smile wryly, the guard turns around and carries on packing his webbing with cartons of cigarettes. Clyde makes the last few steps to the bottom of the pit and kneels, puts his rucksack in front of him whilst one of the workers slowly walks towards Clyde and kneels next to him.

'Good afternoon Sir' said the worker

'Good afternoon Felix' said Clyde

Clyde opens the rucksack to show Felix the contents of the rucksack.

'There's medicine, food and cigarettes' said Clyde

Clyde looks to Felix and then to the rest of the workers who are looking back at him, as he looks at the workers they immediately return to digging as they were before he arrived but they're not working hard because they're scared, they do so because unlike many of the German soldiers Clyde takes an interest in their health and wellbeing, they also appreciate the effort he goes to in foraging them supplies that keep them alive as at other points along the coastline the forced labour do die in high numbers.

'Thank you, Sir' said Felix

'No problem. You know the score, if you get caught with these I will deny all knowledge' said Clyde facetiously as he smiles at Felix 'and you'll be shot for stealing'

Felix smiles wryly and looks to the floor nodding in agreement, he and the other workers had taken a real shine to Clyde because not only was he helping them he seemed to be a nice man who was quite cheerful in desperate situations.

'I understand Sir' said Felix as he stared at Clyde in admiration

Clyde looks around and up to the guard watching over the workers, the guard quickly turns away and looks towards the mainland knowing that he must turn a blind eye as he is benefitting from his dealings, Clyde closes the rucksack, stands up and walks away from it leaving it on the ground. Felix quickly picks up the rucksack and passes it to another worker who buries it in a hole in the sand, Clyde climbs up the embankment and walks towards the tent.

Later that evening Clyde is asleep in his tent, he wakes up and sits up in his camp bed. He is sweating and is out of breath, he pulls the covers from him and leans over to his bed side table and picks up his water bottle, closes his eyes and pours water all over his head. As the beads of water drip from Clyde's face he stands up and starts to get dressed quickly and as he puts on his last boot he stands up, takes a drink from his canteen and begins to walk towards the exit of the tent but then stops, his legs buckle and he must grab hold of the supports for the tent which in turn causes the tent to waver slightly. His initial thought is he's having a heart attack or had caught cholera from the labour workers and he tries to get out of the tent to alert the nearest medic to his emergency.

'Argh' said Clyde

Clyde pours water over his head again and stumbles towards the exit and falls to the floor just before the exit, a bright red light fills the tent and Clyde instantly disappears.

Bunker – Present Day

A dull sound of water dropping onto metal brings Clyde around from his slumber, he wakes up lay on a metal floor in a dimly lit room.

'Jesus' said Clyde

He leans upright and rolls his neck to alleviate the stiffness due to being lay on the floor in an awkward position, as his eyes adjust to the darkness he realises he is in the original metal room in the bunker.

'No, no' said Clyde

Clyde blinks a few times then squints to gain his vision then slowly stands and uses the walls to support him on his unsteady feet then stumbles out of the dome and over to a table nearby where he had left his jacket before himself and Karl had used the dome, he picks up his jacket and puts his hand inside the jacket pocket and pulls out his mobile phone.

'No, no, it can't be' said Clyde as he looks at the time and date on his phone, he has been gone from the present day for just two minutes. He looks around the room intensely and stands more upright as he quickly scans the room hoping to find Karl in the room, maybe he survived and zapped back around the same time as he had.

'Karl, Karl, are you here mate?' said Clyde

Clyde shines the light from his phone around the room and onto the floor checking for any blood stains or any marks to signify that Karl had returned.

'Karl?' said Clyde

He shines the torch from his phone around the dome and along the floor to try and find Karl or at least a footprint of Karl's in the vain hope that somehow he'd made it back. Over the last few months the memory of Karl had never strayed too far away from Clyde's thoughts, he was the reason he'd stayed on in the role in the German Army so that he could kill Stechen, with him zapping back to present day all the feelings he felt just after Karl was shot came flooding back.

'Karl?' shouts Clyde

Clyde puts on his jacket and walks towards the exit of the bunker, he crawls through the dark hole and through into the woods outside. He stands up outside the bunker and squints to look which direction he had left his car in the previous visit, after all it was 12 months ago when he was last there.

'Karl!' shouts Clyde hoping Karl had made it out of the bunker and into the woods, he waits for a moment and listens intently for a reply.

'Karl' shouts Clyde

Again, Clyde awaits a reply

'Sod it' said Clyde as he walks briskly then breaks into a jog through the woods towards the direction of his car.

Moments later Clyde is jogging through the field and spots his car parked at the side of the field, Spike is stood on the passenger seat barking at Clyde and wagging his tail with vigour pleased to see his master, but not as please as Clyde is to see him.

'Spike' said Clyde as he jogs over to the side of the car and opens his passenger side door, bends down and hugs Spike who returns the affection by licking Clyde's face and ears.

'Spike, I've missed you boy' said Clyde

Clyde then looks around to see Karl's car is still there, he looks at his phone and attempts to phone Karl. The phone rings and rings until he reaches Karl's voicemail.

'Karl, if you get this message mate phone me back ASAP' said Clyde

Clyde looks towards the forest in the distance to see if he can spot Karl walking out from the woods, he then looks again at his phone and again towards the forest, the fields are empty. Clyde looks at Karl's car then to his own car, he then leans in to his car and pulls out a book makers pen and a betting slip and walks towards Karl's car, he then leans against the car bonnet whilst he writes a note.

'Karl, I made it out, fuck knows what's happened, phone me ASAP, I want to know if you're ok, cheers, Clyde'

Clyde puts the note behind Karl's windscreen wiper then walks towards his own car and gets inside, starts the engine, has one more look towards the forest where there is still no sign of Karl then drives away.

Chapter 8 – A Helping Hand

An hour or so later Clyde approaches the gates to the army base at Hameln and is driving slowly and is a little coy about what might be waiting for him at the base. He pulls over outside the gate house and looks towards the entrance, a solider in the gate house notices Clyde in the distance and walks outside of the sentry and gestures towards him. Clyde looks at the sentry who is waving at him, it's Private Paul Jackson who he knows quite well, he served alongside him in Iraq a couple of years earlier.

'Yes, Jacko' said Clyde

Clyde drives towards the gates to where Jacko is guarding the gate.

'Good afternoon Corporal, is everything ok? said Jacko

'Yes mate, everything's fine. How's it been today?' said Clyde

Spike climbs over Clyde's lap to the open window, Jacko reaches in and strokes Spike.

'Yes, not too bad. I saw Frau Kirsch earlier' said Jacko with a cheeky grin on his face

Frau Kirsch is a German woman Clyde had a fling with a few weeks previously and despite Clyde efforts to break it off she keeps popping up in the same places that he goes to, the only safe place where she doesn't stalk him is inside the barracks because she's not allowed in due to her being a civilian.

'Oh yes?' said Clyde

'She was looking for you…and she was pushing a pram' said Jacko as he started to laugh at his own joke

'Listen Jacko, I've not got time to mess about pal' said Clyde shooting down any attempt from Jacko to generate banter 'Tell her I've been posted to the Falklands if she comes back. The fucking weirdo'

Jacko smiles as he knows how often she stalks Clyde.

'Will do' said Jacko

Clyde looks in his rear view mirror then back to Jacko.

'Have you been far?' said Jacko

'Just been into the countryside' said Clyde

The barrier opens, Clyde notices

'Sorry Jacko, I've got to get moving' said Clyde

'Ok Corporal, I'll see you later' said Jacko

Jacko takes a few steps backwards and looks behind Clyde's car, Clyde looks to Jacko.

'Hey Jacko, have you seen Karl?' said Clyde

Jacko looks back to Clyde.

'No Corporal, he hasn't been through here whilst I've been on duty' said Jacko.

'Right, ok, if you see him tell him to phone me ASAP' said Clyde

Jacko nods.

'Will do Corporal' said Jacko

Clyde drives on into the barracks and the gate closes behind him.

Minutes later Clyde walks into his living room and Spike runs in behind him, he sits on his couch and places his laptop onto the coffee table, opens it and awaits as it loads, Spike is just around the corner in the kitchen drinking out of his water bowl and Clyde leans forward to see Spike. Water is dripping from Spikes thirsty mouth all over the kitchen floor, Spikes tail starts wagging as he stops and looks back at Clyde.

'Bloody daft dog' said Clyde

By now the laptop has loaded and Clyde searches for events that happened during World War 2. He opens a webpage about the massacre at 'Le Paradis' where the British soldiers were massacred, Colonel Stechen was hung by a military court in 1949. Clyde is shocked by what he reads because he was there when it happened, he searches for other events that happened during the war and opens a webpage about espionage during the war, as he scrolls down the page he opens up a link to another page in the hope of finding an agent he can meet up with in the region to help him in killing Stechen.

'Jean Chevalier infiltrated the German Army due to his Fathers ancestry in late 1938 working for the French Government to pass on information about the mobilisation of the German Army, once the war started Chevalier was stationed in Lille and worked as part of a hit squad taking out German high command through giving intelligence to the British 'Special Operations Executive' or 'SOE' as it was known, which later on after the war would be absorbed by MI6. In late 1943 he was caught meeting up with members of the Resistance and hung in the town centre of Lille' said Clyde

Clyde looks at the photo of Chevalier.

'Chevalier. I think me and you need to meet up' said Clyde

Clyde clicks on the laptop to print the photo of Chevalier, then stands from his chair and jogs up the stairs, seconds later he jogs back down the stairs holding a piece of A4 paper with a photo of Jean Chevalier on it. He then walks over to a doorway underneath the stairs opens the door to access underneath, he pulls out a ruck sack and walks over to his book shelf and places a few books into the rucksack and walks to the front door then exits his house.

Clyde then gets into his car then drives off heading for the countryside leaving Spike behind in the house a moments later stops at the gate with Jacko walking out to meet him, Clyde lowers his window.

'Off out again are you Corporal?' said Jacko

'Yes, I think I've left my wallet in the fields' said Clyde

'Good luck finding it' said Jacko

'Hey, have you seen Karl yet?' said Clyde

Jacko shakes his head.

'No, I can't say I have. When I do I'll tell him to phone you' said Jacko

By now the barrier is lifting, Clyde notices and is in a rush to get back to the bunker just in case Karl has somehow zapped back and is struggling to get back to his car.

'Right then Jacko, I'll see you later' said Clyde

'See you later Corporal' said Jacko

Clyde exits the camp and drives off to the countryside.

German Countryside

An hour later Clyde crawls through a hole in the ground, he struggles to stand up in his usual position as he is pushing a rucksack which is in the way so he crawls a little further. He stands up and walks slowly over to the metal room whist shining his torch around the bunker in the hope that Karl would be there.

'Karl?' shouts Clyde

Clyde still searches in vain for his best friend whilst shining his torch around the room.

'Karl?' shouts Clyde

Nothing, no noises can be heard in the bunker other than Clyde own footsteps on the concrete floor.

'Fucking hell' said Clyde

Clyde makes his way through the bunker and towards the dome and as Clyde approaches the dome and puts the rucksack onto the floor, takes off his jacket revealing he is still wearing the German officers uniform. He opens the door to the metal room, steps inside whilst closing the door behind him and then pulls down on the switch.

The room fills with a bright red light, Clyde hovers inside the dome and in the bright red flash he disappears.

French Countryside – May 1941

The Sun is burning high in the sky as Clyde walks along a dirt track at the side of the woods which shades him from the suns glare. As he walks along the dirt track he looks further ahead to see a farm house, this is the farm house which he was originally taken prisoner in along with Karl until Stechen came along.

Clyde stops and stares at the farm house from a distance, he slowly pulls out a cigarette and lights it with a match, he throws the match to the floor and rubs it out with his foot. With his first drag on the cigarette he hears a motorcycle start with its engine sounding like it's coming from within the courtyard of the farm just ahead, this is what he expected.

Clyde turns to look to the direction he'd walked from then back to the farm house where now a motorcycle and side cart are driving towards him, he takes another drag from the cigarette and slowly blows the smoke from his mouth waiting for the motorcycle to approach. A voice can be faintly heard over the sound of the motorcycles engine which is approaching quickly.

'I can't hear you' shouts Clyde as he stands on the dirt track smoking his cigarette without a care in the world, a far cry from the last time he was in this situation.

He takes another drag then flicks his cigarette to the floor and rubs it out with his foot, he blows the smoke slowly from his mouth into the direction of the motorcycle which is now closer. The passenger fires one shot into the direction of Clyde startling and annoying him, Clyde is wearing full German officer uniform and didn't expect shots to be fired at him, it may be because Clyde is in the shadows and the soldiers in the motorcycle and sidecar can't identify his apparel.

'Jesus' shouts Clyde as he looks to see whereabouts on the floor the bullet hit

'Put your hands up' shouts the motorcycle rider

Clyde looks towards the motorcycle which is 30 metres away, he can see the motorcycle clearly in the morning sun however Clyde is stood in the shadow of the nearby trees. The motorcycle rider gets off the motorcycle and pulls out his pistol, the soldier in the sidecar mans the machine gun which is mounted to the sidecar and aims it at Clyde.

'Identify yourself at once' said the motorcycle rider with a commanding authority

The motorcycle rider loads his pistol and walks towards the shadows aiming towards Clyde who then steps out from the shadows making himself visible to the approaching motorcycle rider.

'Captain Lukas Wolf, 43rd Assault Engineers' said Clyde brazenly

The motorcycle rider's facial expression changes from stern to subdued, then lowers his pistol and turns to look at his accomplice then back to Clyde, as he does he quickly puts his pistol back into its holster realising his error.

'I beg your pardon Sir, I didn't mean to startle you' said the rider as he fumbled with his holster 'I saw a figure in the trees, it could have been…'

'It's ok, take me to Calais' said Clyde dismissing the rider's apology, he didn't care too much for reprimanding the soldiers, he just wanted to get back to Calais to make plans in meeting with Jean Chevalier

'Yes Sir' said the rider

Clyde and the rider walk back towards the motorcycle.

'Sir, if you don't mind me asking…but…why you are walking in the woods?' said the rider

The rider smiles as he's just making polite conversation, he doesn't mean anything by it, Clyde stops and pulls out his notepad and pencil, the rider stops and is shocked by Clyde's reaction.

'How dare you question a commanding officer, what is your name and unit Corporal?' said Clyde as he gets ready to write down his name

The motorcycle rider is shocked that such an innocent question could provoke such a strong reaction and maybe he shouldn't have questioned a senior rank especially an officer.

'Sir, I am Corporal Gretz of the 6th Infantry Division' said the rider as he looks wearily to Clyde

Clyde spots an opportunity to scare the rider and his accomplice, he can't allow subordinates to question him especially asking why he's so far from Calais without transport or accomplices, he'd look like he's up to no good for certain and he doesn't want Jaeger sniffing around.

'Gretz? Is that a Jewish surname?' said Clyde

'No Sir' said the rider

Clyde stares at the rider with contempt, the passenger in the sidecar looks away to anywhere other than Clyde as his eyes are repelled from locking eyes with Clyde through fear.

'It sounds very Jewish to me, are you sure?' said Clyde

The rider purses his lips and looks to the machine gunner as if asking for him for support in his claim of ethnicity but that is short coming, he then looks to the floor.

'Sir, I'm almost certain it's from Saxony' said Gretz with subdued resistance

Gretz looks increasingly worried, Clyde looks at the motorcycle machine gunner cower as best he can behind the powerful weapon.

'And what is *your* name and rank?' said Clyde

The machine gunner briskly gets out of the sidecar and salutes Clyde hoping to impress him with his discipline.

'Sir I am Private Kauffman, Sir' belted out the machine gunner with gusto

Clyde weighs Kauffman up as he writes his name in his notebook slowly, he does this to add to the tension.

'Are you Jewish?' said Clyde

'Sir, no Sir' said Kauffman nervously and a lot quieter than the last time he answered to Clyde

Clyde stares at both men as they squirm like naughty school boys being reprimanded from their headmaster.

'You look Jewish, the both of you look Jewish' said Clyde

Both Gretz and Kauffman look at each other worryingly and then look to the ground, Gretz fidgets with his hands determined to change the subject of questioning their heritage.

'Sir, you wish to go to Calais?' said Gretz hoping that Clyde would take him up on the offer and forget the question of their ancestry

'Don't interrupt me' shouts Clyde as he steps closer to Gretz and goes face to face with him 'Stop fidgeting'

'Sir' said Gretz as he cowers away from Clyde and looks to the side and puts his hands behind his back, Clyde steps away from Gretz and stares at the men with a furrowed brow and grits his teeth as a show of force.

'I have a good mind to call Captain Jaeger to investigate the both of you' said Clyde

Kauffman fidgets with his hands as Gretz looks to the floor, Clyde thinks that dropping Jaegers name into the mix may scare them both into doing what he asks.

'Undo the side cart' said Clyde

'Sir?' said Gretz

Gretz and Kauffman both look up from the ground and look at Clyde, both are surprised.

'You heard what I said' said Clyde

Gretz looks at Kauffman.

'Kauffman, do as he says' barks Gretz as he's desperate to do what he can to get Clyde on his way

Kauffman rushes over to the motorcycle and takes a spanner from a compartment and both Gretz and Kauffman quickly undo the sidecar. Kauffman holds up the sidecar to prevent it falling to the floor, Gretz turns to see Clyde mounting the motorcycle.

'Sir?' said Gretz

Clyde kick starts the motorcycle and turns to Gretz.

'Is there anything else you request?' said Gretz

'Get back to your posts' said Clyde

'Yes Sir' said Gretz

Kaufman and Gretz salute Clyde and start to walk away, Clyde stops and points at the side car lay on the ground.

'Hey. Take that bloody thing with you' said Clyde

'Yes Sir' said Gretz

Clyde revs the engine a few times and turns to look at Gretz and Kauffman who are picking up the side car, the soldiers look at Clyde.

'Shalom fotze's' said Clyde

Clyde rides off on the motorcycle and Gretz stands up to watch resulting in the sidecar falling to the floor and into Gretz injuring his ankle.

Chapter 9 – Making Friends

Once Clyde had returned to Calais and had gotten back into the swing of things with regards to the construction of pill boxes, he makes the trip to Lille in the hope of finding Jean Chevalier to reach out to him and form some sort of alliance. With Clyde's knowledge of the future and Chevaliers contacts they could make an efficient team.

Again, Clyde stays at Le Grand Hotel where he had attended the awards dinner and where both he and Anna had spent the night together long ago, secretly he hoped to bump into Anna as well and if he did he'd be happy, just as long as Captain Jaeger wasn't in the region.

After two unsuccessful days searching for Chevalier, Clyde impatiently makes his way to a popular bar with the German officers in the hope that he finds his man. He had already burnt the picture of Chevalier as he had his image ingrained in his memory after looking at it so much over the past week or so and after all, Chevalier had a distinctive look about him, he was tall with brown hair and eyes, medium build, in his late 40's and had a roman nose and a strong jaw so even if he saw him from a distance he could recognise him.

Inside the bar, Clyde sits on an old wooden chair and as he leans back as he stubs out a cigarette into the ash tray on the wooden table, three German officers walk past Clyde to sit down at the table next to him, the officers are in high spirits as they call to the bar man for a round of beers. A pretty waitress carries three large glasses of beer over to another table nearby, one of the glasses is knocked from her hand and smashes on the floor, nobody in the bar takes notice but the waitress casts a strained look over to the barman who laboriously starts to pour another beer. Above the noise in the bar a shriek pierces the smoke-filled air as a prostitute is jovially man handled by an officer on a far table, the prostitute slaps the officer in the face then kisses him. Clyde looks around the room and catches the eye of the waitress.

'Sir, another Brandy?' said the Waitress

'Yes please, and a cigar' said Clyde

'It'll be with you shortly' said the waitress.

The waitress takes a liking to Clyde as unlike the other officers in the bar Clyde is polite whereas the others are unruly, as the waitress walks away Clyde notices the entrance door is closing, three officers have entered the bar but Clyde cannot see due to another group of officers stood up singing out of tune blissfully ignorant that their makeshift incoherent chant is annoying Clyde.

For God's sake shut the fuck up thinks Clyde

Clyde leans forward on his chair and places his forearms onto the table as he hunches closer. Each of the three officers are walking past the group with Clyde watching intently, the first officer walks past, it isn't Chevalier, the second walks past, it isn't him either.

'Sir, your brandy' said the Waitress as she takes his attention away from the new arrivals

Clyde looks up to the waitress and leans back so she can place the brandy onto the table and leaves a cigar next to the brandy.

'Thank you' said Clyde

Clyde looks back over to the group who have just walked in to see them sit down, the three officers sit down with the last remaining officer with his back to Clyde, this is the officer that he couldn't identify, he is tall with brown hair, that is all he can make out.

'Come on, turn around' whispered Clyde to himself

The waitress walks past the new arrivals and the officer with his back to Clyde turns to get the waitresses attention, she is stood just in front and to the right of him making it difficult to make out his identity so Clyde moves his table slightly to get a better view. The waitress begins to take their order, Clyde moves his chair slightly closer in the hope that he may be able to identify the mystery officer from the side if he turns to the side.

Come on, turn around thinks Clyde

An officer bumps into Clyde's table knocking his glass onto the floor spilling his brandy.

'I'm so sorry Captain' said the drunk officer as he pats Clyde on the shoulder and looks around for the waitress then puts his fingers into his mouth and whistles, the waitress turns and looks at the blundering officer, the new arrivals from the table she is serving also look over to see the officer pointing at Clyde's table, Clyde puts his hand over his forehead embarrassed by the attention and looks towards the waitress.

'Another brandy' shouts the inebriated Officer

The waitress nods, the officer slaps Clyde on the shoulder and walks off, Clyde looks back over to the waitress serving the officers and the one which Clyde hadn't been able to identify looks him square in the eye, this is Chevalier.

'Shit' said Clyde as he immediately looks away, then looks to his cigar which is on the floor, he picks this up and then looks to Chevalier who is still staring at him.

Clyde looks towards the bar to see if his drink is on the way, he just wants to divert attention away from himself and make it look like he wasn't looking at Chevalier as he's afraid he may scare him off. The barman nods at Clyde as he'd heard the drunken officer shout the request across the bar and proceeds to prepare the drink, Clyde then looks over to Chevalier who has now gone, he spots a figure move in the corner of his eye and looks to that direction, Chevalier is walking into the bathroom. Clyde's chair screeches across the wooden floor as he stands up then walks briskly over to the bathroom, he pushes the bathroom door open as another officer walks out, Clyde walks in to see Chevalier using the urinal and is making it look as though he didn't notice anyone walk in. Clyde closes the door and walks over to the urinal and begins to use it a couple of metres away from Chevalier.

'Chevalier, I am Captain Lukas Wolf, I've come here to speak to you' said Clyde

Chevalier says nothing, he finishes using the urinal and walks away to wash his hands, Clyde continues to use the urinal with his back facing towards his target.

'I've been looking for you Mr Chevalier' said Clyde as he stares straight ahead whilst making it look like he's peeing, he turns around whilst zipping up his flies 'I know what you're up to and…'

Chevalier punches him in the face knocking him to the floor then pushes a chair in front of the door handle to stop anyone else coming in, he then kicks Clyde in the stomach which brings a groan from Clyde as he lies on the floor with a bleeding nose. Chevalier pulls a ligature from his pocket and crouches behind Clyde and throws the ligature over his head around his throat, Clyde quickly leans back and slides his hands in between to ease the strain as Chevalier attempts to strangle him.

'Who told you about me?' said Chevalier

Clyde struggles to speak but pulls the ligature away slightly.

'Me, nobody else knows' said Clyde

Chevalier pulls tightly on the ligature, Clyde struggles to pull the ligature away but manages to do so cutting his fingers as he does and bites Chevaliers thumb, Chevalier screams in pain and Clyde manages to wriggle out from the ligature.

'I'm on your side' pleads Clyde

Clyde reaches to his pistol and releases it from its holster and loads it. Clyde rolls to one side then kneels up pointing his pistol at Chevalier who is nursing his thumb which is bleeding, Clyde has blood dripping from his nose from the punch and now has blood in his mouth due to biting Chevaliers hand.

'I'm British' said Clyde through his reddened teeth

Clyde unbuttons his top three buttons from his shirt and pulls his shirt down to reveal a Royal Engineers tattoo on his upper arm whilst Chevalier watches on unperturbed.

'See for yourself' said Clyde as he makes sure Chevalier can see the tattoo clearly 'British Army, Royal Engineers'

Chevalier looks at the tattoo then back to Clyde who is holstering his pistol and nods in acceptance that Clyde may be indeed British.

'Do you always fight so dirty?' said Chevalier

Clyde smiles and pulls his shirt back over his arm.

'You were about to strangle me, what did you expect?' said Clyde

Clyde holds his hand out to help Chevalier get up from the floor who then gets to his feet and acknowledges the gesture from Clyde.

'You shouldn't have sneaked up on me' said Chevalier

Clyde looks in the mirror and wipes the blood from his nose, he cups water from the tap and sips water from it then spits into the sink and readjusts his uniform.

'I had to do what I had to do' said Clyde

Clyde tightens up his collar as Chevalier wraps a napkin around his hand then moves the chair away from the door, Clyde again wipes blood from his nose with a napkin then throws it into the basket.

'We need to speak in private' said Clyde

'Where do you suggest?' said Chevalier

'Come to my hotel room' said Clyde

Chevalier stares at Clyde trying to judge even further whether he is really British or this is to lure Chevalier out as a spy and kill him, he's no fool, he has taken precautions and is armed but also has a cyanide pill in the back of his watch ready to take if he is picked up by the Gestapo.

'Ok, let's go' said Chevalier

Clyde and Chevalier exit the bathroom and walk through the bar, Chevalier gestures to the officers he came in with to say he is leaving then both men exit the bar.

Outside, the empty streets are dimly lit, the sound of a truck driving past overshadows the sound of Clyde and Chevaliers footsteps on the cobbles. Chevalier stops for a moment, lights his pipe and then continues to catch up with Clyde.

'How long have you been on the inside?' said Chevalier as scours the area to make sure there isn't anybody in waiting ready to pounce and arrest him and not give him enough time to take the suicide pill

'Just over 12 months' said Clyde

'I take it on behalf of the SOE?' said Chevalier

Clyde smiles as he knows how ridiculous his story will sound, he will never tell anyone he'd come from the future but being an Englishman in the German Army reaching out to the SOE sounds just as bizarre.

'It's a strange one, technically no I've done it off my own back with a view to keeping less people in the loop' said Clyde

Chevalier stops.

'So you're a maverick?' said Chevalier

Again Clyde smiles as he can't try and lie to Chevalier, that wouldn't play in his favour and it would make him out to be a liar maybe getting him killed in the process, its best to keep it simple he thought.

'In a way, yes' said Clyde

'Nobody knows about you from our side?' said Chevalier

'Nobody' said Clyde

Chevalier reaches into his pocket.

'This doesn't feel right' said Chevalier as he reaches for his pistol not willing to take any chances on what he deems a charlatan, it's not worth the risk, Clyde notices.

'What are you doing?' said Clyde

Chevalier is aiming his pistol at Clyde underneath his jacket to disguise it.

'Taking precautions' said Chevalier sternly 'Turn and walk'

Chevalier prods Clyde in the back with the pistol and pushes him to make him start walking.

'There's no need for this' said Clyde

'Shut up and walk' said Chevalier

Clyde walks slightly in front of Chevalier into the hotel foyer, the concierge on the desk waves at Clyde.

'Good evening Jerome' said Clyde

'Keep walking' whispers Chevalier

Clyde and Chevalier approach the elevator and walk inside, Clyde pushes the number of which floor he is staying on, Clyde closes the gates on the elevator and the lift gradually moves up into the darkness of the hotel.

Moments later the elevator slows to a halt and Clyde opens the gates with both men exiting into the corridor which is well lit.

'You can put that away now' said Clyde

'I'll decide when it's ready, keep walking' said Chevalier as he again nudges Clyde with the pistol encouraging him to walk quickly

Clyde stops outside a room then looks at Chevalier, he then reaches into his pocket and slowly pulls out a key which he holds in front to show it isn't a weapon.

'This is the room' said Clyde

'Is anybody else with you?' said Chevalier

'No' said Clyde

Clyde opens the hotel room door, Chevalier gestures with his pistol for Clyde to enter first and as he walks into the room and Chevalier quickly reaches in front of him with a rag and holds it in front of his mouth, Clyde struggles for a second and then drops to the floor unconscious.

A while later Clyde wakes up and looks around the room, Chevalier is sat in front of him holding a syringe, Clyde's legs are tied together and his hands are tied to the chair.

'What's going on?' said Clyde as he panics struggling to get out of the ropes 'What are you doing?'

'More precautions' said Chevalier

'Untie me now' said Clyde as he struggles against the restraints

'What made you take it upon yourself to go under cover?' said a soft British voice from behind Clyde

Clyde struggles to turn to look behind him but his head is also tied to the chair.

'Take this from my neck' said Clyde

'I'll ask you again. What made you take it upon yourself to go under cover?' said the voice

Clyde again struggles to look around to see who the British person is speaking to him, it's the first British accent he'd heard for a long time and welcomed it, he just wanted to look the person in the eye whilst he spoke to them.

'No, no. It's better if you just answer the question' said the cool calm voice 'Please don't struggle'

Clyde looks at Chevalier with a piercing gaze.

'I was in the Royal Norfolk Regiment; my regiment was slaughtered at Le Paradis…' said Clyde

'Please don't insult our intelligence, we've seen the tattoo on your arm, Royal Engineers?' said the voice

Clyde looks at Chevalier who is smiling.

'Yes' said Clyde

'We have no records of any former Royal Engineers under cover in the region, would you care to explain?' said the voice

Clyde looks back to see who is speaking but struggles due to being tied up.

'Don't struggle, just look ahead an answer the question please' said the voice

Chevalier slaps Clyde with the back of his hand as he's growing impatient with him not answering the question and trying to turn around even though it's impossible.

'Answer the question!' said Chevalier

'It's better if I don't' said Clyde

Chevalier again slaps Clyde in the face.

'No. I think you'll find it's better if you do' said Chevalier

'Just let me go, kill me or whatever you've got planned. Or let me prove that I am working for the British' said Clyde

Clyde looks at Chevalier.

'I'm overseeing the construction of the Atlantic Wall, I'm sure I can help' said Clyde

Chevalier looks behind Clyde to where the British voice is coming from. Clyde tries to look around to see who has been questioning him but can't turn around, he struggles then looks back at Chevalier.

'There is something you can do for us' said the voice

'What's that?' said Clyde

'We require some information' said the voice

'Ok, what information is that?' said Clyde

We require signals from ship to ship, ship to shore' said the voice

Clyde nods.

'That shouldn't be a problem, I can access those' said Clyde

Chevalier puts the syringe down and reaches into his jacket and pulls out a cigarette holder and places it onto the table.

'That's a cigarette holder?' said the voice

'Obviously' said the combative Clyde

Chevalier stands ready to give Clyde more than a slap if he carries on with the attitude clenches his fist and looks for permission from the British agent behind Clyde which isn't forthcoming.

'It's also a micro camera' said the British voice

Clyde looks again at the cigarette box.

'Simply use it to take photos of the signals and then pass it to Chevalier at the earliest opportunity' said the voice

Clyde thinks over what has been asked of him.

'How do I contact him?' said Clyde

'Meet me in the bar where we met earlier' said Chevalier

'Ok' said Clyde

'And if you get caught, destroy the camera' said Chevalier

'I understand' said Clyde

'Oh, if you mess up and get caught' said the British voice and then paused for a moment 'Then hard cheese old boy, you're on your own'

Chevalier stands up and moves towards Clyde with a rag in his hand.

'Wait, who are…' said Clyde

Chevalier muffles the last question as he holds the rag in front of Clyde's mouth until he can no longer resist and passes out.

After the meeting, Clyde knew he could really come in from the cold if he succeeds with this mission of taking photos of the signals, he knows the photos will help an important mission but he doesn't know which one, Chevalier made sure he didn't ask any questions when he knocked him out with the chloroform.

Northern France - Sea Defence Construction

A few days later Clyde walks along a timber constructed path on the sand and walks past the mess test for the German soldiers guarding the construction on the beach, he approaches the communications tent and walks inside to see one soldier manning the radio. The radio operator notices Clyde walk in so he stands and salutes.

'Sir' said the soldier

Clyde salutes back then looks around.

'Private, go and fetch me some coffee' said Clyde abruptly

The soldier hesitantly looks at the radio then back to Clyde.

'But Sir, I've been ordered to man the radio' said the Private

Clyde stands up straight puffing his chest out and stares at the soldier with a striking and imposing stance.

'Are you disobeying an order private?' said Clyde

The private looks at Clyde and then back to the radio.

'Sir, but…' said the Private

'Coffee, now' said Clyde

The Private takes one more look at the radio and then back to Clyde.

'Yes Sir' said the Private

The private hesitantly exits the tent, Clyde quickly moves to the exit and looks outside, there is nobody around, he quickly rushes to the back of the tent where there is a filing cabinet, Clyde opens the cabinet and reaches inside to where he pulls out a file containing the signals he needs to take photos of.

Meanwhile, inside the mess tent the private is pouring a cup of coffee when a Sergeant creeps up on him.

'Roth, you're supposed to be manning the radio are you not?' said the Sergeant

The Sergeant stands beside Roth with his eyes glaring at him which causes him to back away and looks at the Sergeant.

'Yes Sergeant, I know Sergeant, Captain Wolff sent me for coffee' pleaded Roth

'Right, we'll see about that. Come with me' said the Sergeant

Inside the communications tent, Clyde is taking photos with the mini camera one page after another until he hears the hurried footsteps walking down the wooden path outside, Clyde looks towards the entrance and listens attentively then realises that he will soon have company. He had made good progress and only had one more sheet left to photograph and he didn't have long left before he was gate-crashed.

'Shit' said Clyde

He takes one more photo then puts the file back into cabinet and rushes over to the radio and sits down quickly putting the head set on as he slumps into the chair expecting Roth to walk back in alone.

The Sergeant and Private Roth walk into the tent, Private Roth is holding a cup of coffee, Clyde turns to look at them with surprise, he stands up quickly and thinks of an excuse as now Roth has his Sergeant with him, Clyde will have to think on his feet so as not to raise suspicion from the Sergeant, he doesn't trust any of the soldiers who are stationed at the beach as their all quick to stab people in the back.

'Where the hell have you been private?' shouted Clyde

Private Roth looks surprised by Clyde's outburst; the Sergeant turns to look at Roth.

'But Sir, I went for coffee' said Roth

Clyde strolls over closer to both men stopping in front of them and stares at Roth.

'You go for coffee in your own time, not when you're supposed to be manning the radio' said Clyde as he stares Roth in the face then turns to the Sergeant 'Have a word with him Sergeant'

Clyde attempts to walk past the Sergeant and the Private.

'Just one moment Captain' said the Sergeant

Clyde turns to look at the Sergeant who has walked over to the radio, the Sergeant picks something up and hands it to Clyde. It is his micro camera disguised as a cigarette case which Clyde had left behind.

'Thank you Sergeant' said Clyde

Clyde walks out of the tent and puts the camera in his inside pocket, the Sergeant knocks the coffee out the Privates hands and starts to berate him. Clyde walks across the timber walk way and towards his squad car which is parked nearby, he gets into his car, starts the engine then drives away.

A few hours later Chevalier is sat down reading a newspaper in the bar where he met Clyde, Chevalier is sat in wooden built booth with a cup of coffee slightly to his right, Chevalier hears the noise of someone sitting down in front of him and lowers his newspaper down slightly to look over it to see Clyde sat in front of him who seems to be very pleased with himself.

'Good afternoon' said Clyde

Chevalier folds his newspaper up and places it onto the table then looks at Clyde.

'You have a habit of jumping up on people' said Chevalier

Clyde raises his eyebrows at Chevalier then holds out the cigarette case.

'Would you like a cigarette?' said Clyde as he holds the cigarette case proudly

Clyde slides the cigarette holder/micro camera across the table to Chevalier who in turn picks it up, takes a cigarette out and puts the camera in his inside pocket, he lights the cigarette and looks back to Clyde. Clyde is looking at Chevalier expecting some more information on what the signals are for, after all Clyde had been asked to retrieve the information and had proved himself or so he thought, maybe now he would be a legitimate agent privy to learning more about what the information was for.

'So, is everything ok?' said Clyde

Chevalier stands up and attempts to leave, he looks back to Clyde who waits expecting to be given even just a snippet of information from Chevalier.

'So, what next?' said Clyde

Chevalier looks to the entrance door to the street outside and then back to Clyde.

'Meet me at the café over the road next Friday at Noon. Good day to you' said Chevalier

Chevalier attempts to leave and Clyde leans more towards him as he feels as though he can speak freely as the bar is empty other than the bar man sweeping the floor.

'Is that it?' said Clyde

Chevalier carries on walking away from the booth and doesn't turn back, he just carries on walking without acknowledging Clyde.

Chapter 10 - Operation Chariot

A British sailor stands behind a signal lamp on a ship, alongside him is an Officer from the Commandos watching on, this is HMS Campbeltown disguised as a German destroyer flanked by a flotilla of small motor boats each filled with commandos. The sailor frantically sends Morse code messages to the shore via the signal lamp and then worriedly turns to the officer.

'Sir, I don't think they've bought it' said the Seaman

'Well lad, it's too late to turn back now' said the Commando Officer

The Sailor had used the signals that Clyde had pilfered from the communications tent some weeks before, it had taken time to get the photos back to England and then time to plan the raid on St Nazierre or what was known within the Allied hierarchy as 'Operation Chariot'.

The plan was to disguise an old destroyer, the HMS Campbeltown, as a German destroyer and pack it full of explosives with a plan of slipping past the gun batteries on the estuary of the River Loire using stealth in sailing up the estuary at the right tide and using the signals if needs be to get close enough and ram the dry dock gates at St Nazierre allowing the explosives on the ship to blow the dock gates to pieces flooding the dry dock taking it out of use.

The dry dock had previously been used by the German warship the Bismarck which had wreaked havoc in the North Atlantic sinking merchant vessels carrying raw materials, aid and military equipment from America to Great Britain almost starving the British into submission. The dry dock is also used to house German U-Boats and despite aerial attack the construction of the sub pens had been strong enough to withhold the attacks. The Bismarck used St Nazierre as it was the only dry dock large enough to carry out repairs on her otherwise she would have to sail up the English Channel or the GIUK, the sea that separates Greenland, Iceland and the UK risking attack from the British home fleet protecting this part of the sea and also risking aerial bombardment from the RAF, so the port of St Nazierre meant a lot to the German Navy.

After a lot of hard work, the Bismarck was sunk a year earlier and the Germans were preparing to commission the Tirpitz, which was a similar sized ship to the Bismarck and the British were concerned that this may be deployed to the North Atlantic, however, if the dry dock at St Nazierre was put out of use the Germans would put the Tirpitz to use elsewhere as they won't want to take a gamble, they'd still have their U-Boats and other ships in the Atlantic and keep the Tirpitz in safer waters closer to Germany.

After the effort to sink the Bismarck the Royal Navy didn't want to allow another ship of her size to roam freely in the Atlantic as the battle for the Atlantic had turned in the Royal Navy's favour, the Tirpitz could swing that battle the other way and as they say, a 'stitch in time saves nine', this led to Operation Chariot being planned.

The Campbeltown would be supported by a flotilla of small boats and they were tasked with bringing back the commandos after the mission but every commando knew that this was a one-way ticket.

Once the Campbeltown hit the dock gates the explosives would be put on a timer and the commandos would storm the docks and destroy any ancillary equipment such as the pump house and the winch houses, they were also being tasked in destroying the tug boats. Once this was done then each commando was told to do his best in getting back to England and not to surrender unless they had exhausted all ammunition, the group of commandos were eager to take the fight to the Germans as they'd been training in Scotland for months without any action, the commandos were fresh but very well trained and very enthusiastic.

The moonlight shines down onto the commandos in the motorboats as the small flotilla of flimsy but well-armed boats each follow HMS Campbeltown into the estuary. The Seaman stands behind the signal lamp and looks towards the shore in wait for the response from the shore.

'Come on' begged the agitated Seaman as he watches intently on for a return signal but the return doesn't come soon enough.

'Just wait lad' said the Commando Officer

There are lights coming from the shore but this isn't Morse code signals, it's the flash from the artillery rounds and the sound of the shell raining down on them accompanies the flash milliseconds later.

'Jesus' said the Seaman

'We're on lads' shouts the Commando Officer

A round hits the water next to the motorboat sending a spray of water all over the occupants of the small boat, the shore line lights up further when the other gun emplacements begin to fire upon the fleet including anti-aircraft fire and small arms fire. A flare is fired into the night sky from one of the gun batteries illuminating the small armada heading to the estuary.

The size of HMS Campbeltown dwarfing the flotilla of motor boats puts into perspective how vulnerable the motorboats are, HMS Campbeltown fires back at the shoreline lighting up the area around it making the motorboats stand out even further.

A motor boat is hit with anti-aircraft fire and explodes mainly because of the high-octane fuel powering the boat, the screams of all on board is drowned out by the sound of the injured commandos in another motorboat which had been strafed with machine gun fire.

'Bloody hell' said the seaman as he moves from the signal lamp and over to the Vickers machine gun mounted to the side of the ship and starts to fire short bursts at the muzzle flashes in the darkness

The commando officer walks quickly to the inside of the ship to a crowd of ardent looking commandos.

'Right chaps, two minutes to landing' said the Commando Officer

The officer then loads his sten gun, the ships cabin is filled by the sound of machine guns being loaded with the sound of the big guns firing from the Campbeltown and artillery rounds exploding in the sea next to the ship. One commando is sipping from his hipflask; he nudges the commando huddled next to him.

'Jones, have a swig of this' said Bourhill as he holds out the hip flask

Jones takes a swig from it and passes it back to Bourhill who screws the cap back on and stuffs it into his webbing. Bourhill is a tough looking man, he was a coal miner from Fife in Scotland and was in the territorials before volunteering for the commandos. Bourhill had dark hair, blue eyes with high cheek bones and a constant scowl on his face, but with this he was deemed a handsome chap.

Jones was from South Wales and he too was in the territorials but was thinner and looked less menacing and was generally more jovial than Bourhill, but most people were, it was probably down to him having a job in the offices at the coal mine than on the coal face like Bourhill who was a shot firer so had experience with explosives, Jones played on the wing for a decent Rugby Union side in South Wales before the war and was very quick at running.

'Brace yourselves lads' calls a sailor who'd just popped his head around the door to alert the commandos to the impending collision 'Hang onto anything you can'

The commandos move and adjust themselves amongst the rattle of steel on steel where their weapons knock parts of the ship, the sound of machine gun fire hitting the ship is drowned out by the almighty crash of the Campbeltown ramming the dock gates sending the ship onto an angle as it lifts the bow onto the top of the dock gates, the commandos struggle to keep their footing and many fall to the floor, the rest of the commandos quickly help them back to their feet.

A tall and athletically built commando stands up at the doorway and looks around to the commandos who are all looking back at him, this is Sergeant Farrell who was a career soldier, he'd joined the Army in the 1920's and had served in Ireland, Turkey, India and Somalia so was vastly experienced. He had the archetypal moustache of a Sergeant and the typical voice of a Sergeant, one that could shout across a parade ground packed full of soldiers and you'd still hear what he was saying. He was a man who didn't suffer fools but had a good side to him albeit one that anyone rarely saw from him. Farrell had been a thorn in his commanding Officers side since the start of the war, his commanding officer was a University graduate who'd joined the Army straight from University and didn't take any of the advice from Farrell and after a minor altercation was offered the chance to join the commandos or be bumped down to a Corporal, Farrell chose the commandos.

'Right lads, let's go' shouts Sergeant Farrell

The commandos let out a boisterous call as they all exit the cabin and onto the ship's deck. Machine gun fire and artillery fire land in and around the position of the Campbeltown, the commandos pick up wooden ladders from the deck of the ship and proceed to lay them from the ship to the dock and scurry across them onto the dock side. Sergeant Farrell stands at the edge of the ship as if he is immune to the machine gun fire being fired into his direction.

'Get a bloody move on lads' shouts Sergeant Farrell 'This isn't Blackpool Promenade. Move it'

The commandos scurry off the ship and storm the docks killing anybody they come across, a few commandos are shot dead from the German defences.

Bourhill and Jones run alongside the dock towards the pump house, meanwhile just around the corner a German soldier cautiously crouches behind a concrete barrier aiming his rifle towards the direction of the Campbeltown awaiting the next person to rush out so he can shoot them. Jones and Bourhill run along the dock side and stop at a large wooden crate, Jones peers around the side of the crate and spots the German soldier aiming his rifle towards them, the German fires a shot and hits the wooden crate, Jones quickly ducks back behind the crate.

'Shit' shouts Jones as he tries to duck but slips due to his hob nail boots and falls backwards to the floor behind the crate then quickly regains his feet.

Bourhill lies on the floor and props his Bren gun onto the floor just behind the crate.

'I'll cover you. You run to the right and flank him' shouts Bourhill

'Righto' said Jones

Bourhill shuffles to his right bringing the concrete wall into view where the German soldier is hiding and he waits for the right moment for the soldier to come into view, the German slowly pops his head over the wall and fires a shot hitting the floor and ricocheting next to the crate, Bourhill squeezes the trigger of his Bren gun and fires a volley of shots intermittently towards the direction of the German soldier. The German soldier ducks quickly behind the concrete wall and Jones makes a dash sprinting 30 metres to the right and ducks behind a cluster of steel barrels, Bourhill looks to Jones who is giving the thumbs up, Bourhill continues to fires intermittently.

A grenade is slung over the concrete wall towards Bourhill and it hits the floor next to him but bounces and skids along the concrete floor, Bourhill and Jones watch in anticipation as it skids past landing in the sea and explodes throwing a spray of water into the air, Bourhill fires towards the wall again as Jones sprints whilst hunched over gripping his sten gun aiming towards the concrete wall, as he approaches the wall Jones leaps over the wall, crouches and fires a few shots into the German soldier who simultaneously falls to the floor and drops the grenade he had just primed ready to throw, Jones spots the grenade and leaps head first over the wall landing on his side as it explodes, Jones turns back to Bourhill and gestures for Bourhill to join him immediately.

Seconds later Bourhill joins Jones as they both crouch behind the wall in front of the pump house as intense machine gun fire starts firing onto their position pinning them behind the wall. As the zips and cracks make it difficult to hear Jones points to a direction behind the wall to where he believes the machine gun fire is coming from, Bourhill leans in to hear Jones speak.

'A couple of yards behind the wall' shouts Jones

Bourhill leans in so that Jones can hear him.

'The pump house?' shouts Bourhill

Jones nods at Bourhill then slowly tries to peer above the wall as the machine gun fire had died off, hopefully someone had shot or blown up the machine gun nest on the roof of a building nearby he hoped. Jones looks back to see three other commandos rush up to the large wooden crate and give the thumbs up to him, these are Davies, Peters and Harris. Jones gives the thumbs up back then aims his Sten gun over the wall ready to shoot anyone that made themselves visible. The three commandos sprint across the dock side and each dive to the floor and take cover behind the concrete wall, one of the commandos leans in to Bourhill.

'Are you taking the pump house?' said the commando

Bourhill nods at the commando then looks at Jones.

'Aye' said Bourhill

'Ok. Ready when you are' said the commando

'Ready?' said Bourhill as he looks to Jones

Jones nods.

'Go, go, go' shouts Bourhill

Jones goes first and Bourhill is right behind him with the three commandos quickly following behind as they make the dash towards the pump house, Jones reaches the pump house door which is closed, he tries to open it with the handle but it is locked, just as he is about to turn and inform the others Bourhill as quick as he can kicks the door just above the handle smashing the lock from the door and flinging the door back so quickly that the door is ripped from its hinges and lies half hanging off at the side of the doorway, Bourhill then rushes into the room with Jones and the five commandos following quickly behind into the dimly lit pump house.

Inside the pump house are the windings and motors for the pumps, the room is damp and smells of oil and grease, in the corner of the room is a steel stair case with stairs leading both to the roof and lower down in the pump house basement which is around 20ft deep.

Bourhill heads first and checks the pump room for German soldiers as three of the commandos take off their back packs and start to fit the explosives to the windings and the motors, Jones heads to the stairs and aims his sten gun looking down then up the stairs securing the area, as he looks up the stairs he spots a German soldier walking cautiously down, Jones fires a volley of shots hitting the German in the chest dropping him to the floor and as the German hits the steel steps with a thud Bourhill rushes over and aims his Bren gun down the stairs in order to assist Jones.

Behind Bourhill are two more commandos each with a large backpack full of explosives and each carry a Colt 1911 pistol holding them ready to fire upon the enemy, Bourhill nods at Jones who then slowly walks up the stairs with one of the commandos who carries the explosives, Bourhill does likewise but down the stairs with his accomplice.

Jones creeps up the stairs and steps over the dead Germans body whilst maintaining a solid aim down the sights of his Sten gun aiming it up the stairs as he goes ready to pull the trigger upon sight of the enemy, the commando behind him also aims his pistol over Jones' shoulder as he follows closely behind. Jones and his accomplice climb two flights of stairs and as they reach the top they see a door which is wide open leading to the roof of the pump house, Jones crouches at the top of the stairs and peers over the last step to see two German soldiers manning an Anti-Aircraft gun emplacement firing fiercely towards the direction of the Campbeltown, Jones ducks quickly before any of the Germans spot him and the commando looks up at him, Jones holds up two fingers gesturing that there are two more Germans up on the roof. Both Jones and the commando creep up the stairs aiming their weapons at the soldiers and as they reach the last step one of the Germans notices them at the stairwell and pulls his rifle up to his shoulder getting ready to fire at Jones.

'Alarm' shouts the German solider

Jones fires his Sten gun dropping the German to the ground and the German firing the anti-aircraft gun glances at Jones then holds his hands up as quickly as he can. The commando with Jones rushes out aiming his pistol at the last remaining solider with Jones checking the rest of the roof, the roof is only small and just enough space to keep the anti-aircraft gun on it, the commando rushes up to the German and pulls him from his seat by his collar backwards to the floor then kicks him in the side of the ribs then punches him in the face, the German pulls out a concealed pistol and shoots the commando in the chest, Jones notices and quickly fires a volley of shots into the Germans face killing him instantly, Jones scrambles over the dead German and drops to the floor to apply first aid to the commando but he had already died as he was hit in the heart, Jones is kneeling half on the corpse of theGerman with his hands on his knees and looks to the heavens taking a deep frustrated breath as he takes in the fact that the commando was shot, he wishes he'd have just shot the German as soon as he saw him rather than accept his surrender, after all this was a smash and grab raid, it wasn't conventional warfare because if he did accept the Germans surrender, where would he keep him? With that it came at a price too, one of his comrades was shot dead due to it. *I should have shot him; I should have just shot him* Jones thought.

'Bastard' shouts Jones through gritted teeth

After a moment of consolation Jones reluctantly takes the explosives from Harris's rucksack and plants them on the anti-aircraft gun, after a few minutes he stands up and rushes towards the stairs running down into the main pump house to where Bourhill and two other commandos are.

'You ready?' said Bourhill as he notices the blood on Jones' uniform in the dimly lit room, the question of whether the other commando was killed doesn't need to be asked, call it telepathy or body language or the blood stains, Bourhill knew for certain that he was dead.

'Yes, let's go' said Jones

Bourhill, Jones, Davies and Peters make a dash for the wall, whilst running Peters is shot in the side of his thigh dropping him to the floor clumsily, the other commandos dive over a wall and use it as cover from the barrage of machine gun fire. Behind the wall is another commando, Terry Armstrong who is firing a Bren gun over the wall towards German positions and doesn't bat an eyelid at the commandos.

'Where's Peters?' shouts Davies as he looks around searching for him comrade, Bourhill looks over the wall to see Peters wriggling on the floor halfway between the wall and the pump house holding his leg which is bleeding heavily turning the concrete floor beneath him dark with blood, Bourhill bobs his head back down quickly.

'Shit. He's been shot' said Bourhill

Peters writhes along the floor in an attempt to get to the wall neglecting his weapon as he goes, he just wants to make it to safety. Davies watches the struggle and nudges Armstrong and nods towards Peters then crouches up as if to gesture he's getting ready to rescue Peters, Jones nods at Davies as he knows what the plan is and will assist in the rescue operation, both men stand up quickly and jump over the wall making a dash through the oncoming machine gun fire as they scamper towards Peters who is 20 metres away, the intensity of the gun fire causes them to take cover behind an old oil drum and pins them in that position, bullets hit the oil drum rapidly making the commandos huddle up for cover tighter together, as they do Armstrong manning the Bren gun and Bourhill open fire towards the distant muzzle flashes in the darkness causing the Germans who are firing at them to cease and take momentary cover themselves.

'Go, go, go' shouts Bourhill instructing Jones and Davies to quickly stand up and rush over to Peters and grab him by his webbing straps which go over his shoulders and drag him backwards along the concrete dock floor whilst bullets fly over their heads in both directions.

'Come on' shouts Bourhill to the rescuers as he fires his weapon over their heads.

Jones and Davies reach the wall and Bourhill leans over and helps pull Peters over the wall to which they all take cover behind.

'Bloody hell Peters, are you ok?' shouts Davies as he holds the bleeding thigh of Peters inspecting the wound and cutting away the fabric of his trousers to inspect the wound closer, Jones crudely wraps a tourniquet around the top of the thigh in a bid to stem the bleeding as Davies pulls away to torn trousers and wipes the wound ready to dress the wound.

'I'll be alright' said Peters who pulls out a cigarette and lights it then passes the cigarettes to the other commandos

Right at that moment the pump house explodes spewing smoke and rubble across the dock area with the commandos taking cover to shield their eyes from the debris and dust. Seconds later Bourhill leans up spitting the small pieces of dust and rubble from his lips and smiles at Davies who is finishing off dressing the wound on the leg of Peters.

'Right then. Let's get back to the boats' shouts Bourhill as he glances at the hastily dressed wound which looks as good as it is going to get. Bourhill and Armstrong stand up and take pot shots at the muzzle flashes in the distance whilst Jones and Davies carry Peters back to the dock and alongside the Campbeltown.

Bourhill and Armstrong sprint along the side the Campbeltown just behind the others, each of the commandos look in bemusement at the ship because it is still intact.

'Why hasn't it blown up?' said Bourhill

Jones looks back to the bow of the ship then back to Bourhill.

'Don't know' shouts Jones

Jones and Davies carry Peters and are just in front of Bourhill and Armstrong, they're all looking into the water to find a boat amongst the darkness.

'There, there's a boat' said Jones

The commandos briskly rush up to the water's edge and take off their webbing, boots and lay their weapons onto the floor. The boat is floating a few metres from the docks edge, it had not been tied up due to the confusion and commotion of the raid earlier on but was within a short swimming distance.

'I'll get the boat. You fetch my gear' said Jones moments before he dives into the water feet first, Bourhill is distracted by something behind him, a rustle in the bushes, Bourhill turns quickly, kneels and aims his weapon at the bush.

'Don't shoot' calls the voice

'Who is it?' shouts Bourhill with assertion

'It's Williams and Anderson' replied the voice in the bushes

'Come on then, come out' said Bourhill as he stands up 'this is the last boat'

Williams and Anderson scurry out from the bushes and crouch next to Bourhill and the others and look to the water to see Jones pulling himself over the side of the motor boat.

'How did you get on?' said the blackened Williams whose uniform was singed due to fire and smoke.

'We took out the pump house' said Bourhill as he glances as Williams tarnished uniform and notices the burns on his left arm.

'We did two search lights, then the order came to scarper so we're here' said Anderson

Bourhill nods towards the burnt arm 'You want to get that seen to'.

Williams looks at his left arms and notices the burns for the first time, he hadn't been able to inspect it due to the darkness but under the dim moonlight he could make out the ghastly wound.

'Blooming heck' said Williams softly as if it were only a fly bite 'I'll dip it into the sea, that'll sort it'

Jones starts the engine of the motorboat as two more commandos come running down the dock side next to the Campbeltown with the sound of their hob nailed boots clanking on the concrete as they sprint, they stop abruptly and slightly skid on the concrete next to Bourhill, Armstrong, Williams and Anderson.

'Is there room for us?' said the other Commandos

'There's plenty room lad' said Bourhill

Jones reaches the dock in the motorboat and the Commandos each cumbersomely climb down from the dock and into the motorboat, Bourhill picks up Jones' webbing, boots and weapons and passes them to Williams before jumping across himself. The Commandos stand holding their weapons looking towards the darkness of the dock, Anderson looks around to Jones who is at the wheel.

'What are you waiting for?' barked Anderson impatiently

'Waiting to see if anyone else needs a lift' replied Jones acidly

'We were the last ones this side, we got split up from the rest, there's Germans all over the place' said Anderson frantically 'you'd better get moving'.

'Just hang on for a bit' interjected Bourhill

The Commandos hear footsteps sprinting down the dock.

'Wait' calls a voice 'wait for me'

The sound of the hobnail boots hitting the concrete rapidly as the commando sprints gets louder as he quickly approaches.

'Wait for me it's Logger' said the voice

Logger runs and jumps into the boat knocking Williams to the floor.

'Watch where you're bloody going' shouts Williams as he pushes Logger of him

'Go, go, go' shouts Logger as he looks to Jones at the wheel 'What are you waiting for there's Jerry right behind me'

Bourhill looks at Jones and then to Logger who is crouched down looking to the direction he came from.

'Come on, let's go. They're bloody here, what did I tell you?' said Logger

Logger fires a burst of shots from his sten gun into the darkness of the docks and a loud scream of pain is heard followed by shouting in German, from where the shouting is coming from the bright flash from the end of a machine gun firing in to the boats direction accompanied with the undeniable sound of the MP40 making the Commandos dive to the deck of the boat and for Jones to open the throttle on the boat.

'Jones, get us out of here' shouts Bourhill as he fires his weapon towards the docks.

Logger fires another burst towards the Germans on the dock side and Williams starts to fire the Lewis gun mounted to the side of the boat, the muzzle flash from the Lewis gun lights up the boat making it an easier target of the German machine gunner.

'Argh' shouts Logger in pain as he falls back clutching his eye

'Have you been hit?' said Anderson

'Argh, my eye. I've got something in my eye' calls Logger in serious pain

Logger drops to his knees and hunches over holding his eye, the other commandos return fire to the dock side and Anderson leans in to get a closer look at Loggers eye.

'Ok, keep still, let me have a look at it' said Anderson

Logger drops his weapon and leans up slightly holding his eye which is dripping with blood.

'Argh' calls Logger as he moves

Anderson pulls Logger back so he can get a better view of his eye, a large wooden splinter had pierced just below his eye and was rubbing on his eyeball on the inside. The splinter had come from the boat due to the machine gun fire hitting the boat earlier on. Jones mans the wheel and steers the boat as it makes a slow but steady getaway and the commandos on the boat fire frantically at the muzzle flashes on the dock side.

Morning breaks at St Nazierre as a large group of captured Commandos and sailors are being marched from one part of the town to another, the Campbeltown can be seen from where they are marching and it's still perched on top of the dock gates, many German Officers are stood on the bow of the ship having their photos taken whilst German soldiers prowl around the ship guarding it as some sort of trophy of a failed attack on the port. Without warning, HMS Campbeltown explodes with an almighty thud spewing smoke and shrapnel into the sky killing many Germans and destroying the dock gates flooding the dry dock. Among the cries for help from the injured German soldiers there is a fire raging from the ship and many German soldiers run to the aid of their comrades through the plumes of thick black smoke.

Inside one of the buildings, a British Naval officer dressed in a white woollen roll neck jumper, navy blue trousers and a naval officer's cap looks out of the window whilst smoking a pipe and drinking a cup of tea and notices the smoke bellowing from the destroyed ship, he turns to the rest of the captured Commandos.

'Job well done chaps' said the officer.

Chapter 11 – Too Close for Comfort

A few weeks later Clyde is sat in the driver's seat of his squad car which is camouflaged by bushes and trees as it is parked just slightly inside the edge of the tree line of the forest, he'd learnt his lesson last time about not being prepared with a vehicle with him having to steal a motorcycle from two soldiers stationed at the original farmhouse and he didn't want the hassle of doing that again so he made the effort to drive to the area in which he reappears in.

Clyde takes a deep breath and then looks at his watch, the time is 2:15am, he takes a sip of water from his canteen then places it down on the passenger seat, then looks again at his watch, 2:15am.

'Urgh' said Clyde as he gets the sickly feeling in his stomach that he gets when is he about to go back, he holds both hands on his face, a bright red light fills the car and illuminates part of the forest then he wakes up lay on the floor of the dome in the bunker.

He struggles to stand and uses the side of the wall to aid him in standing up, he slowly stumbles out of the dome and into the bunker room and fumbles his way to the nearby table, he runs his fingers across the table and locates his jacket then puts it on.

Clyde then proceeds to leave the bunker cautiously walking towards the light where the tunnel is and as he approaches he gets on all fours and crawls out, once outside he squints as his eyes adjust to the little light there is in the woodland then starts walking in the direction of where he parked his car.

An hour later, Clyde walks swiftly up the stairs of his house and opens the boiler cupboard door, he pulls out a pole to which he uses to unhook the catch on his attic door dropping the door down and the ladders attached to it slide down before Clyde pulls them down so that they reach the floor of the landing.

Clyde climbs up the ladders into his attic and reaches around the floor and switches the lights on casting a light over his army equipment such as his Bergen, helmet, boots, tent, etc. He climbs up into the attic then walks along the timber floor to the other side and crouches down beside a large ammunition crate.

Clyde pulls out a key attached to a nail on the inside of one of the rafters and opens the padlock on the ammo crate, inside are a set of two way radios with ear pieces, a Colt 1911 hand gun with ammunition, an AK47 with ammunition, gold coins with Arabic writing on them and another smaller box. Clyde pulls out the small box, it's roughly the size of an egg box and opens it cautiously, inside is filled with straw and wood shavings and as he rustles his hand around inside he pulls out a piece of plastic explosive, on the side it says 'Semtex-H', he places the 'Semtex' back into the small box and looks around the large ammo crate. Clyde pulls out what looks to be a detonator and places it on the floor, then he pulls out the small box and the 2 way radios with ear pieces and carries them back to the loft hatch, he switches the light off and then climbs back down the ladders holding his equipment.

Once Clyde is back down he walks into another room and picks up a small rucksack which he stuffs the small box and 2 way radios inside, he then folds the ladders up inside the attic and then closes the door to it. Clyde picks up his rucksack and then walks down the stairs.

An hour later Clyde is stood inside the dome holding his rucksack, he pulls down on the lever inside and then a bright red flash fills the room and Clyde wakes up on the floor of a field with morning just breaking. He staggers to his feet and slowly walks over to the woods nearby hoping that his squad car that he'd left previously would still be there, he moves some vegetation uncovering the squad car which he pushes past branches and opens the door, he climbs inside, starts the engine then drives away with small saplings scraping the side of the squad car as he passes through.

Clyde pulls up outside of the café in Lille, he gets out of the squad car, looks around the area to make sure he isn't being followed then walks over to Chevalier who is sat outside of the café reading a newspaper and drinking coffee, as he approaches Chevalier looks up to see Clyde sit down at the table. Chevalier looks around, folds his newspaper up and places it onto the small round table and then back to Clyde who is leaning back on his chair and places both hands on top of his head.

'It was a success' said Chevalier

Clyde smiles and nods cockily.

'Good, I'm glad I could help' said Clyde

A waiter approaches the table and stops beside Clyde.

'1 coffee please' said Clyde

Chevalier looks at the waiter 'I'm ok, thank you' the waiter bows slightly then walks away.

'What do we do next?' said Clyde as he stares at Chevalier in anticipation of their next move, Chevalier leans closer to Clyde to prevent any eavesdropping.

'We need weapons, explosives and medical equipment for the resistance fighters' said Chevalier softly so as not to be overheard

'Ok, that shouldn't be a problem' said Clyde as he thinks he could pilfer most of what Chevalier is asking for as he does have access to most of the left over weapons from when the British fled France at Dunkirk a couple of years earlier.

He also has a large number of explosives that he can take as they go through a lot of them breaking up rocks whilst building the sea defences, the medical equipment he can get but not in large quantities if that's what Chevalier has in mind.

Clyde is about to speak as the waiter approaches the table but he stops as to keep their conversation discrete, the waiter lays down a cup of coffee on the table with a small plate and a biscotti beside it, Clyde turns and nods at the waiter as a show of thanks.

'Thank you' said Clyde

The waiter walks away, Clyde pulls out a cigarette case and takes two cigarettes out, passes one to Chevalier and then lights one for himself and takes a swig of coffee.

'We need somebody who can order the equipment so we can, as you may say, help ourselves to it' said Chevalier

Chevalier doesn't want Clyde to take the items himself he just to needs to order them and tip Chevalier off so the resistance can ambush the supply trucks which makes it easier for Clyde, all he has to do is order what Chevalier needs but making sure at least 19 out of 20 trucks do make it through to keep any suspicion away from him, Clyde nods his head as if to say he can do it as he puts his coffee cup back onto the table.

'Ok. What do we need and where do I order it to?' said Clyde

Chevalier looks around to make sure nobody is around them and able to listen in then leans closer in to Clyde.

'We need as much of anything you can get hold of especially explosives' said Chevalier

'Ok, I can get hold of explosives quite easily I'll just say the area in which we are digging is rocky terrain underneath the sand' said Clyde confidently

Chevalier nods his head and leans a little closer to Clyde.

'Precisely, you let me know when they will be arriving and I'll take care of the rest' said Chevalier as he leans back smoking his cigarette

'No problem, leave it with me' said Clyde

Clyde takes a sip of coffee and stubs his cigarette out in the ash tray when a woman walks past with blonde hair which catches Clyde's eye, he turns to take a closer look at the woman as he feels he recognises her.

'Anna?' calls Clyde

The woman stops and turns around, it is Anna Jaeger but she doesn't spot Clyde sat outside the café so she carries on walking. Clyde and Anna hadn't be in contact with each other since the one night stand at the Grand Hotel, perhaps Jaeger suspected something was amiss and pulled her out of the area or perhaps the guilt had gotten the better of Anna and she pushed for the move away. Clyde thinks Anna still looks as beautiful as she did the night she'd spent at the hotel with him as she's dressed smartly, her blonde hair had grown an inch or two since and it bounced lazily as she walked along the street.

'Anna' calls Clyde as he stands up and walks over to Anna who had now turned around and looks befuddled to see Clyde.

'Lukas. How are you?' said the surprised Anna

Clyde is smiling stood in front of Anna and is pleased to see her, Anna is also but does a better job at hiding it.

'I'm great, how are you?' said Clyde

'I'm fine' said Anna as Clyde fidgets with his cigarette case for a moment as both of them are a little lost for words in the awkwardness of the meeting

'So, what brings you to Lille?' said Clyde

'We're stationed here due to my husband… you remember, Captain Jaeger?' said Anna

Clyde stays silent for a moment and nods secretly thinking to himself '*Yes, I remember that bastard*' but doesn't dare say it.

'Yes, yes I do' said Clyde

'Yes, well. Here we are' said Anna

The awkward meeting isn't going to how Clyde thought it would, there was obvious sexual tension but the words seemed to vanish like dust in the wind before he could think of something half decent to say to her.

'Come and join us' said Clyde as he smiles and steps to one side as if to usher Anna to their table, Anna looks over to see Chevalier sat on his own and is apprehensive about gate crashing.

'Thank you, but I don't want to disturb you both' said Anna

'Nonsense, I insist' said Clyde

'Sorry I can't, but it would have been nice to catch up with you' said Anna, the comment seemed genuine enough.

Anna smiles with a glint of regret in her facial expression as deep down she would have liked to chat with Clyde but there was something holding her back, Clyde could sense this and felt that if he took the chance and used a bit of persuasion then he thought he could get her to spend some time with him again, throughout this Chevalier ignored Anna and tried his best to keep a low profile, Anna had the occasional glance over to Chevalier to get a better view of who Clyde was sitting with.

'Why don't we catch up later? Me, you and *Captain Jaeger*?' said Clyde probingly

Anna again smiles and looks to the floor as she knows he isn't currently with her, she was on her own in Lille and she suspected that Clyde knew it and saw that tact of Clyde's offer wasn't to catch up with Captain Jaeger, it was a polite offer with a hidden agenda and not very well disguised, Anna knew it.

'I'd love to but he's out of town' said Anna with faux naivety

Clyde smiles knowing that he'd backed her into a corner knowing that Anna couldn't have an excuse not to meet up later and had teed Anna up for the next question perfectly.

'Why don't you come by yourself?' said Clyde

Anna shakes her head knowing that the last time they went out they ended up sleeping together and she was married, she had felt rotten inside every time Captain Jaeger had looked her in the eye for the following few weeks after it and didn't want to go through it again, even if she did have a soft spot for Clyde and was struggling to hide that fact.

'I'm sorry, I can't' said Anna

Anna turns to walk away but looks out of the corner of her eye secretly wanting Clyde to chase after her and convince her to go, she was playing hard to get.

'Goodbye Lukas' said Anna

Clyde quickly catches up to Anna and starts to walk beside her.

'One drink, that's all' said Clyde

'Goodbye Lukas' said Anna

'No funny business I promise' said Clyde

The guilt pangs in Anna's stomach causes her to stop, looks around and then advances closer to Clyde pointing her rigid finger into Clyde's chest.

'There will never be any funny business, ever. So leave me alone' said Anna as she prodded Clyde

'One drink and I'll leave you alone' said Clyde

'Please, I have things I need to do today, please… leave me be' said Anna

Anna starts to walk away but Clyde walks quickly alongside her stooping so that their eyes are on the same level, Clyde is a lot taller than Anna.

'Come on, live a little. You could get hit by a bomb tomorrow and you'd regret not coming out for a drink with me' said Clyde

Anna trying to look as though she is fed up with Clyde stops, tries hard to conceal her smile and Clyde smiles trying to coax Anna to allow the smile to come through her fragile stern facade.

'One drink?' said Anna

'Yes, one drink' said Clyde

Anna stops and looks around, she looks to the floor and then back to Clyde.

'Ok, but you keep quiet, ok?' said Anna

'Absolutely' said Clyde

'Just one drink, ok?' said Anna

'Just one drink' said Clyde

'No funny business' said Anna

'Lots of funny business' said Clyde

Anna purses her lips and looks sternly at Clyde who starts to laugh.

'Ok, ok. No funny business' said Clyde

Anna has a wry smile on her face.

'Good, shall we say 8pm at 'Le Grand Hotel' in the bar?' said Clyde

'Hmm. We shall see' said Anna as she walks away, Chevalier now stands beside Clyde and both men stand there watching Anna walk away.

'See you there' shouts Clyde

Both Clyde and Chevalier watch Anna walk gracefully away.

'You know, you were one step from clubbing her over the head and dragging her back to your hotel' said Chevalier

'She'll be coming back to my hotel anyway later, so I wouldn't need the club' said Clyde

'In your dreams hot shot. She'll more likely stand you up' said Chevalier

'No' said Clyde as he laughs off Chevaliers comment 'If she turns around to look at me, she'll be spending the night with me'

Anna continues to walk away but doesn't turn around, Clyde still stands there.

'She's forgotten about you already' said Chevalier

'Keep watching' said Clyde

Anna stops and turns around, Clyde blows her a kiss and Anna smiles and continues walking away.

'What did I tell you?' said Clyde

Chevalier shakes his head and walks back over to the table, Clyde turns and goes and sits back down with Chevalier.

Later on that evening, Clyde sits in a booth in the empty hotel bar, it is a sea of dark green leather and mahogany, as he knocks the beer mat on the table the sound echoes around the room, the ticking of the clock takes Clyde's attention away from the beer mat, he wonders whether Chevalier was right and he's been stood up, but Chevalier would never know as Clyde wouldn't tell him if he had been to spare the embarrassment, *where the hell is she?* wonders Clyde as a waiter walks up to the table.

'Another Brandy Sir?' said the waiter

Clyde nods, the waiter picks up the empty glasses from the table and places them onto his silver tray and walks away. The door of the bar opens and footsteps drown out the sound of the clock with high heels hitting marble slightly faster than the clock is ticking, Clyde puts down the beer mat and looks around the corner of the booth to see Anna walking effortlessly into the bar, she notices Clyde and continues to walk towards him with the barman and the waiter each stopping in their tracks to look at her as she has a long crimson dress which fits where it touches, her hair is long and wavy and bounces as she walks as do the tops of her breasts which are slightly framed by the low neck line of the dress and the side of her charcoal fur coat, Clyde stands wide eyed looking at Anna from the booth and welcomes her with a kiss on the cheek, he looks towards the waiter and barman who turn away quickly to make it look like they weren't staring at Anna, Clyde didn't mind, he wasn't going to get overprotective of his date as she was already married to somebody else, he glances at the clock to see that she was nearly two hours late, he didn't mind as she looked exquisite.

'Did you get here ok?' said Clyde knowing she was rather late

Anna glances at the clock 'Yes. I'm sorry if I'm late' said Anna

'If? It's a bloody damn certainty that you're two hours late' thought Clyde as he smiled at Anna, the waiter walks up to the table placing Clyde's glass of brandy onto the table placing a mat underneath as he does so in a gentle fashion, he then stands awaiting Anna's order and tries in vein not to stare down Anna's cleavage but his eyes keep being drawn to them as if his head was tied to them by elastic, the waiter tries his hardest not to look especially in front of Clyde.

'What would you like Mademoiselle?' said Clyde

'I'll have a vodka martini please' said Anna

'One vodka martini please' said Clyde as he watched in amusement at the squirming waiter as he struggles to keep his eyes from Anna's breasts as she pulls her shoulders back and slides her fur coat of the back of her shoulders rocking from side to side in the process.

'Thank you' said Clyde as the waiter walks away, they both sit down, the open bosom of Anna's dress catches Clyde's eye, she notices causing him to look away and then back to her face.

'Do you remember the last time we were here?' said Clyde with a glint in his eye and a wry smile on his face, Anna blushes.

'How could I forget about this place?' said Anna shyly

'Ah, so you remember?' said Clyde

'Of course I do' said Anna

'Same here' said Clyde as he leans back in his chair cockily 'I rather enjoyed it'

Anna smiles as does Clyde, the waiter brings the vodka martini over and places it onto the table in front of Anna whilst sliding a mat underneath the glass trying not to look at her breasts.

'Thank you' said Clyde to the waiter who walks away quickly

They both pick up their drinks, Clyde reaches his glass out and winks.

'Bottoms up' said Clyde

Both Anna and Clyde smile reminiscing about the last time they were there.

'You know… for days after… my husband was asking questions' said Anna nervously as she cradled her drink.

I'll bet he was, the fucking weasel Clyde thought. He wasn't stupid, he knew he didn't want to raise suspicion from Captain Jaeger after their one night stand and wanted to probe Anna for information, just in case Jaeger came sniffing around again.

'What sort of things was he asking?' probed Clyde

Anna smiled, seemingly embarrassed of what she was about to say.

'He wanted to know…' said Anna shyly 'He wanted to know…why I was so happy'

'And what did you tell him?' said Clyde with a smile breaking unrepentantly on his face

Anna looks to the table not knowing how to say the next bit, she felt embarrassed just in case it scared Clyde off, she took a deep nervous breath.

'I told him I was happy' said Anna in a matter of fact way

'Is that all he asked?' said Clyde thinking that Jaeger may have been probing about him, he thought he might have asked Anna who she was out with that night and questions like that.

'He asked if I went anywhere whilst he was away' said Anna as she took a sip of her drink 'I told him I went into Lille to meet an old friend from school and that was all really'

Thank fuck for that Clyde thought, Captain Jaeger hadn't really asked about him.

'So…why did you move away?' asked Clyde as he takes a swig of brandy

'We had to. I told him I was happy to be in Lille and wanted to stay' said Anna

After the one-night stand Anna had left the area, Clyde wanted to see more of her even if she was married to most dangerous man in Northern France but that was not to be as Captain Jaeger had moved them both out of the area or they'd both been stationed somewhere else. *I wonder what would have happened if they'd stayed in Lille* Clyde thought, *we'd have been caught probably, Jaeger is a weasel but he's not stupid, it was probably for the best.*

'So, *you* wanted to stay?' said Clyde as he tilted his head and nodded slowly

'Yes, I wanted to stay' said Anna as she looks to the floor and slowly raises her eyes to meet Clyde's 'But my husband…I don't know…. I think that maybe *he* thought something was amiss… and we moved away straight after but I wanted to stay'

Surely Captain Jaeger knew something had happened Clyde thought, maybe he was playing with fire and should have left things the way they were and just allowed Anna to walk down the street, if Jaeger investigates Clyde that may put the dampers on any arrangements he'd made earlier with Chevalier but he couldn't help himself, he'd drunk most of a bottle of brandy and Anna looked sensual. He hadn't slept with a woman since Anna and now he had half a chance of doing it again he would take the chance and worry about the repercussions when he'd sobered up. *Fuck Jaeger, I'll just fucking kill the bastard if he finds out* thought Clyde, brave on Dutch courage.

'Was there something you wanted to stay for?' said Clyde as a slow wry smile broke on his face, Anna smiles and twirls her hair with the index finger looking back at him.

'Yes… of course' said Anna brazenly

Anna picks up her drink and takes a larger than normal gulp finishing it off.

'And what was that something?' said Clyde, his heart rate was rising, he had Anna in the palm of his hand and was going in for the kill, *I'm glad I booked the hotel room* Clyde thought.

Anna pauses, she again looks to the table, smiles and then looks back at Clyde.

'I'd never felt more alive or more… wanted' said Anna

Clyde tries to feign modesty as his heart rate rose further and felt a twitch in his groin as his libido awakened. They both smile as previously he'd given Anna a night to remember, people in the 1940's didn't much sexual experience but Clyde did, he had plenty.

He thought he had Anna eating out of the palm of his hand but Anna had other plans, she was a temptress and had a great sense of humour, for a German.

'You know it was a shame we moved, I got real enjoyment from treating those wounded soldiers' said Anna

Clyde spits his brandy as he coughs in surprise, Anna has caught him off guard.

'What? You didn't think I meant you did you?' said Anna

Anna smiles and raises her eyebrows whilst Clyde wipes the brandy from his mouth and laughs as does Anna.

'Well, there aren't any wounded soldiers around here so how are you going to get your kicks?' said Clyde

'Oh, I think there's a wounded soldier sat close to me' said Anna as she reaches across the table and holds Clyde arms gently 'but he only has a bruised ego'

'Really?' said Clyde as he raises his eyebrows in surprise, Anna winks back at him to prove it was jest.

'You've got the devil in you' said Clyde as he feels his pulse in his groin and sits more upright to try and disguise it.

Anna smiles, Clyde pulls out a cigarette and lights it then blows smoke into the air of the dimly lit restaurant.

'I see you've been making friends?' said Anna

Clyde thinks Anna must be talking about Chevalier.

'Do you mean the guy before?' said Clyde

'Yes, who is he?' said Anna

'Major Chevalier, he's a good friend of mine' said Clyde

Anna smiles then slips her right foot from her high heeled shoe and slides it up Clyde's leg stopping at the top rubbing the side of Clyde's thigh, he smiles and looks passionately into her eyes, she slowly moves her foot onto Clyde's throbbing genitals and rubs them with her foot, she smiles when she realises he is erect.

'That's nice' said Clyde

Anna smiles as she carries on rubbing softly with her foot.

'Do you want to go upstairs?' said Clyde with intent

Anna nods and Clyde quickly stands up and holds out his hand to help Anna from the both, she picks her coat up and Clyde downs the rest of his brandy, the waiter looks towards Clyde.

'Bottle of Bollinger and two glasses to room 658' said Clyde

'Yes Sir' said the waiter

Clyde and Anna walk quickly out of the bar and into the foyer, Clyde looks around as they walk through the bar making sure they aren't seen and they walk into the elevator and the door closes behind them as they kiss passionately inside.

Chapter 12 – Moth to the Flame

The wave's crash against the bottom of the cliffs with the water spraying high over the top of them, above the cliffs are the forced labour workers from various parts of France, who by now are looking very thin, bang away at the rock with pick axes making little, if any, progress.

A small group of seagulls fly overhead appearing to taunt the labour workers with their call as they circle above, one of the labour workers stops to look at the seagulls probably wishing to trade places with the bird rather than be where he was. In his hometown of Lyon, he had run his own butchers shop and worked hard during the depression in the 1930s to keep his business afloat, he was too old to fight in the French army so when the Vichy regime came to power, he along with other men of similar age in Lyon were conscripted to build the Atlantic wall.

Clyde is stood above the workers watching them struggle to break the hard rock, a young officer, Lieutenant Shultz, walks up beside Clyde and stands next to him as they both watch over the workers.

'We'll never meet the deadline if we carry on using pickaxes, we need explosives. Sir' said Lieutenant Shultz, who wasn't frustrated with Clyde, he was frustrated with the higher management of the project.

'I know that and so do you, but they've put a stop to it' replied Clyde

A few weeks had passed by since Chevalier and the resistance had started to pick off the supply trucks to the region where Clyde was taking the explosives, weapons, food etc. and had nipped it in the bud, they stopped sending the supplies by truck and started air dropping food and medical supplies and stopped sending explosives altogether, just in case they fell into the wrong hands.

'How the hell can those bunch of idiots expect us to meet our deadlines?' said Lieutenant Shultz, who then realises he shouldn't be making his personal opinions know to anyone else within the Army as he knows anyone who rocks the boat are dealt with swiftly, the young lieutenant didn't want to end up buried in the woods with a bullet in his head from Captain Jaeger as he had a wife and child back home in Dortmund but he'd slipped up due to Clyde being an approachable person.

'I'm sorry Sir… it just frustrates me' added Lieutenant Shultz to make sure he doesn't get reprimanded

'Me too, but it is what it is' said Clyde

'I just…I don't know…we can't help if trucks and trains are hijacked by the resistance' said Lieutenant Shultz

Clyde looks down to the struggling workforce and thinks of some way of helping the workers and getting the rocks broken up quicker so that they can meet their deadlines.

'How many grenades can we spare?' asked Clyde intriguingly

Shultz's eyes look down to the left as he tries to remember how many grenades there were from memory then back to Clyde wondering what he planned to do with them.

'There's two crates in total, that won't last long if we use them to break the rocks' said Shultz

Clyde nods his head in thought, looks to the floor then back to Shultz.

'Yes, yes I agree. They'd be gone in a day if we used them to break the rocks' said Clyde as he shakes his head 'The simple fact of the matter is that we need explosives, regardless of whether things are going missing'

'Precisely' said Shultz

Shultz turns around to see a squad car pull up next to the tents, out of the squad car steps Captain Jaeger. Clyde turns and notices Jaeger waving to him then gestures for him to join him, Shultz looks at Clyde.

'Who's that Sir?' asks the Lieutenant

'That's Captain Jaeger, of the Gestapo. Leave him to me' said Clyde as he walks away.

The colour drains quickly from Shultz's face, he had nothing to hide but he'd heard about Captain Jaeger, he'd heard that once he was investigating a quartermaster who was selling food and medicine to local French women, he wasn't always being paid with money so he always had a woman to warm his bed.

Captain Jaeger had been tipped off by one of the Quartermasters jealous colleagues, Jaeger investigated and thought that the quartermaster could be blackmailed or honey trapped into giving valuable information to an allied female spy so decided he'd have to kill him to prevent this, one of Captain Jaegers female colleagues had met up with the quartermaster, benefited from some goods and went back to his quarters to repay the debt as they mostly did.

Fifteen minutes later, the orderly Corporal in the barracks had been alerted to the quartermaster's room to find him dead, lay naked with his penis chopped off and stuffed inside his mouth. The woman was never to be seen again and there was no evidence to suggest it was Jaeger, but that was the rumour that cautiously went around spreading fear like wildfire.

Lieutenant Shultz walks away nervously, Clyde waves to Jaeger and begins to walk over the sand dunes towards him, Jaeger waits outside the tents as Clyde approaches.

'Captain Wolf. It's good to see you again' said Jaeger

Jaeger reaches his hand out and Clyde shakes his hand in a firm grip with both men trying to out squeeze the other.

'Captain Jaeger, it's always a pleasure' said Clyde

Clyde can't get the thought of himself and Anna out of his head whilst he is looking at Jaeger which brings a smile to Clyde's face, knowing that he'd slept with his wife twice and the thrill of that filled him with nervous excitement and bravado.

Captain Jaeger didn't reach his position in the Gestapo by being a yes man and was a good judge of character and good at reading people and could tell with Clyde's facial expression that he was smirking, but why?

'Is something… *amusing* you, Captain?' said Jaeger as he mimicked the smirk

'No, no. I'm just pleased to see you again Captain' said Clyde, with the smirk slowly leaving his face

Captain Jaeger stands in front of Clyde and smiles whilst nodding his head slowly.

'Is there somewhere we can talk?' said Jaeger

Clyde nods.

'Yes. Follow me' said Clyde

Clyde had a feeling that Jaeger might drop by after the equipment being stolen and also what had happened again with Anna but he felt confident he had covered his tracks unless Anna had said something about the affair, if so, then Clyde would have nowhere to hide and someone like Jaeger would kill him where he stood or with his rank and contacts he may be moved to somewhere not as pleasant or cushy as Northern France, he may be posted to the Eastern front with the massive push into Russia.

Clyde liked it in Northern France and felt he could aid the war effort on a bigger scale for the British and eventually gain revenge in killing Stechen for killing Karl and the British soldiers if he stayed there, so despite his pride he'd have to swallow it and try his best not to antagonise Captain Jaeger, after all, it's in his best interests not to.

Clyde leads Jaeger towards the tent and a soldier walks past them both and salutes as he walks by.

'Private' said Clyde

The Soldier stops and turns.

'Yes Sir?' said the Private

'Fetch us some coffee' said Clyde

'Yes Sir' said the Private

Clyde ushers Jaeger into a tent which has a table and chairs inside for the officer's mess, there is one other officer in the mess, a young 2nd Lieutenant who notices Captain Jaeger and fearfully stands up, makes his excuses then leaves.

Captain Jaeger has a fearsome reputation within the Army in France as he is known as the rat catcher, he's very good at sniffing out double agents, French resistance fighters and anyone else who rocks the boat and sees that they are dealt with, usually a bullet to the back of head once the guilty party turns away thinking that they'd pulled the wool over Jaegers eyes.

Clyde did not fear Jaeger as much as the others, he felt as though he was slightly untouchable or at least a little of out of reach for Jaeger due to being seen as the favoured officer in the region as he had made such good progress in building the Atlantic Wall, he was associated with Stechen and Brigadier Freidrich and also his supposed act of gallantry at the start of the war.

'Please, sit down' said Clyde

Both Clyde and Jaeger sit down facing each other, Jaeger puts his hat onto the table facing up and begins to pull each of the fingers of his leather gloves off one by one in a precise manner.

'I'll not beat about the bush Captain' said Jaeger

'By all means, please, don't feel the need to Captain' said Clyde

Jaeger nods and finishes removing his gloves and throws them into the top of his hat on the table then smiles.

'Ok. So I assume you're aware of the hijackings of equipment designated to be delivered to this site, am I correct?' said Jaeger

Shit thought Clyde *he isn't beating about the bush.*

'Yes' said Clyde trying to look calm and composed

'The equipment such as explosives, weapons, ammunition, medicine and rations?' said Jaeger

'Yes, yes. I am aware' said Clyde politely, *what's your point?* he thought.

'Equipment *you* yourself ordered for the camp?' said Jaeger who then smirked

'Yes' said Clyde

What is he getting at? Clyde thought. He didn't like the way the conversation was heading and adjusts his seating position slightly and his facial expression changes from a smirk to a stern looking expression.

'Equipment… that only *you* knew about' said Jaeger

Jaeger smiles and nods, if he was a peacock his tail would be fanned out in the air.

He's on to me, shit, he's on to me Clyde thinks.

'I'm not sure where you're going with this, but yes, I did order the equipment' said Clyde trying desperately to keep his composure.

Captain Jaeger stays silent, he stares at Clyde smiling and tilts his head and holds his chin with his left hand and Clyde can't stand the awkward silence.

'Captain, I'm not sure what your point is?' said Clyde abruptly

Captain Jaeger holds out his hand as if to calm Clyde then sits more upright.

'I'm sorry Captain, am I making you feel uncomfortable?' said Jaeger

Clyde shakes his head and moves his body position in the chair back slightly.

You've got me, you sneaky bastard thinks Clyde

'No, not at all' said Clyde, though he was.

'Sorry, my mistake' said Jaeger

The Private walks into the mess with a pot of coffee, two cups, a small jug of cream and a bowl of brown sugar cubes. Clyde starts to tap his foot on the timber boards on the floor of the tent as he watches the Private place the percolator, cups, sugar lump bowl, small jug of cream and cutlery onto the table. Clyde wishes Jaeger would just leave right now, he'd got what he wanted, he already knew something was amiss with Clyde and despite his bravado at the start he just wanted to run away or just kill Jaeger.

'Thank you Private' said Jaeger

The Private moves quickly away as he knows he's in Captain Jaeger's vicinity and doesn't want to stick around any longer than he needs to. Captain Jaeger takes a cup from the tray and fills his cup with coffee very carefully and precisely not to spill a drop, he then pours another cup for Clyde.

'Thank you Captain' said Clyde whose mood has now changed to a more solemn vibe rather than belligerent as he was initially, Jaeger seems to have grown more in stature.

'Sugar?' said Jaeger

'No thank you' said Clyde

Jaeger takes a lump of brown sugar from the bowl and drops it into his cup using the tongs provided, he then stirs the cup exactly 9 times. Clyde pulls out his cigarette container and opens it towards Jaeger.

'Cigarette?' said Clyde

'No thank you' said Jaeger

Clyde pulls out a cigarette and lights it, he puts the box back into his inside pocket. Captain Jaeger picks up the small jug with the cream in, he takes out a spoon and starts to take the top of the cream a small bit at a time and places it into his cup, Jaeger notices Clyde is watching and looks back to him.

'I know what you're wondering' said Jaeger

'What's that?' said Clyde

'You're wondering why I'm taking the cream from the top' said Jaeger

'Well, yes, I suppose so' said Clyde

Jaeger smiles.

'The cream rises to the top and I like cream' said Jaeger

Clyde takes a drag on his cigarette then looks to Jaeger and nods his head.

'A lot do' said Clyde as he thinks he'd love to do nothing more than throw the coffee into Jaegers face and then strangle him

"Yes. Everyone likes cream, however, I'm taking a little at a time, this way, nobody notices' said Jaeger

'You fucker, you sneaky fucker, just come out and say it you bastard, just fucking say that you're on to me' Clyde thought.

'Take as much as you like Captain, we have plenty' said Clyde

'That's not the point, we all like the cream. If I were to take all the cream then there would be none left for anybody else, people might be reluctant to give me the milk just in case I take all of the cream and then the chef wouldn't be happy' said Jaeger

'No?' said Clyde in faux nativity

'No, chefs by nature are aggressive and know exactly how much cream there should be' said Jaeger

Clyde looks to the floor and then up to Jaeger, Clyde has a tough stern look on his face and a slight scowl, Clyde doesn't like Jaeger and the feeling is mutual but they both do the dance of pretending they like each other.

'I get your point' said Clyde bluntly

'Now if someone on the camp had a cat and happened to be siphoning off cream to feed, let's say their pet cat, what do you think the chef would say?' said Jaeger

'I don't think he would be too happy about it' said Clyde

Just leave, please just leave the camp. I've had enough of you, you've got me thought Clyde

'And you're exactly right' said Jaeger

Jaeger passes the jug to Clyde then pulls out his own packet of cigarettes and takes one out and lights it, Clyde notices that he'd refused to take one of his before and now he's smoking his own, *'does he not trust me? Obviously not'* thought Clyde.

Clyde pours the milk into his coffee and stirs it, then stubs out his cigarette and takes a swig of the coffee, Jaeger is sat opposite drinking his coffee and smiling at him.

'The milk and the cream aren't for the cat, the cat has no right to the cream' said Jaeger

Clyde nods and rolls his eyes impatiently, the story is boring him, he gets the point but Jaeger seems to be revelling in the tortuous conversation.

'If I were the chef I'd kill the cat, but that's just me' said Jaeger

'You're entitled to your opinion' said Clyde

Jaeger takes a sip of coffee then places the cup back onto the table.

'Also, you may have heard about the raid at St Nazierre?' said Jaeger

Clyde nods his head, he didn't expect Jaeger to ask about this, he assumed he'd ask about the missing equipment, maybe even ask a question about Anna or something along those lines but not St Nazierre.

The raid had caused ruction amongst the coastal defence officers not just because it caused colossal damage and hamstrung the German Atlantic fleet allowing the shipping lanes to move more freely but also as someone had given signals to the British, Jaeger had been deployed to find out who had done it and panic had set amongst the soldiers on the coast, unbeknown to Clyde, as he'd been preoccupied with Chevalier and Anna.

'Yes Captain, I think most people have' said Clyde

Don't go there, please, don't go there thought Clyde.

'Yes I suppose they have done, by now' said Jaeger

Clyde nods.

'After the raid I took a trip to St Nazierre' said Jaeger

'I hope you had a safe journey?' said Clyde

'Yes thank you, I was speaking to a few of the guards on duty that night and I also spoke to a few of the prisoners' said Jaeger

'Ok' said Clyde whose stomach was in knots, he had restless legs and just wanted out of the conversation.

'The guards tell me that the ship that was used in the raid was sending signals to the shore, that these signals weren't the signals that are used for the Atlantic fleet and that these signals were used for ship to shore through the English Channel' said Jaeger

Shit, he thought.

'Right, so what are you saying?' said Clyde brazenly, giving too much away seemingly on the defensive.

'The signals, I believe, were stolen from the Atlantic Wall by someone in the position to do so… then passed to the enemy' said Jaeger

Clyde moves his hand under the table a little closer to his pistol and releases the strap that holds the pistol in the holster ready to pull it out and shoot Jaeger if needs be, after all, if he did get found out he'd be shot on the spot himself so decided to get prepared and shoot first when the time comes.

'I also spoke to a few of the prisoners, not many spoke but some were persuaded' said Jaeger

'Persuaded?' said Clyde

'Yes, *persuaded*' said Jaeger with a grimace on his face indicating he enjoyed whatever he did to the prisoners.

Clyde slowly and quietly pulls the strap back so he has easy access to his pistol, Clyde's heart beats strongly and quickly as the adrenaline kicks in, he thinks to himself that he is the highest ranking officer on the camp and he gets on well with the other officers, maybe if he killed Jaeger in some way shape or form he could get away with it, maybe even get the forced labour to hide Jaegers body in the sand dunes or under part of the construction.

'I'm sure they'd have rather kept their teeth and finger nails but I digress, yes, they were persuaded' said Jaeger

Jaeger takes his cup of coffee and takes a long gulp.

'They gave me information that cemented my original thoughts' said Jaeger

Clyde leans forward slightly to make it easier to pull out his pistol.

'And they were?' said Clyde

'That we have a spy in the camp' said Jaeger

Jaeger drinks his coffee and places the empty cup back on to the table slamming it down causing Clyde to jump.

'Wonderful coffee Captain' said Jaeger

Clyde takes another swig of his coffee and Jaeger stands up and picks up his hat with his gloves inside.

'Captain Wolf. Thank you for your hospitality but I must be on my way' said Jaeger

Jaeger starts to put his gloves back on, Clyde stands up.

'Was there anything else you wanted Captain? You've not been here long' said Clyde

'No, no' said Jaeger

'Would you like some food perhaps?' said Clyde

'No thank you, I must be leaving to file my report' said Jaeger

'Are you sure Captain, I can have the chef make you some sandwiches for the long trip back' said Clyde

'No, it's quite alright, I've been posted just a few miles away so I'm local' said Jaeger

Shit, if he's local there's only me he could suspect thought Clyde

'It was good seeing you' said Clyde

'Yes, good seeing you also, if you hear anything about the cream, sorry… I've got that on my mind now' said Jaeger as he chuckled to himself 'If you hear anything about the equipment going missing or anything that seems suspicious do get in touch'

'Yes… I will' said Clyde

Jaeger looks down to see Clyde's holster undone.

'Sorry Captain Wolf but your holster seems to be undone' said Jaeger

Jaeger laughs, Clyde looks down to his holster and slowly clips the holster back together then Jaeger begins to walk out of the tent and Clyde follows, as they exit the tent they stop, shake hands and again briefly try to out squeeze the other. Clyde waits at the tent entrance and Jaeger makes his way to his car.

'Goodbye Captain' said Clyde

'Yes, see you soon' replied Jaeger without turning around.

See you soon? What does he mean by that? Is he threatening me? thinks Clyde

Clyde watches on as Jaeger approaches his squad car.

'Oh, Captain' shouts Clyde

Jaeger turns around and looks at Clyde and tilts his head as to listen closely to what Clyde will say.

'Yes?' said Jaeger

Jaeger stands outside of his car with the key in his hand.

'Do give my love to Anna won't you?' said Clyde who then smirks

Jaeger looks to the floor, then out to sea then looks back to Clyde and for a moment looks embarrassed and covers his mannerisms and composes himself quickly then smiles at Clyde.

'Yes, yes I'll do that' said Jaeger

Clyde stands outside the tent smiling as Jaeger gets into his car and drives away, Clyde waves him off.

'Shit' whispers Clyde

Chapter 13 – Back Against the Wall

Chevalier sits outside of the café in Lille whilst drinking coffee looking out onto the square in the town, the streets are quite busy with civilians and German troops patrol the square. Clyde walks up to Chevalier and sits down at the table.

'Good morning' said Chevalier nonchalantly

Clyde sharply leans towards Chevalier.

'They're onto us' said Clyde anxiously

Chevalier sits more upright then leans in towards Clyde raising his eyebrows as he does.

'I'm sorry what?' said Chevalier

'They're onto us' said Clyde a bit quieter this time

Both Clyde and Chevalier are speaking in hushed tones, Clyde looks around to the nearby tables and then moves into whisper to Chevalier.

'The Gestapo, they're onto us' said Clyde

Never the one to be ruffled by the thought of being rumbled as a spy Chevalier looks relaxed at the news Clyde has brought.

'How can you be sure?' said Chevalier

'Captain Jaeger paid me a visit' said Clyde

Chevalier leans back into his chair and picks up his newspaper and begins to read it ignorantly, Clyde looks around and holds his hands out to gesture that he is confused with Chevaliers actions.

'What are you doing?' said Clyde

'You may have been followed here, I don't want to be compromised' said Chevalier

Clyde looks around, there are many people in the square and too many people around to pick out if anyone is watching them.

'Quickly, tell me what he said to you' said Chevalier

Clyde leans in closer to Chevalier.

'He knows about the supplies going missing' said Clyde

'No shit. Everybody does' said Chevalier

Clyde shakes his head in disbelief, he feels Chevalier isn't taking him seriously enough.

'No, he knows it's me, I can tell' said Clyde

'Why. What makes you think that?' said Chevalier

'It was what he was saying, he was probing and basically luring me into doing something or saying something that would blow my cover' said Clyde

Chevalier knows about Jaeger from a mutual acquaintance he'd served with at the start of the war, his friend Francois Tallec who was another spy who Jaeger had sniffed out and shot. He would have caught Chevalier had Tallec broke whilst being tortured and Chevalier didn't want to get caught, not because he didn't want to die, more so that his friend had given his life to allow Chevalier to keep up the fight and he didn't want his friend to have died for nothing, he wanted to do his best to so that Tallec's memory lived on.

'You'll have to get him off our tail' said Chevalier

'No problem, what do you suggest?' said Clyde

'I said *you* get him off our tail… I'll play no part in it' said Chevalier

Clyde feels like a leper, like Chevalier has disowned him at the first hurdle. *Typical bloody Frenchman* he thought.

'Just find a way, you must do it as soon as possible' said Chevalier

Clyde cannot think on the spot about how to keep Jaeger from investigating him further, he knew for the time being he would have limited access to Chevalier and would have to keep his head down but that may not be enough, he would have to pull the rabbit out of the hat to get the attention off him or kill Jaeger, he still had promises to keep in killing Stechen so he didn't want to kill Jaeger if he didn't have to as he'd never get his chance to get at Stechen because he may have to go on the run.

'Right, ok' said Clyde in deep thought as he tried to think of a plan.

'We need to be careful, we need you where you are. We have plans that you can help with' said Chevalier

'What plans are they?' said Clyde

'I can't tell you just yet, you've been breached' said Chevalier

Clyde shakes his head then looks in deep thought, he holds his finger and thumb either side of his chin as he thinks.

'I'll sort something out' said Clyde

Clyde smiles and nods his head slowly.

'Don't tell me the details, just get him off your tail' said Chevalier

Chevalier stands up throws a few coins into the street in front of their table and the civilians in the street fight to pick up the coins causing a ruckus so if anybody is following either Clyde or Chevalier the crowd will obstruct their view or distract them so that Chevalier and Clyde can slip away unnoticed, Chevalier walks briskly away as does Clyde in the opposite direction.

Clyde's Hotel Room – Northern French Coast

The hotel room is lit merely by a gas light, a little old fashioned to what Clyde is used to but none the less part and parcel of the 1940's. Clyde brushes one page of his book over piercing the room's tranquillity with the noise of the page turning and then leans over to his bedside table to stub out his cigarette in the glass ash tray.

'*Dieppe*' thought Clyde

Clyde knew that Dieppe was the failed invasion of Northern France in August 1943, the Allies managed to get a foot hold in Northern France but were pushed back weeks later and most of the soldiers at Dieppe died trying to save the foothold in France, Clyde wondered whether he could save those lives and also get back on board with the High Command with Jaeger lurking in the background, this tip off would surely cast aside any doubts of Clyde's commitment to Germany and would also get Jaeger off his tail, it could be a masterstroke as he'd also save British and Canadian lives.

Clyde knew he could put things back right again if things went pear shaped as it would lead to more people looking to Clyde as a good strategist with his finger on the pulse and his opinions would carry more weight and add to that he knew the future.

Despite the potentially fewer lives lost at Dieppe Clyde is racked with guilt, he knows many thousands of allied troops will be slaughtered but he tries to kid himself, he tries to convince himself that there won't be much of a difference in the amount of people killed, he also tries to convince himself that if the allies are met with resistance at the beach head then maybe fewer people will land and fewer people will die, in fact what Clyde thinks he is doing is a favour, a good thing maybe or so he thinks.

Northern French Coast – Sea Defence Construction

The wave's crash against the rocks on the beach casting a spray of water over the workers laying barbed wire on the cliffs edge, Clyde walks past and into the communications tent. The canvas tent is drenched due to the spray from the crashing waves and the rain, inside the tent pots are catching leaking water from the ceiling.

Clyde stops for a moment, looks back out of the tent to sea and inside he wrestles with his conscience as to whether to go through with tipping off the Germans about Dieppe but he'd already made up his mind, it just didn't sit easy with him. He looks down at the ground and takes a deep breath then walks over to the radio operator.

'Sir' said the radio operator as he salutes Clyde

'At ease, get me Brigadier Freidrich' said Clyde

Clyde walks back over to the doorway and looks out to sea, he watches the waves crash on the rocks below casting a spray over the already drenched workers, a trickle of water drips from the tent doorway onto Clyde's neck but he doesn't flinch, he has too much on his mind to let it bother him.

'Sir, Brigadier Friedrich' said the radio operator

Clyde looks to the floor, takes a deep breath then walks over to the radio operator and picks up the head set and microphone.

'Good morning Brigadier, how are you today?' said Clyde

'Good morning Captain Wolf, I'm very well thank you, it's good to hear from you again. What brings me the pleasure of your call?' said Friedrich

Clyde lets out a sigh, looks to the floor and then looks to the doorway out to sea.

'Brigadier…' said Clyde apprehensively

'Yes?' said Freidrich

'Brigadier… I have reason to believe that the Allies are planning to launch an amphibious landing at Dieppe… in the next couple of days' said Clyde who then takes a deep breath as the weight is lifted from his shoulders.

The radio falls silent for a moment, Clyde breathes a little easier as he'd done the hard part, it was finally done and he just had to give more information when questioned but he had already thought of a story to tell Freidrich.

'Yes? What makes you suspect this?' said Freidrich

'Over the last few days we have seen quite a few RAF mosquito reconnaissance planes flying overhead' said Clyde

'And?' said Friedrich

'We also picked up two prisoners digging up samples of the beach' said Clyde

This was a lie; Clyde knew it but it could swing things for him to get Freidrich to get on board.

'And this means?' said Freidrich

Clyde feels as though Freidrich doesn't believe him, maybe he doesn't have the friends in high places he thought he did after all he only spent the evening with Stechen and Freidrich two years earlier, maybe they'd forgotten him.

'Sir, I have reason to believe they are taking samples of the beach to see whether the beach will take tanks, vehicles and so on' said Clyde

The line goes quiet, Clyde looks at the radio operator who turns away so it doesn't look like he is listening in to the conversation.

'Sir?' said Clyde

'Yes, yes Wolf. I'm thinking' said Freidrich

Clyde looks back through the doorway out to sea hoping that he believes Clyde and backs him up.

'Very well. I will place everyone in the region on full alert and push the 302nd static infantry division into the region' said Freidrich

The tension leaves Clyde, but only to be replaced by guilt at the thought of going against the Allies. *I hope I've done the right thing, I really do* thinks Clyde.

'Very well Sir' said Clyde

'I'll notify Field Marshall von Rundstedt' said Freidrich

'Good day to you Sir' said Clyde

'Thank you Wolf, good day to you' said Freidrich

Clyde knows the Germans will bite, they cannot afford to fight the war on two fronts due to the intense fighting in the East, if Clyde didn't come up with a way to get himself out of trouble with Jaeger suspecting something was amiss then he too could find himself on the Eastern Front, a popular destination to send troops as a punishment for even suspecting something about them or worse, he could be shot.

He only wanted to kill Stechen and once he'd done that he'd escape to Spain then either make his way to Gibraltar or England, that was the only reason keeping him in under cover in the German army, that and he did like Anna but she came and went too often.

Clyde really wants to stay in Northern France as he doesn't have to worry about being killed, well, only by the resistance but this is being covered by Chevalier. He would have tipped the underground movement off about him, the Allies won't be attacking any time soon so Clyde can go about his business as a high ranking undercover agent in a bid to help the war effort. Military history is one of Clyde's hobbies, he knows exactly what happened during the war but keeps his books safe with him just in case he needs to look anything up.

Dieppe was due to fail anyway, in fact it hindered the actual D-Day due to the Germans having egg on their faces after 1,500 troops captured a decent chunk of the French coastline, only due to the mismanagement of supplies on the Allies side meant that they were forced back into the sea, captured or killed. Afterwards the Atlantic Wall construction trebled, therefore in Clyde's eyes counterproductive, maybe Clyde was doing a good thing he thought but if it was detrimental he was in a position to help things and put things right again.

Atlantic Wall – September 1942

The seagulls fly over the beach and pierce the sound of the waves with their calls, Clyde sits on a chair outside taking in the sun whilst smoking a cigarette and wearing a pair of club master sun glasses. A soldier walks out of the tent with a piece of paper in his hand and looks really pleased with himself, he stops next to Clyde and salutes.

'Sir, a telegram for you' said the Soldier

Clyde who is slouched in the chair lifts his head into the direction of the soldier then holds out his hand and leisurely takes the paper from him. The solider stands there looking for a reaction from Clyde who is now reading the letter, Clyde sits up in his chair and rubs his forehead with his left hand as he reads the letter.

Dear Major Wolff,

First of all, I'd like to say you did very well with your intuition as your immediate actions led to the foiling of the invasion at Dieppe just a few weeks ago. If it weren't for your actions we could now potentially be fighting the war on two fronts, thank you.

Secondly, as reward, I wish for you to attend an awards ceremony to receive the Order of the German Cross.

The awards night will be at Le Grand Hotel in Lille on 3rd of October at 7pm.

Yours gratefully,

Adolf Hitler.

Clyde looks to the floor, then out to sea not knowing what to do or say.

'Fuck' he whispers under his breath.

The soldier is still stands beside Clyde in anticipation of the news having read the message himself. The soldier, who sees the perplexed look on Clyde's face quickly marches back to the tent out of the way as Clyde looked agitated.

Clyde leans to the side of his chair and rests his head on his hand still looking out to sea, he takes out a cigarette and lights it amongst the breeze from the sea, then he takes a quick look at the letter again, he folds it up and places it in his inside pocket.

He'd been promoted due to the tip off about Dieppe where approximately 1000 allied troops, mainly Canadian, had been slaughtered on the beach and now he'd received a telegram from Adolf Hitler.

What am I doing? He thought.

He had mixed feelings as he felt the guilt and the shame but also the excitement and relief of getting Jaeger off his case, he now had a free reign with Jaeger out of the picture.

Clyde thought about the awards evening and how different it will be as opposed to the last time he attended one, this time he was prepared and had connections with people, mainly Chevalier and the resistance, who could be tipped off about the other high ranking targets who would be in attendance. The last awards evening had Heinrich Himmler in attendance, but with the recent kidnappings and murders of Nazi officials and German officers in France, Clyde felt the guest list may not be as glamorous but worth a shot anyway and the first thing he wanted to do was to get in touch with Chevalier to inform him so they could pass the information back to the British or the resistance and makes plans for the event.

Chapter 14 - Retribution

A squad car rolls across the crisp and dried leaves scattered in the gutter blowing them onto the pavement and the car slowly stops with the screech of the drum brakes. The door opens and out comes a tall soldier with a muscular build, he is a Corporal in the German Army, this is Hans who is acting as Clyde's bodyguard whilst he is away from his posting, he walks around to the front of the car and onto the pavement and opens the passenger door to which Clyde steps out from, Clyde looks up at 'Le Grand Hotel' and smiles as the memories flood back of when he and Anna had stayed there.

The bell boy walks up to the back of the car whilst Hans opens the boot, the bell boy pulls out the luggage and walks back to the entrance, he places the luggage onto the floor and waits at the entrance.

'Hans, check us both in and then make your way to the café around the corner, I'm meeting an old friend' said Clyde

'Yes Sir' said Hans

The bell boy opens the door for Hans as he walks in through the entrance and quickly follows himself with the rest of the luggage.

After a few minutes, Clyde walks up to the front of the café whilst looking through the window and spots Chevalier sat inside drinking a cup of coffee and reading a newspaper. Clyde opens the door to the café and walks inside, the café is almost empty apart from Chevalier, the waiter and the chef who is cleaning the dishes in the back of the café and the clanging of dishes combined with the music from the wireless radio is the only noise in the café. Chevalier looks up to see Clyde and puts his newspaper down on the table and nods to the waiter, the waiter takes notice and walks away into the kitchen to give them some privacy.

'Good morning' said Clyde with a sense of excitement as he walks up to the table and sits down in front of Chevalier, a far cry from the last time they met when Clyde was agitated by the threat of Jaeger.

 'Good morning to you also... Major' said Chevalier

Clyde smiles in a slightly embarrassed way due to Chevaliers veiled insult, Chevalier doesn't know Clyde tipped off the Germans about Dieppe as he wouldn't have known about it but he suspects he'd done something to earn his award and promotion but he didn't know what.

'You'll have to be careful getting promoted so quickly, or you too will end up on our list' said Chevalier

Both Clyde and Chevalier smile, *many a true word said in jest* Clyde thought, the waiter brings out two cups of coffee and replaces the ash tray with a clean one and then walks away.

'Thank you Pierre' said Chevalier as he places a lump of sugar in his coffee and begins to stir it.

Clyde takes a sip of coffee.

'We've been ordered to carry out an important mission' said Chevalier

After the previous couple of months keeping his head down due to Jaeger being around him Clyde is excited and honoured to be trusted to be allowed back in the loop, he thought he may have compromised his cover and may not be involved in any more important missions due to that.

'Ok, we must be quick' said Clyde as he looks over his shoulder to the entrance 'my bodyguard will be with us shortly'

'No problem' said Chevalier who sat in his chair and sipped his coffee nonchalantly, then slowly pulls out a brown A5 envelope from his inside pocket and slides it across the table to Clyde.

'Memorise it, then destroy it' said Chevalier as he looks towards the entrance making sure nobody is about to join them, the staff in the café keep themselves to themselves as they are a front for the resistance, they know when to stay out of the way.

Clyde picks up the envelope and begins to open it, Chevalier watches on.

'At the check in desk there is a parcel that has been left for you, it's under the name *Big Bertie*' said Chevalier

'Ok' said Clyde as he opens the envelope and slides out the photograph, he looks at the photograph quickly and then holds it over the ash tray, taking his lighter out of his pocket then burns it over the ash tray and begins to smile, Chevalier notices and looks intriguingly at Clyde.

'What's the matter?' said Chevalier

Clyde smiles wryly.

'No, nothing. It's…. it's about time we took out this target' said Clyde with butterflies in his stomach with the excitement.

Clyde takes a sip of coffee and places the cup down onto the table and lights a cigarette with the burning photograph and blows smoke into the air.

'The package will contain the room key and all the equipment you need, it's a spring-loaded detonator so needs to be installed under the bed so that late tonight when he goes to his room, as soon as he puts pressure onto the bed it will detonate' said Chevalier

'Yes, no problem' said Clyde as he holds the burning photo over the ash tray to ensure it is destroyed.

'That should give you enough time to collect your medal' said Chevalier who then grins as he enjoys teasing Clyde about his promotion.

'Stop it' said Clyde sternly

Chevaliers mouth is grinning but his eyes are steely and serious as if he doesn't trust Clyde, mainly due to Clyde gaining promotion when it looked as though he was caught. Either way Chevalier would always be a hard man to win over and gain his trust, he was naturally sceptical and untrusting.

Clyde shakes his head whilst still holding a small section of the photograph and turns it in a way to catch the flame so that the piece he was holding burns, he then places it into the ashtray to finish off burning.

'After you've set the explosives meet me outside and we'll get the hell out of there' said Chevalier who's now behaving normal as the smile struggles to leave his face

'No problem, I'll meet you right after I've collected my medal' said Clyde

A smile slowly breaks out on Chevaliers face, this time his eyes smile too, the door to the café opens, in walks Hans who notices Clyde sat down at the table and walks over, stops then salutes both men.

'At ease Hans' said Clyde as Hans stands with his feet shoulder width apart with both hands behind his lower back 'I need you to run a few errands for me'

'Yes Sir' said Hans with aplomb

Clyde reaches into his inside pocket and pulls out a piece of paper, he then hands it to Hans. The list consists of difficult items to find, drawn up by Clyde to keep his bodyguard away from him whilst he carries out the mission. Hans is supposed to be at Clyde's side wherever he goes but that would prevent the mission from going ahead and needed to be kept occupied and out of the way, if Hans was questioned afterwards he wouldn't be able to say where Clyde was, Clyde had already organised to be with Chevalier all day in the quiet café until the dinner later in the evening and they'd be each other's alibi if anything happened or either men were questioned.

'Here's a list, meet me back here in two hours' said Clyde

Hans takes the list and holds it in his right arm at his side as his left arm is neatly tucked behind his back as he stands at ease.

'Yes Sir' said Hans

Hans salutes and then walks out of the café with Clyde and Chevalier staying silent as they watch him walk out, Hans exits the café and both men turn to look at each other.

Chevalier watches Hans walk past the window in the opposite direction of the hotel then looks at Clyde and pauses for a moment.

'How are you finding it now… with the bodyguard?' said Chevalier

'It's because of us they've sent him' said Clyde as he raises his eyebrows and smiles 'Any officer at the rank of Major upwards to be escorted when away from their posts as a form of *close protection*'

Chevalier gives a patronising nod.

'How long have you been in Lille?' said Chevalier

'About… 20 minutes, why?' said the defensive Clyde

'In that time, how long have you been with Hans?' said Chevalier who raises his eyebrows as if to suggest something

Clyde looks to his left and shakes his head as to guess a time scale.

'Two minutes, something like that' said Clyde who didn't understand where Chevalier was heading with the questions

'He's not much use then is he?' said Chevalier as he stares at Clyde

'What do you mean?' said Clyde

Chevalier smiles and leans forwards towards Clyde.

'He's supposed to be close protection yes?' said Chevalier

Clyde looks at Chevalier for a moment confused but with a sense of apprehension of answering the question.

'Yes' said Clyde

'He's not been with you much?' said Chevalier

'No. What's your point?' said Clyde impatiently

'Is he slowing you down or getting in the way?' said Chevalier

What Clyde thinks is Chevalier is proposing to kill Hans whilst on his errands on Clyde's behalf if he's getting in the way. *He's thinking of killing Hans* thinks Clyde as he leans closer to Chevalier assertively and holds his hand up to Chevalier as if to quell any plans to kill Hans.

'Listen. Don't even *think* about killing him, he's a good man' said Clyde firmly

Chevalier laughs thinking Clyde had gone soft and began to enjoy his role a bit too much whereas Clyde liked Hans as he was stationed at the Atlantic Wall and had worked alongside Clyde for the past 18 months and he'd got to know him quite well in that time.

'A good Nazi?' huffed Chevalier in a sarcastic manner 'That's a first'

Clyde shakes his head and seems agitated.

'No. He isn't a Nazi. He's a good man, he has a family which he's close to… and he has children' said Clyde

'What? Nazis can't have wives and children?' huffs Chevalier

'He isn't a Nazi' interrupts Clyde 'He doesn't buy into all that stuff. He's a conscripted soldier and a bloody good one too. Don't fucking touch him'

'Ok, ok. I'll make sure he isn't harmed' said Chevalier who was taken aback by the protectiveness shown by Clyde towards Hans

'Well, make sure of that. He doesn't deserve it' said Clyde sombrely

Chevalier nods and sips from his cup of coffee seemingly surprised at Clyde jumping to the defence of a German soldier.

'Where have you sent him to?' said Chevalier

'I've just sent him shopping for things which are hard to find, just to keep him busy and out of the way' said Clyde

Chevalier raises his eyebrows and doesn't look bothered, he isn't bothered where Hans goes or what he does just as long as he doesn't get in the way because if he does, Chevalier will kill him whether he's a good man or not. Clyde swigs the rest of his coffee and stands up ready to leave the café.

'Well. I'll be off then' said Clyde

'Good luck' said Chevalier

'Thank you. I'll see you shortly' said Clyde

Clyde walks out of the café and through the streets back to the hotel.

A few minutes later he enters the foyer and stops to look around. In the foyer are many German officers with their bodyguards each being waited on by the bell boys checking in their luggage, Clyde looks for the baggage claim desk which is empty, behind the desk is a portly fellow who is sat down slightly out of view reading a newspaper. Clyde walks slowly up to the desk and waits, the portly fellow behind the desk does not look away from his newspaper, Clyde coughs and the portly fellow looks up very slowly but does not speak.

'Hello' said Clyde

The portly fellow still stares at Clyde but does not speak.

'I'd like to check out my bag' said Clyde quietly

The portly fellow lets out a sigh and slowly places his newspaper down onto the desk and stands very slowly.

'Name?!' said the portly fellow

Clyde looks around the foyer and then leans in towards the portly fellow.

'Big Bertie?' said Clyde

The portly fellow looks at Clyde for a few seconds, then looks around the foyer and moves quickly into the back area, Clyde also turns around and looks around the foyer.

'Sir' said a new man behind the desk.

The new man is younger, more athletic looking and looks more serious holds a brown leather satchel, the portly fellow is stood behind him looking to the floor.

'Yes' said Clyde

The new man stands brazenly behind the desk not intimidated by the presence of the Germans in the foyer.

'Sir, who did you say the bag was for?' said the new man

Clyde looks around to his left and right quickly to make sure he can't be heard.

'Big Bertie?' said Clyde uncertainly

The man slowly puts the satchel onto the desk and slides it towards Clyde. Clyde lets out a sigh of relief and reaches out grabbing the satchel.

'Thank you' said Clyde

Clyde takes the satchel and walks across the foyer to the elevator, he gets inside and the bellboy looks at Clyde.

'Sir, which floor do you require?' said the bellboy politely

Clyde looks at the bell boy confused, he'd been more worried about making sure he got the package and he already knew the target, the one thing he didn't know was which room he had to go to. *Shit, which room is it?* Clyde thought.

'I'm not sure' said Clyde as he turns away from the bellboy cautiously opening the satchel, the elevator is still on the ground floor with the doors wide open waiting for Clyde who rummages through the satchel. Two German Officers walk into the elevator and look at Clyde rummaging in the satchel.

'Sir which floor do you require?' said the bellboy

'Hang on' said Clyde

'Four' said one of the Officers

The Officers look at Clyde who pulls out a key.

'Room 320' said Clyde

'Floor 3 then Sir?' said the bellboy

'If that's the floor I need, then yes' barked Clyde as he was embarrassed

The bellboy sheepishly pulls the doors shut and pulls a lever making the elevator rise through the building, Clyde smiles and nods to the other Officers who smile back. The elevator slows to a stop and the bellboy opens the doors.

'Floor 3 Sir' said the bellboy

'Thank you' said Clyde

Clyde exits the elevator; the doors close behind him and he walks along the corridor.

165

302, 304, 306 said Clyde to himself as he walks a bit faster as he knows the room is quite a few doors down.

'310, 312' whispers Clyde under his breath

Clyde carries on walking down the corridor looking at the room numbers.

'318, 320' said Clyde

Clyde stops outside and looks around the corridor to see if anyone is watching, he presses is ear to the door to see if he can hear anybody inside, the room inside is silent, Clyde knocks on the door and wait.

Clyde listens for movement inside the room to which there isn't any, he knocks again quickly to which there is no answer, he presses his ear again to the door and then looks around the corridor.

Clyde breathes a sigh of relief and then inserts the key into the door causing a scratching sound of brass on brass to echo up the corridor due to the marble floors and plastered walls. He slowly turns the key inside the lock, pulls the handle down and opens the door and cautiously steps inside listening intently.

'Hello?' said Clyde

Clyde waits silently for a reply and the room stays silent, he closes the door behind him and quickly searches the bathroom, then the bedroom.

'Hello?' said Clyde

Clyde walks into the living room to where there is a desk and also a few couches in this spacious room, he walks through the room and over to the balcony to check there, he looks through the French doors leading to the balcony but it is empty.

Right, let's get cracking thinks Clyde as he quickly moves to the bedroom, he puts his satchel onto the floor and sits on the bed to get a feel for how firm it is, he notices that there is a lot of movement in the bed, a little too springy so that any pressure on the bed would set the explosives off.

He moves to the floor kneeling down opening the satchel and pulls the contents out onto the floor. Clyde notices there is a large explosive device and a pressure triggered detonator that is all. '*This better not blow up in my face*' thinks Clyde as he looks over the seemingly ancient explosives.

Clyde is lay on the floor reaching under the bed and is fixing the explosives underneath, he primes the charge and then installs the pressured detonator under the bed then he hears a noise outside of keys in a lock and he stops still and looks under the bed towards the door.

'Shit' whispers Clyde

Clyde quickly stands up and hides behind the doorway as he hears a door open, he cautiously looks around the door way but the entrance door is still closed. *What the hell?* Thinks Clyde

He rushes over to the entrance and looks through the spy hole to see someone else in the room across the corridor closing the door behind them, '*thank god for that*' thinks Clyde as he breathes a sigh of relief as now he has enough time to double check the bomb and leave the room unseen.

The brown satchel is still on the floor of the bedroom, Clyde rushes back into the bedroom to pick it up, he checks that everything is ready with the bomb and then walks briskly out of the bedroom and up to the exit door. Clyde looks through the spy hole to see if anyone is around but the corridor seems empty, after all with the marble floor the slightest noise would echo up the corridor and Clyde can't hear anybody walking in the corridor so it must be empty. He looks back around the room to see if he has left anything behind but he hasn't, he has the satchel over his shoulder and the key in his hand, he opens the door, looks up and down the corridor which is empty and steps outside.

He locks the door then walks towards the elevator breathing a sigh of relief as he takes out a cigarette, lights it and begins to smile triumphantly as he smokes it. As he approaches the elevator the ping from the elevator stopping on that floor echoes down the corridor, Clyde stops and is stood a few metres from the elevator, he looks around to see if there is anywhere to hide but the doors open quickly and out walks a large blonde haired solider carrying two suit cases followed by an officer, Clyde looks at his watch in the vain hope that whoever walks out of the elevator doesn't recognise him.

'Wolf?' asked the Officer

Clyde stays silent just staring at his watch hoping that whoever said his name takes the hint and walks past him.

'Lukas Wolf!' said the Officer with gusto 'Good to see you old friend'

Clyde looks up and is shocked to see Stechen, he fakes a smile.

'Lieutenant-Colonel Stechen' stuttered Clyde as he stares wide eyed in shock

Stechen smiles.

'*Colonel* Stechen, to be precise' said Stechen with great pomposity

Clyde salutes Stechen, the bell boy is still stood inside the lift awaiting Clyde.

'Are we staying on the same floor?' asked Stechen

Clyde looks to the bell boy then back to Stechen.

'Yes, we must be' said Clyde

'Which room are you in?' asked Stechen who smiled excitedly

Clyde looks at the bellboy hoping that he doesn't hear as he'd previously told the bellboy that he was in 320 which was Stechens room.

'Room 318' said Clyde quietly out of earshot of the bellboy, who was still waiting just behind them.

'Hoffman' snapped Stechen 'Which room is mine?'

The soldier carrying the luggage is stood holding the suit cases, he places them onto the floor and looks at the key.

'320 Sir' said Hoffman

The bell boy looks at Clyde as if to tell them that there must be a mistake as they have the same room.

'Come to my room for a drink before we go down' said Stechen

'I couldn't possibly, I've…' said Clyde

'Nonsense, I insist' interrupted Stechen

'Sir…' said the bellboy as he stealthily moved out from the elevator and stooped with his head bowed.

Stay out of this boy thinks Clyde as he looks at the bell boy with scorn, he knows he is about to drop Clyde in the shit.

'You can go' said Clyde authoritatively 'Go on, leave us'

'But Sir, I think…' said the bell boy who tried to move closer to the men and still had his head bowed

'Don't disturb us' said Stechen quietly and caustically as he stared deep into the soul of the bellboy 'Or I'll have your head'

The bell boy looks sheepish with his head bowed, he knows both Clyde and Stechen have the same room number but doesn't think he is doing anything wrong other than notifying them, the bellboy knows that Clyde or Stechen could be put up in another room quite easily and just wants to help but feels intimidated by them both so stays quiet as his manager can deal with the fallout from the mix up or rooms, he doesn't get paid enough to risk upsetting a Colonel.

'Please leave' said Hoffman sternly as he stands toe to toe with the bell boy overbearing him with his height and frame.

Hoffman is an imposing figure, the bell boy takes notes and promptly steps back not raising his head to look at any of the men, he closes the door on the elevator and it moves to the floor below.

'Come on' said Stechen who snaps his fingers very close to Clyde's face like a master may do to their dog 'my room, now'

Hoffman picks up the luggage and starts to walk down the corridor looking at the door numbers, Stechen walks down the corridor and Clyde hastily follows not knowing what to do.

'We could go to your room if you like?' said Stechen

Clyde smiles and fumbles with his satchel.

'It's better if we go to yours… Sir' said Clyde

Stechen nods, looks at Hoffman walking down the corridor and back to Clyde.

'If you wish' said Stechen

'What am I going to do? How do I lose him without him figuring out somethings wrong? Shit! The slightest nudge on the bed and we'll be blown to pieces' panics Clyde

Hoffman is further ahead and puts the luggage down outside the room, he takes out the key, opens the door and walks into the room with Stechen behind him and Clyde hastily behind.

Don't fucking go into the bedroom, please thinks Clyde

All three men walk into the living room and Hoffman places the bags onto the floor, Stechen notices and coughs boorishly to get Hoffman's attention. Stechen clicks his fingers and points to the bedroom.

'No, bedroom, chop chop' said Stechen as he clicked as his fingers on his right hand in turn and slapped the top of with his left making a sound like a horse galloping, he kept doing this whilst walking around inspecting the accommodation.

Shit, not the fucking bedroom thinks Clyde as he's nervous about anybody going into there, the slightest pressure on the bed whether it be from a person or a bag will set off the explosives killing them all, obviously, he doesn't want to die as he still has plans to help the war effort and also wants to go back to the future. Clyde's body temperature rises as he gets anxious and becomes flustered, he takes off his jacket and holds it over his arm.

'I… beg your pardon Sir… may we have a drink first?' said Clyde

Hoffman stops and then looks at Stechen expecting to be asked to pour drinks for both men.

'Very well. Hoffman, get us some Brandy' said Stechen who still paced the room like a caged animal clicking his fingers and slapping the top of his hand in one smooth motion as he walked.

Hoffman crouches to the floor and opens up the luggage and pulls out a bottle of Napoleon brandy and places it on a table, Stechen walks over to the table and takes off his hat and jacket placing them onto the hat stand then sits down and stares at Clyde pointing to the seat beside him.

'Sit down' instructed Stechen who then smiled wickedly

Hoffman walks over to the desk and picks up two brandy glasses and walks over to Stechen and places them onto the table, Clyde hangs his jacket on the hat stand then walks over and sits down beside the table. Stechen begins to pour two glasses of brandy and Hoffman walks over to the luggage and picks them up, Clyde watches attentively.

No, not the fucking bedroom thinks Clyde as he internally plans some way to get rid of Hoffman or at least stop him from going into the bedroom because he may knock the bed.

'How about some cigars?' said Clyde

Hoffman stops reluctantly, Stechen looks at Hoffman.

'I don't have any' said Stechen

Upon this news Clyde decides to lay it on thick of how much he'd like a cigar as Hoffman would be sent downstairs for them and be out of the room long enough for Clyde to try and kill Stechen if he wandered into the bedroom and he could rig something up so that Hoffman sets off the explosives once he returns, he just knows he has to get rid of Hoffman as Stechen had slipped through Clyde's fingers once before and this time he was sure he'd kill him, it was his only chance.

'I could really smoke a cigar right now; it goes well with the brandy' said Clyde

Stechen looks at Clyde and nods.

'Hoffman, fetch some cigars at once' said Stechen

Hoffman places the luggage onto the floor again.

'Yes Sir' said Hoffman trying to quell his feelings of resentment of being made to act as a flunkey, he'd served in the SS and was promoted quickly due to his valour and all it landed him was a posting to baby sit a spoilt brat, he just wanted to get back out into the field killing the enemy, it was what he was good at.

Hoffman walks over to the door and exits the room, Stechen looks to Clyde.

'I do enjoy a cigar with my Brandy' said the smiling Stechen who then grabbed Clyde's knee

'Yes, me too' said Clyde who was uncomfortable with the hand on his knee, it was evident in his facial expression

Stechen stands up, walks over to the French doors and looks out onto the balcony to the streets below, Clyde hopes he stays there and doesn't walk into his bedroom.

'So, how did you find out about Dieppe?' quizzed Stechen

Clyde stands up and walks over to stand next to Stechen to get close to him should he veer into the bedroom. *I knew about it all along and I would have let it happen, but I had to pull a rabbit out the hat, otherwise Jaeger would have had my arse on a plate* thinks Clyde but would never let the words pass his mouth.

'I had a gut instinct then I saw a few things that didn't add up, well, it looks like I was right' said Clyde

'Hmmm' said Stechen prominently as if not believing the story 'I find that strange'

Stechen turns to look at Clyde who is squirming inside but has a cool and calm facade.

'Sir?' asks Clyde as he is intrigued by Stechens remark.

'I find it strange how the gut works and that you get a feeling something isn't quite right and it usually isn't' said Stechen

Stechen walks towards the bathroom and Clyde follows closely behind, a little too close and that doesn't go unnoticed, Stechen walks into the bathroom and runs the tap on the basin running a sink full of water.

'We had a long journey Wolf' said Stechen who stares into the mirror with a lot of vanity as he stands upright puffing out his chest and raising his chin turning to look at his jaw line.

Clyde stands at the door watching Stechen who swills his face with water three times and stands with his eyes closed due to the water on his face.

'That feels good' said Stechen

Stechen squints as he looks around the bathroom and then to Clyde.

'Well?' barked Stechen as he squinted towards Clyde holding out his hand 'Fetch me a towel'

Shocked at the way he's being spoken to Clyde looks around the bathroom and then back to Stechen

'Sorry…there isn't one' said Clyde who frowns whilst looking at Stechen unimpressed

'What sort of shit hotel is this, I'll have their heads, French bastards, I'll show them, yes you watch' mumbled Stechen under his breath as he barges past Clyde into the bedroom, Clyde quickly follows and grits his teeth and gives Stechen a dirty look from behind as he walks past as he knows the time has come to kill him.

He'd thought about killing him for the previous few years and now was filled with nervous excitement, his heart starts to beat faster, he has a flutter in his stomach and his palms start to go clammy as he was also nervous about Stechen going anywhere near to the bed as both men would be blown to pieces. Hoffman was due back anytime soon, if Clyde was going to kill Stechen and rig the room to explode once Hoffman came back his window of opportunity was closing fast.

'I wonder if there's any in here' said Stechen

Clyde stands close to the bed to prevent Stechen going anywhere near it as he is looking through the wardrobes to find a towel.

'Ah, found you' said Stechen

Clyde gulps as he thinks indecisively whether to kill Stechen here and now or make his excuses and leave, after all he doesn't need to worry about seeing Stechen again so doesn't mind upsetting him in leaving the room without saying anything. Clyde is sweating from his forehead profusely and is breathing heavily as the adrenaline kicks in with what Clyde knows could happen and will happen. Stechen wipes his face with the towel and then looks at Clyde who has sweat bead running down his brow and he looks nervous which is duly noted.

'Are you ok Wolf?' said Stechen who seemed to have changed from being a spoilt brat to very humble as he sensed danger

Clyde is nervous and really looks it now, the facade has well and truly dropped, he looks to have given the game away.

'Yes Sir' said Clyde unconvincingly

Stechen looks at Clyde with suspicion now, the look on Clyde's face along with the sweat has made him think something isn't right.

'You look a little sweaty' said Stechen who holds out the damp towel ready to throw it 'take this'

Stechen throws the towel towards the right of Clyde and looks to be hitting the bed but Clyde just saves the towel from landing on the bed quickly looking up in shock at Stechen who looks back with more suspicion, Stechen senses something is amiss so crouches to the floor quickly to see what is under the bed.

'Sir…' said Clyde who moves slowly towards Stechen who is crouching on all fours looking underneath the bed and spots the explosives and then looks up to the approaching Clyde. They stare at each other silently for a maximum of two seconds but feels like an eternity to both men.

'Alarm! Alarm!' shouts Stechen hysterically

Clyde rushes towards Stechen and puts his hand over his mouth and drags him back into the living room aggressively dragging him out of the bedroom just in case he knocked the bed as Clyde knows the time has come to kill him. Whilst being dragged away and into the living room Stechen manages to pulls Clyde's hand down from his mouth.

'Alarm!' shouts Stechen

Clyde hears Hoffman outside the room insert his key into the door lock so hastily pushes a chair with his foot so that the chair sits directly under the door handle to prevent Hoffman from getting back in the room.

Outside Hoffman is knocking on the door unaware of what is going on inside and is perplexed of how he can't get back inside.

'Sir?!' calls Hoffman through the thick oak door

Stechen is struggling with Clyde who has his hand over his mouth, Stechen drops to the floor out of Clyde's grasp and rolls away.

'Help!' shouts Stechen as he cowers on the floor.

Clyde kicks Stechen in the face knocking him onto his back and then proceeds to stamp on his face multiple times as he tries to cover up, after a few stamps Stechens nose and mouth are bleeding heavily and he is screaming like a pig with each blow.

'Sir?! Hang on' shouts Hoffman who is still outside and starts to barge into the door with his shoulder.

Stechen spits blood onto the floor as he turns over in an attempt to push himself up from the floor. Clyde lands a kick in his face wrapping his boot around his jaw which knocks him out cold breaking numerous teeth along with his jaw, by now Hoffman has opened the door slightly, Clyde notices Hoffman is making progress and quickly hides behind the door as it springs open knocking the chair across the room into a side board, Hoffman is holding his pistol in front of him as he walks into the room and notices Stechen lay face down on the floor unconscious with splashes of dark red blood on the carpet beneath his head.

'Sir?' said Hoffman

Clyde rushes out and grabs Hoffman's arm which is holding the pistol and keeps Hoffmans arm straight so that the pistol points away from them both, Clyde then head butts Hoffman repeatedly bursting Hoffman's nose and then puts out his right leg and throws Hoffman to the floor with Clyde going with him with Hoffman landing on his back and Clyde landing shoulder first into Hoffman's sternum winding him causing hin to let go of the pistol which falls to the floor.

Stechen still is lay on the floor struggling to gain consciousness.

Clyde is lay on top of Hoffman facing the opposite way to his adversary, Clyde's right arm is underneath Hoffman's right arm and neck so he begins to squeeze in an attempt to choke Hoffman who in turn struggles as he feels his head is going to burst due to the pressure put on his neck.

A gurgle then a cough is heard as Stechen wakes up and clears the blood from his throat but still lies on the floor.

Clyde keeps the grip tight whilst Hoffman flails his legs as he panics, after a few seconds Hoffman reaches out with his left arm furiously grabbing Clyde's testicles squeezing them as tightly as he can to which Clyde releases his choke hold and falls backwards onto his back holding his genitals in pain.

Stechen is starting to get to his feet but is struggling to stand up on his own so grabs hold of a nearby desk and struggles to see what Clyde and Hoffman are doing.

'Hoffman?' mumbled Stechen through his broken jaw and missing teeth

Hoffman stands up and looks around for his pistol, Clyde crawls back along the floor and looks around for a weapon, anything will do so he can hit Hoffman with it. Hoffman cannot find the gun so picks up a large brass lamp from the sideboard and pulls out the plug and starts to swing it at Clyde who quickly gets to his feet and moves back with each swing taken at him. Clyde picks up a vase, dummies to throw it whilst Hoffman flinches, Clyde then throws the vase and misses Hoffman who ducks, Clyde looks around as he walks backwards to find something to hit Hoffman with who is swinging the lamp viscously back and forth.

Stechen is still struggling to see as one of his eyes have closed due to the swelling and still cannot stand up unaided by the desk, he struggles to see the fight properly.

'Kill him, just kill him' mumbled Stechen who then spits blood to the floor and takes a deep breath struggling to stay on his feet

Hoffman swings again at Clyde who moves backwards falling into the French doors smashing them as he does and lands on his back on the balcony cutting his hands and back on the broken glass.

'Bastard' shouts Clyde as he quickly looks at his cuts then back up to see Hoffman rushing out to kick him in the face but Clyde moves backwards grabbing Hoffman's leg with one hand and with the other he takes the cable from the lamp and wraps it around Hoffman's neck then lifts him over his shoulder and over the balcony, the lamp gets caught on the iron railings resulting in the hanging of Hoffman from the balcony killing him instantly, the sound of Hoffman's neck breaking causes Clyde to look away wincing and back into Stechen.

Hoffman's body swings from side to side on the balcony railings like a pendulum.

Stechen is still holding onto the desk looking towards the balcony and knows his time is up, he looks to the floor to see if he can find Hoffman's pistol but his vision isn't what it should be.

'Wolf, what are you doing?' said Stechen fearfully

Clyde limps into the room from the balcony and over to Stechen, he has cut most of the back of him from falling back through the French doors.

'Wolf, I beg you, please' said Stechen who starts to cry as he picks up a letter opener from the desk and drops to his knees. Clyde notices this and walks over cautiously closing the entrance door to the hotel room on the way, Stechen notices that the door was open all this time and a sense of regret fills him as if he'd have been able to see the open doorway he'd have attempted to leave the room or at least alert someone else.

 Clyde pulls out a ligature from his pocket and wraps it around his hands.

'Please, Wolf, please, why?' begged Stechen

Stechen is kneeling and shuffling backwards slowly, Clyde kicks him in the chest with the sole of his boot knocking him to the floor, Stechen turns over onto his front and attempts to crawl towards the door. Clyde clambers on top of him wrapping his legs around his waist as he wraps the ligature around his neck. Stechen struggles and pulls out the letter opener and tries to cut the ligature, the ligature is steel wire and is unable to cut it, Clyde notices and pulls tighter.

'My name isn't Wolf. Its Corporal Bradley Clyde of the British Army' said Clyde

Stechens feet kick everything that is around knocking a small table over and the vase which was on top which smashes, Clyde lowers his legs from Stechens waist and wraps them around the top half of Stechen legs to stop them flapping around.

'This is for the slaughter of the British soldiers at '*Le Paradis*' and also for killing my best mate Karl' said Clyde

Stechen takes the letter opener and starts to weakly stab Clyde in the thigh multiple times.

'Argh' shouts Clyde

Clyde drops the ligature and grabs Stechens hand holding the letter opener stopping him from stabbing him, Stechen gasps for breath and coughs up a small amount of blood. Clyde holds Stechens hand with the letter opener pulls it backwards and pushes it slowly towards Stechens throat struggling as he does so as his foe attempts to fight back.

'Jaeger will get you' said Stechen

Clyde laughs.

'Not if I get him first' said Clyde

Clyde pushes the letter opener into Stechens throat repeatedly causing him to gargle on his own blood as he struggles to breathe, Clyde takes out the letter opener and stabs him again multiple times in the throat until Stechens body goes limp and is pouring blood from his mouth and throat.

Clyde pushes Stechen away and stands up and looks around and notices Hoffman hanging from the balcony, he rushes out to the balcony and looks below, due to the time of day it is dusk and the street cannot be seen clearly from the balcony, Clyde struggles as he pulls the lifeless body back over the side and into the living room and places him onto the floor.

Clyde reaches into Hoffman's inside pocket and pulls out a cigar, he lights the cigar and walks over to the table where the brandy is and dips the end of the cigar in the brandy and starts to smoke the cigar.

Stechen is lay on the floor dead in a pool of blood coming from his throat. The large bottle of Napoleon brandy sits on the table still open, Clyde picks it up and pours it over the floor, Clyde spots a decanter of whiskey on the desk and pours that onto Stechens body then walks over to the mirror and stands with his back to it and looks back over his shoulder to see his wounds from falling backwards through the glass earlier, Clyde has cuts on the back of his thighs and the back of his arms, he pulls his trousers down to see the cut in more detail on his thighs and notices a small piece of glass in his thigh, he pulls it out and pours a small amount of whiskey onto his hand and rubs it into the wound.

'Bastard' seethed Clyde as he looks to the heavens in pain

He takes off his jacket and shirt and cleans the wounds on the back of his arms with the whiskey. Clyde then rips one of Stechens white shirts to use as makeshift bandages to dress his wounds, he does so then takes off Hoffman's trousers and wears them. He can get away with his own jacket over the top of his torn uniform as he had hung it up earlier on.

Clyde then picks up one of the heavy suit cases and carries it to the bathroom, once in the bathroom he takes out the draw strings from the bath robes and ties them together and then walks into the bedroom where he opens up the large wardrobe to finds the iron which he slides the cord through the handle of the suitcase then ties the cord to the bath robe draw strings. He moves the bed side cabinet next to the bed and places the suitcase on the edge of the cabinet which is higher than the bed, he carefully runs the cord and draw strings across the bed and over to the entrance, he ties the end of the bath robe draw string to the door handle inside and closes the door, the bath robes are tight enough so that the next person the open the door will pull the string causing the suitcase to fall onto the bed setting off the explosion.

Clyde who is still smoking the cigar limps along the corridor to the elevator and presses the button and waits for the elevator to arrive still smoking the cigar, the elevator pings and the doors open, inside is the bell boy. Clyde steps inside the elevator and looks a lot rougher than earlier or so the bell boy thinks, Clyde has ruffled hair, trousers that look a little too big for him, the top three buttons on his shirt have been torn off and there are specks of blood on his face.

'Ground floor please' said Clyde who notices the bell boy staring at him 'oh, we like to wrestle when we get drunk. We're old friends you see'

The bell boy closes the doors, pulls a lever and the elevator moves down towards ground floor, the bellboy thinks whilst he has Clyde alone he may be able to tell him about the rooms.

'Sir. I think there's some mistake with the rooms' said the bell boy

'Yes, there dam well is' said Clyde

Clyde is still smoking his cigar in the lift.

'Sir, I've been ordered to report anything suspicious, I hope you don't mind' said the bell boy

'Suspicious?' laughed Clyde 'It's quite simple, you've double booked the rooms'

'But Sir, if you're a Major… you should be on floor 1' said the bellboy

Clyde pulls out his wallet, opens it and pulls out a decent sum of money, a week's wages for the bellboy and stuffs them into the bell boy's top pocket.

'Ok, go and fetch my bags from room 320' said Clyde

'Sir?' said the bell boy

'Go and fetch my bags, room 320' said Clyde assertively

'But Sir… I'm to report this' said the bell boy

Clyde takes more money from his wallet and puts it into the bell boys pocket, so much money was inside that it bulged out and almost fell out.

'Go fetch my bags, right now!' said Clyde

'Yes Sir, right away' said the bell boy

Clyde passes the bellboy the key for the room.

'Just let yourself in' said Clyde

The elevator stops, the bell boy opens the doors and Clyde exits the elevator. The bell boy looks to be shocked as he has been given two weeks' wages to get Clyde's bags right now, the bellboy wonders what he'll spend the money on but he had the bags to get then report what had happened.

'Well hurry up then' said Clyde

'Sorry Sir, I'll get right there' said the bell boy

The bell boy closes the doors and Clyde walks through the foyer to the exit trying desperately not to limp, he looks bad enough without drawing attention to himself limping, he exits the hotel and spots Chevalier across the street sat on a bench.

Clyde takes a drag on his cigar and walks across the street, Chevalier notices Clyde's uniform is all tatty and looks to have been involved in a fight but more importantly Clyde is ridiculously early so something must have gone wrong, still it doesn't stop him from having a friendly dig at Clyde.

'No time for medals then?' said Chevalier

Clyde slumps back onto the bench.

'Stick your medals up your…' said Clyde

A room on the third floor explodes spewing smoke, broken glass and bricks onto the street below, the room bursts into flames as do the other rooms either side of 320. Clyde turns to Chevalier and they both smile.

'Job well done' said the exhausted Clyde

177

Chapter 15 – Wrong Turn

Clyde is sat in his squad car in the countryside and can only been seen due to the moon light cast upon him, an owl makes its call in the dead of night, a bright red flash fills the car lighting up the surrounding trees and bushes, Clyde disappears.

Bunker – Present Day

Moments later, Clyde wakes up on the floor of dome in the bunker and struggles to stand up unaided, he then slowly stumbles towards the table outside the dome and follows the light from his torch which he left there on his last visit. Due to him only being away for a few minutes in real time means the batteries won't run out despite him being in the past for a year. He picks up the torch and shines it onto the history book he left on the side in the hope that it had updated itself with the changes he had caused in the past. With trepidation, he picks up the book and opens it, reads it for a moment then drops to his knees in shock. *Fuck, what have I done?* panics Clyde

In late 1943, the Germans had produced the world first atomic bomb due to the heavy water plant at Vemork in Norway, they dropped the first bombs in January 1944 on Coventry, Derby and Liverpool docks ending the war with Britain immediately.

Germany invaded Britain in March 1944 with little resistance and had taken over the whole Country by the end of April with skirmishes in the North still taking place.

With Great Britain out of the war the American and Canadian forces had no launch pad to mount the attack on Germany other than Spain which was neutral and out of the war, for the time being, later on Hitler moved troops through France and into Spain and Portugal to prevent this from happening. Hitler also sent troops into Ireland before they had chance to allow the Americans and Canadians to be based there.

Hitler started to concentrate his forces on America hoping that a few swift strikes would get them to sign a peace treaty and mounted sea attacks on merchant vessels with his submarines, then launched V2 rockets at New York from aircraft carriers and threatened to drop an Atomic bomb on New York, Philadelphia and Boston unless a treaty was signed, President Roosevelt was due to sign a peace treaty with Hitler allowing Germany full control of Europe but due to the stress had to step down as President and Harry S Truman took over the US Presidency and signed the treaty.

Germany dropped an atomic bomb on Stalingrad and Moscow causing the immediate cease fire from the Russians. At the time of the bomb dropping both sides were at a stale mate and the eastern front stretched from St Petersburg to the Caspian Sea incorporating Moscow.

Overnight after the ceasefire from Russia, Hitler ordered a wall similar to the 'Maginot line' to be constructed from St Petersburg to the Caspian Sea by Organisation Todt using Russian slave labour.

A peace treaty was signed between Truman and Hitler in Johannesburg in July 1945 basically handing Europe over to the Nazis. Winston Churchill, his cabinet ministers along with the Royal Family and many British civilians fled to America or Canada via Ireland before the country was captured, any fighting aged males were taken to be used as slave labour to build up the sea defences on the coast.

With the USA, Great Britain and the Commonwealth out of the war Japan invaded Australia in late 1945, after months of fighting and stiff resistance from the Australians alongside New Zealanders, Pacific Islanders and the rest of the British forces which were in the east.

With help from the Germans with equipment and troops, Japan took over most of Australasia and Asia and was ruled by the Japanese Emperor.

By 1948 the combined Allied Naval fleet had wiped out the German Atlantic fleet and had the Atlantic clear of German ships ruling out the threat of more V2s fired at US cities and ruled out the threat of atomic weapons being used against them.

In the early Summer of 1948 the US, Canada and the rest of the British troops which retreated to North America landed on the East Coast of Ireland and later on mounted an invasion of England at Southport in 1949, they took Liverpool and opened the port to have more troops and supplies sent directly to the front. In December 1951 the Germans retreated across the English Channel to Northern France with much of Great Britain destroyed.

By now the US had developed their own Nuclear weapons which they proceeded to drop on Dortmund and Hamburg, the Germans were unable to launch their atomic weapons at the USA so surrendered and the USSR moved troops in quickly taking control of all of Germany to the French border.

The US, Canadian, French and British forces remained in France on the Maginot line indefinitely, with the Russians taking the German scientists at the wars end they were the first on the moon, the Vietnam war didn't happen and the USSR had spread communism from France to most of Asia and were making headway into Africa.

The USSR was the major world power than the USA and in the mid 1950's had taken over the Nordic states of Finland, Norway, Sweden and Denmark.

Clyde has read enough, he knew he had to go back at once and change things for the better and get things back on track, he knew he couldn't achieve perfection but he had to try.

Clyde knew the one thing he needed to do was to help knock out the heavy water plant at Vemork, he remembered watching the films as a child about the 'Raiders of Telemarck' and that it had to be done by Commandos but that mission was carried out in February 1943 as he remembered but with Clyde changing events that happened in the 2ⁿᵈ World War that created an alternate future perhaps *he* had had some effect on Vemork. He knew he would have to put plans into place to destroy the heavy water plant at Vemork as soon as possible, he also knew that he had to put the plans for D-Day into action whether the allies were working on the plans or not, he had to get things back the way they were. Clyde breathes a huge sigh, places the book back onto the table, stands up and then walks inside the dome pulling the lever.

'Arggh' shouts Clyde

A bright red light fills the room and Clyde wakes up on the floor of a field in the countryside, the glare of the sun temporarily blinds Clyde as he struggles to see properly but through experience he knows which direction his car is in so slowly stands to his feet and walks towards the woods. Clyde walks towards the blurred outline of the woods, he rubs his eyes and now can see a bit better, he spots his car camouflaged with the fallen branches and shrubs so walks quickly over to it, he pushes the branches away from the car, gets inside the car, starts the engine then drives away determined to make changes for the better so as not to create a Nazi dystopian wasteland for the future generations.

Lille - June 1943

A few days later Clyde is sat down in the café in Lille drinking his coffee and is looking towards the front door, he taps his foot on the floor quickly and taps his fingers on the table impatiently waiting for Chevalier to turn up.

The door opens and in walks Chevalier and immediately looks at Clyde, he walks over and sits down across from Clyde who had phoned him a few hours earlier and arranged for them to meet as soon as possible as a matter of extreme urgency.

'What is it? You're making me nervous' said Chevalier

'Now listen to me, this is of the utmost importance' said Clyde

Clyde gets a cigarette out and lights it and takes a long drag from it.

'Go on' said Chevalier

Clyde blows the large plume of smoke into the air as he still taps his foot against the table leg.

'Are you aware of Vemork?' said Clyde

Chevalier looks around the café, furrows his brow and then looks back to Clyde as if he shouldn't have mentioned it.

'Yes' said Chevalier

'What's being done about it then?' said Clyde

'We're bombing it on a regular occurrence' said Chevalier

'Not good enough' said Clyde who sits back into his chair shaking his head from side to side in disagreement 'It's just not good enough'

'It's in the middle of Norway so we bomb them, setting them back, disrupting them and so on…' said Chevalier

'Not good enough' said Clyde as he impetuously shakes his head and smokes profusely on his cigarette. His body language is erratic, he is clearly agitated and Chevalier has picked up on it.

'What's the matter with you?' said Chevalier sternly 'Pull yourself together'

'I'll tell you what it is' said Clyde who stubs out his cigarette and lights another 'They're not far away from developing the atomic bomb, that's what's up with me. You say, *pull yourself together*, ha'

Chevalier shakes his head in a dismissive fashion.

'Nonsense' said Chevalier

Clyde leans closer to Chevalier.

'Nonsense? Now you listen to me, they're very close to…' said Clyde

'We have people on the inside' interrupts Chevalier 'They're nowhere near building one'

'Listen' snaps Clyde as he bangs his fist down onto the table shaking the coffee cup and attracting attention to himself, he realises this and leans closer to Chevalier and lowers his tone 'I'm telling you, they will have one developed by the end of the year and will drop them on England'

Chevalier looks at Clyde as if his stance has changed slightly from dismissive to a more curious position, more willing to listen.

'How do you know all this?' said Chevalier

'It doesn't matter how I know, it's what I know' said Clyde quietly then takes a long drag on his cigarette and blows a large plume of smoke into the air 'Now what I suggest is we launch a commando raid on Vemork and knock it out from the inside but also keep up with the aerial bombing too'

Chevalier sits back on his chair and looks a little rattled with how Clyde is behaving, Chevalier knows things must be serious and true if Clyde is acting the way he is as he's not one to panic unless there is something majorly wrong.

'Ok, I'll put it to the SOE' said Chevalier

Clyde leans quickly and aggressively towards Chevalier.

'You won't just *put it to them*!' said Clyde

Chevalier looks shocked.

'You will insist! Is that clear?' said Clyde

Chevalier stares at Clyde who is wide eyed and clearly getting more agitated the more Chevalier plays the issue down.

'Yes. Clear' said Chevalier

Clyde takes another drag on his cigarette, the waiter walks over to take Clyde's order.

'Sir...' said the waiter

'Not now Pierre!' roared Clyde

The waiter looks at Chevalier as if to say '*What have I done*?' Chevalier shakes his head at Pierre who takes the hint and walks away.

'And another thing' said Clyde

'Yes?' said Chevalier sarcastically

'I need a meeting with the SOE' said Clyde

'Ok, I'll set something up' said Chevalier

'Well I need it ASAP, ok?' said Clyde

Despite their friendship, Chevalier has never known Clyde to behave in this manner, not even when Jaeger was closing in on him or he'd just killed Stechen and had a narrow escape. He feels as though he is being kept out of the loop and he doesn't like it, he'd built up a good relationship with Clyde over the years and he wanted to find out what the bee in his bonnet was.

'What's up with you?' said Chevalier

Clyde stubs his cigarette out quickly in the ash tray and lights another.

'I'm a little on edge, you know… about Vemork' said Clyde

'No kidding' said Chevalier who smiles to try and break the tension

Clyde's facial expression shows clearly that he does not appreciate Chevaliers one liner.

'Take the piss if you want, I'm not bothered, just get it sorted' said Clyde

'Ok, I get it' said Chevalier who isn't trying to joke anymore, he's deadly serious 'Leave it with me and the next time we meet we will have sorted it'

'Ok. Well, we better had of sorted it, that's all I have to say' said Clyde

Clyde looks to the café entrance as the door opens, it is Anna, and Chevalier looks at Clyde in disappointment about him carrying on his affair with Anna after what he'd been through after the last time with Captain Jaeger, but with Clyde being Clyde he just couldn't help himself.

Whenever she was in the area they'd meet up and spend the time together, even though it could go months at a time without seeing each other somehow every couple of months Anna would show up, they'd sleep together then Captain Jaeger wouldn't be far behind sniffing around again and Chevalier thought it was dangerous and had told Clyde on a number of occasions but the warnings fell on deaf ears.

'You're getting in too deep my friend' said Chevalier

Clyde leans over to Chevalier and whispers.

'Where do you think I'm getting my information from?' said Clyde

Clyde was bluffing, the only information he got from Anna was were Captain Jaeger was and sometimes who he was with, it came in handy sometimes but most of the time Anna just said that he was away and hadn't told her where he had gone. Clyde stands up, waves at Anna and looks back at Chevalier.

'I'll see you soon' said Clyde as both men look at each other like an old married couple who'd just argued then made up.

'Goodbye' said Chevalier who nods at Clyde and ignores Anna as he doesn't like her getting involved with Clyde as if cold be the death of him if Jaeger finds out, Clyde walks away over to Anna, they kiss then both exit the café onto the street and start to walk away.

'I don't think he likes me' said Anna

'He does, he just has a funny way of showing it' said Clyde who smiles at Anna 'So, where would you like to go?'

'Let's go to the restaurant in the hotel' said Anna

'Ok. Lead the way' said Clyde.

Lille Park – July 1943

A few weeks' later Clyde walks across the park to see Chevalier sat on the park bench feeding the pigeons with crumbs of bread and walks towards him and sits down next to him.

Just one week earlier the heavy water plant at Vemork had been destroyed by a combined force of the British SOE and Norwegian Commandos. The Germans were furious, they no longer had the ability to create heavy water in order to manufacture an Atomic weapon capable of finishing the war.

'I see Vemork went well?' said Clyde contentedly

Chevalier smiles but looks at the pigeons and throws another small piece of bread to them.

'I told you I'd sort it' said Chevalier

Clyde smiles as he remembers how much he panicked about it and rightly so, now he was relieved it was out of action, he just had to wait until he flashed back to the future to see if there were any repercussions.

'You did well' said Clyde

Chevalier throws a small chunk of bread to the pigeons.

'What about the SOE meeting?' said Clyde

'It's arranged for tomorrow at noon' said Chevalier

'Ok. Where do I need to go?' said Clyde

'Make your way from here to Arras, you'll need to find a small village called Caucort 10 miles North West of Arras, once there just wait and someone will pick you up' said Chevalier

'As easy as that?' said Clyde

Chevalier nods and turns to look at Clyde.

'As easy as that' said Chevalier

French Countryside (just outside Caucort)

The day after, Clyde is driving along a country road and looks to be lost as there aren't any road signs to direct him to either Arras or Caucort, he isn't far away from Caucort but he needs to find out exactly where he is so he pulls over to look at his map. He lays his map on the steering wheel and gets out his compass to get his bearings.

Right, I'm here, I need to be there, three miles West should do it thinks Clyde

Clyde puts his map and compass back on to the passenger seat and drives away.

After a few minutes driving he comes to a very small village that has long been evacuated by its citizens, there is nobody in sight other than the odd stray dog and the eerie village sends a chill down Clyde's spine. He can smell the rotten food and long burnt out houses that had opened their blackened insides for all to see. He looks at his watch, the time is 11:30am, he looks in his rear-view mirror but still there is nobody in sight, he opens his window and tosses his cigarette out and rests his arm on the side of the door, he picks up his map and looks at it.

'Yes, you're in the right place' said a British voice

Clyde looks to where the voice came from as he's surprised to hear a British voice, the first one he'd heard for a very long time and that gave him comfort. Stood at the side of his car the British man wearing civilian clothes and holding a sten gun aiming it at Clyde's head and two resistance fighters flanking him on either side, there would have been others hidden in the buildings surrounding him he thought.

'Come on, get out' instructed the British man

Clyde turns the engine off then gets out of the car.

'Give him your keys' said the British man who gestures to the man on his left

Clyde looks to the resistance fighter and passes him the keys for the car, the resistance fighter gets into Clyde's car then drives off quickly to somewhere else in the town. Clyde hoped that his reception would be a little warmer but he agreed with the precautions the British man was taking, he'd have done the same.

'So… you know who I am?' said Clyde

The British man looks composed and seems very placid in his mannerisms, he was around 5ft 8 with a stocky build, around 40 years of age with brown short hair. He had a hint of an East Midlands accent, maybe Derby or Nottingham Clyde thought.

'Yes. We know who you are, but we don't take chances, as you can appreciate' said the British man

The British man quickly flicks the end of his sten gun upwards twice to gesture to Clyde.

'Hands up' said the British man

Clyde raises his hands and his pistol is taken from him by one of the other resistance fighters and is searched.

'Does anybody know you're here?' said the British man solemnly as Clyde is frisked, he thinks that if he tries to make light of the situation the British man may have a sense of humour, after all, he is British and he's the first one he's spoken to for a long time.

'Well…I've got a feeling you guys know' said Clyde

'We didn't order a comedian' replied the British man with contempt 'Does anyone know you're here?'

Clearly Clyde had misjudged the man which was a shame, he wanted a bit of banter with an Englishman for a change, he only had Chevalier whom he could laugh with.

'Other than the person who set this meeting up, no nobody' said Clyde

'Good. I'm agent Newbold, come with me' said Newbold

Newbold walks down the side of a building with Clyde slightly behind and the other resistance fighter trudging behind, Clyde then notices he wasn't aiming his weapon at him anymore. Newbold turns whilst walking and looks at Clyde who still has his hands raised.

'You can put your hands down now' said Newbold

Clyde lowers his hands and continues to walk just behind Newbold down the alley. As they approach a doorway Newbold stops and points to the ground.

'Mind the wire, you don't want to blow us all to smithereens' said Newbold

Clyde steps over the wire cautiously as Newbold watches on.

'There's a good chap' said Newbold

They walk through the doorway and into the building to where Clyde and Newbold sit at an old weathered wooden table with a radio and some sort of typewriter attached to it.

The resistance fighters each guard the windows and the entrance door watching on lazily, they don't need to worry too much about anyone gate-crashing them as they have their own sentries on duty throughout the village, if anyone approaches someone will raise the alarm.

'Right' said Newbold who sits upright and ready to type in anticipation of what Clyde will tell him 'So what is it you want to tell us?'

'I want to get a message across about the invasion' said Clyde

Newbold looks at Clyde in bemusement, as the only invasion he could think of was the one at Sicily a few months before and the one at Italy that happened the week before.

'Sicily or Italy?' asked Newbold who thought, *what use is this information so long after the invasion had happened*?

'Neither. I'm talking about Northern France.' said Clyde

Here we go again thought Newbold who sighed, he stares at Clyde as though he is wasting his time discussing things that are so blatantly obvious as the Allies wanting to invade the French mainland, he'd had these type of meetings before by agents in the field who thought they could get close to Hitler and assassinate him or people who thought they had good information but it ended up as false, he'd learnt his lesson and was cautious when speaking to new agents especially if they had grand ideas.

'I'm not aware of any plans to invade France. We're currently over stretched in other areas, mainly North Africa and the Far East. Not to mention the Italian campaign we've just embarked on' said Newbold

Newbold raises his eyebrows and gives a quick grin as if to mock Clyde, he then rests his arms on the table away from being ready to type therefore dismissing Clyde's 'master plan'.

'Listen to me, there may or may not be a plan for invasion but that's why I'm here, to start things' said Clyde

Newbold looks at Clyde as if he is having delusions of grandeur, *bloody invasion, ha, why hadn't we thought of that already?* Newbold wanted to say but he would not allow the words to pass his lips, he'd risk a smack in the mouth from Clyde if he did.

'Well go on then' said Newbold pretentiously 'enlighten me'

Clyde glances at the resistance fighters around the room 'I'd prefer to tell you in private if that's ok?'

Newbold nods to the resistance fighters who then take notice then walk out of the room.

'Well? Go on then' said Newbold

'We need to start the plans for invasion' said Clyde as he leans a little closer to Newbold clearly adamant in what he is saying.

'As it stands Germany pose no serious threat in the Atlantic, we need to step up in planning for the invasion of Northern France' said Clyde

Newbold smiles haughtily, Clyde knows he isn't buying into anything he is saying, Newbold shakes his head.

'What's up?' said Clyde bluntly

'No. Nothing' said Newbold

'So why did you smile?' said Clyde

Newbold smiles again.

'It sounds to me like you're having delusions of grandeur old boy' said Newbold

Clyde isn't happy about being antagonised by Newbold in the snotty manner that he is, Newbold doesn't mean it though, it's just the way he comes across as he is by nature slightly aloof and from his experience he's learned the hard way of buying into grand plans that have been ill thought out.

'Now listen to me, I have the ears of the high command in the region, if I speak, they listen' said Clyde

Newbold looks at Clyde but cannot comprehend what he is trying to get across but thinks there may be something worthwhile Clyde has to say as he'd been behind enemy lines carrying out work for the SOE for a few years so he gives him the benefit of the doubt and hears him out.

'If I were to tip them off about an invasion plan in a location other than where it is supposed to happen, then they would pull troops together and send them to that region making it a little easier to gain a foothold' said Clyde

Newbold sits upright and holds his hand on his chin in thought.

'Do you understand?' said Clyde

Newbold doesn't flinch or reply, Clyde shakes his head in disbelief as he doesn't seem to be getting through to Newbold.

'I understand what you mean…I honestly do…' said Newbold

'Well. Hoorah for that' interrupts Clyde

'…but where do *you* suggest we invade?' said Newbold as he leans further back into his chair

'Normandy' said Clyde

Newbold looks at Clyde with a mocking smirk on his face.

'Normandy? Blast, that's the widest stretch' said Newbold who then laughed

'Exactly. So they won't suspect it' said Clyde who was fast losing patience

Newbold shakes his head in disbelief.

'You must be mad. So you think it would be a good idea to invade at the widest stretch?' said Newbold mockingly

Both men stare at each other as if the other person is stark raving mad.

'Yes' said Clyde

'I'm sorry, I think you're bang wrong' said Newbold

'It's the widest and most complicated stretch yes I agree…' said Clyde

'Yes, I'm glad you're speaking sense, now do carry on' interrupted Newbold

'…and that's the reason why they wouldn't suspect it' said Clyde stressing his point

Newbold looks at Clyde for a moment and appears to agree with Clyde, that landing at Normandy *could* catch them off guard.

'We have to do it. I just know it would be successful' said Clyde as Newbold shakes his head and smiles pretentiously.

'We can't just go and make plans from every hunch from everyone who *just knows* something will be successful, we use hard facts boy and logic' said Newbold

'Well here's a hard fact for you…I planned, designed and built the sea defences at Normandy and that is the weakest point of the Atlantic wall' said Clyde with great pride 'I purposely made it like that. I also have the plans for the sea defences along that part of coastline'

Newbold sits up in his chair and now seems to have bitten, he seems to be interested in Clyde's plan as he didn't know Clyde had planned, designed and built the sea defences, perhaps he did have something worthwhile to add to the mix and back up his reputation.

'Where are they?' said Newbold

'The plans?' said Clyde

'Yes' said Newbold who nods

'They're sewn into the rear seat lining of my car' said Clyde

Newbold leans closer to Clyde and looks in awe of him, he can't believe a chance meeting would bring him the plans for the Atlantic Wall. The British had aerial photographs and knew exactly where they were or at least had a good idea but with the actual plans they'd know the weak points of the structures and how to attack them making an amphibious landing on the Northern Coast a more plausible idea.

'Also, I do have the ear of General Freidrich' said Clyde

In the previous few years Brigadier Freidrich had been promoted to General, he'd risen steadily up the ranks until Clyde tipped him off about Dieppe and that piece of information got both Clyde and Freidrich dually promoted.

'Ok?' said Newbold who pretends he doesn't know who Freidrich is but he is well aware of his social standing with the top brass in Northern France.

'All it would take is a phone call to tip him off about us invading at Calais and the troops and tanks will be moved to that region' said Clyde

Newbold is impressed, he seems to have warmed to Clyde and his ideas and willing to put them forward to the SOE so sits upright and begins to type on his typewriter.

'You need to do your bit too; you'll need to make it look as though you're going to invade at Calais or they'll never buy into it' said Clyde

Finally, Newbold starts to type on his typewriter.

'Well, I'll put it to them and see what they think' said Newbold as he carries on typing.

'You can't just *put it to them*. You must be adamant. This *has* to happen' said Clyde

Newbold stops typing.

'Like I said, it isn't my decision but I will be adamant in my typing, I can assure you of that' said Newbold

'Jerome' calls Newbold looks to the doorway, seconds later the door opens and one of the resistance fighters walks in to the room.

'In the lining of the rear seat of this gentleman's vehicle are papers I'd like you to retrieve' said Newbold

Jerome nods and turns away as to walk back outside.

'Oh Jerome?' said Newbold

Jerome pops his head around the door to look at Newbold.

'Don't go hell for leather on the seats won't you. Don't make it obvious' said Newbold

Jerome nods at Newbold then walks out of the room and Newbold begins to type again, Clyde pulls out a cigarette and lights it, he offers one to Newbold.

'No thank you, I prefer the pipe' said Newbold

'Once the invasion begins, a warrant will go out for my arrest' said Clyde

'Don't count your chicken's old boy, we need to take this one step at a time' said Newbold

Newbold stops typing then packs tobacco into his pipe.

'One day will come where I'll have to cross over, especially if my cover is blown' said Clyde

'Yes, we can have someone pick you up' said Newbold who strikes a match and lights his pipe

'That's what I'd like, I want to cross back over but not until the invasion' said Clyde

Newbold smiles as he puffs away on his walnut pipe 'That's if it goes ahead' said Newbold

'I really want to cross back over' said Clyde

'You're not the only one you know' said Newbold

'Yes, yes I know that. I just don't want to be caught with my trousers around my ankles once the fun starts' said Clyde

Newbold laughs and leans back on his chair.

'What a marvellous expression' said Newbold

Newbold stokes his pipe then lights it again puffing out the smoke as he does.

'Don't worry, we'll make sure your pants are kept firmly up' said Newbold

Jerome enters the room and lays the papers onto the table in front of Newbold.

'Thank you Jerome' said Newbold

Clyde stands up and stubs his cigarette out in the ash tray.

'Ok. Well, the balls in your court now Newbold. I've done all I can to convince you, now it's your turn' said Clyde

'I'll try' said Newbold

Clyde shakes his head 'You better...

'Just kidding old boy' interrupted Newbold 'The drawings look pretty good, I'm sure they'll come in handy further down the line but I will tell them what you told me. I'm sure in future there will be plans for retaking France and this bit of information and you yourself can help us, that you can be sure of'

'Good. I'm willing to do whatever's necessary to help' said Clyde who stands up ready to leave, he'd given Newbold the drawings and told him about invading at Normandy, it was up to him to convince the others that this plan was worth pursuing. Currently, the Allies had pushed the Germans and Italians out of North Africa and had invaded Sicily and Italy, the so called soft underbelly of the 'crocodile' of Europe which was hard on the top with the Atlantic wall and supposedly soft underneath due to there being no sea defences and the Italians were deemed easier to defeat than the Germans.

'That's good to hear. We'll be in touch further down the line' said Newbold

'How will you contact me' said Clyde

'Let us worry about that, we'll be in touch' said Newbold

'Ok. Good luck' said Clyde

Clyde exits the building with Jerome ushering him to his vehicle, Jerome hands the keys back to Clyde who then gets into his vehicle then drives away.

Chapter 16 – Back in the Headlights

A few days later Clyde walks along the street in Lille with Anna walking hand in hand and as they approach the café they kiss then go their separate ways, Clyde walks into the café to where Chevalier is.

'Good afternoon' said Clyde

Chevalier stands up and meets Clyde at the entrance quickly and ushers him to the window and points towards a man stood over on the other side of the wide street.

'You see that man over the road with the black coat on?' said Chevalier

Clyde stoops to look under the curtains and out through the window.

'Yes' said Clyde

Chevalier takes a step backwards and holds his hands out akin to a magician revealing his latest trick.

'He works for Jaeger' said Chevalier

The look on Clyde's face changes, he also goes a little paler.

'He's been following you lately, hadn't you noticed?' said Chevalier

Clyde still in a daze sits down on the nearest chair and holds his hands over his face because he feels so stupid, he's surely been caught and this time Jaeger will pin something on him and take him out due to him being seen with Anna. Surely now he'd be killed by Jaeger or the best he could hope for would be him sent to the Eastern Front, he'd rather die he thought.

'Well, no, no I haven't' said Clyde

Chevalier walks away and is frustrated with Clyde as he has warned him all along that being with Anna will land him in trouble.

'Shit! You've had it this time. He's on to you' said Chevalier

Chevalier paces the room shaking his head thinking that Anna knows about Chevalier and he too may be invested or stitched up by Jaeger. Both men aren't afraid of being killed, they're afraid of being killed and therefore preventing them from carrying out their tasks and missions, they'd gladly die if their death meant the Allies won the war.

Clyde sits by the window sheepishly looking at Chevalier pace around the empty café.

'And sleeping with his wife isn't helping… right under his bloody nose as well… shit!' said Chevalier

'Don't bring her into this…' said Clyde

Chevalier stops still and looks at Clyde in an intimidating way.

'Listen to me you fool. You'll have us all shot or at best you'll be on the Eastern front, is that what you want? Tell me, is that what you want?' barked Chevalier

Clyde looks distraught and holds his head in his hands and looks to the floor.

'Don't say I didn't warn you' said Chevalier sternly

Clyde takes a deep breath then looks back at the man in the black coat who is looking over to the café.

'Shit' said Clyde

Chevalier nods in agreement quickly.

'Yes, you're right. Shit indeed' said Chevalier

Clyde who is feeling very sorry for himself looks back to Chevalier for some sort of moral support.

'What do you suggest?' asked Clyde sheepishly

'We do what we should have done a long time ago, we get rid of Jaeger' said Chevalier

Clyde suddenly perks up a bit and sits more upright in the chair, if Jaeger was taken care of then that would get him off his back and allow Clyde and Anna to spend more time together.

'Ok, when?' said Clyde

'There's a dinner in Brussels for the New Year celebrations' said Chevalier

'And what?' said Clyde

'And we take him out, we get on the inside and we take him out' said Chevalier

'How?' said Clyde

Clyde looks at Chevalier who stops pacing the room and sits at the table next to him. Both men sit in silence as they think of ways to kill Jaeger for a few minutes.

'I know what we can do. I have something that will do the job' said Clyde

'Well whatever it is, arrange it. We need to get rid of him as soon as possible' said Chevalier

The last time Clyde went back to present day he brought back with him the Semtex explosives with remote detonators and a pair of two way radios, he believed he could put them to good use, using them on Jaeger would be the best way.

Lille - December 1943

Later that evening Clyde is sat in a hotel room looking out of the window at the falling snow, behind him sitting on the edge of the bed is Anna Jaeger who looks as though she has been crying, Anna's eyes are reddened and she still is upset.

'I'll leave him' sobbed Anna 'I'll pack my bags and I'll leave'

Clyde turns around to look at Anna.

'Ok, do that. Then go and stay with your Mother in Berlin for a few weeks, then come back to meet me here. We can start a new life together' said Clyde

Anna wipes a tear away from her eye with a handkerchief, Clyde walks over to the bed and sits next to her and puts his arm around her to comfort her.

'Don't worry, everything will be ok, just stay out of harm's way for a while. Ok?' said Clyde

Anna pushes Clyde back and stands up, walks over to the window and then looks back to Clyde.

'I can't go back to him, I can't, I can't…' sobbed Anna

Clyde stands up and walks quickly over to Anna and hugs her tightly.

'Hey, hey calm down, don't get worked up about it' said Clyde

Anna bursts into tears, Clyde rubs her back as he hugs her.

'It is what it is, we just need to move on' said Clyde

Anna pushes Clyde back so she can see his face.

'I love you' said Anna

'I love you too' said Clyde

Anna hugs Clyde as he kisses her forehead and looks towards the window.

Brussels - New Year's Eve 1943

Inside a Hotel room, Clyde is sitting on a windowsill in a bay window looking to Chevalier who is dressed smartly in his Officers uniform ready for the party and he is holding the Semtex and the remote detonator. These are the most advanced weapons Chevalier has seen which isn't surprising as they're from 60 years into the future, he's also impressed with the two-way radio and ear pieces.

'I can't believe it, they're amazing' said Chevalier excitedly

Chevalier is smiling, he is impressed by the technology that Clyde has managed to get hold of yet doesn't know that it's from the future. Chevalier also wears a discreet ear piece which is connected to a two-way radio, Chevalier presses his ear piece.

'Hello, hello' said Chevalier

The sound of Chevalier speaking on the two-way radio blasts out from the radio perched on the windowsill, Chevalier starts laughing and Clyde smiles.

'I don't know where you got these from but they're amazing' said Chevalier

'They're great aren't they? Radios subtle enough so nobody can see them' said Clyde

'Well, I'm amazed' said Chevalier

Chevalier holds the detonator of the explosives and holds his finger on the trigger.

'So you just pull the trigger and it explodes? No wires?' said Clyde

'No wires. It's triggered by radio waves' said Clyde

Chevalier suddenly looks shocked and puts the detonator down on the bed.

'So can the wireless set it off?' said Chevalier

Clyde smiles, stands up and walks over to the bed and picks up the detonator.

'No. It works in the same way; you have to set the charge before it's live' said Clyde

Chevalier doesn't look to have understood how it works and doesn't seem to trust the explosives.

'Just leave it with me anyway, just stick to your job as the spotter' said Clyde

Chevalier breathes a sigh of relief as he doesn't have to deal with the complicated explosives.

'Ok. Once I identify Jaeger I'll keep my eyes on him, you plant the explosives under the seat of his car and make your way back here and when he is ready to leave I'll let you know and you do the rest?' said Chevalier

'Precisely. Are you ready?' said Clyde

'Yep, ready' said Chevalier

'Good luck' said Clyde

Chevalier walks out of the door and Clyde looks towards the entrance to the hall where the event will be held through binoculars looking at the guards on duty outside the entrance.

'Alpha 1, communications check' said Chevalier

'Bravo 1, hearing you loud and clear' said Clyde

'Roger' said Chevalier

Chevalier walks across the snowy street and on to the side of the road where the hall is, a vehicle stops outside the entrance to the hall, Clyde looks closely at the concierge walking out to meet the occupants of the vehicle. The concierge opens the door for the Officer and his wife who both step out of the vehicle, Chevalier watches on intently.

'Negative' said Chevalier

'Roger' said Clyde

Clyde watches the driver drive past in the car and around the corner to a car park where the vehicles will be kept throughout the evening, the driver then gets out of the vehicle and walks to the back entrance of the hall, all of which Clyde can see from the hotel room.

Chevalier is approaching the entrance to the building, he'd managed to get on the list for the party via the French Resistance, one of them worked at the hotel and had wrote his name on the guest list.

'I'm going in' said Chevalier

'Roger' said Clyde

Clyde looks through his binoculars to the hall entrance to where Chevalier is walking into the foyer. Another car pulls up at the entrance, the concierge walks out to open the door of the car where another officer and his wife exit the vehicle. Chevalier is watching from just inside the entrance and notices it isn't the target.

'Negative' said Chevalier

Clyde is watching on through his binoculars and can also see that it isn't Jaeger.

'Roger' said Clyde

Clyde watches as the car drives away from the entrance splashing the slushy ice onto the pavement as it drives away passing the building where he is watching from then drives around the corner to the car park, he also watches the guards patrol the car park. It's very easy to understand how the German war machine rages on so well with the discipline of their soldiers, they run like clockwork, this could also be their downfall especially tonight as Clyde is watching them and timing them to make sure he goes at the right time and has enough time to plant the explosives.

Clyde looks back to the hall entrance, there aren't any cars arriving and only the concierge waiting outside with five German soldiers.

'Looks cold out there tonight' said Clyde

'It is' said Chevalier

'Any sign of him?' said Clyde

'He's not here yet. You should see who's in here. It would be like shooting fish in a barrel if we tried to kill them all' said Chevalier

Chevalier is excited at the fact that they could do a whole lot more damage if they concentrated on primarily bombing the whole hall rather than just Jaeger but knows they have to kill Jaeger now before their cover is blown.

'Hold that thought, there's a car pulling up' said Clyde

The car pulls up at the entrance, the concierge opens the door to the car, an officer steps out of the car alone and walks into the building.

'Negative' said Chevalier

'Roger, I could identify him from here' said Clyde

Clyde looks to his table which is on the other side of the room to where the brandy is, as he's nervously excited he thinks it's best to have a bit of Dutch courage to calm his nerves and warm him up a bit.

Clyde glances up and down the main street, looks around the area through his binoculars to make sure nobody is arriving and seeing that the coast is clear he dashes over to the table and pours himself a drink carefully.

'He's arrived' said Chevalier

Clyde stops pouring his drink.

'What, when?' said Clyde

'Just now, his car is outside now, just driving off' said Chevalier

'Shit' said Clyde

Clyde puts the bottle down and rushes to the window, slams his glass of brandy onto the table and picks up the binoculars quickly looking through them to see Jaegers car being driven past him and towards the car park.

'Right, I've got the car, over' said Clyde who makes sure that it is Jaegers car as he can now see the rear of the car.

'It's a positive I.D. It's definitely him, over' said Chevalier who was stood in the foyer watching Jaeger walk in.

Let's get rid of Jaeger once and for all Clyde thinks as he drinks the whole glass of Brandy he had just poured.

'I'm ready to go, over' said Clyde

Clyde puts on his jacket, hat and gloves and picks up a rucksack containing the explosives, detonator and a wire coat hanger, his clothing is all in white so to camouflage him in with the snowy surrounds outside.

He opens the room door and jogs down the stairs and waits at the buildings entrance and looks to his watch.

'23, 22, 21, 20' whispers Clyde under his breath

Clyde opens the door slightly to see a Soldier on the other side of the road walk past.

'15, 14, 13, 12' whispers Clyde

He again looks at the guard who has turned the corner around the street out of sight from Clyde.

'3,2,1' said Clyde

Clyde walks out into the street checking both ways quickly, he then sprints across the road jumping up at the lamp post next to the chain link fence of the car park and climbs over the fence. Once on the other side he crouches behind a car and looks all around the area through the windows of the car then looks to his watch and whispers to himself.

5,4,3 Clyde thinks to himself as he ducks down as a soldier walks past the fence without the slightest suspicion of what is going on. Clyde then slowly shuffles past the cars in the carpark making sure he doesn't make any noise or gets spotted by anyone, he also walks close to the cars and stays in the shadows so that his footprints aren't as visible. He carries on moving past cars looking at their registration plates and after four cars he spots Jaegers car.

'Bingo' whispers Clyde, *I've got you now you bastard* he thinks.

Clyde moves up to the driver's door and slowly stands up taking the wire coat hanger out of his rucksack, he pushes the coat hanger down the side of the window and unhooks the lock opening the door, he then looks around to see if there's anyone around to hear to which there is not.

The car park is dead silent with an odd howl of wind blowing the falling snow into a swirl in the air. Clyde opens the door and puts the rucksack on the floor outside taking out the explosives, he inserts the detonator inside the plastic explosives and then places it underneath the driver's seat. A car is heard driving down the street approaching the car park.

'Shit' hissed Clyde quietly

He climbs into the back of Jaegers car and leaves the door ajar watching the approaching car drive into the carpark and attempt to reverse park into a space. *That's it, park the car then fuck off, come on, hurry up* thinks Clyde to himself.

The driver gets out of the car then spots another car driving down the street and onto the car park, the driver of the first car starts to walk towards the hall back entrance but in doing so will have to walk past Jaegers car.

Clyde looks out of the car window to the floor to see whether his footprints in the snow would be visible to anyone walking past and notices he had left the rucksack on the floor outside of the car.

'Shit' whispers Clyde. *If he walks past here he's going to see that rucksack, I've got to move it now* he thinks.

The second car pulls into the car park, Clyde ducks behind the driver's seat as the first driver walks past the car but doesn't notice the rucksack. As he walks a few yards past he stops, turns around and looks towards the second car that has parked up.

Please no, keep fucking walking, just walk away thinks Clyde

Clyde knows he has to act fast if he is to retrieve the rucksack, there isn't anything valuable or anything that could give Clyde away inside the bag but if anyone noticed it they may walk towards it to pick it up thinking that it had been dropped by a comrade and once outside Jaegers car may notice Clyde hid behind the seats or notice the footprints and suspect something is amiss.

After a moment thinking about the option of leaving it where it is Clyde thinks it's just better to pick the bag up somehow and stay hidden.

The second driver opens his door and at the same time Clyde opens his, snatches the rucksack back into Jaegers car and when the second driver closes his door Clyde closes Jaegers in situ as to disguise the noise.

The drivers both walk towards each other as they seem to be old friends and they meet halfway across the car park right in front of Jaegers car, Clyde slides further down behind the seats praying for help in staying hidden.

'Is everything ok?' said the second driver

The first driver looks down the side of Jaegers car where the rucksack was and then looks at the second driver.

'Yes, fine. How are you?' said the first driver.

They both walk away into the back entrance of the hall, Clyde watches through the window of Jaegers car as the drivers walk into the building and once they're inside he gets out of the car and closes the door.

'Everything ok?' said Chevalier over the radio which made Clyde duck, he'd forgotten about the ear piece and hearing the voice shocked him. *Fucking hell, you frightened the bloody life out of me* he thought.

Clyde taps three times on the microphone to indicate to Chevalier that he can't speak as he may make noise, they didn't have radio silence as they believed nobody would be listening in to the frequency anyway. The snow keeps falling all around Clyde as he looks around the empty car park then moves to the fence which he jumped over previously and hides behind a car then looks at his watch.

A soldier walks past Clyde in the same motion he did previously, he waits a few seconds and then jumps up and climbs over the fence, a dog barks in the distance, Clyde crouches to the floor but there's nobody around, he then briskly walks over the road to the building where the observation post is set up, he opens the door to the building, checks the streets behind him, enters the building then closes the door, runs up the stairs into his room and then sits at the window.

'It's planted. We're good to go' said Clyde whose cheeks were red and his fingers numb as he warmed them by cupping them and blowing into them

'Good to hear, let's sit tight until home time' said Chevalier

A few hours later Clyde sips from his glass of Brandy whilst lay on the bed and holding the detonator looking at a small photo of himself and Anna inside his wallet and wonders if she's ok in Germany with her Mother. After Jaeger was out of the way then he could see her all the time, it may be frowned upon that she is a widow but that didn't quell any feelings from either party in the affair, both of them clearly wanted to be together and it was only a matter of time until they could be.

'He's on the move, I repeat he's on the move' said Chevalier

Clyde gets up from the bed and moves over to the window, picks up the detonator and is holding the binoculars with his left hand and looks towards the entrance.

'I'm ready' said Clyde

Jaegers car slowly pulls up outside the venue and the driver gets out and walks to the entrance, Captain Jaeger walks out of the building and towards his car.

'Come on you bastard' said Clyde who sits upright ready to pull the trigger

Jaeger stops and turns back to the entrance and waits.

What's he waiting for? Get in the bloody car thinks Clyde as he looks again at Jaeger who now turns and walks towards the car but is speaking to somebody walking out of the building.

'Come on, come on' said Clyde

Jaeger is stood at the entrance speaking to the driver and hands him some money as a tip, the driver is pleased and walks away wishing him a good evening.

'Get in the car, come on' said Clyde

Jaeger looks back inside the building and gestures at someone inside then starts to walk towards the driver's side of the car.

'That's it, keep going' said Clyde who holds the detonator desperate to pull the trigger blowing Captain Jaeger to pieces

Jaeger opens the car door and sits inside.

'Do it' said Chevalier

Clyde takes the safety off the remote detonator whilst still looking towards Jaegers car, however, something catches his eye.

'Anna?' said Clyde

Anna Jaeger walks out of the building towards the car and then the bellboy opens the car door for her, Anna gets into the car sitting in the passenger seat and the bellboy closes the door.

'Do it now' said Chevalier

Clyde sits forward in his chair looking at the back of Anna's head through his binoculars. The blonde hair flows in the rear window swinging from side to side as the car moves over the slippery cobles.

'Wait' said Clyde whose legs had gone limp and he had a sickly feeling in his stomach

'Wait?! Do it, do it now' instructed Chevalier

Clyde pauses, puts his binoculars down and looks at the detonator.

'Pull…the…switch…now' said Chevalier

The car starts to drive further away, Clyde turns the safety on the detonator back on and places it on the table then holds his head in his hands.

'I can't, it's Anna, she…' said Clyde

'You're a fool' interrupts Chevalier acidly

Clyde looks out of the window to see Chevalier walking very sternly and quickly towards the hotel looking up at the room which Clyde is in.

A few moments later Chevalier barges open the door aggressively and walks into the room.

'What the hell was that?!' barked Chevalier

'I couldn't, Anna was with him, I…' said Clyde

Chevalier walks briskly over to Clyde who is sat at the table in front of the window and picks up the detonator and rapidly presses the trigger on the detonator and looks out of the window in anticipation of the explosion.

'Has it exploded?' said Chevalier

Chevalier continues to pull the switch and looks out of the window, he then looks at the detonator and takes off the safety then presses the switch and looks out of the window.

'It's too far away, it won't work' said Clyde

Chevalier continues to pull the trigger rapidly, he looks out of the window then lets out a sigh and shakes his head.

'All that planning and you lose your bottle?' said Chevalier

'Why didn't you tell me Anna was with him?' said Clyde as he stood up

'Why do you think?' said Chevalier who eye balls Clyde 'She's collateral damage'

Clyde squares up to Chevalier.

'You can't say that' said Clyde who prods Chevalier in the chest with his finger

'Why can't I? What's more important? You getting your kicks or getting Jaeger off our backs, for good?' said Chevalier

Clyde stays quiet and looks at the floor.

'Very, very stupid' said Chevalier

Chevalier switches off the detonator and puts it into his pocket.

'From now on I take control of the detonator' said Chevalier

Clyde stays quiet and sits down as Chevalier starts to pack up their clothing into the bags they brought with them.

'He'll find the explosives you know, in the morning when it's light' said Clyde

Chevalier takes out a cigarette and lights it then sits on the edge of the bed, he then blows smoke into the air.

'We better get it back then, or we're as good as dead. Aren't we?' said Chevalier

Clyde looks at the floor then over to Chevalier and both men stare at each for a moment.

'Ok, we go tonight' said Clyde

'We go now. Do you know where he lives?' said Chevalier

'I have an idea' said Clyde

Chevalier stands up, stubs his cigarette out and looks at Clyde.

'Let's go' said Chevalier

A few hours later Clyde and Chevalier are sat in a car facing away from Jaegers three storey terraced house about 40 metres away, Clyde is sat in the driver's seat and is looking through the rear-view mirror and Chevalier is leaning forward looking through the side mirror.

The streets are dimly lit by the street lights and have freshly fallen snow on them with the one set of tyre tracks in the snow solely from Jaegers car and a few odd footprints on the pavement from the guards that patrolled the area every now and again.

'Is that his car?' said Chevalier

'Yes, that's it' said Clyde

Chevalier stubs his cigarette out into the ash tray inside the car and winds his window up.

'Right. I'm going' said Chevalier

Clyde grabs Chevaliers arm to prevent him getting out of his seat.

'I'll go' said Clyde

Chevalier shrugs Clyde off and holds his hand up.

'No you won't, I can't trust you to do it now. I will go' said Chevalier

Chevalier opens the car door then starts to walk down the street with his feet crunching the snow as he walks along the quiet street, Clyde is watching through the rear-view mirror.

As Chevalier approaches Jaegers car, he looks around before pulling out the wire coat hanger and uses it to open the driver's door, he then climbs into the back seat and puts his hand under the seat pulling out the explosives.

'Halt!' shouts a voice

Chevalier stops then looks up from behind the driver's seat and Captain Jaeger is half dressed and pointing his pistol at him through the car door.

'Get out. Come on, get out' said Jaeger

Clyde looks through the rear-view mirror.

'Shit' said Clyde

'Alarm! Alarm!' shouts Jaeger

Chevalier sneakily places the C4 onto the back seat and slowly raises his hands in the air outside of the car as he exits the vehicle, he is also holding the detonator in his right hand and to Jaeger it looks like a pistol.

Two German Soldiers come running along the street from the opposite end to Clyde and many of the other houses in the street switch their lights on and people look through their windows to see what is going on.

'Alarm, alarm' shouts Jaeger 'Put your weapon on the ground'

The German soldiers stop and aim their weapons at Chevalier who slowly bends down to place the detonator on the floor and looks over to Clyde.

Clyde is watching through the rear-view mirror and is slouched back sitting low in his seat with the rear-view mirror dipped so that he can see from his lowered position.

'Good luck my friend' whispers Chevalier

Jaeger looks towards Clyde's car and then back to Chevalier who now pulls the trigger on the detonator causing the c4 to explode inside the car blowing Chevalier, Jaeger and the two soldiers up and shattering a lot of glass windows in the street.

'No' said Clyde

A lot of people in the street cautiously come out of their front doors to find out what the explosion was, Clyde starts his engine then looks through his rear-view mirror to see the smouldering bodies on the floor beside the blown-up vehicle and then drives away.

Chapter 17 – Turncoat

Among the vast swathes of oaks, beech's and poplars Clyde is parked in the countryside in his squad car, he looks at his watch, the time is 2:15am, he looks out of the side window and up to the moon, then a bright red light fills the car and lights up the surrounding trees and he wakes up on the floor of the dome in the bunker back in present day.

Clyde wakes up on the cold floor of the dome, he stands up and slowly struggles to walk over to the table outside of the dome, he rubs his eyes so he can see better and picks up his torch which is easy to find due to it still being switched on from the last time he was here. He picks up the torch and shines it on the table to find the history book which he picks up, opens and reads.

In 1943 Allied Commandos destroyed the '*Heavy Water Plant*' at Vemork, this prevented the Germans from developing the atomic bomb.

'Yes' said Clyde as he fist pumps the air in jubilation 'Thank god for that'

The Allies invaded France at Normandy on June 6th 1944 known as D-Day, they fought all the way to Berlin where both the Allies and Soviet troops closed in on the City. Hitler escaped in a plane flying from Tempelhof airport in Berlin and fled to the Balkans where many German troops were located.

Hitler regrouped and started off another front with troops based in Italy and Austria launching an attack to reclaim Germany, it failed but it cost so many lives after Germany and the Balkans were bombed using two atomic bombs in August 1945 creating a giant wasteland in central Europe that still would be radioactive 50 years later leaving it uninhabitable in some places with the fallout causing premature cancers in people from all over Europe.

The war with Japan ended when Hiroshima and Nagasaki were targeted with Atomic bombs in September 1945.

Things didn't end up that way as Clyde remembers, so Clyde must have altered the past and there was only one thing for it. He had to either kill Hitler or destroy the Tempelhof Airport runway to prevent Hitler from escaping Berlin as the red army took the City, maybe then things would turn out the way they were supposed to. But then again with Clyde going back if he tampered with any plans he could alter the future even further, he knew he had to help the Allies and do nothing for the Germans even if it meant him having to escape and cross over to the Allies prematurely, it would be difficult to make it to Spain but he only had a month to wait until the Allies landed at Normandy where he could hand himself over to the first group of Allied soldiers he came across.

Clyde places the book and torch down onto the table and walks back into the dome and pulls the lever, a bright red light fills the room.

'Argh' screamed Clyde

Clyde disappears from the dome and wakes up on the dewy grass in the French countryside, he struggles to his feet and slowly walks over to his car, he pulls back foliage that disguised his squad car, he gets inside, he starts the engine then drives away skidding and wheel spinning on the damp grass as he drives off.

Lille Park – May 1944

Clyde is sat on a park bench in Lille remembering the last time he and Chevalier had spoken to each other on that same bench, he felt guilty of the way they parted ways and that following his heart ultimately led to Chevaliers death but then again, he gave his life so that Clyde could carry on with the missions.

Now that Jaeger was out of the picture Clyde had a bit of breathing space not just with the mission but also with Anna and this was a weird feeling as the thrill of being caught had gone. This was also the second time where Clyde had hesitated and not acted on his friend's advice resulting in their death, as it did with Karl when he wanted to make a break for Spain a few years previous and now with Chevalier.

Clyde felt alone in the world, he had limited access to anybody else as Chevalier was the one to contact the SOE, he looks into the distance and is in deep thought. *What do I do now? I don't know anyone but Chevalier, how do I get in touch with Newbold? Maybe if I travel to Caucort will he still be there?*

'Good afternoon old boy. Don't turn around' said Newbold

Clyde carries on looking forward.

'Do you recognise my voice?' said Newbold

'Aye' said Clyde

'Good. Now just keep looking forward' said Newbold

'What took you so long to get in touch? said Clyde

Newbold pauses as he waits for a child on a bicycle pass, Clyde still stares straight in front of him.

'After the Chevalier episode… we needed to lay low' said Newbold

Clyde nods in agreement, *God bless his soul.*

'We want to take you up on your offer' said Newbold

Newbold must have passed on the information that Clyde could help with the D Day landings and had been tasked with getting back in touch with him to formalise those plans.

'Yes, go on' said Clyde

'You pull troops away from where you originally proposed' said Newbold

Clyde sits up, *they've listened to me, I can really help with the invasion.*

'No problem, I can do that. Is everything good to go?' said Clyde

'You know the rules as well as I do, I can't say too much. We'd like to take you up on your offer regarding Calais' said Newbold

They've bought it, they're going to invade at Normandy thinks Clyde

'We'll sort the rest. When it all starts, you need to find Colonel Carmont' said Newbold

'Ok. I'll do what I can' said Clyde

Colonel Carmont, when it all kicks off find Colonel Carmont.

'Everything else ok?' said Newbold

'Yes, I just have one thing to ask' said Clyde

'Yes, go on' said Newbold

Clyde runs his tongue over his bottom lip and looks around to make sure nobody is trying to listen to them but makes sure he doesn't look at Newbold.

'Destroy the runway at Tempelhof airport as soon as you can and make sure you do a good job of it' said Clyde

'Ok' said Newbold, he was puzzled, *what would the point in destroying the runway as we'd need to rebuild it once we took Berlin?*

'I need you to completely take it out of use' said Clyde

Newbold pauses.

'May I ask why?' said Newbold

'No, you may not. Just make sure it is done' said Clyde

'Very well' said Newbold

Clyde stays silent for a moment.

'Good luck' said Clyde

Clyde turns around but Newbold is gone, Clyde stands up to look around but can't see him. He then walks over the road to the café, he opens the door and walks inside. The waiter, Pierre, is stood at the counter reading a newspaper.

'Pierre, has Anna been in today?' said Clyde

'Sorry Lukas, no' said Pierre

Anna hasn't been seen since the explosion outside Jaegers house, whether or not she was caught up in the explosion or attended the funeral he would never know. The only person who could have found out was Chevalier but he was dead, she may have gone back to her Mothers in Berlin or may still be living at the same house as she did before, all he knew was since Jaeger had been killed she had kept out of the way and made no attempt to contact Clyde.

'If she calls in don't forget to tell her to come and see me as soon as possible over at Calais, I'm not going be around for a while' said Clyde

Pierre quickly folds his newspaper up and puts it behind the counter.

'Ok Lukas, no problem' said Pierre

Clyde stares at Pierre for a moment, he knows what is about to happen soon and there would be a chance of civilians being caught in the crossfire, Pierre may be caught up in it as he is part of the resistance.

'Stay safe Pierre' said Clyde

'You too' said Pierre

Clyde then walks out of the café.

Northern French Coast - 28th May 1944

The wind blows through the gap in the pill box piercing the eyes with its icy gale as Clyde looks out to sea then back to the troops manning the post, you'd have thought it was Winter by the current temperature and the storms in the sea.

'Take a break guys' said Clyde

The soldiers inside the pill box each walk out and begin to chat amongst themselves, they can now go for a hot cup of coffee and a smoke which is long overdue. Clyde waits until the last soldier exits then picks up the radio.

'Yes, hello, it's Major Wolf, I'd like to speak with General Freidrich' said Clyde

Clyde waits, holding on to the radio and struggling to look out to sea as the cold wind blows into his eyes, he turns away and looks to the floor.

'Hello Wolf' said Freidrich

'Hello General, it's been a while since we last spoke' said Clyde

'Yes Wolf, it has, a lot has happened since' said Freidrich soberly, he had Stechen on his mind and wanted retribution for his death and had taken a lot of it out on any French resistance fighters or anyone suspected of being so, still he felt unfulfilled.

'I'm sorry about what happened to Otto, I know how much he meant to you' said Clyde

'Yes, yes, he did. He thought very highly of you Wolf' said Freidrich

'We got on well together. He was a good friend' said Clyde

'Hmmm yes' said Freidrich which was followed by a momentarily awkward silence 'so how can I help?'

Clyde takes a deep breath as a way of combating the nerves he is experiencing.

'Do you remember Dieppe, Sir?' said Clyde

'Yes, I remember' said Freidrich

Clyde pauses for a moment taking another deep breath and breathes out slowly.

'I'm having the same signs again Sir' said Clyde awaiting the reaction from Freidrich

'What signs are they Wolf?' said Freidrich

Clyde takes a large gulp as he swallows.

'We've had almost the same thing happen here at Calais over the past few days that happened at Dieppe, Sir' said Clyde

Freidrich pauses, Clyde gets even more nervous as he breathes slowly in and out to ease his nerves.

'So, what do you thinks happening then?' said Freidrich

'Sir, I have reason to believe they are planning an invasion… at Calais' said Clyde ominously

The line falls silent for a moment, Clyde hopes that just mentioning this will start alarm bells ringing in the upper echelons of the German Army and hopes his word carries more weight after foiling the invasion at Dieppe.

'They wouldn't stand a chance' said Freidrich pompously

Clyde is flustered, he looks around the room wondering how to convince him to move troops to Calais. *Think, come on, think.*

'What makes you think that, Sir?' said Clyde

'Well *you* should know. I think you know full well they wouldn't invade at Calais' said Freidrich

The look on Clyde's face changes, the nerves affect him even more now as he starts to breathe rapidly as things don't pan out as he expected them to. *Dieppe, shit, think.*

'Sir, what about Dieppe. I saw the signs and I was right with that....sir' said Clyde

Clyde decides to remind the General of his previous tip off in the hope that he'd forgot and a reminder may prompt him to take Clyde's side and take action.

'We had our suspicions before you let us know, you just enforced the belief. So no, they won't attack at Calais that can be sure' said Freidrich

Clyde looks out to sea and then back to the floor. *Fuck, come on, think.*

'Is that all Wolf?' said Freidrich

'Sir…' said Clyde

'Is that all?' said Friedrich

With Freidrich dismissing the idea of an invasion at Calais Clyde knows he has to think fast and come up with something else that will help the invasion, the Allies had hoped that troops and tanks will be pulled away from Normandy to make the invasion a little easier.

Shit, come on Clyde think. Prove it, prove you know they won't invade Calais, prove it against the other Generals, you're full of shit Freidrich. War games, plan war games on the 5th or 6th of June, get all the top brass away from their posts. How do I suggest it?

'What about the others, do any others believe they would invade at Calais?' said Clyde who thinks his next question will be a challenge to appeal to his competitive side.

'Maybe one or two, but they're wrong' said Freidrich

'What makes you think they're wrong, Sir?' said Clyde

'I'm sorry Wolf, it sounds like you're questioning my authority, I hope I'm wrong' said Freidrich sternly

Shit, I've pissed him off. Come on Clyde.

'Sir, I sincerely apologise. I think the emotion of the Allies invading at Calais has got to me, once again I apologise, Sir' said Clyde

'Well, there's very little chance of it in my opinion.' said Freidrich who couldn't sound any more arrogant or pompous if he tried.

Clyde thinks on his feet; he stands up straight taking in a deep breath then looks out to sea.

'Sir, would it be worth moving more troops and armour into that area, Sir?' said Clyde

'Listen to me Wolf, I respect what you have done for the war effort and I like you because of your friendship with Otto but don't for one second think that you can make suggestions to me and undermine my authority and leadership' said Freidrich who catches Clyde off guard

Shit, it's gone, I've blown it.

'Sir, I'm sorry Sir' repented Clyde

'Well... it's because of what you've done in the past I'll take that suggestion on board, but if you ever question me again, I'll have you hanged' said Freidrich

Clyde looks to the floor knowing his plan has almost failed, his plans to help the invasion are in tatters.

Freidrich said he'd take the information on board, he didn't say he would do it, he didn't say he wouldn't either.

'Is that clear?!' said Freidrich

'Yes Sir' said Clyde

Freidrich puts the phone down on the other end without saying goodbye, Clyde had really burnt his bridges.

'Fuck' said Clyde

He did say he would take it on board, he did so he might actually move troops over to Calais, hopefully.

215

Clyde's plan and promise to Newbold has gone completely, not only had he not been able to pull troops out of Normandy but he didn't manage to organise the war games and get the military top brass away from their posts on the day of the invasion.

He must think on his feet, he pulls out a cigarette and lights it and sits down whilst thinking of a plan. Then it came to him, if he can't convince General Freidrich to move troops out of Normandy or convince him to take part in war games then maybe he could trick him and others into it, maybe not into moving troop numbers but certainly trick them into competing in war games.

Clyde still had his letter from Adolf Hitler to congratulate him from last time so maybe he could send out forged letters demanding certain high ranking officials attend the war games at Rennes. The invitees would surely attend without question and the day after that's just what Clyde did.

Chapter 18 – Over the Line

05:00hrs - 6th June 1944

A few days later underneath a full moon, Clyde walks out of the farm house, careful not to make a sound, the moon casts a light over the side of the farm so Clyde can just make out his squad car.

'Sir?' said a voice

Clyde is startled, he turns around to see a soldier stood guarding the farm house.

'Yes?' said Clyde

'Is everything ok Sir?' said the Solider who was looking at Clyde curiously

'Yes, everything's fine, I'll be back soon' said Clyde

Clyde opens the door of his squad car, gets inside and drives away slowly so as not to make it look suspicious, as he drives along the country roads he can only see where he is going due to his car headlights and once he's drove for a few hours along the country road Clyde pulls over to the side, parks his car and then gets out and looks at the sky above.

The faint hum of aircraft engines overhead can be heard along with the crickets in the surrounding countryside. Clyde takes his binoculars and looks to the skies where he can just make out the planes flying above in the sky. *It's happening, bloody hell its happening* he thinks.

He moves around to the front of the car and sits on the bonnet, pulls out a cigarette, lights it and begins to smoke it whilst looking at the sky through his binoculars, in the distance he can see the white silhouettes of parachutes falling gracefully from the sky, searchlights come on in the distance and anti-aircraft guns start to fire at the sky lighting up the armada of planes and gliders flying above.

'Flipping heck' said Clyde

Clyde has a front row seat to watch D-Day take place, he'd decided to wait a few miles inland from Sword Beach on the outskirts of Caen so he can meet up with the British landing party and turn himself in and eventually meet with Colonel Carmont.

06:00hrs – 6th June 1944 – HMS Saumarez – English Channel

As dawn breaks a seaman is stood in the crow's nest smoking a cigarette aboard HMS Saumarez when he spots the French Coast, the seaman then throws his cigarette to the floor and looks again through his binoculars then frantically picks up the phone and winds it up.

'It's in sight, the French coast is in sight' said the seaman

A group of Naval Officers look towards the coastline through binoculars.

'Right chaps, get ready to open fire on my command' said the Admiral

'Aye aye Sir' said an Officer

The Officer then walks briskly back inside to the bridge and the Admiral stands and looks out to the French coast and takes in all the smells and sounds that are going on around him, he knows this day will live long in his memory and he wants to absorb everything, after a moment of reflection he looks to the officer.

'Fire' said the Admiral

'Fire' said the Officer holding the phone

The armada of ships open fire on the French coast line, the bright flash from the turrets is followed with a large bang, a whistle and then an explosion of sand on the main land. The officers on the deck watch on as the barrage of shells explode on the coast, a formation of Spitfires flies over the armada with a faint hum from their engines.

Meanwhile, inside a gun battery on the coast, the soldiers inside are frantically loading and firing the heavy guns towards the ships at sea, outside of the gun battery German soldiers rush to their defensive positions from nearby tents and buildings are being blown to pieces in the process by the RAF who fly overhead in Spitfire and Hurricanes.

A German truck parked at the side of the tents is blown up by a Spitfire flying overhead, two Soldiers rush to their machine gun nest but are blown up by the shelling from the ships and chaos ensues the German defensive positions.

Clyde is on a hillside watching the naval bombardment through binoculars with a cigarette hanging from his mouth as it is stuck to his bottom lip, he watches with amazement as a Spitfire flies low overhead fresh from bombing the beach in the distance, he ducks as it passes then looks to his car and thinks about getting in it and driving off but quickly decides against getting back inside as he too may be bombed by the plane.

He rushes over to his car, pulls out a rucksack and then begins to run away down the hillside to a farm track, the sound of the Spitfires engine grows louder and Clyde hides in a bush next to the track and has a clear view of the car he had just abandoned, the Spitfire strafes the ground hitting the squad car and it bursts into flames.

'Bloody hell' said Clyde who is excited and also wary of getting killed, he needs to be careful

The Spitfire flies over Clyde and back to the coast to pursue its attack on the gun positions.

Clyde stands up and begins to walk down the farm track but stays close to the hedge rows along the road just in case he needs to hide, the battle rages on in the distance but he notices the shelling has stopped, this means the troops will be landing shortly, his squad car explodes in the distance behind him causing him to dive to the floor.

Jesus, that was close he thinks as he looks back at the remains of the burnt and blackened car.

June 6th 1944 – German Army Headquarters - Rennes

In a large room in Rennes, the German High Command are huddled into a room with a large map of Northern France on the table with various pieces to show the whereabouts of troops and tanks, friend or foe and they're completing the war games. As the Generals do their best to look as if they know what the other team will do once they make their move, it's like a large game of chess.

'If we move the 2nd Panzer Division from Amiens up to Calais to wait until they have a foothold then drive them out into the sea, that way the Naval bombardment will be lessened as they'll have their own on the beach and panic will ensue' said one General teaming with arrogance as he winked at one of his team members.

A Corporal rushes into the room and looks around for the most important officer in the room, the colour has drained from his face as he looks shocked, he walks quickly over to Field Marshall Von Rundstedt and salutes.

'Sir, we have reports they are commencing naval bombardment at Normandy and are beginning to launch an amphibious landing' said the Corporal as he struggled to catch his breath 'there are reports of paratroopers landing but we can't confirm it'

The officers in the room begin to speak amongst themselves, Von Rundstedt looks scornfully at General Freidrich and then back to the Corporal.

'Thank you Corporal' said Von Rundstedt.

General Freidrich slumps lower in his chair and leans over to speak to his aid.

'Sergeant, you put the notice out to arrest Major Lukas Wolf at once. Shoot on site if they must' said Freidrich

'General Freidrich?' said Von Rundstedt

Freidrich sits up in his chair.

'Yes Sir?' said Freidrich

'Please, come with me' said Von Rundstedt

Freidrich looks to his aid and then gets up and walks out of the room with Von Rundstedt.

Unbeknown to Clyde, General Freidrich had taken his advice and thought he could capitalise on the information of an impending invasion and thought he could play it in his favour as Clyde was promoted last time and honoured by the Fuhrer because of Dieppe, Freidrich had ambitions and got greedy deciding to take the credit for the invasion at Calais for himself.

General Freidrich had always had ambition and had stepped on a few people in the process of reaching General, the next step was Field Marshall and he had his eye on Von Rundstedt's position as commander in the West but Von Rundstedt wasn't going anywhere despite his old age and pig headedness.

Freidrich thought him as a relic and only there as window dressing, he had done well in the past but it was time for him to move on and allow the new blood to come in, that new blood being Freidrich.

Field Marshall Von Rundstedt wasn't stupid, neither did he suffer fools gladly nor reach his lofty position without keeping an eye on career assassins like Freidrich. With all this in mind it was clear that neither man saw eye to eye, with Von Rundstedt believing Freidrich to be an empty suit and a complete waste of time, he believed Hitler had kept him in France as he could not stack up to being a battle commander in Africa, Italy or Russia so kept him tucked away in France just because he enjoyed his company.

General Freidrich had the plan of secretly moving divisions of troops out from Normandy and towards Calais a few days before D-Day so that Von Rundstedt may not find out in time so that when the invasion began at Calais, Freidrich could come to the rescue and repel the invasion making him a hero and undermining Von Rundstedt and hopefully retiring him with himself stepping into that role.

With all this in mind General Freidrich knew he'd been caught with his trousers down and once the news broke that he had moved the troops then he'd surely be hanged as a traitor or given cyanide pills to take on the promise that he'd he given a hero's funeral and a heroes cover story, maybe this was where he was being taken by Von Rundstedt, maybe there were two Gestapo officers waiting in another room ready to send Freidrich to meet his maker.

Mathieu – Outskirts of Caen

Clyde hears an engine from a truck further down the road so jumps into the hedges, crouches and hides in anticipation, he doesn't know whether it will be friend or foe driving towards him and either way he is dressed in full German army officer uniform so needs to be careful to say the least.

As the engine noise grows louder he notices a disturbance in the hedges further along the track in front of him towards the sound of the truck. *Did something move, is there someone there?* He thinks.

The truck now comes into view, it is a German truck carrying troops to help defend the coast, the hedges move again and Clyde can see a British Paratrooper edging his way out of the bushes holding a Piat anti-tank weapon. *This is amazing* he thinks.

Clyde ducks down slightly as the truck moves closer to the Paratrooper in wait and as it comes within 20 metres the Paratrooper fires the Piat at the truck and the cabin of the truck explodes, the truck veers to the right crashing into the hedge. The soldiers in the back of the truck fall about inside and a group of Paratroopers rush out from the hedges and fire their Sten guns at the Germans killing them instantly inside the back of the truck.

Clyde watches in amazement as this is his chance to turn himself over, at last he can be free from the shackles of the German army and be free from the threat of being caught as a spy. *What if the Para's shoot him? What if they don't believe him, surely the word has been passed down that he would be crossing over? Maybe they didn't get the memo?*

He thinks to himself that he needs to be very careful when alerting the Para's, he remembers who he needs to ask for. *Colonel Carmont, ask for Colonel Carmont.*

A Para throws a grenade into the back of the truck and it explodes, Clyde flinches, the Para's all rush to their Sergeant and crouch at the side of the hedges looking at a map, Clyde quickly takes off his jacket and throws it further into the hedge, he picks up his rucksack and stands up. *Fuck it, here goes nothing.*

'Lads... don't shoot... I'm British' said Clyde who steps out from the hedge with his hands raised

The Paras hear this, they quickly turn and aim their weapons at Clyde and quickly spread out, one Para rushes over whilst aiming his Sten gun at Clyde.

'I'm on your side, I've been told to ask for Colonel...' said Clyde

The Para hits Clyde in the face with his weapon knocking him to the floor.

'Fucking turncoat are you?' said the Para

The Para pulls out his knife and sits on top of Clyde holding it to his throat ready to slit it once ordered to.

'Carmont, ask Carmont, Colonel Carmont' shouts Clyde in the fracas

The Sergeant quickly rushes over to Clyde and crouches next to him.

'Just hold it for a moment Edwards' said the Sergeant

'I'm British, I'm from Lancashire, I...' said Clyde

Edwards and the Sergeant look at each other and seem at least convinced due to his accent, Edwards thinks of a way of getting Clyde to speak more.

'British? Who won the Ashes last time around then?' said Edwards

Clyde looks up at Edwards and then to the Sergeant who by now is using the radio.

'Cricket or Rugby League ashes?' said Clyde

'Either' said Edwards

'I don't bloody know I've been in France for five years' said Clyde

'Not good enough sunshine' said Edwards

The Sergeant puts down his radio.

'What's your name?' said the Sergeant

'Bradley Clyde, but I've been under the name Major Lukas Wolf' said Clyde

The Sergeant speaks again on the radio; Edwards's looks at Clyde as a few other Para's gather around them.

'Scalp him Edwards' said Gregory

Clyde looks up in panic to Gregory who is smiling, clearly joking at the expense of his dignity as he is lay on the floor fretting.

'Just hold on lads, he checks out, you can let go of him now Edwards' said the Sergeant

Edwards stands up and puts his knife away, as Edwards looks down to slide his knife back into its pouch Clyde punches him in the face knocking him to the ground, the Paras look stunned, Clyde stands over Edwards who has fallen back to the floor.

'We'll call it even then eh?' said Clyde

The Sergeant moves closer to Clyde and holds his arm out in front of him just in case he goes for Edwards again, Edwards quickly gets to his feet brushing himself off as he does he moves towards Clyde.

'Come on, you jerry bastard' said Edwards

'Leave it Edwards' said the Sergeant

Edwards stops, looks at his Sergeant then brushes his backside and back of his thighs then slowly walks away staring at Clyde and would love nothing more than to finish Clyde off.

'You said our name was Clyde?' said the Sergeant

'Yes' said Clyde

'You'll have to stick with us for the time being, until someone can pick you up' said the Sergeant

Clyde stares back at Edwards.

'No problem' said Clyde

The Sergeant turns to the other paratroopers.

'Right lads, let's go to rally point C and brew up' said the Sergeant

The Para's quickly disperse past the smouldering truck, Clyde has a quick look inside to see the dead troops burning, the smell makes him feel nauseous, it smells like shit and burnt bacon.

As mid-day is approaching, Clyde and the Paras sit in a ditch and they're all smoking cigarettes, some of the Paras boil water to make a cup of tea when a Bedford truck drives towards them accompanied by a Sherman tank and an armoured car, a Para walks out into the road and holds his hand up to the truck.

The convoy stops and a few soldiers jump out of the back of the truck and cover the area, Clyde walks out of the ditch and up to the truck. Clive Stapleton, a clean cut, slim built gentleman jumps out of the front of the truck and walks up to Clyde and holds his hand out.

'Hello, Arthur Stapleton SOE' said Stapleton

Clyde and Stapleton shake hands.

'Bradley Clyde, alias Major Lukas Wolff' said Clyde

They stop shaking hands and Clyde takes a drag from his cigarette, he turns away blowing the smoke.

'It's an honour to meet you Sir' said Stapleton

'It's nice to finally be in safe hands' said Clyde

Stapleton looks around to see the Sergeant walking up to him.

'Thank you for taking care of him' said Stapleton

'It's my pleasure Sir' said the Sergeant

'Right then Major, jump in the truck and we'll go and see Colonel Carmont' said Stapleton

Clyde turns to the Sergeant and shakes his hand then waves to the other Paras and then gets into the front of the truck along with Stapleton.

'Well, we're still in bandit country so keep your eyes peeled' said Stapleton

Stapleton passes Clyde a pistol and the convoy starts to drive away, Clyde puts the pistol inside the top of his trousers so that is wedged between his belt and his stomach.

'Oh, you'll probably want to get out of that uniform, take one of the jackets from the truck, it'll make you look more human' said Stapleton

Clyde leans into the back of the truck and grabs a smock jacket then opens the window of the truck as it drives past the Paras.

'See you later lads' said Clyde

Edwards is nursing his reddened cheek looking fiercely towards the truck, Clyde notices and winks back at him.

Hermanville-Sur-Mer

As morning breaks the convoy of vehicles drives along a road leading into a town that has been untouched by the battles that raged across Normandy on D-Day and slows to a Military Police checkpoint at the edge of the town. The truck pulls alongside the checkpoint and a Military Police Officer walks towards the truck, Stapleton leans slightly over the driver towards the window. An endless convoy of tanks, trucks and troops slowly advance in the opposite direction heading for Caen.

'Hello Corporal, we're looking for Colonel Carmont' said Stapleton

The military police officer turns and looks towards the town and holds one arm in front to give directions.

'Follow the road into Town. He's using the old church hall; you can't miss it' said the Corporal

'Thank you Corporal' said Stapleton

The tank and armoured car pulls over to let the truck drive through and into the town. As the truck drives through the town many civilians wave to the truck and some pass flowers and bottles of wine to the troops inside, all inside the truck are overwhelmed by the generosity shown in adversity by the civilians, the troops in the back start to drink the wine from the bottle and pass it around the truck, one passes the bottle to Clyde who takes a swig and passes it to Stapleton, he declines and the driver takes the bottle and takes a swig then passes it into the back of the truck.

A few minutes later the truck comes to a slow-moving stop as civilians stand in the way of the truck preventing it from moving and many civilians try to hug or kiss everyone on board. The driver attempts to drive and has to keep stopping intermittently shaking all people on board the truck as it comes to a halt, the driver turns to Stapleton and shakes his head and nods to the civilians in the street stopping them and the convoy moving in the opposite direction.

'We won't be able to get through this lot Sir' said the Truck Driver

Stapleton looks at the civilians in the street, there are more coming towards them and the streets are already packed, he then looks at Clyde.

'Looks like we'll have to walk through old chap' said Stapleton

Clyde looks to the crowded streets and can see the church up ahead.

'Come on then' said Clyde

Clyde struggles to open the door and get out of the truck as French women try to pat him on the head and kiss him, Clyde is laughing as is Stapleton.

'I bet you didn't expect this did you Clyde?' said Stapleton

'I can't say I did' said Clyde

Stapleton climbs down from the truck and is kissed on the cheek by an old man who mumbles something in French, Clyde laughs.

'It's over there Clyde' shouts Stapleton

Clyde gives the thumbs up to Stapleton as it's hard to hear him as the civilians make noise all around, meanwhile the troops on the back of the truck struggle to even get out of the truck, French children climb into the truck preventing the soldiers from getting off, Stapleton looks to the Soldiers and raises his arms to gesture there's not much they can do, as he does so an old woman hugs Stapleton.

'Looks like you're flavour of the month around here Stapleton' said Clyde

Stapleton and Clyde wade through the kisses, flowers and pats on the back and approach the entrance to the church hall, outside of the barbed wire fence stand two military police officers guarding it, the MP's notice Clyde and Stapleton and pull back the fence barbed wire gate to allow them in and then close it quickly behind them.

'Its bloody bedlam out there Sir' said the MP

'You're not wrong Corporal, which way is it to Colonel Carmont?' said Stapleton

The MP turns and points to the entrance to the church hall.

'Right through there Sir, you can't miss him' said the MP

'Thank you Corporal' said Stapleton

Stapleton and Clyde walk through the entrance to the church hall, inside is a crudely set up communications headquarters for the region and countless officers on radios communicating frantically to whoever is on the other line, maps hang from the walls and chalk boards are being constantly updated.

Colonel Carmont is at the other end of the church hall speaking on the radio and looks up and notices Stapleton, he gestures for them to wait. Colonel Carmont is the typical British Army Officer of yesteryear, he was in his mid-50's with dark hair, sun burnt weathered skin wrinkled like a walnut with a neatly trimmed moustache.

'We'll just wait here for a moment' said Stapleton

'Righto' said Clyde

Clyde looks around the room to see a few Officers looking at his trousers and boots, he still has German Army Officers uniform on under his smock jacket he took from the back of the truck, Stapleton notices and stops a Lance Corporal as he walks past.

'Excuse me Lance Corporal, Major Clyde here needs a uniform as soon as possible, can you see that it is done?' said Stapleton

The Lance Corporal looks Clyde up and down to size him up for uniform and notices the German uniform and seems to be confused with Clyde attire.

'Right away Sir' said the Lance Corporal

Colonel Carmont walks up behind Stapleton and Clyde, he notices Clyde's German army trousers and then raises his eyebrows in confusion whilst looking to the Lance Corporal.

'Ah, Stapleton, good to see you again' said Colonel Carmont

Colonel Carmont stands proudly with his hand outreached and shakes Stapleton's hand vigorously.

'Yes Sir, it's good to see you too' said Stapleton

Carmont looks at Clyde not knowing what to expect from his attire, he has a slight suspicion it may be the man who is crossing over today and hopefully it is, he thinks.

'And who might you be?' asked Carmont

Clyde is used to saluting British army officers due to his days in the Royal Engineers, he notices the pips on Colonel Carmonts shoulders and stands to attention and salutes.

'Sir, I'm Bradley Clyde, Sir' said Clyde

Carmont grins then holds his hand out again vigorously shaking hands with Clyde.

'I was Major Lukas Wolf in the German Army until this morning' said Clyde

Carmont stares at Clyde and grins, he seems happy to see him.

'Ah, so you're our inside man then?' said Carmont

'Yes, I suppose I am' said Clyde

'Well, you did a wonderful job Major during your time undercover' said Carmont

'Thank you Sir, but if truth be told I'm not really a Major' said Clyde

Carmont looks at Stapleton then back to Clyde and smiles.

'Well, you are now old chap' said Carmont

Clyde looks at Stapleton who smiles at Clyde.

'And I'd like you to carry on your work' said Carmont

Surely this doesn't mean he goes back undercover, Clyde thought, his cover had been blown with arranging the war games and he didn't want to risk it.

'I'm not sure I understand Sir; I will have been compromised due to the invasion' said Clyde

'No Major, I'm not asking you to go undercover again, I'm sure we'll find other uses for you' said Carmont

'Yes Sir, I'm happy to help Sir' said Clyde

'Anyway, there's a warrant out for your arrest if I recall correctly. Is that true Stapleton?' said Carmont

Clyde is surprised, he turns to look at Stapleton as if to ask why he'd been kept in the dark, Stapleton smiles wryly.

'Yes Sir' said Stapleton

Stapleton had other agents on the inside ready to come back over to the Allies and news was that they'd set a high bounty on Clyde's head, a bounty of 10,000 Reich's marks, just over £1000, probably about £1,000,000 in today's money.

'Very well Major, first things first, we'll need you out of that ghastly uniform at once, you don't want to be scaring the natives' said Carmont

'Yes Sir, at once Sir' said Clyde

'See that it is done Arthur. Oh, Clyde?' said Carmont

'Yes Sir?' said Carmont

'Meet me back here once you've got your new uniform and we'll have a chat' said Carmont

'Yes Sir' said Clyde

'Cheerio' said Carmont

Carmont walks away, Clyde turns to look at Stapleton.

'Right, I just need my uniform' said Clyde

'Come with me' said Stapleton who leads the way to the quartermaster's stores.

Hermanville-Sur-Mer – British Army Headquarters

An hour, later Clyde walks proudly through the church hall wearing his brand new British army uniform complete with the crown on his shoulder to signify his rank as Major. He loves the fact that British soldiers salute him rather than the Germans, he feels at ease and more at home now. He just has one thing in the back of his mind and that's Anna, if he can meet up with her then he'd be happy to see out the war behind a desk or even on the front line, he just wanted Anna and he wouldn't settle until he had her in his arms again.

Clyde walks up to Colonel Carmonts office and knocks on the door.

'Yes?' calls Carmont from inside the room

Clyde opens the door and walks inside closing the door once inside.

'Looking better already I see' said Carmont with a glint in his eye

'It sure feels better to be wearing this Sir' said Clyde who couldn't help looking pleased as punch

'Do sit down Clyde' said Carmont

Clyde doesn't sit, he walks over to one side of the room and points at a large map on the wall.

'Just before I do I want to show you something on a map, if you don't mind Sir' said Clyde

Clyde looks at a map pinned on the wall of Northern France and points to Rennes, Carmont is stood next to Clyde.

'Sir, the high commanders in the region are in Rennes, I sent them there to play war games so they'd be away from their posts when the invasion began' said Clyde

Carmont looks at Clyde.

'What an awfully brilliant thing to do' said Carmont

'If you can get me a more detailed map of Rennes, I can show you the building in which they were in so the RAF can wipe them out' said Clyde

Carmont thinks the plan over and wonders if they'd not already left the building but at least it would be worth the try just in case some had stayed behind.

'They've probably pretty much dispersed by now I'd think, but hey ho, let's give it a try then eh?' said Carmont

'Yes Sir' said Clyde

'Do sit down with me' said Carmont as both men sit opposite each other at the desk.

'Right, what to do with you? I'm right in thinking you have a lot of information with regards to German positions, numbers and so on yes?' said Carmont

'Yes Sir' said Clyde

'Ok, you'll be attached to us and we'll command the battles from here' said Carmont

Clyde doesn't want this and his facial expression clearly shows his feelings, he doesn't want to be stuck behind a desk, not until he'd met back up with Anna making sure she was safe anyway. He'd more or less stayed out of the action when operating as a spy on the German side but did get his hands dirty on a few occasions when he carried out missions to kill high ranking targets, now he was back on the British side and wanted to go full throttle in getting involved in the fight as it was what he was used to and what he was good at and truth be told, he missed it.

'Sir, with all due respect I'd *much prefer* to be out in the field' said Clyde

'Really?' said Carmont

'Yes Sir, I've been sat behind a desk for too long' said Clyde

Clyde notices Carmonts last few years would have been sat behind a desk as he does seem to be carrying more weight than he probably once did.

'No offence Sir' said Clyde

'No, none taken Major. I appreciate your honesty' said Carmont

Carmont leans back in his chair and is in deep thought about what to do with Clyde, he wants to get out into the field but with what he had done behind enemy lines it may be a waste to let him command the rank and file soldiers, he deserved more.

'How would you feel about leading a section of commando's?' said Carmont

Clyde nods his head in agreement with the idea as he'd done the all arms commando course whilst with the Royal Engineers and had earned the right to wear the green beret of the Royal Marines Commandos.

'I'd be over the moon Sir' said Clyde

'Very well, I'll see that it is done. For the time being stick close to Stapleton and tell him everything you know' said Carmont

'Yes Sir' said Clyde

'The first thing you must do is tell him the location of the building at Rennes and have it blown up' said Carmont

'Yes Sir' said Clyde

'And once more Major, thank you for your efforts. You don't need me to tell you how important your actions have been' said Carmont

Clyde allows a moment for that comment to sink in.

Yes, I have done well thank you very much. Hopefully I'll get a medal for it thinks Clyde with great pride

'Thank you, Sir' said Clyde humbly

'Cheerio Clyde' said Carmont

Clyde stands up, salutes Carmont then exits the room.

Chapter 19 – Out into the Field

Clyde waits in Carmonts office looking at the maps on the wall and looks at the progress in which the Allies had taken in Northern France, they had gained a good foothold but were a way off from Lille, he couldn't wait for the liberation of Lille as he hoped that Anna would be waiting for him.

He hadn't seen her for a few months and not since Captain Jaeger had been killed by Chevalier in the unfortunate suicide bombing outside their home, he hoped that Anna wasn't harmed in the blast but had no idea of whether she was alive or dead so he couldn't wait to get the chance to go back to Lille and see if she is still there or to see whether she took his advice in the end and went to stay with her Mother in Germany.

Clyde then looks at a map of Rennes and the building that he had identified a few weeks earlier and was bombed but they'd missed most of the high-ranking Germans though a few were killed in the attack.

The door opens and in walks Colonel Carmont with a Sergeant, Clyde stands up and salutes Carmont and the Sergeant, they both salute back.

'Major Clyde, this is Sergeant Farrell' said Carmont as he walks past, Clyde and Farrell shake hands. Farrell looks granite tough, although around 5ft 9 he had presence. He had brown hair, a broken nose and high cheek bones and was stocky but without an ounce of fat on him and when he shook Clyde's hand he nearly broke it, it was something Farrell liked to do to people he was introduced to who were officers or may be of importance, it was a form of inverted snobbery. Clyde squeezes back and does his best not to let Farrell know he'd been out squeezed.

Farrell was from Scotland and had worked as a cattle farmer before the war and he suited that job because he looked like a bull due to his height, build and no nonsense attitude that had gotten him promoted to Sergeant.

'Do sit down chaps' said Carmont

Carmont sits down at his desk in front of Clyde and Farrell.

'As you know, Jerry is still firing those ghastly doodlebugs or flying bombs, whatever you want to call, them at London. The RAF are struggling to destroy the launch sites since they started using mobile launch sites in Holland' said Carmont

Carmont places a map onto the desk pointing at an area in Holland, Clyde and Farrell shuffle their chairs closer to the desk to see the map in more detail.

'In this area here, this is where we think they are launching them from. What we plan to do is drop your squad into this region and set up an observation post. From there you'll need to keep your eyes peeled for rockets and radio in their position, time and direction as best you can. That way the clever fellows here can work out when they will hit England and set up our defences against them and try to work out where they have been launched from' said Carmont

Clyde nods in agreement with the plan, he likes it, he remembers seeing an old clip of a Spitfire flying next to the V1 rockets and tipping them causing them to crash.

'It's a very cunning plan Sir' said Clyde

'It is Major; it will surely help in our fight against them. We're pushing Jerry further and further back but they still are in range of hitting London so until then we need to do what we can to prevent it' said Carmont

Farrell leans back in his chair and looks intriguingly at Carmont.

'Will we be working alone Sir?' said Farrell as he clenches his fists which perch on top of his knees.

'There will be other patrols in the area for increased accuracy, but they will be miles away from yourselves so you won't encounter them, or at least you shouldn't encounter them' said Carmont

'When do we go Sir?' said Clyde

'Tomorrow at dawn. We'll be parachuting you in' said Carmont

Clyde nods and Carmont smiles whilst looking at the two men pleased with his plan. *I've never bloody jumped out of a plane before* thinks Clyde

'Any questions?' said Carmont

'How long will we be in the field?' said Clyde

'Hopefully a maximum of three to four weeks, it depends on the success of the mission and how far we can advance. We'll keep in contact either way' said Carmont

'Will we have any support if we're compromised?' said Farrell

'Well. Depending on availability there may be air support' said Carmont unconvincingly, Farrell shakes his head.

'So, we're on our own then Sir?' said Farrell, Carmont gives a sympathetic smile

'I'd love to guarantee it Sergeant but you know from experience how things work' said Carmont

Shit, we really will be on our own behind enemy lines thinks Clyde

'What about supplies?' said Clyde

'Dawn air drops every three days to a designated position. Anyway, we'll have a final briefing at 16:00 hours ok?' said Carmont as he seemed preoccupied in getting both men out of the room 'That'll give you time to digest the information and come up with any questions or any input'

Clyde and Farrell both nod.

'Sergeant, can you introduce Major Clyde to the squad please?' said Carmont

'Yes Sir' said Farrell

'Very well, see you both later' said Carmont

Clyde and Farrell stand up, they both salute Carmont then exit the room and begin to walk down the corridor side by side.

'So, what's your background, Sir?' said Farrell

Clyde's glad he's asked this question, he can put a marker down and tell him about his past. He assumes Sergeant Farrell will think of Clyde as nothing more than a pencil necked, university graduate who probably went to private school and will hinder the squad behind enemy lines by doing things by the book, as his experience has taught him, he didn't like officers, none of the rank and file soldiers did.

'Well then Sergeant, I'm originally a Corporal in the Royal Engineers, I've been under cover in Germany since 1940 overseeing the Atlantic Wall construction' said Clyde

'Oh, so you were promoted from the ranks, Sir?' said Farrell

'Yes Sergeant' said Clyde *but not through arse licking or being a sycophant, I've bloody earnt* it he wanted to say.

'So what sort of things did you do over the last few years? If you don't mind me asking, Sir' said Sergeant Farrell

This cheeky bugger doesn't believe me

'No, I don't mind at all. I passed on information about the St Nazierre raid, assassinated a few high-ranking Officers and pulled the high commanders to Rennes for war games for D-Day' said Clyde

Go on, pick the bones out of that.

'Now that must have been living on the edge, Sir' said Farrell

'I almost got caught, a few times' said Clyde

'Flipping heck' said Farrell

'So what's the squad like then?' said Clyde

'They're the cream of the crop, Sir' said Farrell who smiles wryly as if the comment was said in jest.

Sergeant Farrell opens a door to a room, Clyde walks in first and Farrell follows, inside the room are five men sat on the floor around their equipment, cleaning their weapons and smoking, they notice Clyde enter the room and stand up and salute.

'Right lads, this is Major Clyde, he'll be leading the mission' said Farrell

The commandos each say hello in an unorganised manner.

'You can do better than that' barked Farrell

The commandos let out a colloquial hello with gusto.

'That's better lads' said Farrell pretentiously

Clyde knows how it feels to be introduced to your new commanding officer and from experience he knows the lads don't really care about him until he proves himself in the field of battle, so he wants to come across naturally as unlike many of the other officers at that time he wasn't gentry and he'd come from a poor working class background and wanted that to come across to the commandos.

'Please, don't stand on my watch' stressed Clyde as he wanted the commandos to go about their business

'Don't take it off your wrist then' said Morris under his breath

'Shut it Moz' said Farrell

'That's ok Sergeant, I don't mind the banter. Please continue what you were doing before I arrived' said Clyde

The commandos sit down on the floor and continue what they were doing previously though Morris stays standing.

Morris was a typical spiv from London. He was average height, slim build, in his early 20's with slick black hair and had a cheeky sense of humour to go with it. At first Morris comes across as abrasive and cocky which meant that a few of the commandos ended up punching him but as time went on they grew to like him and the fact that he was the butt of a lot of the jokes from the other commandos as he wasn't book smart but he was street smart.

'So Sir, what did you done before this posting, if you don't mind me asking?' said Morris

Bourhill looks at Smith and shakes his head, Clyde wants to have a close relationship with the commandos but didn't expect them to be so upfront and forward.

'Shut it Moz' said Farrell who lurched forwards ready to smack Morris in the mouth for being insolent

'It's ok' said Clyde ushering Farrell to stand aside 'I've been under cover in the German Army since 1940, my cover was blown on D-Day so I've come back over' said Clyde

'Did you get to meet old Adolf then?' said Morris who looks at Farrell for his reaction, Clyde smiles.

'No, I didn't, otherwise I'd have killed him. I did meet Himmler though' said Clyde

'That's what I said' said Morris as he looks around to the other commandos 'why didn't you kill him then?'

'*Himmler*' snapped Bourhill 'not *Hitler*. You daft bugger'

All the commandos laugh at the expense of Morris who stands there looking peeved off.

'He's not the sharpest knife in the draw Sir, you'll have to excuse him' said Bourhill

The commandos laugh.

'Maybe I'm not the brightest, but I'm a top-class infantryman' said Morris proudly, none of the commandos can disagree with that comment.

Clyde looks at Farrell as if to ask if he can back up the claim, Farrell looks back at Clyde and nods his head.

'It's a bloody good job you are Moz' said Bourhill

'Thank you' said Morris bashfully

'Otherwise you'd be back in the factory, making holes for polo mints, wouldn't you lad?' said Bourhill

All the commandos and Clyde laugh, Bourhill grabs Morris's leg.

'Sir, this is Private Morris, our medic, I'm sure you'd have a good grasp of what he's like by now' said Farrell

Clyde smiles and nods at Morris.

'Morris, do you want to introduce the lads?' said Farrell

'Yes Sergeant. With pleasure' said Morris who turns to look at Bourhill so he can rib him first as a way of getting his own back and smiles in anticipation of making Bourhill look silly.

Bourhill hated Morris when they first met and had on a couple of occasions given Morris a black eye and a burst lip, one occasion when they were training in Scotland they managed to find a local pub and after a few drinks Morris started teasing Bourhill about how bad Scotland was. After five minutes of berating Scotland albeit tongue in cheek to wind Bourhill up Morris ended up flat on his back knocked out cold with Bourhill being held back by some of the other commandos, but since then they served together and had become good friends.

'This is Lance Corporal *Frank Bourhill*' said Morris with fervour

Bourhill nods at Clyde.

'He's our sniper. He's a typical Jock though, drinks like a fish and won't buy a round' said Morris

Bourhill kicks at Morris but he moves away.

'He's that tight he only ever breathes in' said Morris

The Commandos all laugh, Bourhill sits up and tries to grab Morris.

'Once, I saw him pull out a shilling from his wallet and the sunlight made the King squint' said Morris

All the commandos laugh.

'You cheeky bugger' said Bourhill

Bourhill grabs Morris and pulls him to the floor and tries to wrestle with him.

'Come on lads. Behave yourselves' said Farrell sternly

Bourhill lets go of Morris, Morris stands up, Farrell turns to Clyde.

'They're the best of friends really' said Farrell

'Right, this is Private Thomas Smith or Smudge as we call him, he's into explosives, he's a Kiwi Rugby player hence his cauliflower ears' said Morris

'Good to meet you Sir' said Smith

Smith was in his late 20's and was powerfully built, his Father was a Maori and his Mother was English, he had served in the New Zealand Army until the chance came to join the newly formed commandos. Smith was a gentleman and a true warrior, he always seemed to be smiling but could change into aggressive in a heartbeat, he too had an altercation with Morris when they first met as Smith didn't drink alcohol as he was a devout Christian and Morris didn't seem to understand why he wouldn't drink. One night in the local pub whilst training in Scotland Morris kept ordering gin and tonic for Smith and told him it was Scottish lemonade.

After a few drinks Morris couldn't help but laugh as Smith stumbled when he stood up to go to the toilet, then he let slip that he'd spiked his drinks and Smith knocked out Morris' two front teeth, it took five commandos to hold him back from Morris but as with Bourhill they too became good friends after serving in the field together.

'Next up, Corporal Arthur Clarke, he's our signals man, loves the sound of his own voice and likes to think of himself as a bit of a lady's man' said Morris

'Hello Sir' said Clarke

Clarke was of average height, average build and had slick dark hair swept neatly back, he was very fond of bryllcream and using too much aftershave. He was from a working-class background but liked to take care of his looks. He wasn't married as he liked to play the field and rather than spend his money on horses or in the pub he liked to wine and dine the local women and spend money on nice suits.

'Although I don't know why, the bloody tide wouldn't go out with him' said Morris

All the commandos laugh.

'You're only jealous Morris' said Clarke who smiled, he was at ease with himself and didn't mind Morris jesting the way he did.

'Last but not least is Private Harry Evans or Taff as we know him' said Morris

Evans was in his late 20's and hailed from the Rhondda Valley in South Wales, he was married with two children and he was a placid man, it took a lot to get a rise out of Evans as he was so laid back, but make no mistake, he did have a mean streak. Due to his outlook on life on first thoughts he may have been judged as lazy, he was one of the most driven, fit and most organised men in the group and sometimes his laid back attitude and slow drawl led people to think that he wasn't intelligent when in fact he had passed his 11 plus and attended a secondary modern, in those days only the cleverest boys attended such schools.

'Hello Sir' said Evans

'He's from Wales, where the men are men and the sheep are scared' said Morris

The commandos laugh and look at Evans in wait of one of his usual brilliant one liners to put Morris back in his place.

'Well, you'd know all about that wouldn't you Moz?' said Evans

All the commandos laugh a lot louder than usual, Clyde looks confused and looks at Farrell who is awaiting Evans' response.

'Don't start that Taff' said Morris whose tone has changed completely

'Go on Taff, tell Major Clyde the story' said Farrell

Evans smiles as he sits up and smiles, it's a tale he's told before but it never gets old.

'Ok' said Evans as he glances at Morris 'One day on exercise in the Brecon Beacons…'

'No, no, you're wrong…' interrupted Morris

'Stay out of it Moz' barked Farrell as he looked at Morris, he then spoke softly 'Go on Taff'

'Ok, there were lots of sheep and we'd been out there for two weeks' said Evans

'Don't believe a word Sir' interrupted Morris who looks at Farrell staring back with his eyes burning into him

'Anyway, all I'll say is Moz was caught in a compromising situation with a sheep' said Evans who opens his hands out as if to say, make what you will of it.

All the commandos laugh and Clyde does also.

'Sir, I was having a pee and Evans walked over and heard a noise in the bushes and shone his torch onto me and a sheep was stood in front of me, that's all' said Morris

All the commandos laugh even louder now as they love this story being told to new ears.

'Honestly Sir, I was having a pee, I hadn't a clue it was there' said Morris

'Acchh bollocks' snarled Bourhill in his Scottish accent 'Why do you still send it flowers then Moz?'

All the men except Morris laugh, Bourhill laughs loudest at his own joke as he doesn't really get to tell many funny ones.

'I've even heard you talk about her in your sleep' said Bourhill who again laughs the loudest.

'Honestly Sir, I wasn't' said Morris

Evans looks at Clyde and winks as if to say Morris is right and they're only winding him up, Clyde smiles and nods. Morris turns to Evans and tries to slap him around the ear, Evans catches his arm and pushes it away and laughs.

'They're a good bunch Sir' said Farrell

'I can tell that they are' said Clyde

The commando's laughter dies out and they look to Clyde awaiting him to tell them about himself.

'Right then, so that leaves me' said Clyde who looks around the room to see all the commandos staring back at him in anticipation 'Originally I'm from the Royal Engineers I'm an assault engineer'

The commandos look at Clyde and nod in appreciation, at least he's no pencil neck.

'Since 1940 I've infiltrated the German army and played a part in organising the St Nazierre raid. I've assassinated a few high-ranking Officers and pulled back the German High Command from the front line with a bit of deception for today's invasion' said Clyde

The commandos look impressed, Farrell looks at his watch, and the time is 15:30hrs, Clyde notices.

'That's it really. I'm sure there'll come a time when we can talk in more detail' said Clyde as he knows the commandos have to get ready for the mission.

'Right lads, we have a full briefing at 16:00hrs in Colonel Carmonts office, then we've got to be good to go at 20:00hrs, ok? See you all later' said Farrell

Farrell and Clyde exit the room.

Countryside – French/Belgian Border

Morris looks out of the gap in between the sand bags looking out into the countryside through his binoculars, the countryside is eerily quiet, there's not even a hint of noise from the wind or from birds singing in the trees.

'We've not seen anything for weeks' said Morris

'I know' said Clarke who looks fed up as he's cold, damp and hungry 'At least we're not on cold rations anymore'

Morris continues to search the nearby countryside, if a V1 rocket was fired they'd certainly be able to hear it as it was so quiet.

'Get a brew on Clarkey, I could murder a cup of tea' said Morris

Clarke laboriously crawls over to his rucksack and pulls out a paraffin stove and prepares it ready to boil the water to make a cup of tea, Morris looks out into the distance through his binoculars.

'It's getting bloody cold now, it must be what? October? November?' said Morris

Clarke sets up the stove and lights it and as the flame burns he puts his hands over the flame then rubs them together to warm them up.

'It's mid-September Moz' said Clarke

'Bloody hell' said Morris as he shook his head in disbelief

Clarke puts a mess tin on the floor and pours water into it from his canteen then places the mess tin on top of the paraffin burner, he then pulls out a tin of corned beef and places that into the mess tin to warm up for their breakfast, Morris watches on.

'Corned bloody beef, if I never eat corned beef again it'll be too soon' said Morris

'Shut your bloody moaning Moz' said Bourhill who is just waking up and seems groggy, he leans up and rubs his eyes then pulls out his cigarette case and throws a cigarette to Morris, one to Clarke and lights one for himself and blows out the smoke.

'It is bloody cold though, I'll give you that Moz' said Bourhill

Bourhill leans forward and warms his hands on the stoves flame and rubs them together whilst holding the cigarette in his mouth. He then leans back and picks up three enamel mugs from the side of the observation post then pulls out three tea bags from his rucksack and drops a tea bag in each cup then passes them to Clarke.

'Robin, this is wren' said Clyde over the radio as he was in another observation post a small distance away, Clarke picks up the radio holding it to his ear.

'Go ahead Wren' said Clarke

'Pack your gear up, we're moving out tonight at 22:00hrs' said Clyde

Morris, Clarke and Bourhill smile as all three manage to hear what was said over the radio.

'Received over' said Clarke

'I'll pop over shortly, keep your eyes peeled' said Clyde

'Roger' said Clarke

Clarke places the receiver back onto the radio, all three men look at one another as they smile.

'Bloody hell eh? I thought we were here for the duration' said Clarke

'If I'd have had corned beef one more time… I'd have turned myself in' said Morris half joking

'Aye, what if the Germans fed you corned beef once you did?' said Bourhill

'Then I'd go berserk and kill them all. End the war single handed, no more bloody corned beef for me thank you' said Morris

Clarke warms his hands on the stove alongside Bourhill, Morris is still looking out into the countryside, Bourhill then crawls to the exit of the observation post.

'Just going for a pee lads, I'll check the perimeter too' said Bourhill

'The brews will be ready in five minutes' said Clarke

Bourhill picks up his rifle and exits the observation post slowly, Clarke continues to warm his hands on the flames.

'What are you going to do when it's all over Clarkey' asked Morris as he scanned to countryside through his binoculars

'I don't know, probably work down the pit' said Clarke as he continued to warm his hands and smoke his cigarette

'I've heard its good money. I might try for that too' said Morris

'Are there any coal mines down in London Moz?' queried Clarke as he looked to Morris intriguingly, Morris turned around in deep thought.

'No, no I don't think there are' said Morris

'Well you're knackered then, aren't you?' said Clarke

'Yes, I suppose I am' said Morris who then smiled as he turned back to search the horizon

'My Uncle George works at the one down the road from my house, the last time I saw him he said he'd get me a job there once I get de-mobilised' said Clarke

There is a rustle outside the observation post, Morris and Clarke look towards the entrance and Clyde crawls in.

'How you doing lads?' said Clyde

Clarke and Morris seem pleased to see Clyde as they haven't seen any of the other commandos for the past two days and want to pick his brains about when they'll return to base so they can eat proper food, get clean, warm and dry.

'Good Sir' said Clarke who exchanges glances with Morris 'So what's happening tonight then?'

'As you'd have probably guessed by now, they're not launching the doodlebugs from this area anymore' said Clyde

'We haven't seen one for a while' interrupted Clarke, Clyde nods to hurry Clarke as he wants to finish what he was saying.

'The reason being is they can't reach England now as we've almost pushed them out of France' said Clyde as he lets that information sink in, Morris and Clarke grow wide smiles as it's the first they've heard about how the Allies were doing in France for quite some time, they both fist pumped the air jubilantly.

Clyde had his own reasons to be cheerful, it now gives him the chance to see whether Anna remained in Lille or went back to Germany.

'So, with that in mind, there's no need for us to be here' said Clyde

'That sounds good to me Sir' said Morris who along with all the other commandos had no real idea whereabouts they were, whether they were in France, Belgium or even Germany they did not know for certain. What they did know is that they were parachuted behind enemy lines some weeks before.

'We're to pack up and head west and meet up with the 103rd Royal Artillery' said Clyde

Morris and Clarke both look at each other as if surprised to find out that the artillery is so close, they'd been behind enemy lines for so long and thought they still were as they didn't have much contact with headquarters other than radioing in whenever they saw a rocket, thought they hadn't seen one for weeks.

'Artillery? I thought we were behind the lines, Sir?' said Morris

'We've not been behind the lines for a good few weeks so I'm told, we're pushing into Holland as we speak' said Clyde

Again, Morris and Clarke look at each other and seem happy as they both have smiles on their faces but they still can't believe they're not behind enemy lines anymore.

'Bloody hell, we've been keeping low and there's nobody about' said Morris

243

'That's it Moz, but they were still firing the doodlebugs, but not from anywhere around here' said Clyde

'So…do you think we'll be going into Holland or Germany after this Sir?' said Clarke

'I don't know Clarkey, we'll find out once we're back. Let's get packed up and get ourselves something *proper* to eat' said Clyde who along with all the others was sick and tired of at first being on cold rations then onto half rations for the last two weeks as supplies were low.

'I'm with you on that one Sir' said Morris

Bourhill crawls into the observation post.

'Everything's clear out there' said Bourhill as he crawls in and notices Clyde 'Sorry, good morning Sir.

'Everything should be clear mate, we're moving into Holland, we're well behind the front line' said Morris

Bourhill looks to Clyde for him to back up the claim that they're safe, Clyde nods.

'Bloody hell, well that's good' said Bourhill

'We're moving west to meet up with the 103rd Royal Artillery just East of Orchies' said Clyde

'Artillery?' said Bourhill surprised 'We must be bloody miles from the front line. What time are we leaving?'

'22:00hrs' said Clyde

'Great, let's get packed up then' said Bourhill

As morning breaks, the commandos walk along a country road not walking with any apprehension of ambush as they're well behind the lines, Clyde, Smith, Farrell and Bourhill walk on one side and Clarke, Evans and Morris on the other walk single file, Farrell looks through his binoculars towards the distance and notices a convoy further up ahead around 1 mile away and is heading towards them on the dirt road.

'Here we go lads, this must be them' called Farrell

Clyde looks through his binoculars and notices the convoy, he stops and turns to the commandos.

'Right lads, we'll just wait here for them' said Clyde

The commandos stop, with Bourhill scanning the surrounding area through his scope to make sure there isn't anybody around, even though they are well behind the front line the commandos still check just in case.

The other commandos each take off their rucksacks and sit at the side of the road in anticipation of the oncoming convoy.

Ten minutes later the convoy approaches and at the front of the convoy is an armoured car with an Officer looking out of the top of it, the armoured car stops in front of the commandos and the Officer salutes Clyde and he salutes back.

'You must be the commandos then?' said the Officer, a man in his forties with blonde hair and a slightly darker moustache to match.

'Indeed we are. You must be the 103rd artillery? asked Clyde

'That's right, were heading to Lille to meet up with the 12th Royal Engineers' said the Captain

'Lille?' said Clyde

'Yes, that's right. We have space on board one of the trucks further down, just jump aboard' said the Captain

The information takes a little longer than anticipated to sink in, Clyde will be going back to Lille and potentially meeting up with Anna.

'We must be going Major, we're already behind schedule' said the Captain

The Captain salutes Clyde and then smacks the top of the armoured car then it moves away, the commandos each climb into the truck behind the armoured car and the convoy moves on.

Lille, bloody hell. I hope Anna's still there.

Clyde is excited, he's the first into the back of the truck and is grinning from ear to ear, he hopes Anna is still there, he hopes she got caught up in the liberation and was kept out of the loop of the German army and got left behind.

He wonders what Anna will think of his new position in the British Army and whether she will want to be with him, he thinks that's a chance he will have to take, if she loved him before then she should still, regardless of who he fights for.

Clyde leans around the side of the truck to see the commandos walking beside it slowly and gets impatient, they're slowing him down and preventing him from seeing Anna sooner.

'Come on lads, hurry up' barks Clyde

The commandos look at Clyde not expecting an Officer to bark out orders, Farrell too didn't expect it but like a good Sergeant backs up the order with more gusto.

'You heard the Major, come on' shouts Farrell 'Move it, move it'

The commandos scurry to the back of the truck and climb in with great speed, the driver of the truck looks through his side mirror and can't see the commandos anymore, a tap on his shoulder signifies that it time to move on and catch up with the armoured car so it sets off with the rest of the convoy in tow just behind.

Chapter 20 – Familiar Faces

The convoy of vehicles drives slowly through the streets of Lille. Clyde and Farrell are sat at the back of the truck looking out to the crowds of French civilians waving and cheering at the troops moving through the City.

Morris leans out to the back of the truck and waves back blowing kisses to all of the women, the other commandos begin to pull back the canvass on the truck so they can get a better look. As they pull it back they start to wave at the crowd and civilians run up and the commandos pull them up into the truck and wave alongside them, the convoy slows even further as it drives past 'Le Grand Hotel'. Clyde looks up at the Hotel and spots the blast marks from the explosion in Stechens room and points to it.

'Sergeant, you see that room' said Clyde

Farrell looks up to see the scorch marks on the side of an exploded room with its blackened curtains flailing in the wind.

'The one which has been blown up Sir?' said Farrell

'That's the one' said Clyde with a sense of pride 'I planted explosives in there for Colonel Stechen, he slaughtered 100 of the Norfolk Regiment…in cold blood'

Sergeant Farrell looks up and stares at the scorch marks outside the exploded hotel room and shakes his head.

'The bastard' said Farrell as he spits on the road outside 'Good on you Sir'

The convoy moves past the hotel and struggles to move through the crowd, Clyde looks around and then stands up and shuffles through the truck and leans into the driver.

'Where is it in Lille we're setting up camp?' said Clyde

The driver leans his head back but keeps his eyes on the road so he doesn't drive into the back of the armoured car in front if it stops due to the civilians that are congratulating the convoy.

'North West of the City, there's an old stadium we'll be using' said the Driver

Clyde nods as he knows where this is, but it means that the convoy wont drive past Anna's house so he'd have to either go to the stadium first then come back or jump out on the way and walk there.

With Clyde being excited about being back in Lille with the chance of being reunited with Anna if she's still there his mind is already made up.

'Yes. I know where you mean' said Clyde

Clyde shuffles through the truck and back over to Sergeant Farrell.

'Sergeant, there's a bit of business I need to sort out here, I'll meet you back at the stadium' said Clyde

'Ok Sir' said Farrell 'Do you want us to come with you?'

The commandos each look to Clyde awaiting his response, it would mean they had to wait a bit longer for a hot shower, a shave, a good meal and a comfortable sleep. He wouldn't begrudge them of that.

'No, it's ok, I'll be fine. I know my way around here' said Clyde as he gets ready to climb from the truck as it slows due to the crowds in the street.

'See you in a bit lads' said Clyde

Clyde climbs over the side of the truck and jumps to the road below, as soon as he lands he is hugged and kissed by the civilians, the convoy slowly continues to move through the crowd.

'See you later Sir' shouts Morris who is relieved he didn't have to go with him, he was desperate for a decent meal and a hot shower

Morris and the commandos wave at Clyde as he's mobbed by the crowd, Clyde struggles to wave back amongst the handshakes and hugs but ducks down and moves through the crowd and into a back street.

'Vive la France' shouts an onlooker

Clyde smiles at the onlooker and continues to walk down the empty side street, he then hears footsteps behind him and as he turns around to look there are two young boys marching behind him with sticks being held as weapons over the shoulder, he stops and the young boys do also.

'Here you go lads' said Clyde as he pulls out some boiled sweets and hands them to the young boys and pats them on the head then turns and walks away down the street.

Twenty minutes later Clyde gets to the top of Anna's street. Dried out brown leaves blow across the street an elderly resident struggles to brush them up outside her house, he stops for a moment as he spots a black patch on the road further up ahead, this is the place were Chevalier blew both him and Jaeger to pieces, it has been a while but the marks were still visible.

He starts to walk up the street whilst looking around wondering what happened to the other German Officers and whether they had taken Anna with them when they fled the City. In no time at all he was stood at the bottom of the steps to Anna's house looking at the front door, then he looks down to the scorch marks on the cobbled road and then back to the front door and notices there wasn't much damage to the door so perhaps Anna wasn't harmed in the explosion.

What do I say to her? How do I explain I was a spy? Will she even be here?

Then the front door opens and Anna is stood at the door with Clyde staring back.

'Lukas?' said Anna with her eyes wide open in shock

Clyde smiles then begins to walk up the steps.

'Lukas' said Anna as she realises it is definitely him

Anna rushes out and meets Clyde at the top of the stairs and hugs him tightly, Clyde hugs back and kisses her forehead, Anna pulls away and kisses Clyde passionately on the lips.

'Come inside quickly, the Army pulled out of here a while back, you need to be careful' said Anna who grabs Clyde by the arm and pulls him inside the house whilst checking the street for anybody watching

Clyde smiles at Anna and they both walk inside the house into the living room, he then takes off his beret.

'You need to be careful, there are British…troops…everywhere…' said Anna as she looks confused as she looks at the uniform Clyde is wearing as it isn't a German one, it's British.

'Why are you wearing that Uniform?' said Anna

Clyde fiddles with his beret as he looks to the floor then back up to Anna and smiles awkwardly as he looks at her.

'There's something I need to tell you' said Clyde

Anna looks at Clyde and is confused.

'I'm British' said Clyde

Anna takes a step backwards and looks at Clyde in a distrusting way.

'Lukas…but how?' said Anna

'My name's not Lukas. It's Bradley Clyde. I've been undercover since the start of the war' said Clyde

Anna sits down slowly as she struggles to comprehend what she has just been told, she then stares at the floor then back to Clyde.

'But how? Why? Why did you…? I just…don't understand' said Anna

Anna stands up, shakes her head in disbelief and starts to pace the room.

'I'm glad to see you Anna, I didn't think you'd be here, I thought you may have moved out with the other families' said Clyde

Anna stops pacing to look at Clyde.

'I was waiting for you. I wanted us to be together. You said you'd be back for me' said Anna

Did I say I'd come back for her? I thought I told her to stay with her Mother in Berlin for a few weeks? Yes, Yes, I did thinks Clyde

'I thought you were going to stay with your Mother in Berlin?' said Clyde

Anna allows that information to sink in.

'I did, for a few weeks. Then I came back as you told me to' said Anna

Hang on a minute, I asked her to go to Berlin before Jaeger was killed. If she had, then Chevalier would still be alive thinks Clyde

'Why didn't you go to Berlin when I asked you to?' said Clyde

'I went as quickly as I could' replied Anna quickly 'I had to stay and sort out the funeral and put on a brave face whilst I waited for you to contact me'

Clyde looks out through the window and knows Anna has a point.

'But once he died I saw no point in going to Berlin in case I missed you. But you left me in limbo, I didn't know what to do and I got caught up I grief, worry and indecision and I was left behind by the Army' said Anna

Clyde feels guilty, after what happened to Jaeger he had stayed away from her house, he knew she lived there but didn't want to bring attention to himself by walking down a street full of German Officers and dating one of their dead friend's wife. He merely hung around Lille in the Grand Hotel and the café in the hope that he'd bump into her.

Yes, I suppose she's right.

'Well…I'm here for you. I'm back' said Clyde

Anna looks angry.

'I could have been killed. I could have been shot…' said Anna

Clyde walks over and cuddles Anna.

'No, you wouldn't have done. The British wouldn't do something like that' said Clyde

'Don't give me that, what about Dresden?' said Anna as she pushes Clyde back to look into his eyes so she can stress her point 'They've bombed Dresden down to the ground'

Clyde looks out of the window as he's embarrassed, he can't look her in the eye and come up with a good excuse for Dresden, it wasn't his fault obviously, he had nothing whatsoever to do with it. Anna pushes him away and takes a step back.

'That was Dresden…and it was a bombing campaign, anyway you're here, you're safe and you're with me' said Clyde

Anna digests what Clyde has told her, she is struggling to come to terms with the information that Clyde isn't German.

'That's not the point' said Anna as she prods her thin bony finger into his chest 'Why did you lie to me?'

Clyde laughs and grabs her hand pulling it down so he can hold her closely.

'Anna, I needed to, I'm a bloody spy' said Clyde as he hugs her gently
'Anyway, does it matter? I'm back. We can be together now'

'Does it matter you lied to me?' said Anna as she pushes him away again 'Of course it matters'

'Anna, I wasn't lying to you, I love you, I had to do what I did otherwise I'd have been shot' said Clyde as he tiresomely stresses his point to try and get her back on board, he'd been holed up in the countryside freezing his arse off thinking of Anna every day, he doesn't need this palaver. Anna looks away and then back to Clyde.

'You love me?' said Anna with a hint of a smile breaking out along with a raised eyebrow, Clyde notices and sees that he's making progress.

'Yes, I want us to be together' said Clyde as moves forwards and pulls her close, she doesn't resist

'Really?' said Anna naively

'Yes, cross my heart' said Clyde

Anna smiles and rubs her wedding ring finger then looks back to Clyde.

'I love you too' said Anna

They kiss passionately, Clyde runs his hands over Anna's shoulders and starts to undo her top buttons on her cardigan, Anna pulls away.

Don't do this to me, I've not bloody seen you for months.

'Upstairs' said Anna

That's music to my ears.

Anna grabs Clyde's hand and they walk out of the room and upstairs to the bedroom.

A few hours' later Clyde and Anna walk up to the stadium and Military Police officers guard the entrance, as Clyde approaches the MPs salute and raise the barrier for Clyde.

Just inside the compound Morris and Smith walk whilst struggling to holding a mess tin with hot soup, an enamel cup with boiling hot tea, they have pockets filled with scones, cake and sausage rolls and they're stuffing sandwiches into their mouths as they walk, they notice Clyde.

'There's Major Clyde' mumbles Smith through the egg and cress sandwich he'd just taken a large bite from. Morris looks up and smiles through a mouth full of chewed ham, cheese and pickle as he's impressed with the beauty of Anna and impressed that Clyde's managed to get a woman of this high calibre, he smiles wryly as he chews and swallows.

'Bloody hell, there's no flies on him is there' said Morris as he finishes chewing his last bite and swallows 'Two hours we've been in Lille and he's already got a woman. He hasn't even had a shower'

Smith chuckles, Clarke notices Clyde and walks over to Morris and Smith.

'Who's the woman?' said Clarke

'I don't know mate' said Smith as he drinks the soup from his mess tin as he has no spoon

'I wonder if she's got a friend?' said Clarke who was rolling a cigarette

'Yeah' said Morris who took another bite from his ham, cheese and pickle sandwich 'I wonder if she's got…a few friends' mumbled Morris through the food in his mouth

Clyde is kissing Anna goodbye at the gate.

'I'll see you later, I'll come to your house around 9pm' said Clyde

'Ok, I'll see you later' said Anna who couldn't smile any wider if she tried, her bright white teeth stood out like a beacon in the dusky evening along with her blonde hair.

Anna walks away and Clyde turns and walks into the camp and notices Morris, Smith and Clarke stood watching him smiling.

'No flies on you are there Sir?' said Morris

Clyde smiles and walks over to the commandos, the commandos think that Clyde had just met Anna on the street, they have no idea that they have history.

'I met Anna whilst undercover' said Clyde

'Blooming heck, I bet she had the shock of her life when she saw you wearing that uniform eh?' said Morris

'Aye, she did' said Clyde as he smiled 'Where's Sergeant Farrell?'

'He's in the ablutions taking a shower, Sir' said Smith

Clyde notices the commando's pockets are packed with food, it makes his mouth water even though Anna did manage to make him some food, her supplies were scarce, he couldn't wait to get to the officer's mess and see what was on offer.

'Ok, where is the HQ?' said Clyde

'On the half way line Sir' said Morris who then takes a large swig of his soup from his mess tin, he also didn't have a spoon, nobody did.

'Cheers lads, I'll see you in a bit, I need to debrief' said Clyde

'See you later Sir' said the commandos

Clyde walks off and the commandos look at Morris awaiting some quip or smart remark.

'He's already been *de-briefed*, by his Mrs I bet' said Morris

The commandos laugh.

Moments later Clyde walks into a large tent on the football pitch which is the headquarters for troops in Lille, the tent is a hive of activity as Officers bustle about with purpose, Clyde holds his arm out and stops an Officer who is walking briskly holding a brown file.

'Excuse me Major, is Colonel Carmont here?' said Clyde

'Sorry Sir, I don't know of a Colonel Carmont' said the Major as he carries on walking

Shit, where the bloody hell is he? I wonder if Stapleton is here?

Clyde looks around the room to see if he can recognise anyone, he spots a Corporal in his tracks, the Corporal salutes him and he replicates.

'Who's in charge?' said Clyde

'You're better off speaking with Brigadier Somersby Sir' said the Corporal as he points to the Brigadier further down the tent.

'Thank you' said Clyde

Clyde walks over to the Brigadier and waits beside him and as the Brigadier looks at a map of Lille, he glances at Clyde.

'Sir, Major Clyde from the 12th regiment' said Clyde

Brigadier Somersby looks at Clyde with trepidation as he doesn't recognise Clyde.

'Hello Major, what can I do for you?' said Somersby as he cumbersomely turns around. The Brigadier is tall, well-built and well fed with greying ginger hair and a thick moustache. They both salute each other with Somersby doing so with a lot less vigour.

'Sir, we need to debrief, we've been out in the field for a few months and need to know what we are to do next' said Clyde

Brigadier Somersby is clearly involved in other things more important than what to do with Clyde and his commandos, Clyde thought they'd have had a better reception that this but due to the long days and pressure on Brigadier Somersby's shoulders he doesn't want to shoulder any more responsibility if he can help it.

'Who's your CO?' said Somersby as a way of brushing him off, so that he'll pursue his commanding officer

'Colonel Carmont, Sir' said Clyde

Brigadier Somersby now realises that Clyde must be of some importance as he knows Colonel Carmont well, he knows anybody that usually answers to him personally is usually from good stock.

'Oh dear, I'm afraid Carmont is at Arnhem, so you'll struggle to speak to him' said Somersby

Clyde looks at Somersby expecting someone else to have taken over, maybe Arthur Stapleton.

'What about Arthur Stapleton?' asks Clyde as Somersby shakes his head.

'Sorry. I don't know that name' said Somersby as he turns away and looks back at the map with a Captain stood beside him awaiting instruction, Clyde feels aggrieved that he's been brushed off. He's cold, he's hungry and he's tired.

'What does that mean for *us*...Sir?' said Clyde sternly, not meaning to but it came out that way as he was frustrated.

Brigadier Somersby is busy but wants to give Clyde the time of day to have a decent conversation with him but not now and maybe not even later on either. Somersby turns and looks at Clyde apologetically as he sighs.

'Well Major, let's have a chat in my office tomorrow at 11:00hrs' said Somersby

Clyde looks around the tent as to find the Brigadiers office, Somersby remembers that he's new and doesn't know the layout of the headquarters.

'Major, it's just on your left to the back of the tent' said Somersby

Clyde spots the office right at the back past the numerous amounts of other officers in the tent who are engaged in preparations for their own missions and tasks.

'Ok Sir' said Clyde 'What are we to do in the meantime?'

Brigadier Somersby shrugs, he's desperate to get back to the map and his planning, he doesn't have the time for Clyde.

'Just sit tight. Enjoy Lille if you wish' said Somersby

'Very good Sir, see you tomorrow at 11:00hrs' said Clyde

They salute each other and Clyde walks away pushing past the officers in the packed tent as he goes.

Outside the tents an old oil drum has been filled with wood and as the flames rise from the fire inside, the commandos stand around it warming their hands, Sergeant Farrell pulls out a hip flask with Brandy in it and takes a swig of it then passes it around to the other commandos who each take a sip.

Morris pulls out a pack of cigarettes and passes them around and the commandos each take one and light them.

'It's getting bloody cold now eh?' said Smith who had finished his food, he had his arms folded in front of him as he huddled next to the fire with his collar flicked up on his jacket.

'You should be used to it by now Smudge' said Bourhill who wasn't as affected as much by the cold as Smith

'Used to it, yes' said Smith 'Do I like it, no'

Bourhill looks away to see Clyde walking over to them.

'Ey up lads, here's the Major' said Bourhill

The commandos look to see Clyde walking over to them, as Clyde joins them Farrell passes him the hip flask.

'Thank you Sergeant' said Clyde who takes a sip from the hip flask and passes it back to Farrell.

'Right lads, we're to sit tight in Lille until further notice' said Clyde who looked around to the eager commandos 'We're only allowed over the wire *in pairs* and when you do, needless to say, take your weapons with you'

The commandos look at each other and smile thinking that after a long time out in the field they get the chance to enjoy the simple pleasures in life, maybe find the nearest pub and brothel.

As they'd returned to headquarters they had claimed their pay packets so had money to spend and due to the nature of their jobs they didn't know if they'd survive from one day to the next so liked to enjoy spending their money whether it be in pubs, betting shops or brothels apart from Clarke, he didn't really want to stoop so low as to be seen walking into a brothel, he'd usually climb in through the top window and try to charm the women into getting his kicks for free and more often than not, succeeded.

'Are we allowed to drink then Sir?' said Morris

The commandos look at Clyde who looks to Farrell and back to the commandos.

'I don't see why not, just take it easy' said Clyde to the smiling commandos eager to sample the Lille nightlife

'We will Sir' said Smith

'We heading out then lads?' said Bourhill

'I'm up for it' said Evans

'Me too' said Smith

'I'll hang about here Sir. I've seen an old mate of mine' said Farrell

'Ok lads, meet back here tomorrow at 10:00hrs' said Clyde as he looked at the commandos who all seemly had cheeky grins beaming from their faces 'Do take care now won't you lads?'

'Yes Sir' said Morris with aplomb

The commandos all walk briskly away whilst Farrell and Clyde stand beside the fire.

'What will you do Sir?' said Farrell

'I've got to see Brigadier Somersby tomorrow so I'll go back and see Anna' said Clyde

Sergeant Farrell doesn't know who she is, he presumes that it's the woman from before who the commandos were talking about.

'Is that...your Mrs, Sir?' asked Farrell

'Yes Sergeant' said Clyde

Farrell thinks for a moment.

'Do you need a chaperone?' asked Farrell

Clyde realises that he'd walked through Lille on his own earlier without a chaperone, if Anna had been left behind maybe other Germans had or maybe Clyde could get mugged for his cigarettes and wallet in some dark alley and thought if he's going back into Lille, it's probably best he takes Farrell with him.

'I will need one, just to be safe, if you don't mind' said Clyde

'Not at all Sir, I'll be glad to see a bit of the City' said Farrell

Chapter 21 – No Rest for the Wicked

A few days later Clyde stands outside of Anna's front door, behind him in the street is a Bedford truck with the commandos inside all geared up to go back out behind enemy lines to carry on scouting for the new V2 rockets being firing at Antwerp, they were a lot quicker and were much harder to defend against than the V1 they previously scouted. They don't know how long they will be away but this time but Clyde knows Anna will be waiting for him when he returns, he turns to look at the commandos in the truck and then back to the worried Anna who is stood at the open front door.

'I'll be back soon, hopefully in time for Christmas' said Clyde reassuringly to his worried girlfriend

'I hope so, be careful out there' said Anna

'I will. You be careful too, remember if you need any more rations you speak to the Brigadier ok?' said Clyde

'Yes, yes, I know' said Anna

'Well, you're eating for two now, you need to keep your strength up' said Clyde

With the commandos being in Lille for a few weeks, Clyde and Anna had spent a lot of time together. After their first night together Anna had fallen pregnant, she woke up one-day vomiting and had gone to see the local Doctor who'd confirmed she was pregnant, when she told Clyde he was over the moon, he didn't have children and was so in love with Anna he couldn't have asked for more. After that they'd taken a short break in Paris and that was where Clyde had proposed to Anna.

She was still in the early stages of pregnancy and Clyde didn't want her to worry and he wanted to make sure she was well fed whilst he was away, he didn't know how long they would be away for and that worried him but he didn't show it.

'I know; I'll take it easy' said Anna

'If you need anything, anything at all, speak to the Brigadier' said Clyde

'Yes, I know' said Anna

Anna looks up to the back of the truck where the commandos are and they're looking at them both cuddle on top of the steps.

'Time to go, your friends are waiting for you' said Anna

Anna and Clyde kiss and the commandos all cheer, Anna waves at the commandos and Clyde walks out into the street and climbs up into the back of the truck.

'See you soon' shouts Clyde

Anna waves at Clyde and the commandos.

'Take care love' shouts Morris

The truck drives away and Clyde continues to wave at Anna and blows kisses to her.

North-West German Countryside

The faint white silhouettes of parachutes glide gracefully to the snowy ground against the backdrop of the night sky followed by a dull thud of boots hitting the ground at a faster pace and the jangle of the commando's equipment as they land can be heard amongst the coos from an owl nearby.

The moonlight shines upon the commandos as they take off their parachutes and fold them up then take their weapons out to cover the area, the commandos are camouflaged well in their white uniforms to match the snowy environment.

Morris folds his parachute away as Bourhill digs a hole in the snow beside a hedgerow to bury the parachutes in, the rest of the commandos are crouched covering the area whilst Farrell crouches next to Clyde as they look at a map of the area.

'Right, we pitch there at the observation post and monitor that main road' said Clyde as he points at the map with a sharp pencil 'tonight we send out a reconnaissance patrol but still keep eyes on the road'

'Right Sir' said Farrell

Farrell looks around to see Bourhill hiding the parachutes in the hole in the ground and Smith is helping him do so, Bourhill covers the parachutes with soil then snow and looks to Farrell and gives him the thumbs up.

'Right lads, let's move' said Farrell

The commandos jog at the side of the hedgerow for a few miles then Clyde stops and holds his hand up gesturing for the others to stop and crouch also, he turns to Farrell who is behind him and pulls out his map and holds it in between them both, a few hundred yards away there is a farm house with the lights on, Clyde leans in to whisper to Farrell.

'There's no bloody farmhouse on this map, are we in the right place?' said Clyde

Farrell takes the map and looks at it, looks at the compass and looks around to see a village in the distance.

'Yes Sir. Definitely the right place, we need to be over in the woods on our left' said Farrell

Sergeant Farrell looks closely at the building on the map then over to the farmhouse with the lights on.

'You're right, there's no building on this map Sir' said Farrell

Clyde looks closely at the map then looks to the woods on his left and then looks towards the farmhouse.

'Should I take some of the men to check it out Sir?' said Sergeant Farrell

'No. Tell the others to move to the observation post and wait. You and I will check out the farmhouse' said Clyde

Farrell appreciates Clyde's courage, he feels as though he's another Sergeant rather than a Major in the way he commands and jumps into things with both feet and never one to shy away from the hard graft. Farrell turns around to the other commandos and ushers them closer.

'Lads. Me and the Major are going to check the farmhouse out. You lot go and wait at the observation point' said Farrell

Smith looks to the other commandos.

'Right lads. Let's move' said Smith

The commandos walk away into the direction of the woods to their left with Farrell and Clyde moving slowly and cautiously towards the farm house.

After a few hundred yards as they approach the farmhouse Clyde stops and lies on the floor careful not to make a sound but still making slight noise due to the crunch of the snow as they lie down to see underneath the hedge to see the farmhouse clearly.

'Can you see anything Sir?' said Farrell

'No, not properly' said Clyde

Farrell crawls up next to Clyde and looks towards the farmhouse where the kitchen window light is on, the curtains are open and a figure walks past the window.

Clyde reaches for his binoculars and looks through them to the farmhouse to the kitchen window. As he watches in anticipation of identifying whoever's in the farm house an engine can be heard approaching the farmhouse.

'Vehicle approaching' whispers Clyde

Farrell and Clyde lay flat to the floor as a car drives towards the farmhouse casting its headlight into their position for a split second then the vehicle drives towards the house and comes to a halt outside.

Clyde raises his head very slowly, pulls around his binoculars to his eyes and looks through his binoculars to see who the visitor is.

'Who are they Sir?' said Farrell

Clyde looks through his binoculars to see two German officers get out of the car and enter the farmhouse, a figure walks past the window of the kitchen and that too is an officer.

Shit. Bloody Germans.

'That's at least three officers in the building' said Clyde

Farrell puts his hand up to silence Clyde as the crunch of footsteps on snow is heard, Clyde and Farrell duck down further as the sound of someone walking towards them gets louder.

A German soldier walks the perimeter of the farm and approaches the hedge where Clyde and Farrell are, both men keep dead still on the floor against the hedge as the soldier walks past, just in front of the hedge.

Clyde reaches to his webbing and pulls out his knife and holds it in front of Sergeant Farrell's face and gestures for him to kill the soldier, Farrell leans back and grabs the knife then kneels up, crouches and slowly walks after the soldier cutting through the hedge and walks at the same pace as the soldier until he stands behind him and in one swift movement grabs the soldier by the chin covering his mouth with his hand to silence the cries for help, pulls his head back and slits his throat.

As the warm blood spirts over Farrell's hand and wrist the soldier gurgles and chokes on his own blood, Farrell gently lays the soldier down onto the floor as to not drop him which may make more noise, he keeps his hand over the soldier's mouth until he drops out of consciousness.

Farrell then leans down to wipe his hand and wrist on the soldier's uniform.

Clyde crawls through the hedge then slowly stands up and looks at Farrell who is breathing heavily. Clyde then nods to the body as if to say he will help move the body further into the hedge and Farrell nods as if to say he is ready, they then push the soldier's body into the hedge so that it can't be seen.

Farrell then places the soldier's weapon into the hedge and wipes his knife on the soldier's uniform and hands it back to Clyde. Both Clyde and Farrell then quickly but quietly hide the body by scooping up snow and putting it on top of the dead body making sure there is no blood tainted snow on show for anyone else to see and bring unwanted attention to the mound of snow underneath the hedge.

Both men check the area to make sure they've left no trace and in the darkness it looks like they haven't, however, the snow around is slightly pink but impossible to see in the dark, they then scamper back to the other side of the hedge.

Was that the right thing to do? Should I have just left him? Shit, too late now.

Clyde then leans over to Farrell and they both crouch to the floor and look towards the kitchen window.

'There's German officers in the house, we need to get Clarkey to call it in and have the RAF blow it to pieces' said Clyde

Probably shouldn't have killed him, I should have just left him and radioed for an airstrike. What if someone finds the body, shit.

'Can we not just go in and kill them?' said Farrell

'No, if anyone finds the bodies with their throats cut they'll know we're in the area, if it's bombed they'll never know' said Clyde

Farrell looks at Clyde then back towards the kitchen window.

'Come on then, let's go' said Farrell

Farrell and Clyde quickly run alongside the hedge row and over the field to the woods where the commandos are hiding.

Moments later they slowly walk in the dark woods and a feint whistle is heard.

'Over here Sir' whispers Evans

Farrell and Clyde walk swiftly over to the commandos.

'Clarkey, where are you?' said Clyde

'Here Sir' said Clarke

Clyde walks over to Clarke and crouches beside him.

'Get me HQ' said Clyde

'Yes Sir' said Clarke as he gets his radio out and hands the head phones to Clyde.

'Big bird this is little robin, are you receiving over' said Clyde as he is handed a map by Farrell, Farrell points at the area where the farmhouse should be with a pencil.

'I'd like to request a bombing raid ASAP' said Clyde

Clyde looks at the map and works out the co-ordinates.

'Just one farmhouse, they may compromise our mission' said Clyde

Clyde looks closer at the map.

'51.692578, 6.379629 over, I repeat 51.692578, 6.379629 over' said Clyde

Clyde looks at Farrell and then to the map.

'Roger' said Clyde

Clyde hands the headset back to Clarke and looks at the commandos.

'They'll be here at dawn, lets dig in here but be prepared to move on if they send more troops after the air strike' said Clyde

'Righto Sir' said Farrell

The commandos pull out their spades and start to dig a hole in the ground preparing a crudely built fox hole to conceal their position for when dawn breaks but still allowing a good view of the farmhouse a few hundred yards in the distance.

A few hours later as dawn is breaking Clyde, Farrell and Bourhill all look towards the farmhouse. Clyde and Farrell look through binoculars and Bourhill looks through the scope on his sniper rifle whilst the other commandos do their best to sleep.

'Sir, what happens if there's survivors?' said Bourhill as he looks through his rifle scope and not taking his eyes away from the farmhouse 'Do you want me to take them out?'

'If anyone is *outside* at the time of the bomb hitting then yes, take them out' said Clyde

Clyde watches a soldier walk out of the house and look around, probably looking for the guard who was on duty the night before who had been killed by Farrell.

'Here's one Sir' said Bourhill

'Keep your eye on him, as soon as the bomb drops take him out' said Clyde

The soldier starts to patrol the perimeter of the house towards the hedges that separate the garden from the fields and is looking around trying to find the soldier who was on duty the night before.

'What about the body Sir?' said Farrell

Clyde looks towards the hedge where the body has been hidden, it is well hidden but the snow around the body has a pink tinge to it.

'Shit' said Clyde

'What's up Sir?' said Farrell

'Look at where the body is, the snows gone pink' said Clyde

Farrell looks to where the body was hidden and the pink snow around it, he then looks to the solider outside who is looking around.

'Bourhill can take him out, if you want to, Sir' said Farrell

Clyde thinks it's best to try and leave it until the very last moment to kill the soldier, he would have liked to do it silently but they stood no chance of getting across the field in the dawn light without being seen, they had no choice to wait and see if the soldier spotted the body then they'd be left no choice than to take him out.

Bourhill could hit him from the distance quite easily but once the shot was fired the people inside the farmhouse would come out and investigate, once they saw the body they would raise the alarm and with the small village not far away there was no telling how many soldiers there were in the village. Clyde thinks maybe they should have just left the soldier to walk past them the night before rather than kill him.

'Have you got eyes on him Bourhill?' said Clyde

'He's in my sight Sir, I can take him anytime, you just say the word' said Bourhill confidently

Where's this bloody air strike?

Farrell looks towards the village through his binoculars.

'I can't see any movement in the Village Sir' said Farrell

'Just keep your eyes on the soldier' said Clyde

The soldier walks along the hedge row looking around the fields and towards the woods.

'He can't see us from there' said Bourhill

An engine can be heard faintly in the distance; the soldier looks towards where the sound is coming from.

'I think that's our air strike Sir' said Farrell

'Bourhill' said Clyde

'Yes Sir?' said Bourhill

'As soon as the plane drops the bomb, take your shot' said Clyde

'Yes Sir' said Bourhill

The sound of the plane's engine can be heard now as it gets closer, the soldier drops his rifle from his shoulder and aims it towards the spitfire that is flying towards the house and as the sound of the engine changes due to the spitfire dropping in altitude.

Bourhill adjusts the sight on his rifle slightly and removes the safety catch ready to fire, Clyde and Farrell watch on through their binoculars.

'Sir?' said Bourhill

'Wait for it' said Clyde

The Spitfire gets closer and closer and as the soldier notices the plane is a Spitfire he fires at the plane diving towards the farmhouse, he has no chance of hitting it but fires at it nonetheless, the shot misses and the soldier then runs away towards the farmhouse, the Spitfire flies overhead and drops its bomb onto the farmhouse.

'Fire' said Clyde

Bourhill fires a shot at the soldier hitting him in the back dropping him to the floor as the house explodes with the Spitfire flying over the explosion.

'Good shot' said Clyde

'Thank you Sir' said Bourhill

The Spitfire flies into the distance and turns and comes back to check the damage, the house has been destroyed and there are no survivors.

Clyde turns to Bourhill and pats him on the back, Bourhill continues to look through the scope on his rifle.

'Right, keep your eyes peeled lads, if anyone survived...kill them' said Clyde

The spitfire's engine grows louder as it flies over the village then back over the farmhouse and then fades off into the distance.

Clyde, Farrell and Bourhill watch on.

'Have you seen anything Sir?' said Farrell

'No, nothing' said Clyde 'What about you Bourhill?'

'Nothing Sir' said Bourhill

Morris slowly crawls up alongside Bourhill.

'Does anyone fancy a brew?' said Morris

'You've already been told Moz, it's cold rations only' said Farrell sternly as Morris laughs

'Only joking Sarge' said Morris as he smiled

Chapter 22 – Stolen Goods

Clyde and the commandos are sat on a Bren carrier as it drives through the snowy streets of Lille, this time there are no crowds, kisses or cheers as the reality sets in of the cold winter and harsh reality that the City needs to rebuild itself financially from the war. The locals grow hungry and war weary and with the cold Winter upon them the reality of it all hits home harder.

The solitary Bren carrier crushes the freshly fallen snow beneath it as the odd civilian walks along the street, Morris flicks a cigarette to the road and a woman passing in the street picks it up and starts to smoke it.

'It's bloody desolate' said Evans

'Its bloody cold' said Smith

Sergeant Farrell takes out his hip flask and holds it out to Smith.

'Here, have a swig of this' said Farrell

Farrell passes Smith his hip flask, Smith struggles to take the top off due to his numb fingers.

'Thanks Sergeant' said Smith

Smith gradually opens the lid with his cold and numb fingers and takes a swig and passes it back to Farrell who holds his hand up.

'No, pass it around' said Farrell

The commandos each take a sip of the whiskey in the hip flask and Clyde sits quietly at the back, Farrell leans back.

'Everything ok Sir?' said Farrell

Clyde is in a daze; he blinks to bring him out of his daydream then he looks at Farrell.

'Sorry, yes Sergeant. I'm just wondering about how Anna is' said Clyde solemnly 'I said I'd be back for Christmas and well, we weren't'

'There's nothing you can do about that Sir' said Farrell as he tried to reassure him

Clyde raises his eyebrows as to agree with Farrell.

'Are you going to see Anna first or go back to HQ?' said Farrell

'I'll go to Anna first; I'll get out at the next corner' said Clyde

'Righto Sir' said Farrell

Evans passes the hipflask back to Farrell, Farrell passes it to Clyde who takes a sip and passes it back, Farrell puts the lid back in and puts it into his pocket. Clyde leans forward and taps the driver.

'Stop here will you please' said Clyde

The Bren Carrier slows to a halt and Clyde climbs cumbersomely out due to his cold and aching bones, the commandos look to Clyde who turns around.

'I'll see you all back at HQ lads' said Clyde

The Bren carrier starts to drive away, the commandos lift an arm or hand to gesture their farewell to Clyde, they'd had a tough time out in the cold and harsh wilderness for the last few months and were cold, tired and hungry.

'See you later Sir' said Sergeant Farrell

The Bren Carrier drives away and Clyde waves back at the commandos, he starts the short walk up the steps to Anna's front door then knocks at the door with his numb knuckles hurting with each knock on the oak door.

Clyde waits for a moment and blows into his cupped hands to warm them up then knocks again, still no answer.

He loses patience so walks over to the window and looks inside but can't see Anna, he walks back over to the door and knocks again but still no answer.

Come on, where are you? It's bloody freezing out here.

Clyde walks down the side of the house and around the back and up to the back door.

Please let the backdoor be open.

Clyde then knocks on the door, looks through the back window then tries to turn the door handle. The door handle opens; Clyde pushes the door open slowly then walks inside the kitchen.

'Anna?' calls Clyde

He walks through the kitchen into the hallway and looks up the stairs.

'Anna?' he calls again then he stops, listens and waits.

Come on, where are you?

'Anna?' said Clyde

Clyde turns and walks into the living room and walks up to the window, as he stands in front of the window he looks up and down the snowy street to see if he can see her, he then turns around and sits down on a chair thinking she may have gone out and it's best to wait there for her to return. He looks at the coffee table to see a burnt piece of plastic, he leans forward and picks up the burnt plastic then he stands up quickly in shock.

'Shit' shouts Clyde

Clyde realises that the burnt piece of plastic is the detonator of which Chevalier had detonated the explosives, he slides it into his pocket then runs upstairs and into the bedroom and opens the wardrobe, the wardrobes are empty. Clyde quickly moves over to the draws and one by one he quickly opens the empty draws.

'Shit' said Clyde

She's fucking gone. She's fucking left me. Fuck.

Clyde runs down the stairs and opens the front door and runs to the next house and knocks on the door frantically, the door is opened briskly by an elderly woman who is unimpressed with Clyde banging on her front door.

'Yes?!' said the woman abruptly

'Have you seen Anna?' said Clyde

The old woman doesn't know her by name but assumes he means next door as she knew most people from the street, even the Germans who had commandeered the houses nearby and had since fled.

'The woman from next door?' said the woman

'Yes, Anna from next door, have you seen here lately?' said Clyde

The old woman thinks for a moment and seems to not want to tell Clyde what she is about to. Clyde can tell she has something to say.

'No, no I haven't' said the old woman

Liar

'Are you sure? You don't seem so sure. Nobody is in any trouble' said Clyde

The old woman ponders for a moment.

'She said she was going back home with her husband' said the woman as she tried to close her door with Clyde putting his numb foot in the way to stop it, wincing as it jams into his cold and wet foot.

Fucking hell that hurts.

'Her husband?' asked Clyde as the old woman peered from the half closed door.

'Yes...her husband...he's just got out of hospital...after the...explosion' said the woman hesitantly as Clyde moves his foot from the door allowing her to slam it.

Clyde looks away into space in deep thought, Captain Jaeger isn't dead and he's taken Anna away with him the crafty bastard.

'Fuck' shouts Clyde as loud as he can and the word echoes up the street with gusto

Clyde walks away and then looks up at Anna's house as he walks past, he pulls out the detonator and looks at it as the walk turns into a jog as he starts to run down the street determined to get back to headquarters and the commandos as soon as possible as he's devastated that not only Anna has gone but Jaeger is still alive and must be holding Anna captive.

A few minutes' later, Clyde jogs down the snowy street back to headquarters. Tanks and other military vehicles move slowly down the street and in the space between vehicles Clyde looks across the other side of the street and notices a red cross vehicle serving hot food and tea to a group of soldiers and notices it's the commandos. He then dodges through the traffic and up to the commandos who are sat on a wall eating sandwiches and drinking tea as they warm themselves next to an old oil drum which has logs burning away inside.

Morris notices Clyde jogging towards them and nudges Evans to look at Clyde.

'That was quick Sir' said Morris who nudges Evans again and winks at him as if to say Clyde doesn't last long in the bedroom.

Clyde doesn't take any notice of Morris but instead looks at Sergeant Farrell and stands in front of him.

'Sergeant, we need to get to HQ quickly' said Clyde

Clyde starts to walk briskly away, Farrell stands up from the wall and picks up his rucksack whilst holding a cup of tea and follows quickly spilling his hot tea on the white snow as he follows.

'What's the matter Sir?' said Farrell

Bourhill tries to pass Clyde a sandwich, Clyde shakes his head and then looks at Farrell.

'I'll tell you on the way' said Clyde

Clyde looks to a convoy which is passing through the town slowly.

'Come on, let's get onto this tank' said Clyde

Farrell throws the tea out of the cup onto the floor and hands the cup to Bourhill, both Farrell and Clyde jog up alongside a Sherman tank.

The tank commander notices and ushers the driver to stop for a moment, the tank stops and both Clyde and Farrell climb onto the tank sitting on the top, the tank drives away slowly into the distance. Farrell looks to the rest of the commandos who are still eating sandwiches and drinking tea watching Clyde and Farrell.

'Lads, meet us at HQ once you've finished' shouts Farrell

Minutes later Clyde barges into Somersby's office abruptly, Brigadier Somersby is sat down speaking with another officer and is caught mid conversation as Clyde walks in accompanied by Farrell.

'Brigadier, I have a favour to ask' said Clyde

Somersby stops and looks at Clyde and seems a little befuddled, the officer meeting with Somersby is shocked and turns to look at Clyde.

'I'm sorry Major but I'm in the middle of something, if you'd please come back later… and bring your manners with you' said Brigadier Somersby

'I'm sorry Sir but this really can't wait' said Clyde

Brigadier Somersby isn't impressed with the manner in which Clyde has burst into his office and started making demands, he breathes a loud sigh of dissatisfaction then looks at Clyde in a pretentious way.

'Well go on then. What is it?' said Somersby

Clyde stands beside the officer, Farrell stands at the door and closes it gently behind him, then salutes Somersby.

'Sir' said Farrell

Somersby salutes Farrell then looks at Clyde.

'Spit it out lad' demands Somersby

'I need to go to Berlin' said Clyde

Somersby looks at Farrell and then to Clyde.

'My God Major. Have you lost your mind?' said Somersby

Clyde lights a cigarette and blows out the smoke quickly.

'It's just…well…my pregnant fiancé has been kidnapped and I believe she has been taken to Berlin' said Clyde

Somersby struggles to comprehend what Clyde is asking, he didn't know he had a fiancé and there were more important things going on at the time rather than rescuing his fiancé, anyway, shouldn't his fiancé be in England, Somersby thought.

'What? Berlin?' said Somersby as he smirks at the other officer in the room as he finds the idea amusing

'Yes, Berlin. I've thought about it, if we…' said Clyde

'Hang on just a minute. How do you know she's been taken to Berlin?' said Somersby

'I can't, what we need to do is…' said Clyde

'Well how the hell can you be certain she's still alive?' said Somersby who realises he may have overstepped the mark with his last remark 'With all due respect'

Clyde looks back to Farrell then to Somersby.

'Well, I can't be certain of anything' said Clyde

Somersby sits back in his chair and folds his arms and looks at Clyde.

'Well I can't let you go then' said Somersby

271

Clyde looks back at Farrell and then back to Somersby still puffing on his cigarette.

Think. Come on, think. Just come up with a bullshit reason. Anything will do.

'But Sir. I've got another reason to go' said Clyde

Somersby leans forward in his chair ready to listen to whatever stupid plan Clyde will put forward.

'Spit it out then' said Somersby

'I could kill Hitler' said Clyde confidently

Somersby and the officer look at each then both laugh, Somersby stands up and picks up his pipe and lights it and starts to puff away on it.

'Don't be naïve Major. Don't you think we've already tried that' said Somersby

Maybe the plan to kill Hitler was a little naïve but Clyde had to think on the spot of another reason to go to Berlin, albeit a farfetched reason.

'Why not? I'm willing to put myself on the line to do it' said Clyde

Somersby smokes his pipe and looks at Clyde in a condescending way.

'The wars over, the Red Army are closing in on Berlin and he's in hiding, you won't get anywhere near to him' said Somersby

'What if we went in and set up an observation post for bombing raids?' said Clyde as Somersby shakes his head

'Forget about it Clyde, he'll be dead in a few days at the hands of the Soviets' said Somersby

Clyde is pissed off that he doesn't have permission to go to Berlin and not only that he is unhappy of the way Somersby and the other pompous bastard had made him look stupid in front of Sergeant Farrell in the way that they dismissed and mocked him.

'What do I need to do to get to Berlin?' asked Clyde

Again, Brigadier Somersby looks at Clyde with contempt whilst seeming to share an in joke with the other officer in the room as they keep looking at each other grinning at the expense of Clyde.

'I'm sorry old chap but it's completely out of the question' said Somersby

Somersby stands up and walks towards Clyde putting his hand on his shoulder.

'Was there anything else?' said Somersby

Clyde looks at Somersby, then looks at Farrell.

Fuck you Sir, I'm going anyway.

'No thank you Sir' said Clyde

'Very well, I'm glad you're back and in good shape Clyde, we'll have a debriefing later' said Somersby

No we fucking won't

'Yes, ok Sir' said Clyde

Farrell opens the door and both Clyde and Farrell salute Somersby then walk out into the foyer of the building where a Military Police Officer is arguing with the commandos.

'What's going on?' asked Sergeant Farrell who demanded to know, the MP turns to Farrell and is glad to see someone of a decent rank who may help him reprimand the unruly mob of commandos, he has no idea Clyde and Farrell are part of the group.

'Sergeant I've asked these men to move outside, they're blocking the exit' said the MP

'It's bloody freezing outside' interrupted Smith

Farrell looks at Smith then to the MP, the MP then notices Clyde and salutes him.

'Sorry Sir' said the MP as he didn't notice Clyde was a Major 'I asked these men to move outside, Sir'

Clyde stops and looks at the commandos who are all weary, cold and dirty then looks back at the MP. The commandos watch Clyde for his reaction, they think they'll be in trouble and be punished at the hands of Sergeant Farrell for the commotion.

'And what did the lads say?' said Clyde

The Military Police Officer looks coy and slightly embarrassed of what he is about to say to an officer.

'Sir… they told me to piss off, Sir' said the MP

Clyde nods and looks at the commandos then back to the MP.

'Well piss off then!' said Clyde

'Sir?' said the MP wo was shocked, he'd never known an officer to speak to anybody in that manner before.

'You heard' said Clyde

The MPs face goes red with embarrassment and turns and walks away amongst the laughter from the commandos.

'What now Sir?' asks Sergeant Farrell

'Get the men ready to go, we're going tonight' said Clyde

'Where?' said Sergeant Farrell

'Berlin' said Clyde

Farrell looks at Clyde and smiles.

'Glad to hear Sir' said Farrell

Clyde spots Stapleton sat at a desk using the phone.

Stapleton, you beauty.

Clyde walks up to him, Stapleton notices and looks up to see Clyde holding his finger on the telephone cutting off the phone call, Stapleton puts the phone back onto the receiver.

'I have a favour to ask' said Clyde.

A few hours later the commandos are boarding a Halifax bomber each kitted out in civilian clothing with weapons and back packs, Stapleton is speaking to Clyde outside of the plane and seems rattled. The noise of the plane's engines makes it difficult to hear.

'If anybody asks, I'll tell them you tried to stop me ok?' said Clyde

Clearly not happy about him being implicated in the ad hoc mission Stapleton looks nervous, he enjoys his job and if he's caught he'd end up doing some menial task as a way of punishing him, he doesn't want that, he enjoys the serious stuff.

'Yes but I'll be court marshalled Sir' said Stapleton

Clyde looks away then back to Stapleton.

'I tell you what…' said Clyde

Clyde punches Stapleton in the eye, Stapleton stumbles back then holds his eye which has reddened and is shocked that he had been assaulted.

'That was uncalled for' said Stapleton

'It'll back up your claim though' said Clyde

Stapleton looks at Clyde in disbelief, Clyde climbs aboard the plane and reaches out to pull the door closed.

'Cheerio' shouts Clyde

Stapleton moves backwards nursing his bruised eye as the chocks are pulled from the wheels of the plane, Stapleton looks back to see a Military Police car driving quickly towards the airstrip, he then looks back to the plane to see Clyde looking at the Military Police car and then to him.

Clyde points at his eye then points at Stapleton. Stapleton nods his head then starts to walk over to the direction of the Military Police car and the plane slowly moves down the runway.

Moments later the plane is taking off whilst the Military Police Officers are quizzing Stapleton outside of the car on the airstrip.

Chapter 23 – Rescue Mission

In the midst of the night, in the German countryside, Clyde hides his parachute in the nearby bushes and then crouches next to Sergeant Farrell, the commandos hide their parachutes whilst Clyde and Sergeant Farrell look at a map.

'Right Sergeant, we're here and we need to be here' said Clyde as he points at the map with a sharp blade of grass.

'Looks like we've been blown off course' said Clyde

Farrell looks at his watch then back to the map.

'Right, its 22:35 now, we've got 6 hours before dawn so we've got plenty of time to get there' said Farrell

'Right then, let's get moving' said Clyde

The commandos move silently and slowly away into the dark countryside.

Hours later as dawn breaks over the German countryside Bourhill guards the rear of a barn looking through a small opening out into the surrounding area, Clyde is looking at the map of Berlin as he sits next to Farrell, Clarke is looking out of the barn doors which are slightly ajar and Farrell is cleaning his rifle whilst boiling water on his stove and just at the side of him Morris, Evans and Smith are asleep on bales of hay.

'We're twenty miles away from Berlin' said Clyde

'How long have we got before the Russians close in Sir?' said Farrell

Clyde looks to Farrell then back at the map which has the Red Army's positions outside of Berlin on it.

'I'd say going from this information, we've got one maybe two days to get in and out' said Clyde as he looks seriously at Farrell 'In two to three days the Red Army will be closing in on Berlin and we don't want to be around when they stroll into town'

'We're do you think Anna will be Sir?' said Farrell

'Wherever Captain Jaeger is, that's where Anna will be, so she's bound to be at the Gestapo headquarters' said Clyde

Farrell smiles at the audacity of the commandos going into Berlin and straight to the Gestapo HQ.

'I can't believe we're going into to Berlin' said Farrell as he looks up at Clyde 'You've got balls of steel Sir; I'll give you that'

Clyde smiles.

'At dusk we move, we cover twenty miles and get into position before dawn. We can't afford to mess about with this one' said Clyde

'Right Sir' said Farrell

The day after, Bourhill, Morris and Smith are hiding in a bombed out building with Bourhill looking through the scope on his rifle towards the Gestapo headquarters watching young boys dressed in German army uniform push a 30mm cannon past the headquarters, Smith looks on through binoculars.

With the end of the war in sight and the Germans clearly beaten and lacking men of a fighting age they armed the young boys and the old men of Germany in an attempt at putting up a fight, though it didn't even prolong the war, it just meant that old men and young boys were killed as a result of Hitler's stubbornness.

'They're only bloody kids' said Bourhill

'I know mate, it's a shame' said Smith

Morris is sat back in the room out of view manning the radio whilst typing Morse code to the other group of commandos hidden in a building nearby.

In the other building, Clyde, Farrell, Clarke and Evans disguise themselves amongst the rubble in another bombed out building. Clyde and Farrell look through binoculars at the headquarters as Clarke listens to Morris sending Morse code over the radio and Evans guards the room.

'Sir, Bravo 1 are in position and have reported a 30mm cannon outside the HQ' said Clarke

'Ok, tell them to hang tight, we'll move out once they disperse' said Clyde

Clyde looks through the binoculars to see the Hitler youth struggle to push the cannon past the headquarters, he decides it's best they wait until the cannon has been moved past as it doesn't matter what the age the person firing the cannon is, it will still cause destruction and they don't fancy storming the HQ if that's nearby for the Gestapo to call on in support.

Two people walk briskly out of the headquarters and begin to shout at the boy soldiers pushing the cannon, Clyde recognises one of them, it's the man he's come to track down in Berlin, Captain Jaeger.

'That's him, that's Jaeger' said Clyde with vigour as his eyes light up, he knows Anna must be inside the HQ if Jaeger is here

Farrell looks on through his binoculars intrigued to see what Jaeger looks like.

'Looks like you did a job on him Sir' said Farrell

Jaeger stands outside of the building, he cuts a shadowy figure now as he walks with a limp, his scars cover the right side of his face with half of his hair missing and is missing an eye which is covered with an eye patch. Jaeger continues to shout at the youths as they struggle with the 30mm cannon.

'I'm surprised he's still alive' said Clyde

The Hitler youth stop pushing the cannon and one of them tries to run away as they believe the resistance they're putting up is futile, Jaeger pulls out his pistol and shoots the boy and he drops to the floor with blood pouring out of his back from the wound from Jaegers dead eyed shot to his spine.

'The fucking bastard' said Farrell

The rest of the Hitler youth start to push the cannon faster now and Jaeger stops to look around, he tries to put the pistol back into its holster but he struggles as he is missing a few fingers on his right hand, the side that took the brunt of the blast when Chevalier took him out. Jaeger and his accomplice walk back inside with Jaeger limping heavily.

'Clarke, tell Bravo 1 that is our man. The scumbag with the eye patch' said Clyde

'Righto Sir' said Clarke

Clarke begins to tap Morse code on the radio.

Meanwhile back at the other building Bourhill and Smith look across to the Gestapo headquarters as Morris listens to the radio.

'That was Jaeger, that's our man' said Morris

Bourhill watches on thought his scope aiming it at Jaegers back as he walks back into the building.

'The bastard with the eye patch?' asked Bourhill

'That's the one' said Morris

Bourhill looks through his scope moving it up to Jaegers head as he limps inside.

'I can take him now' said Bourhill

We can take him now, over typed Morris

Morris looks at Bourhill who has his rifle aimed at Jaegers head with very little time left to take the shot, they need a decision now if Bourhill is to take it. Morris receives a Morse code message.

'Negative, stand down' said Morris

Morris puts the radio down.

'Hold your fire, we don't want to give them an early warning' said Morris

Back at the other building Clyde, Farrell, Clarke and Evans are taking off their rucksacks and trying to get rid of as much equipment as they can to allow them to move in and out of the HQ as quick as possible for a smash and grab raid, Clarke picks up the radio and begins to type in Morse code.

'Bravo 1 we are about to move into position, stand by, over' typed Clarke

'Just so we're clear gents, Evans moves behind the building and cuts the power and communications. Once that's done then me, Farrell and Clarke burst into the HQ killing as many as we can. Clarke, you stay at the entrance guarding it with cover from Bravo 1, we'll let Evans through the back door and then proceed to locate Anna' said Clyde

The commandos listen intently.

'Try to take Jaeger alive, if Anna's not here, he'll know where she is. Is that clear?' said Clyde

'Clear' said the commandos

'Whatever happens, we get out and we move *East* across the *Charlottenberg Bridge* and rendezvous *five miles east* into Spandau at the rendezvous point, any questions?' said Clyde

The commandos are crouched and look at each other as they all know they want to ask to same question, with Anna being Clyde's pregnant fiancé they feel apprehensive about asking the question.

'What if she's not there?' said Evans

'Then we grab Jaeger instead and torture the bastard until he tells us where she is' said Clyde in a matter of fact kind of way

The commandos smile.

'Can't say fairer than that then Sir' said Clarke

The commandos realise that she may not be there, only Clyde fully believes she is but the commandos are willing to follow Clyde anywhere. As they are professional soldiers they get on with the job in hand after one more glance at each other, they all know they are taking a huge gamble.

Clyde is dead set on Anna being held there, he believes Captain Jaeger would keep Anna close as he wouldn't have sneaked into British held Lille and taken Anna back with him to let her stay any place other than by his side, he was a control freak.

'Any more questions?' said Clyde

'No' said the Commandos

'Right then, let's go' said Clyde

The commandos move briskly out of the room one by one aiming their weapons in the direction in which they are heading as they move through the building eventually exiting it moments later and take cover behind a wooden kiosk, they then move away one by one rushing from cover to cover along the short stretch to the gestapo headquarters.

In the other building Bourhill is watching the other commandos move towards the headquarters.

'I see them' said Bourhill

Clyde and the commandos run across the street stopping every 10 yards to guard their position, Sergeant Farrell looks back to see if anyone is behind them and looks forwards to the HQ.

The commandos reach the front of the HQ and look to Clyde, Clyde nods for them to proceed. Clarke bends down and picks Clyde up onto his shoulders so he can see through the high window to see how many enemies are inside the room so they know how many and whereabouts in the room they are so they can storm the building with great speed and accuracy.

'There's seven in the room, Anna isn't in this room. We have three on the left in the far corner, two guards at the entrance and two others just to the right of the entrance, get the grenades ready' said Clyde

Clarke lowers Clyde to the floor and he climbs down from his shoulders, Sergeant Farrell passes Clyde a grenade, Clarke pulls out a grenade and Evans walks to the corner of the building ready to run around the back to cut the power supply to the building.

'Evans, go' said Clyde

Evans rushes around the back of the building out of sight whilst Clyde, Clarke and Farrell each have a grenade in hand as they crouch next to the entrance, Clyde leans back slightly and looks to see the lights inside the building go off as Evans cuts the power supply.

'Go, go, go' said Clyde

Sergeant Farrell and Clarke both throw a grenade each through the window smashing the glass as they do, Clyde throws his grenade into the entrance and they crouch back down outside of the building.

The grenades explode inside the building causing the rest of the windows to shatter as Clyde, Sergeant Farrell and Clarke burst into the room shooting startled and wounded Gestapo officers and within twenty seconds the room is clear.

'Clarkey. Let Evans inside then guard the front door' said Clyde

'Yes Sir' said Clarke

Clyde and Farrell rush to the back of the room to a stairwell, Clyde slowly peers his head around to see down the steps and a shot from a pistol ricochets off the side of the stone wall, Clyde ducks and falls back with Sergeant Farrell catching him keeping Clyde on his feet.

'Shit' said Clyde

Sergeant Farrell hides around the side of the stairwell and fires his sten gun aimlessly around the corner and down the stairs hoping to hit whoever is at the bottom, Clyde stops him from firing anymore.

'Jesus, accurate fire Farrell, Anna may be down there' said Clyde

'Sorry Sir' said Sergeant Farrell

Clyde peers again down the stairs at a lower level this time to see the Gestapo officer lay on the floor bleeding heavily from his abdomen and the officer notices Clyde, the Gestapo officer struggles to decide whether to try to stop the bleeding or reach for his pistol which he dropped when he was shot. Meanwhile Sergeant Farrell leans around the door and fires a volley of shots into the Gestapo Officer killing him instantly, Sergeant Farrell smiles wryly at Clyde due to the reprimand he'd had moments before.

'Accurate enough Sir?' said Farrell jovially

Clyde and Farrell move swiftly down the stairs and when they reach the bottom Clyde slowly peers around the side to see the cells, Jaeger is limping towards one of the cells, and Clyde nudges Farrell.

'He's here, on his own' whispers Clyde

Both Clyde and Farrell smoothly creep out from the side of the stairs and aim their weapons at Jaeger who stands behind Anna holding his pistol against her head.

Clyde is relieved that she's still alive and is indeed at the Gestapo headquarters, his intuition was right but he doesn't feel that confident that they'll live happily ever after just yet as Captain Jaeger holds his pistol to her head.

Anna seems shocked to see Clyde; she smiles nervously because she has a pistol pointed at her head. She looks to have been treated well though, she was clean and looked healthy, she wore a thick black duffle type coat and wasn't showing much of a baby bump, hopefully she hadn't miscarried and hopefully Somersby had been giving her double rations. She wore black leather gloves, a charcoal fur hat, a long navy dress and walking boots.

'Whoa, whoa, whoa. Easy now' said Clyde

Jaeger is moving backwards to another door towards the back of the cells, Sergeant Farrell is accurate with his sten gun and feels he can hit Captain Jaeger without hurting Anna but doesn't feel confident enough to do it due to the earlier reprimand.

'Stop right there' said Farrell

'Lukas' calls Anna as she is dragged backwards slowly and awkwardly by Jaeger

'Let her go Jaeger, the wars over, you're finished' said Clyde

Jaeger carries on moving backwards slowly to the doorway with Clyde and Sergeant Farrell moving simultaneously, Sergeant Farrell is growing impatient as he feels he can make the shot to Captain Jaegers head without harming Anna.

'I can take him Sir' said Farrell through gritted teeth

Clyde shakes his head as he doesn't want to take the risk of hitting Anna.

'What do you want?' said Clyde

Jaeger says quiet and opens the door at the back of the cells.

'Don't move! Sir, I can take him' said Farrell confidently

Clyde is caught between letting Farrell take a shot at Jaeger and making sure Anna is unharmed. Clyde is also confused that Jaeger isn't speaking, maybe it's due to the blast he thinks, maybe he was injured that badly that he couldn't speak anymore or had damage to his brain.

'What do you want?' asked Clyde sternly, he was growing impatient at Jaeger as he wasn't answering back, this made Clyde feel that something wasn't right 'Just let her go'

Jaeger opens the door at the back of the cell block, once it's open there are stairs which lead up to the front of the building and Jaeger slowly walks backwards outside whilst using Anna as a shield.

Clyde and Farrell slowly follow and as they do four soldiers start to aim their rifles inside the cell block from outside.

'Put your weapons down and come outside' shouted Jaeger

Jaeger is now outside still using Anna as a shield with four German soldiers aiming their rifles towards Clyde and Farrell.

'What do we do Sir?' said Farrell

'On my mark, make a dash backwards up the stairs' said Clyde

German soldiers shout from the top of the stairs inside the building at the shock of finding the dead bodies, Farrell and Clyde realise that they're surrounded.

If they go up the stairs they risk being shot by the shocked soldiers, if they allow themselves to be taken prisoner by Jaeger for a few minutes at the front of the building in the hope that Bourhill will provide sniper cover and take a few of them by surprise.

Where the fuck are Evans and Clarke if there's Germans behind us at the top of the stairs?

'Leave it, let's take our chances outside with Bravo 1 covering. Maybe Evans and Clarke will be there' said Clyde

'Hey. Put your weapons on the floor and get outside' shouts Jaeger

Clyde and Farrell reluctantly put their weapons onto the floor and walk slowly outside with their hands in the air, as they walk outside they notice Clarke acting sheepish stood outside and looks to have been beaten up as his clothes are torn, his left eye has closed due to swelling, his nose is broken and his mouth is bleeding and there is no sign of Evans.

'Where's Evans?' said Clyde

'He's dead Sir' said Clarke solemnly as he looked to the floor

One of the soldiers starts to push Clarke towards the building next door, ready to shoot him against the wall.

'Sir what's happening?' said Clarke

Captain Jaeger lets go of Anna and aims his pistol at Clyde.

'Move. Come on, up against the wall' said Captain Jaeger

'Sir, do we need blindfolds?' asked one of the soldiers

'No, we don't. Let them watch' said Jaeger

Clyde and Farrell look at each other knowing they could be shot if Bourhill and the other commandos don't intervene soon.

'Come on, up, up against the wall now, move' shouts a soldier

Clyde, Clarke and Farrell each move apprehensively to the next building along.

'Come on Bourhill' mumbles Clyde

Clyde, Farrell and Clarke each line up against the wall of the building and three soldiers aim their rifles at them, one of the soldier's guards Anna and Jaeger stands whilst struggling to put his pistol back in its holster.

Meanwhile a shot rings out hitting one of the soldiers in the side of the face dropping him to the floor, Evans is stood on the corner of the building holding his pistol and one of the soldier's notices then quickly shoots Evans in the chest, Evans then falls to the floor dropping his weapon.

Another shot rings out this time from a higher calibre rifle hitting another soldier in the back of the head creating a red mist from the exploding head covering the other soldier next to him, Clyde rushes out and rugby tackles a soldier knocking him to the floor, Clarke rushes to the soldier guarding Anna and knocks him to the floor whilst Farrell picks up a rifle and fires it towards Jaeger who by now is running away pulling Anna with him, they escape down an alleyway.

Farrell shoots the soldier who is wrestling with Clarke in the side of the chest and Clyde stabs the other soldier to death with his bayonet, Clyde then turns and looks for Anna, then looks to Farrell.

'Where's Anna?' said Clyde

'She's gone that way' said Farrell

Farrell looks to Clarke who has been shot in the chest in the melee and then looks to Evans whose body is lifeless on the floor at the side of the building. Two soldiers rush out of the Gestapo HQ from up the stairs from the cell block and are shot simultaneously by a high calibre rifle, this is Bourhill overseeing the commandos.

'Get after them, I'll see to Clarke' said Sergeant Farrell

Farrell passes Clyde a dead soldier's rifle.

'It's loaded' said Farrell

Clyde runs as fast as he can after Jaeger and Anna and Sergeant Farrell crouches and tends to Clarke's wound.

As Clyde rushes towards an alleyway a shot rings out and hits the wall at the side of him prompting Clyde to dive to the floor, Clyde looks up to see Jaeger aiming his pistol at him taking another shot, this causes Clyde to flinch and crawl backwards before firing back at Jaeger from the floor.

Shit, don't fucking hit Anna.

Jaeger hides down the alleyway across the street. Clyde stands up, reloads the weapon then slowly leans around the corner of the alley but can't see Jaeger across the street.

He cautiously moves out into the street over to the alleyway and aims his rifle down the alley, Jaeger leans out from a doorway and takes another shot at him, Clyde crouches and hides at the top of the alley and aims towards the doorway and takes a shot a Jaeger but misses.

Clyde stands up and reloads the weapon but notices the rifle only has one more round in the magazine.

'Shit' said Clyde

Clyde then looks to the doorway where Jaeger is but Jaeger isn't there, he looks down the alley and Jaeger and Anna aren't there either, they must have gone inside the building.

Where the fuck are they?

He looks around and notices that he may be able to cut them both off if he tries a different route, Clyde leans against the wall then checks to see if the coast is clear then pushes himself from the wall and runs as fast as he can to another alley that runs parallel with the building that Jaeger is in and as he reaches the end of the alleyway he crouches at the end and spot's Jaeger and Anna crossing the road from one building to the next.

There you are.

Jaeger is looking in a different direction to which Clyde is as he is expecting him to follow him, Clyde waits until Jaeger enters the next building then rushes across the street and down the next alley as fast as he can and enter the building through an open door further down in the hope of cutting his retreat off.

Clyde aims his rifle to the doorway in which he expects Jaeger to walk through and waits, he licks his lips as his mouth is dry, his head is wet with sweat and he is struggling to aim properly due to his heavy breathing, Clyde holds the rifle in one hand and wipes the sweat from his brow just as Jaeger walks into the building, Clyde quickly holds the rifle with both hands but Jaeger notices and fires a shot at him, Clyde fires back but misses and Jaeger and Anna rush up a nearby flight of stairs.

'Shit' said Clyde as he throws the weapon to the floor and looks around, he's is in the front room of someone's house, there is a Star of David painted on the wall.

He then looks back to the direction in which Jaeger went and looks around to find another stairwell further down the corridor.

Clyde stands up and pulls his knife from its holster and then quickly runs over to the stairwell and looks up. He then slowly walks up the stairs as quiet as he possibly can whilst holding the knife and ready to stab whoever crosses his path next. Clyde hears some footsteps coming from down the corridor approaching his direction and he stops taking a deep breath.

The footsteps get louder as they approach Clyde's position, it definitely sounds like two people running along the floor boards in the building so he takes another deep breath and holds his knife tighter.

Jaeger and Anna run past the crouching Clyde who then jumps out and grabs Jaegers trailing foot causing him to trip and drops his pistol which slides down the corridor and under a sideboard, Clyde moves towards Jaeger with his knife in hand and Anna tries to stop him by hugging him.

'It's so good to see you Lukas' said Anna who when she hugged Clyde didn't seem to have a baby bump at all.

Meanwhile Jaeger takes this opportunity to stand up then picks up a fire poker from the floor and Clyde pushes Anna to one side.

'Move out of the way Anna' said Clyde

Clyde pushes Anna so that she is behind him, Jacger takes a swing and Clyde tries to grab the poker but has to move out of the way quickly, Jaeger then moves back and forth taking swings with the poker trying to hit Clyde in the head.

Clyde tries to slash at Jaeger with the knife but Jaeger just clips his hand with the poker breaking Clyde's thumb.

'Argh' shouts Clyde

Clyde swaps hands with the knife and uses his left hand and tries to slash at Jaeger. Jaeger knocks the knife from Clyde's cumbersome left hand and the knife falls to the floor.

'Argh' shouts Clyde

Clyde rubs his hands together as he moves slowly backwards, Jaeger moves intermittently towards Clyde taking random swings then backing away quickly, Clyde continues to move backwards and as he does he bumps his leg against a fire extinguisher.

'Anna, come with me' calls Captain Jaeger

Anna looks as if she is waiting for Clyde to move out of the way so she can run to Captain Jaeger but Clyde doesn't notice as she's stood behind him.

'Come on Anna' calls Captain Jaeger

Captain Jaeger wants Anna to join him so they can escape to Switzerland and then move onto Argentina, they'd been promised safe haven in Argentina by one of Jaeger's high ranking friends in the Nazi party.

Clyde reaches down not taking his eyes from Captain Jaeger and picks up the fire extinguisher, pulls the pin out and sprays the powder at Jaeger and with the vast cloud of powder streaming towards Jaeger he backs off coughing and spluttering then tries to move down the stairs so that he can breathe and in doing so drops the poker whilst covering his nose and mouth.

Clyde turns back to Anna who looks nervous and shifty as she searches in the powdery air for Captain Jaeger.

'Anna?!' calls Jaeger as he coughs 'Anna, come to me'

Clyde moves slowly to the edge of the stairs ready to finish Captain Jaeger off by hitting him with the fire extinguisher.

Meanwhile, just outside in the street, a Russian tank fires a shell missing its target but it hits the side of the stairwell and blows it up causing the whole facade of the building to crumble into the street.

Clyde, Anna and Jaeger are knocked to the ground amongst the rubble, the dust and the powdery air.

Clyde stands up with his face covered in dust to see Jaeger is moving quickly up the stairs towards him, Clyde stands up quickly, he still holds the fire extinguisher and uses it to push Jaeger back down the stairs, Jaeger stumbles backwards and tries in vain to grab onto something but can't other than the fire extinguisher, Clyde notices and lets go of it causing Captain Jaeger to fall back down the stairs and out through the missing facade and falling 20 feet to the floor outside landing on his back in the street.

Clyde rushes down to the edge of the rubble and looks outside to see Jaeger lay on the floor unconscious, probably even dead he thinks.

'Hey, hey, hands up' shouts a Russian voice

Clyde looks down the street to see five red army soldiers rushing towards Jaeger on the floor, Clyde ducks back inside the building.

'We better get out of here quickly' said Clyde as he turns to look at Anna who is crying and holds a pistol aimed at him.

What the fuck is she doing?

'Anna…'said Clyde

Chapter 24 – Escape Artists

Without warning, she shoots him in the shoulder and he drops to the floor calling out in pain as he does so. The shot to the shoulder is not due to her wanting to maim Clyde but because she is such a bad shot.

Anna again takes another shot at Clyde but misses.

'Anna. What are you doing?' said Clyde

She again tries to fire the pistol at him but it has run out of ammunition, she tries again but the pistol just keeps clicking, Clyde watches her in shock and the colour has drained from his face.

'Anna?' said Clyde

She picks up the knife from the floor and walks towards Clyde, the sound of the Russian soldiers outside can be heard with more clarity now and machine gun fire is heard outside as the Russians fire a volley of shots into Captain Jaeger's torso killing him on the spot.

Clyde looks to the direction of the machine gun fire then back to Anna.

'Anna, what are you doing?' said Clyde

Anna slowly walks down the stairs holding the knife as Clyde holds his shoulder which is bleeding heavily.

'I thought we were having a baby, what are you doing?' said Clyde begging with his eyes as he speaks

She pays no mind to his pleading and stands over him and tries to pull his head back and tries to cut his throat, Clyde struggles and squirms back to the floor as Anna struggles to cut his throat.

She fucking isn't pregnant, she's got no bump and she's wearing her fucking wedding ring. Bitch.

'Argh, fuck you' shouts Clyde

Clyde wriggles on the floor as Anna tries to get a firm grip of him and crouches behind him and tries to pull his head back, Clyde wriggles further down to the floor.

'Fucking bitch. Fuck you!' shouts Clyde

Anna props her knees against Clyde's back to stop him wriggling to the floor, Clyde tries to push her away with his good arm but it causes more pain and he does that whilst trying to wriggle to the floor as Anna struggles to cut his throat.

Anna slices the side of his neck, he doesn't feel it but feels the warm and wetness between his chin and neck as he tries to block her from getting to his throat. She then tries again to wrestle his neck back against stiff resistance as he tries to keep his chin close to his chest as he wriggles away trying to block out the knife.

'Argh, fucking bitch. Fuck you!' shouts Clyde

Farrell runs into the building on the ground floor and over to the bottom of the stairs and aims his Sten gun at Anna and he watches the struggle not knowing what to do, Clyde notices.

'Fucking…stop her' called Clyde is desperation, he couldn't fight back for much longer and knew Anna would have to die, something wasn't right.

Farrell fires a volley of shots into Anna dropping her to the floor with a loud thud.

Clyde is out of breath and is in shock, he'd narrowly escaped death at the hands of the woman he'd come to rescue. He didn't really want her dead, he wanted her to be stopped but Farrell had killed her, the instruction mustn't have been clear enough.

Fucking hell, what if she really was pregnant? What if she really loved me like she said she did?

'You ok Sir?' said Sergeant Farrell who looked at little coy as he'd just killed the woman they were he to rescue

Clyde continues to breathe heavily and nods, he puts his hand on Anna's belly, there is no sign of her being pregnant.

She lied to me?

He then glances at her wedding ring then looks at her brooch around her neck, he opens it up to see a photo of her and Captain Jaeger inside.

Fucking bitch, she played me.

He then reaches into her jacket and locates her identification papers, it turns out that Anna Jaeger worked for the Gestapo along with her husband. Surely she was a honey trap and she'd caught Clyde hook, line and sinker.

What a fucking idiot I've been. I could have been caught. Shit.

'Get me out of here' said Clyde

Sergeant Farrell runs up the stairs and helps Clyde to his feet.

'My arms fucked, I…' said Clyde

Farrell holds a finger up to silence him.

'Someone's here' whispers Sergeant Farrell

The sound of someone running down the corridor alerts Sergeant Farrell to stop holding Clyde and aim his sten gun to the bottom of the stairs in anticipation of the Russian soldiers he's expecting to encounter.

Clyde and Farrell each look towards the bottom of the stairs and Morris, Bourhill and Smith each run out.

'Jesus Christ, you scared the life out of us' said Sergeant Farrell

'Sorry about that Sergeant but the Ruskies are moving in fast. We need to get out of here' said Morris

Morris moves up to Clyde and kneels beside him and starts to wrap Clyde's neck wound with a bandage.

'I know, they're outside' said Clyde as he notices there are a few commandos short 'Where's Clarke and Evans?'

'Both dead Sir' said Morris sombrely

Morris then tries to grab Clyde's arm ready to dress the wound, Clyde reels away in pain.

'Don't worry about that, it's gone straight through' said Clyde

'Don't you want me to wrap it up?' said Morris

Clyde shakes his head.

'No. We've no time for it, come on let's go' said Clyde

Clyde is helped to his feet by Farrell.

'Pass me your pistol Smith' said Clyde

Smith passes Clyde his pistol and Clyde looks out of the hole in the side of the stairwell to see the Russian troops aiming their rifles up towards the demolished gable end, he spots the fire extinguisher on the floor next to Jaegers body.

'Hey. Come out of there!' shouts the Russian Soldier

A shot is fired from one of the Russian Soldiers and Clyde leans back and the bullet ricochets inside the stairwell. The commandos all duck then look at Clyde.

'Jesus' said Clyde

'If they catch us...they'll think we're bloody Germans' said Bourhill

Clyde leans out quickly and fires a shot at the fire extinguisher blowing it up causing the whole of the street outside to be engulfed in white powder and the Russian soldiers to take cover to try and catch their breath.

'Let's go' said Clyde

The commandos each rush down the stairwell with the white powder from the fire extinguisher flowing into the stairwell behind them, Clyde points to the end of the corridor in which he entered the building, Bourhill leads the commandos.

As Bourhill reaches the end of the corridor he kneels and aims his sniper rifle into the street and looks around, the other commandos each run up in turn and crouch behind him.

Civilians are rushing past in the street struggling to carry their possessions and keep together in their family groups, there are old men, old women, women, children and pets taking the opportunity to escape from the Russian troops.

Clyde quickly moves up to Bourhill and leans over him, pats him on the shoulder and points.

'Across the street, into that building' said Clyde

'Go, go, go' said Sergeant Farrell

Morris makes a dash across the street with Smith just behind him, as they cross the street as shots are fired towards them, an elderly woman is caught in the fire and drops to the floor at the side of Smith as he rushes across the street, Bourhill is still in the building and fires back into the direction in which the shot came from.

'Bloody Russians!' said Bourhill

Morris and Smith are across the street ushering the rest to join them, Sergeant Farrell watches Morris and Smith then turns to Clyde.

'Me and you next Sir' said Sergeant Farrell

Clyde nods his head then slowly stands up, Sergeant Farrell also stands up.

'Ready?' said Clyde

Sergeant Farrell nods.

'Go' said Clyde

Clyde and Farrell rush across the street as more shots are fired at them but the shots miss.

Bourhill, Morris and Smith fire back at the Russians which subdues the gunfire. As Clyde and Sergeant Farrell reach the safety of the building across the street Bourhill runs across the street and moments later joins them. Whilst running across the street he notices a group of five or six Russian soldiers firing at him, they must suspect the commandos are Germans. Accompanying the Russians is a T34 tank driving through the street with the soldiers flanking either side of it.

'We need to get out of here quickly, there's a bloody tank heading this way' said Bourhill

The commandos each start to follow Bourhill into the building, Smith crouches down.

'Hang on a minute' said Smith who starts planting two grenades on the floor to detonate when they are moved.

'I'll leave them a little treat' said Smith

Smith places the grenades inside the door and the door frame so that when the door is opened the grenades explode, Smith stands up and follows the other commandos who are rushing through the building.

After a few metres the corridor comes to an end in the distance, Bourhill turns back and looks to Clyde.

'Which way Sir?' said Bourhill

'Keep going and turn right into the room at the end' said Clyde

As the commandos reach the end of the corridor an explosion is heard at the doorway where Smith left the booby trap and screams ring out from the injured Russian soldiers. The commandos look back quickly then look at Smith whilst they run along the corridor.

'Keep going, that should hold them up' said Smith

As they turn right into a room at the end of the corridor they stop at a doorway leading into the street, the street is quite wide, Bourhill stops and looks up and down the street and spots a German squad car with its canvass roof pulled all the way back making for easy access.

'Here, that car, get into it' said Bourhill

Morris runs out of the building and climbs into the German squad car, he fumbles about underneath the steering wheel whilst he hot wires it, starts the engine then looks back to the commandos.

'Come on, get in' said Morris

The commandos run out and each get into the car, Bourhill is in the passenger seat with Clyde, Farrell and Smith in the back seats.

'Come on Morris, go' said Clyde

Sergeant Farrell pulls out a map as Morris drives quickly down the street, both Clyde and Sergeant Farrell look at the map and look around to get their bearings.

'We're here, we need to turn right when we can' said Clyde

The car drives over a pot hole shaking all the commandos in the car making Clyde call out in pain as his shoulder is knocked.

Fucking hell that hurts.

'Moz, do a right' said Sergeant Farrell

Smith looks back to see some Russian soldiers coming out of the building from which they just escaped.

'They're right behind us boys' said Smith

Farrell, Clyde and Bourhill look behind to see the Russian soldiers firing at them but missing, Smith fires his sten gun over his shoulder just to make the Russians take cover.

'Can't turn right here' said Morris

'Next right then' said Clyde

Jesus, it hurts.

Morris continues to drive quickly whilst looking all around to make sure they're safe, Bourhill turns back to Clyde.

'You ok Sir?' said Bourhill

The expression on his face clearly shows that he's in pain but Clyde doesn't have time for feeling sorry for himself, at least, not out loud.

'Yes, I'll be fine, just give me a cigarette' said Clyde

Bourhill pulls out a pack of cigarettes and pulls five cigarettes out and lights them all passing one to each commando.

'We need to get out of here ASAP' said Clyde

Morris drives quickly down the street dodging the large pot holes and debris in the road and slows down as there is a right turn ahead.

'Here we go lads' said Morris

Morris attempts to turn right but is met by a T34 Russian Tank at the end of the street facing them.

'Shit' shouts Morris as he swerves the car away from the tank and the car drops out of gear.

'A bloody tank' said Bourhill

Morris revs but all it does is makes a loud revving noise and the car goes nowhere as it's in neutral.

'Shit' said Morris

'Fucking move Morris' shouts Smith

'Come on Morris' said Bourhill

Morris concentrates on getting the car back into gear and then starts to drive off whilst the other commandos look at the tank which they just drove past, the tank notices the car and the turret starts to move towards them, a crack of machine gun fire from the tank opens up on the car as it drives away.

'Argh' said Farrell

'You ok?' said Clyde

Farrell holds his leg and winces in pain.

'I've been shot' said Farrell

Clyde turns to Smith who slumps into him.

'Smudge?' said Clyde

Bourhill turns around to see that Smith has been shot dead and Farrell has been hit in the leg and wrist.

'Smudge?' said Bourhill

Clyde grabs Smiths wrist to check for a pulse and holds for a second, then he looks up at Bourhill.

'He's dead' said Clyde

'Shit' said Morris who thinks it's his fault that he was dead, he'd panicked when they saw the tank

'Sergeant, are you ok?' said Bourhill

'I'll be alright. Jesus it hurts' said Sergeant Farrell as he pulls out his hip flask and takes a large gulp to try and ease the pain.

Bourhill turns back to look at the tank at the rear of the car, it has moved out of the side street and is now aiming its gun turret towards the car.

'It's aiming at us' said Bourhill who then looks at Morris 'Moz get us out of here'

'It's a bloody dead end' said Morris who drives the car to the approaching end of the street which is a dead end.

The tank fires a shot that just misses the car but hits just to the right of the car throwing the car upside down with Clyde, Farrell and Smiths body thrown from the wreckage and Morris and Bourhill are still inside.

Clyde has a large and raw scrape on the side of his face from where he has hit the road and a broken tooth, he spits out the broken tooth and wipes away the blood from his cheek and tries to stand up using only his good arm which is painful and time consuming. Sergeant Farrell is struggling to stand up due to him being shot in the leg, Smith was dead anyway. Clyde cumbersomely creeps over to the wreckage and peers inside.

'Are you two ok?' said Clyde

Clyde looks inside to see Morris unconscious but slowly waking up and Bourhill with part of the steel door frame of the car embedded into his chest and the wound is bleeding heavily.

'No, fucking hell' said Clyde who turns to look at Sergeant Farrell who is tending to Smiths lifeless body patting him on the back as Smith lies dead face down on the cobbles.

'Bourhill's dead' calls Clyde reluctantly

Clyde reaches in to grab Morris and tries in vain to pull him out with one good arm, Sergeant Farrell now holds himself up against an iron fence and looks towards the direction of the tank.

'The bloody tank is coming this way' warns Sergeant Farrell

The tank fires a shot down the street hitting a building thirty yards away, Farrell limps across the street and stands behind the car wreckage along with an injured Clyde and a groggy Morris who had just been pulled from the wreckage, he then reaches back inside for the map.

'We need to get moving Sir' said Sergeant Farrell as he looks towards the tank which is trundling towards them

Clyde glances at the map, he then looks to the building that was hit by the blast then looks to Sergeant Farrell and holds him up along with Morris, the pain from Clyde's shoulder makes him wince but the adrenaline has kicked in allowing him to do such a thing.

'On three we push as hard as we can and run across into that building, the bridge is on the other side ok?' said Clyde

'Ok' said Sergeant Farrell

'Ready? One, two, three go' said Clyde

Clyde struggles to hold them both up and Morris struggles to walk due to being knocked unconscious in the crash and is only just coming around, Sergeant Farrell has been hit in the leg and they struggle as a unit to move away as quickly as they can, the tank fires its machine gun at them but misses.

'Come on lads, come on' said Clyde as they labour across to the broken facade of the building that was hit by the tank. Farrell looks back to see the tanks turret move towards them.

'It's going to fire at us' shouted Farrell 'Hurry up'

The commandos reach the building and climb over the rubble and into the building, the tank fires another shot above them higher into the building hoping for the building to collapse on top of them and also fires its machine gun towards them but misses. Rubble and glass falls to the floor just outside but doesn't affect them as they dive to the floor.

'Keep moving' calls Clyde

The commandos then crawl across the rubble and further into the building.

'Come on. Push on through' said Clyde

Sergeant Farrell is really struggling to crawl as his leg bleeds over the dust and the rubble, Morris is starting to come around and Clyde crawls using only one arm, he finds that painful but he has to do it or they'll be killed.

'Come on Sergeant, keep moving, keep moving forwards' said Morris as now he's lucid and is fully aware of the situation

As the commandos reach further into the building Clyde stands up and Morris helps Sergeant Farrell to his feet, Clyde looks through the glass pane of a window and can see the Charlottenberg bridge just outside.

'There it is, that's the bridge' said Clyde

The commandos look at each other, Sergeant Farrell smiles and grabs tighter onto Morris and then they walk briskly but clumsily due to them being injured and weary as they approach the door that leads onto the street, Clyde struggles to open the door.

'It's locked' said Clyde

Sergeant Farrell picks up a piece of rubble and throws it through the glass window and smashes all the glass out from the frame then picks up a rug from the floor with one hand and places it on the bottom of the broken window and crawls out through the smashed window, Morris follows and so does Clyde.

All three are lay in a heap on the floor as the tank fires another shot hitting the building on the side in which they entered blowing out the windows on their side where they are lay on the floor, the commandos cover up as pieces of glass fall around them. Glass shatters all around grazing the hands, heads and necks of the commandos, Clyde lifts his head and struggles to see due to the dust from the falling debris and glass.

'Come on we're almost there' said Clyde

Morris and Clyde both take one of Sergeant Farrell's arms over their shoulders to help him walk, Sergeant Farrell and winces in pain at every step and they slowly but determinedly walk towards the bridge.

Moments later they approach the bridge with caution but don't stop, they keep walking as quickly as they can across it and as they reach the other side both Clyde and Sergeant Farrell fall to the floor exhausted at the side of the road.

'I can't go on, I need to get this leg sorted' said Farrell as he holds his leg and writhes in pain on the floor

Clyde looks up to Morris who looks as though he's spotted something, he has, there is a Kettenkrad which is a German half-track motorcycle with enough room on for the rider and two passengers on the back.

'Here we go' said Morris

Morris runs away quickly and a minute later the sound of a motorcycle engine can be heard, Sergeant Farrell doesn't look because he's in pain so assumes Morris has found a normal motorcycle.

'How's he supposed to fit us all on one bike, we're not a bloody circus act' said Farrell

Both Farrell and Clyde look at each other then start laughing but quickly stop because they are in so much pain but start again and all three commandos all laugh loud and hard as Morris rides the bike towards them singing 'The Entry of the Gladiators' tune, the theme music that clowns used to perform routines to. Despite the danger that surrounds them, Morris still shows his sense of humour, it certainly helps ease the tension and for some reason seems far funnier than it should be, mainly due to the impending danger and the narrow escape they'd just had.

'Get up, we can fit us on all on its a little halftrack motorbike' said Morris

Sergeant Farrell and Clyde are both laughing as Morris lifts them up and helps them sit on the Kettenkrad. Clyde turns to look back to the building from where they came from and it's on fire, the sound of a huge battle can be heard that is raging across Berlin and Morris starts to get the Kettenkrad into gear with both Sergeant Farrell and Clyde looking backwards as they drive away.

British Medical Tent – West German Countryside

Brigadier Somersby flanked by Stapleton walks into a field hospital in the West German Countryside, they walk up to a bed where Clyde is lay, Sergeant Farrell is lay in the bed next to him with Morris sat on the edge of Clyde's bed.

Brigadier Somersby is clearly angry as he storms up to Clyde with Stapleton in tow, Morris stands up and salutes Brigadier Somersby who salutes back.

'At ease gentlemen' said Brigadier Somersby

Clyde looks up to see Stapleton with a black eye, he then looks to Brigadier Somersby apprehensively.

'Hello Sir' said Clyde

'Hello Major' said Brigadier Somersby

Stapleton stands beside Brigadier Somersby and is bearing a black eye and looks at Clyde who raises his eyebrows in an apologetic way, Brigadier Somersby looks at Stapleton's eye and then back to Clyde, he doesn't want to be there and wouldn't have made and special arrangement to reprimand Clyde had he not been passing through the camp, add to that the work that Clyde did under cover Brigadier Somersby was told from higher up that he should see Clyde whilst he is there, if it were up to Somersby he'd have sent two military police officers to arrest him forcefully but it wasn't up to him.

'Yes, I'll cut to the chase. What you did was stupid and I cannot defend your actions as you went AWOL and disobeyed a direct order' said Brigadier Somersby

Clyde looks sheepish, as he did disobey a direct order and in the process not only did part of the team die but he lost Anna also and as it turned out Clyde found out where her true loyalties lay.

'I'm sorry Sir' said Clyde

'You put lives at risk and we lost some good men. If it weren't for how busy we will be over the next few months I'd take action but due to what you've done in the past it's easier to dismiss you from the Army, Major Clyde. As of now, you're no longer a member of His Majesties Armed Forces, Stapleton with go through the paperwork with you later' said Brigadier Somersby

Dismissed? That's fine with me, I should be being zapped back to present day any time soon anyway.

'Very good Sir, what about these two?' said Clyde who gestures to Farrell and Morris 'I want to make a point of saying that they only followed *my* orders, please, do not punish them for my insubordination'

'They're being demobilised anyway in the next few months, but we'll need them for the meantime' said Brigadier Somersby

'Ok Sir, so what happened with Hitler?' said Clyde

'Hari Kari old boy' said Brigadier Somersby

Clyde, Farrell and Morris look at each other and smile, Clyde was relieved more than the others as he had the knowledge that in an alternative future Hitler had escaped and with the bombing of the runway at the Tempelhof airport that prevented him from escaping, at last, things were falling into line and getting back to how they should.

'That's great news' said Sergeant Farrell

'Indeed it is, the war with Germany is over, well done to all' said Brigadier Somersby 'though we're still at war with Japan in the East'

'That's good to know' said Clyde 'the end is in sight'

'Indeed' said Brigadier Somersby who was desperate to leave, he looks to Stapleton.

'Goodbye gentlemen' said Brigadier Somersby as he saluted the men then walked away

Clyde looks around and is in deep thought about what to do now knowing that the war is over and things that went wrong were eventually put right, but that came at a cost, he wonders what he will do with himself now that he did what he set out to do, he then turns to Stapleton who has stayed behind and as Somersby leaves the tent he places a punnet of grapes on Clyde's bed.

'Sorry lads, I could only get one punnet' said Stapleton 'You'll have to share'

Morris pulls off a bunch of the grapes and passes them to Sergeant Farrell, he then picks some for himself whilst Clyde takes a few and stuffs them in his mouth.

'So, what are your plans now it's all over Major…sorry, Clyde?' said Stapleton

Clyde thinks to himself for a moment whilst he chews the mouth full of grapes.

'I'm not sure' said Clyde

Clyde continues to chew the grapes then swallows.

'I might do a bit of travelling, you know, see a bit of the world' said Clyde

Stapleton nods and smiles in a friendly manner, Clyde can't help but feel sorry for giving him the black eye which is now tinged with yellow.

'Well…I don't blame you' said Stapleton as he helps himself to the grapes 'You'll have a lot of time on your hands now'

Clyde smiles.

'I've got all the time in the world' said Clyde

THE END

By Rob Kenyon